DATE DUE

Gotcha Down

GOTCHA DOWN

A Novel

Chris Earl

JONES
BOOKS

Madison, Wisconsin

Jones Books
309 N. Hillside Terrace
Madison, Wisconsin 53705-3328
www.jonesbooks.com

First edition, first printing

This is a work of fiction. Real names of places, people, and streets have been included to lend the work authenticity to the reader, especially those familiar with the area. Any similarities between the fictional characters and any real persons, living or dead, is strictly coincidental.

Library of Congress Cataloging-in-Publication Data

Earl, Chris.
    Gotcha down : a novel / Chris Earl.—1st ed.
        p. cm.
    ISBN 0-9721217-6-5 (alk. paper)
    1. Football players—Fiction. 2. College sports—Fiction.
    3. Gambling—Fiction. I. Title.
    PS3605.A75G68 2004
    813'.6—dc22

                                                2004004036

Printed in the U.S.A.

*To Erica, for her unwavering encouragement
and to Sam, whose morning naps made this book possible.*

Acknowledgments

Starting a novel only requires a kernel of inspiration but finishing one requires inspiring people. Digging into how high-level football works was a real education. Thank you to Bob Nielson, Nate Gibbs and Rick Fritz for a look into how a college football team operates in the huddle. Your assistance led to the authenticity of the novel. Thanks. Also, thank you to Joan Strasbaugh at Jones Books for seeing this book from raw to refined. The biggest thanks go to those closest to me. To my wife Erica, who reminds me that the ultimate goal is still just seeing it on the shelves and to little Sam. His morning naps freed up the time to both start and finish *Gotcha Down*.

Table of Contents

1. The Talking Head Returns Home

Clark Cattoor scanned the constant motion of navy-and-white football jerseys on the field below, and said to the sky-blue Madison morning, "This is it."

This, the fourth day of August, was the day he'd worked a decade for. All those frozen winters toiling in the sticks, chasing stories about high school volleyball players, dog mushers, and cross-country skiers, had led up to this, the opening day of college football practice at Wisconsin State.

Just as he'd always dreamed it.

Madison was Clark's place. His town. He'd graduated from Wisconsin State and still had the memories of old glory: Sitting on the shore of Lake Monona with cool drinks and good cheer. Strolling down to the fraternity house. Sitting in the strangling Madison traffic after the Fourth of July fireworks.

Now Clark enjoyed his status as sports journalism royalty. As the main sports anchor at WMA-TV in Madison, he paced the sidelines along with three dozen other sports media types. He remembered the newspaper writers from his college days. All were a shade older and a layer thicker. Sports journalists in Madison tended to stay put. The jobs were that cushy.

Clark watched the head coach of the Boars bark orders during the first drills.

Frank Flaherty was starting his fourth year as head football coach at Wisconsin State. He replaced Bob Monroe, the legend who'd brought the program back to glory and then left for the Philadelphia Eagles in 1999. The shadow of his predecessor turned Frank from a genial, middle-aged guy into an old man with a mean streak. A cigarette dangled from his lips as he watched his players stretch. His stomach revealed one too many fried chicken banquets and not enough exercise. His brown hair was now streaked with gray.

Clark didn't care whether Frank liked him. Clark was no brownnoser. In each of his three stops before WMA-TV, Clark had dug up the dirt on at least one sports institution. Title IX violations, academic fraud—nothing was too hard to uncover. Six months out of school, he'd uncovered a cartel of professional bull riders in Grand Junction, Colorado, who drugged bulls with a potent formula of crystal meth and coconut milk. The bulls would shake because of the drugs, but not as intensely as they normally would. This let riders stay in the saddle longer. Four bull riders and the mastermind, an announcer who served as the rodeo circuit's private bookmaker, still rotted in prison.

Clark was not at football practice to make friends. He had enough of those already. A young 31, he walked the city with his head held high, making eye contact with people just to see who recognized him. Since his divorce, he'd strutted through the bars to see if any leggy women would walk up and say, "Hey, aren't you?" His lean 6'3" frame, dark brown hair, and perpetual tan made him one of the beautiful people of Madison.

A year ago today, Clark had stood on the sidelines for the start of college football practice in Duluth. Now as he stood, arms folded, on the sidelines of the Meadow Hill Seminary, miles south of the WSU campus, he felt a tap on his shoulder, followed by a male voice saying, "Thanks for coming out."

Clark whipped around to see the friendly smile of Jim Tillman.

I really have made it full circle, Clark thought. Jim was the school's long-time sports information director, the middleman between the football team and the media.

Ten years before, Clark Cattoor had been a fan trying to become a legitimate sports journalist. He'd produced and hosted a controversial half-hour sports show on public access television. *Firing Squad*, he titled it. Clark would pop up on the tube and question the school's athletic programs between taking phone calls.

Jim Tillman and the coaches were not amused. Before long, Clark was WSU's Media Enemy Number One. Wisconsin State athletes were instructed not to appear on the show.

Now Jim Tillman had to take care of this former rock in his shoe. Jim was now working for Clark Cattoor, making sure Clark received all of the updated rosters and news releases.

"Thanks, Jim." Clark flashed his porcelain teeth. "Good to see you."

Jim replied with a forced smile. "Anything else we can do for you, just let me or one of my assistants know," he said, and strode away.

As the chatter on the field rose to the hill where the media were perched, Clark looked over the updated football roster. He'd spent the summer catching up on the main players and their colorful backgrounds. He'd read about their histories, on the field and in the police blotter.

Now he watched as the players broke into their groups, sorted by position. The team's cliques formed largely by where you played on the field.

Senior starting quarterback Craig Zellnoff was from the Chicago suburb of Naperville. Craig was penciled in to run the offense for his senior year. He was no pro prospect, to be sure. With imposing brown eyebrows that looked odd below his moppy haircut, Craig was steady. Nothing spectacular, but nothing stupid. The ultimate "even-keel" quarterback. His only vice appeared to be single-malt scotch.

Just weeks into his freshman year, Craig had tossed a heckler through the window of a State Street gyro shop at 3 A.M. All Craig had suffered was a $177 ticket for drinking, when a police officer spotted him sipping from his mini-flask of scotch right after the incident.

No one messed with Craig Zellnoff after that story made its way around Madison.

The black receivers from Florida griped about Madison's winters. Wisconsin State landed the second-rate Florida receivers, not the best in the Sunshine State but certainly more skilled than anything Wisconsin would ever produce. The team's top two receivers, senior Laverneus Wilson and junior "Touchdown" Tyrone Collins, hailed from Miami. Collins was the taller of the two and easily the more flamboyant and talented. The newspapers speculated that Collins would leave for the NFL after the season. Rumors floated that he had signed with an agent, a major no-no in college football. Collins said of NFL super-agent Jerry Copperzweig, "That Jerry is just helpin' me through a few things. He just a buddy."

A buddy with two million in the bank and a contract with Touchdown's name on the last page.

Clark watched the speedy receiver run his strides on the near sideline. His #1 white jersey glistened under the sun. Collins would become an NFL star for someone.

The players from the state of Wisconsin provided few problems for the program. They were simply not talented enough to sign with agents or throw people through gyro shops in the middle of the night. The linemen consisted of corn-fed, husky Wisconsin boys, peaceful big men until the whiskey or the Leinenkugel's took effect—another Badger State tradition.

The program produced scores of NFL linemen, and that trend was continuing. Senior captains Bob Verly and Cory Larkman led an offensive line seen as one of the best in the nation. Bob and Cory had grown up in Wausau, a paper mill town two hours north of Madison, dreaming about playing for the Boars.

Looking down the roster was always a treat for Clark, seeing for the first time that season the 118 names, numbers, heights, weights, and positions. He loved absorbing the hometowns the most. After eight years of hacking around small Wisconsin towns, Clark could peg the location of just about every township in the state.

He wondered if Wisconsin State had a real kicker yet. Last year's 5-7 season should have been 8-4, but missed field goals had doomed the team. Three more field goals and the school would have brought in two million dollars at the Sun Bowl in El Paso.

A few of the new names on the roster came from familiar places, northwestern towns like Spooner, Superior, Maple, Menomonie, Barron, and Amery. Clark had spent more than enough time chasing football games in those towns. One name popped out at him: Number 17—Jake Steffon, PK, So./Fr., 6-1, 190, Fall Creek, Wisconsin.

2. The Kicker

Jake Steffon stretched his hamstrings on the practice field and finally felt at home. So far, his freshman year in Madison had been the ultimate in culture shock. Jake had grown up in Fall Creek, Wisconsin, population 876. The locals pronounced it "Fall Crick." Fall Creek boasted an A&W and a speed trap on Highway 12 that accounted for 8 percent of the city's budget.

Jake played high school football for the Fall Creek Crickets. He was a standout small-town quarterback and a decent placekicker. He and his father often drove 15 miles west to Eau Claire to watch college football games in the fall. Jake's family wanted him to stay close to home and play for Eau Claire. But Jake believed there was more to life than being a hero in one tiny corner of the world. He wanted to see the other corners as well.

Eleven weeks after graduating from high school, Jake arrived in Madison with his possessions crammed into three navy trunks, still clinging to the hope of playing for the Boars. He moved into an imposing skyscraper dorm on the southeast edge of the WSU campus.

He'd received a letter from Wisconsin State his senior year of high school, encouraging him to try out for the football team in the fall. It was a form letter that spelled his last name "Stefen." When he called the football office, he was told the team was "all set" at kicker but that he should stay in shape in case injuries swept through the roster.

As he began his new life, Jake forgot about football. He landed a delivery job three nights a week at Pizza Perfecto, a little shop downtown. The work paid about $15 an hour, most of it in cash. With money falling from his pockets, Jake lived like a king. He walked around his dorm floor with a roll of twenties.

Madison was like midtown Manhattan to the kid from Fall Creek. Temptation loomed around each corner.

By early October, Jake felt the pressures of academic life. Six-week exams approached, and he cut back on the pizza shop for a week. If he could just get by those dreaded blue-book tests, he was in the clear until Thanksgiving.

That same week, Frank Flaherty was dodging the media arrows after a humiliating disaster, a 16-14 homecoming loss to the Indiana Hoosiers. Losing to Indiana was embarrassing. Losing to Indiana in this manner was even worse. The Wisconsin State kicker had missed three field goal attempts, the final one a 22-yard chip shot.

"Man, I could have made that," Jake said to his friends as they walked out of Mendota Stadium after the game.

He sat in his political science class the Monday after and read the headlines in *The Daily Boar*, the school newspaper: "Kicker Puts Coach Frank in Danger."

He turned on Channel 11 that night at six, and watched in shock as Clark Cattoor appeared.

"Hey, Jason, I grew up watching this guy." Jake said to his roommate. "Back in Eau Claire. I didn't know he was in Madison."

Seconds after Clark's gelled hair and tanned face appeared, a tape rolled of Frank Flaherty at the press conference, the Jackson Bank and Let's Go Blue Sports Drink logos behind the coach.

"Tomorrow at four P.M., all students interested in placekicking are welcome to an open tryout at Mendota Stadium," Flaherty said confidently on the videotape. "Bring your student IDs and a strong leg. Females are also encouraged to try out."

Wisconsin State. Forever politically correct, even in the midst of a kicking crisis.

Jake dreamed about returning to that world as he watched Clark come back on TV and wonder, on-air, if he himself had any college eligibility left. Jake quit paying attention to the tube. He looked at his roommate.

"I'm doing this," he said.

Jake was one of 43 wannabe kickers who walked onto the turf at Mendota Stadium on that Tuesday in October for the shot of a lifetime. Two women were in the group. Frank Flaherty was a beggar, so choosing was not a luxury to him.

"I don't need someone to come out here and hit a 50-yarder," Frank said to the kickers. "Just kick it straight. Hit extra points. That's all we're after here."

Jake knew he could do that. His size kept him from attracting interest as a quarterback, but he could still kick. He'd made seven field goals his senior year at Fall Creek, and all but one of the extra points. His junior year, some klutz from rival Augusta had stepped on his right big toe and broken it. Jake had responded by hooking in an extra point with his left foot. Just cleared the crossbar. Looked like a perfect kick in the Saturday newspaper.

Each student was given two field goal tries from 30 yards out. They did not necessarily have to make one, they just had to have that oomph on impact when foot hit leather. Jake was one of only two who had the oomph.

What made the kicks even more difficult was the presence of Frank, chewing gum and wearing his intimidator sunglasses. Frank could be a nice guy to his own players, but he had to be a jerk with the wannabes. Even worse for the kickers, they had to deal with the constant yelling of John Wilcox, a flamboyant media darling who was being touted as the Next Hot Young Coach.

"Don't think about it, it's only your future!" Wilcox yelled as most of the kickers offered spirals that never made it ten feet off the ground.

"Can it, John," Frank yelled. "We need a kicker! We can't chase these guys off yet."

Once Frank turned around, Wilcox simply rolled his eyes, the same motion most of the players made behind Frank's back at one time or another.

Jake missed his first one, wide left. Nerves, he thought.

Jake smacked the second field goal attempt true. No hook, no slice. Straight on. It would have been good from 40 yards out.

"Not bad," Wilcox commented, trying to save face.

"Thanks, Coach Wilcox."

Jake had committed Wilcox's story to memory long before showing up at Mendota Stadium. After all, Wilcox was the author of the "Stefen" letter.

John Wilcox was your typical young, hard-driving assistant football coach. During the team's annual Blue-White spring game, Wilcox always led the bench in jumping up and down and shouting, "Make us proud!" At 29, he'd been a football coach for more than ten years. He came from a career track best described as non-traditional.

The sandy-haired, pudgy-faced Wilcox had grown up in a tiny town in Kansas. He was too small to play football, even in high school, but he'd always wanted to coach. He even went so far as to contact the head coach at Washburn University in Topeka, a small Division 2 school. No football power, to be sure, but an opportunity. Wilcox stepped on campus in the fall of 1993 as a freshman. He immediately joined the team as a quality control assistant, in charge of making sure the team had enough helmets, tape, and shoes. No glamour, but as he always remembered, the world needed ditch diggers, too.

He proved to be no ditch digger, however. His junior year, the offensive coordinator left after a falling-out with the head coach. Wilcox was the offensive line coach at age 20, a remarkable feat. The local media took notice. John craved the attention, the story that a local boy would be coaching players older than he was.

In December 1995, Frank Flaherty needed a special teams coach at Wyoming, a lower-level Division 1 school. The brink of the big time. Frank was in his second season with the Cowboys. He hired Wilcox, who finished at Wyoming in 1997 with degrees in communications and English literature.

John followed Frank to Wisconsin State two years later. By then he was seen as a guru of sorts with kickers. Yet what Wilcox really wanted was the role of offensive coordinator. That was the territory of the long-time offensive coordinator, Randy Munson.

John believed deep down that it would be only a matter of time until Frank sent Munson packing. In the meantime, he became a master of public relations. He sent a box of steaks each summer to the sports departments of the TV stations.

The predictable "boy wonder coach" stories soon followed. Wilcox was soon violating the one principle of sports: Never believe your own press releases.

Things were not always perfect, even for the Hot Young Coach. After the disappointing 6-6 season in 2001, Wilcox walked into the head coach's office and wondered if and when Frank would fire Randy Munson and install him as offensive coordinator.

What Frank said that day shook Wilcox to the core.

"Now, why would I do that?" Frank said from behind the massive desk in his office. "Randy Munson is seen around these parts as the last link to those Rose Bowl teams. The last thing I need is some young assistant with a big head who's never even called his own plays running my system."

Wilcox spent the off-season avoiding his boss. Frank responded by pumping his assistant up to the national media.

Rice called. So did Tulane and Utah State. Even large programs like Kentucky and Missouri were interested in hiring Wilcox as a top assistant.

John did the unthinkable: he turned them all down. He said he wanted a head coaching job at a large school or a coordinator spot at a Top 20 team.

Only two of the hopefuls made the 30-yard field goals during that October tryout—Jake and another wannabe, Greg Cunningham, a fifth-year senior with only weeks of college eligibility. The coaches thanked and dismissed the others.

Frank had the two kick field goals from 40 yards out. Each would get five cracks.

"Whoever makes more MIGHT make my team," he yelled from the sidelines. "Whoever misses more WILL NOT make my team."

Cunningham drilled three of five, all with enough distance, but his right-footed hook sent the first two wide left.

Jake had distance problems but aim was not an issue. He drained his first three 40-yard attempts before coming up just short on the final two.

"Screw it. We need a kicker, and I need to leave," Frank said. He had to go off to the radio studio for another session of hearing it from the callers on *The Frank Flaherty Show.* "We MAY be in touch," he barked to the kickers.

Jake walked the seven blocks to his dorm. It was just after five. He was already late for his shift at Pizza Perfecto. He jogged to his well-used burgundy Bonneville, the Honey Wagon, as his friends back home called it, and headed out into the night.

All evening on his routes, he wondered, Did I show them enough? Did I make it?

Jake was stuck with the jock bug.

Five hours and eighty bucks later, he left the pizza shop and cruised three miles west across downtown to find a parking place near Jackson Hall. Ten minutes later, he rolled up to Room 815A. Jason was out at the library for the night, but Jake saw a note on the door in his roommate's handwriting.

"A COACH WILCOX CALLED. CALL HIM. URGENT."

Jake wrote down the number and phoned the assistant coach. After chatting with Wilcox for a few moments, Jake found himself with a new reason to get out of bed each morning. A jersey with his name on the back would be waiting for him the next day at the stadium. Jake only wished that Wilcox would correctly spell the last name of his next hope.

In the space of one week, Jake went from ordinary student to walk-on football player. First came the clothes. Football players have their own gear, dark blue pants with gray sweatshirts. Jake's sweatshirt read WISCONSIN STATE FOOTBALL, 17. That combination of cotton and nylon was pure gold on campus.

His first days at practice, Jake said precious little. He felt happy to be there. He kicked like it, too. Solid some days, awful on others. Flaherty kept his new kicker on a long leash. He knew Jake would have time to blossom and calm his nerves. The coach figured Jake would be with the team longer than he would.

Jake's first game was a home loss, a listless 20-7 defeat to Michigan. What a rush it was for the kid from Fall Creek, though.

When he breezed out onto the field before the game with the other players, his fresh, royal blue #17 jersey fit him like gladiator's armor. Even as a back-up kicker, Jake felt like a better man. His folks drove down from Fall Creek to watch their son stand around on the sidelines for three hours. The news of Jake making the football team had swept through town. Jake was now the favorite son in Fall Creek.

Jake's father, Carl, told his son the first thing he should do was quit his part-time pizza job. But the store's owner, Bill Millstein, begged Jake to stay, just so he could tell his own drinking buddies that he had a football player delivering his cuisine. Jake and Bill came to a deal: One late shift on Wednesday nights and the long Sunday NFL shift. Packer Sundays typically brought in $200 for a 10-hour shift as Madisonians woke up to the noon Green Bay game, ready to feed hangovers and tip their friendly pizza guy.

Carl Steffon was not terribly pleased, but he trusted his only child.

"Jake, you can always make money, but you're only supposed to do college once," Carl said to him at dinner after his son's first college football game.

"I'll see what my boss wants me to do. I think I can do both."

Jake changed from a student to a Division 1 football player. But for all that, he made it onto the football field just once that season. He knocked through an extra point for his only kick of the year, a harmless pop fly down the middle against Northwestern in the last game of the season.

A year later, Sam Cattanach, Jake's new roommate and the team's starting punter, was holding for the field goal attempt. Jake plowed another field goal between the uprights. The kid did belong. Jake was slowly morphing into an accepted member of the football team.

Older players lived in run-down houses on the south end of campus, near Mendota Stadium, ancient termite holes where the players each tossed in $150 a month to live, five or six to a sardine box. They lived like slobs. One player, departed lineman Kyle Solheim, had made his lack of amenities famous in a *Sports Illustrated* article. The story's opening picture featured Solheim in his mildew-filled bathtub. The 6'6", 330-pound offensive guard was wearing only his boxer shorts, three dozen cockroaches, and a smile.

Jake and Sam rented a typical college bachelor pad in south campus. They'd become fast friends toward the end of last year's football season. Sam was from Neillsville, a larger town just 40 miles east of Fall Creek down Highway 10. Sam didn't own a car, so he would hop in with Jake for a weekend home here and there. Being mere kickers, they spent most of their practice time throwing footballs to each other.

"Just keep them loose for the end of practice," Frank yelled over toward Wilcox.

"Got it," Wilcox said in his media voice. Whenever Frank could not appear at a benefit that required a speaker, Wilcox was always ready. He had that look after each practice. He looked each journalist in the eye, practically begging to answer any questions. He spoke in 15-second sentences, perfect for the TV types. Wilcox knew all this would benefit him one day. One day when he wouldn't waste his own genius keeping kickers loose for the end of practice.

3. The Coach

Craig Zellnoff's status as starting quarterback was due largely to long-time offensive coordinator Randy Munson. Munson had signed on at Wisconsin State in 1991 as the quarterbacks' coach, the year after WSU joined the Big Ten as the second school from the state in the conference.

The Big Ten conference was in a bind after Penn State bolted the league at the last minute. Officials had promised 11 teams for the upcoming television contract.

The conference allowed the Boars to join with a rare exemption: Wisconsin State would never have to play its in-state rival, the University of Wisconsin. This was unheard-of in major college football, but the conference wanted the extra cut of revenue. Both Wisconsin State and Wisconsin sat in the same city, just two miles apart but on different lakes. Wisconsin State had fewer students and far less tradition. It relied on a more exciting team to draw its fan base. The schools worked together to schedule home games on opposite weekends, and the awful Madison traffic prevailed every Saturday in the fall.

Four years after Munson arrived, Wisconsin State reached its summit. The Boars won the Rose Bowl in 1995 and Randy was promoted to offensive coordinator. Two more Rose Bowls were due largely to Munson's wizardry. He was viewed nationally as a horse whisperer for quarterbacks.

At 43, Randy Munson had a full head of straight brown hair. Unlike the other coaches, he was trim, athletic, and occasionally fashionable. The players saw from his mannerisms at practice that Randy Munson had spent some time in their shoes.

Munson worked tirelessly with Craig Zellnoff, a tall, rangy kid with limited talent but good instincts. As bitter as Munson remained about being passed over for head coach, he still put in the 12-hour days at his office. He still reviewed the game films and preached the gospel of Boars football to any talented offensive recruit.

Randy was the only coach who liked Clark Cattoor back then. He'd actually admitted to Clark ten years before that he got a kick out of *Firing Squad*. Before the gag rule came down from Jim Tillman, Randy had even agreed to appear on the show. Clark respected him for offering his time to a rookie just starting out.

Randy did not say a whole lot. Most of his thoughts about his own program were not encouraging. He lacked respect for Frank, seeing him as a cupcake compared with the previous coach. Randy hated the losing seasons. Like the fans, he'd grown accustomed to the annual bowl trips and the kudos. Instead of saying anything, he just worked harder.

Randy had been a star college quarterback for Northern Iowa in the early 1980s. He'd even landed two pro tryouts, the most promising a cup of coffee with the Seattle Seahawks of the NFL in 1983.

Off the field, Munson and his wife Lisa were the parents of three children, Melissa, Scott, and Brett. They'd named their last son after Brett Favre, the great Packers quarterback. Five weeks before Brett was born, doctors discovered that he had Down's syndrome.

Brett's treatments were expensive, and his special school ran the Munsons about $14,000 a year. On top of that, Melissa was checking out private colleges for next year. Randy had some savings, but not enough to cover a six-figure tuition bill over four years.

Randy's anger at not being a head coach ate away at him every night. Flaherty made nearly a million dollars a year. Munson got by on 55 grand. Not bad, except Lisa had to stay home with Brett each afternoon and could not work. They still lived in the same starter home, one that was far too small for five people, much less four plus an adorable red-headed boy who happened to have a few special requests, as Munson often said of his youngest son.

Randy Munson's career should have landed him a nice salary somewhere else.

Munson had helped eight players make the NFL—three running backs, one fullback, three wide receivers, and one tight end. The numerous offensive linemen in the NFL were, technically, on his watch, but he dealt mostly with the fancy aspects of the offense. He spotted a hitch in his quarterback's delivery on the practice field.

"Craig, when the receiver hooks back at seven yards, try hitting him a half-second earlier. Watch what'll happen."

Craig did. The offense was crisper just by that tweak.

Randy found Wilcox's approach especially tasteless. Randy would walk quietly past the media types with dignity while John charmed them.

Randy, though, had his one shot.

He'd interviewed for the head coaching job at Baylor a few years back. Baylor was awful, and he'd remembered the words of his boss, Bob Monroe. A "hot young assistant coach" should never take a job where he would probably go 8-26 in three years and get shown the door. Don't take it, said Bob. Wait for a good situation.

That good situation never came.

The next year, Bob Monroe left the program and took most of his staff to Philadelphia. Randy was the only top assistant coach left behind. Deep down he believed it was because he didn't rub elbows and swap tall tales with the other coaches every night. He had Brett to take care of, after all, Brett's spirits to keep afloat amid the cruel children in the neighborhood.

Even worse, the call had come from Will Terkel, the Wisconsin State athletic director, on that day, the second Friday in December of 1999. Randy never forgot it. It was the day after he'd interviewed for the vacant head coaching job at Wisconsin State, the job for which everyone had him pegged.

Randy had just returned from a day of shopping with Brett. With all the things that made life challenging for Randy, time with his son helped set things right. Brett's quick smile and easygoing personality made Randy remember that football was a living but not his life.

The phone rang just before dinner.

"Randy, it's Will. I just wanted to tell you that we've decided to go another direction with the head coaching position. We'd like to keep you on staff as offensive coordinator. Whether the new coach will keep you remains to be seen."

Over the next three years, the Boars slipped badly, and Randy's star fell with the decline. As the offense sputtered, the phone calls stopped. He kicked himself constantly. Yes, that Baylor job would have meant sure failure, but $250,000 a year to fail wasn't bad.

Flashing back to his present problems, Randy looked past the quarterback drills and focused on Karen Strassel and her unflappable blond hair. Karen was pacing the sidelines. After all, she was in charge of everyone's future.

The school had hired Karen Strassel as the new athletic director in 2000. The 6', 44-year-old former college basketball coach shook hands with the journalists on this first day of practice.

Dressed in a light blue golf shirt with STATE on the left collar, Karen walked confidently. She knew enough to let the coaches do their thing without watching over their shoulders. She'd won 257 games in 13 seasons as the women's basketball coach at North Dakota and Colorado without an AD keeping her under the microscope. If not for the unbearable stress of coaching college basketball, she would have stayed on the bench forever and not moved into administration. Seven years as assistant athletic director at Colorado was her preparation for dealing with Frank Flaherty.

Frank hated her from the start. The previous administration had taken a hands-off approach, as long as the wins rolled in. Now that the bowl games had stopped, Frank felt that Strassel was slowly overstepping her boundaries. She placed limits on the recruiting and expense budgets for the coaches. Karen called it accountability, but Frank called it meddling. Karen considered Frank's football program at Wyoming as one that had succeeded by bringing in thugs and renegades. Karen came from the school of winning with integrity.

Randy, on the other hand, had nothing but respect for Karen. She understood what the coaches went through and demanded only the same level of responsibility that had helped the Boars flourish in the 1990s, when the team played in three consecutive Rose Bowls.

Randy ached for those days and believed Karen could help the athletic department find its way back on the right path.

As the new AD, Karen Strassel had already replaced five coaches in her two years at the school, three of them in the money positions—both basketball teams and men's hockey. Football was still a sacred cow, but once the milk stopped, Frank, too, would be off to the butcher.

4. Under Pressure

The end of the first practice came two hours after the start.

"OK, Steffon, get in here. You want to play this year? You want to be more than a football freeloader?" Frank yelled across the field to the placekicker before lighting up another Winston. Each time the head coach barked an order, the cigarette flew up and down between his lips.

Jake ran out to the huddle. At stake: a 40-yard field goal. Make it and he would run just one wind sprint, a 100-yard dash. The rest of the team would be done for practice. Miss it and the entire offense would run five 100-yard dash wind sprints. While he watched.

Considering his own lack of popularity within the team, due not to his personality but to his role as a kicker, this was the most pressure he'd ever faced with the Boars. Last year, Flaherty had treated him like a water boy with a uniform. This was real responsibility.

"Snap down, ball up, snap down, ball up," Jake whispered to himself. Five seconds and three steps later, Jake's snap down, ball up was on its way into the steamy late morning sky. A little to the right. Jake threw on the body English. Then his hook kicked in, floating the ball back left and through the goalposts.

"Make me proud, baby, make me proud," yelled John Wilcox, jumping up and down.

"Yeah, Zeke!" shouted quarterback Craig Zellnoff, unaware of

Jake's correct first name but very aware that he would have no more running this morning.

"That's it, fellas, I'm gone," Touchdown Tyrone Collins said in his best James Brown voice, adding a shimmy.

"Good job, shooter," Sam said. He, too, was out from running sprints on this one.

"I think we got ourselves a pressure kicker!" Frank yelled. "You guys on the second team better hope for the same thing or else you'll be running so much that *Chariots of Fire* looks like a frickin' shuffleboard game at a nursing home!"

The running complete, Frank brought the players together midfield. "Gentlemen, I like what I saw this first day," he said. "We appear ready to grasp the challenge of this season. Seniors, don't lose that fire in your eyes. Some days will be hell, men, absolute hell. We do this to make you better. Craig, good throws out there. It's obvious you spent the summer working on your timing."

Frank left it with a fiery chant.

"It's the gleam, men! Never lose the gleam! Back here at three."

"BREAK," the players yelled in unison.

Clark watched the parade of blue and white heading toward him, ready to meet the kid from Fall Creek.

"Jake, Clark Cattoor from WMA-TV, good to meet you. Can I grab you for a couple minutes?"

"Sure."

Then the uneasy pause. Clark instantly knew what it was. He often experienced it with fans. Jake needed a few seconds to say that he enjoyed watching Clark's sportscasts.

"Mr. Cattoor, I really enjoyed your sports reports back in Eau Claire. We used to watch you all the time."

"Thank you. I still miss Eau Claire. That job was the most fun I ever had in this business. Loved the town."

Clark then went into his usual questions about the upcoming season. Once he'd wrapped up his interview with Jake, he strolled toward Randy Munson.

The two men shook hands as if they hadn't seen each other in eight years, which was exactly the case.

"Clark, it's good to see you're in the real media now, not just broadcasting from that warehouse downtown," said Munson. In Clark's early days, the public access studio was located inside a furniture warehouse on East Main Street, just behind a power plant. His shows were often interrupted by the plant bells signaling the start of the overnight shift.

That got a hearty laugh from Clark Cattoor, sportscaster.

"Randy, I appreciate that. I really do. You were the only one there for me when I was a nobody."

"You're saying you're somebody now?" Randy asked with a chuckle.

"At least now the program has to pay attention to what I ask."

"We're both older men now," Randy said with a twinkle in his eye. "You're no college kid. I'm no hot-shot assistant. Just a couple guys trying to pay the bills. We should go out for dinner one night after practice."

"Make that a plan," Clark said without hesitation.

They exchanged phone numbers and set a tentative date for Thursday night at the Golden Lasso, a country-western joint off Highway 18.

Clark usually tried not to get too close to his subjects. He drove back to the station telling himself that Randy was a friend from before any of his good fortune.

Things were looking up for Clark Cattoor, and it wasn't even noon.

5. Sleepy Summer Nights

Afternoon practice was a breeze compared with the morning's. A bright sun hung over the field, but cool winds from the west kept the players from getting too hot.

Weather was rarely a concern to Jake. Since he was a protected entity as a placekicker, he spent most of the day's second practice tossing footballs with Sam.

"Steffon! Steffon!"

It was Frank.

Frank came over to the kickers, still beaming from Jake's pressure kick earlier in the day. The head coach sized up his investment and let forth the good news.

"OK. You showed that you can handle some pressure this morning," Flaherty said. "I'm going to turn up the heat a little bit on you right now. As of THIS minute, YOU, Jerry Steffon, are the starting placekicker. Don't screw it up. You will be the one out there for every extra point, every field goal under 50 yards. It's your show now, Jerry."

"Uh, Jake, coach."

"Oh yeah, right."

Hearing it from the head coach, even with the wrong first name, brought Jake an indescribable feeling.

He, too, had made it.

"Good evening. Thanks for calling Pizza Perfecto. This is Jake. How can I help you?"

Despite being a football player who had made it, Jake still hacked away at the pizza factory. Classes were three weeks away, and he was raising some extra funds for the school year.

"That'll be $15.75, and we'll be there in 30 to 45 minutes," Jake told another customer on the phone.

As he hung up, Jake shifted his green eyes to the television Bill kept in the shop. The sports had just come on.

Clark Cattoor, complete with smiling face, burgundy jacket and wine-colored shirt, popped up on-screen to talk about the morning's football practice. Then came on the footage of Jake's practice-ending kick. Right down the middle.

Jake just couldn't help himself. "Look at that, Bill. Who's the man!" he said with his arms stretched.

"Good kick, buddy. Don't screw it up when you get out there for real."

Jake's face came on the tube. "I just hope that I get a chance to prove myself this year," he said on tape. "Kicking has been a sore spot for the team in recent years, and hopefully, I can clear that up."

Clark then carried on about the team's early schedule. The Boars played two of their first four games on the road. They opened at home with Murray State, a typical September cupcake. Then Wisconsin State would fly west to Hawaii to face the Warriors. The final two games before the Big Ten season were at home against Northern Illinois and on the road at Kansas. Wisconsin State expected to win all four. If they slipped, the pressure on Frank would resurface like a long-lost submarine. All of this heat even before the Big Ten opener.

Only two kickers were allowed to travel. Frank would take eight backup cornerbacks before adding a third kicker to the travel team of 85 players. The remaining three dozen would stay home and watch the Wisconsin State road games on TV. Jake was on the traveling team this time around. He'd never been west of Minneapolis, and he dreamed of the trips.

After six hours of driving around Madison, Jake left work with $117 in cash in his pocket. He still had two hours of bar time to fill.

Madison is the French Riviera of the north. Only a quarter of the city's college students remain in summer. The weather is rarely too hot, and the elbow room in the bars downtown makes for a relaxed nighttime atmosphere.

Jake and Sam met at the Brass Tack on State Street. The two kickers, one a placekicker and the other the starting punter, looked like regular students. They weren't huge, muscular men. They didn't wear garish football team sweats. They actually tipped the bartenders. On occasion, a drunk would come up and wish them luck.

As Jake worked over his second Long Island iced tea, a familiar face approached. A tall man with a pencil-thin mustache.

"Jake, I'm Skip Stevens from the *Dane County Tribune*," the man said with a smile. "You know you really shouldn't be here during training camp. Isn't this place off-limits to you guys?"

Whatever buzz was flowing through Jake's body evaporated like an ice cube in a parked car in the middle of July.

Stevens looked squarely at Jake.

"I'll tell you what, though. I know you're a walk-on who has to work to stay in school. I won't tell anyone about this. Just be careful out here."

"Thank you," Jake said.

"Besides, you're the first-team placekicker! You're the one who will keep this whole thing afloat. I'm not gonna tear that apart!"

Stevens laughed before walking out the door.

Upon the departure of the ultimate football brownnoser, both kickers broke out in laughter. Sam started in on Stevens.

" 'You know you really shouldn't be here during training camp?!' " he mimicked. "What kind of bullshit is that? Last year he did a fluff piece on me, on how I came out of the little town of Neillsville to kick for the big, bad football team. Like I'm a damn Martian because I'm from a small town. What a suck-up he is."

"He really won't tell anyone, will he?"

"Of course not. Skip Stevens is a lightweight."

Even so, Jake turned his drinking into mere sipping for the rest of the night.

6. The Plan Is Born

Clark Cattoor cruised east on McKee Road to the Golden Lasso for dinner with Randy Munson. Clark was in a most foul mood. The one piece of mail he'd hoped would never arrive finally had. It was technically from Carol but was signed by Marlin L. Sanders, attorney at law, the same hack lawyer who'd handled Carol's side of the divorce. More court proceedings were in the sportscaster's future.

Clark had signed the divorce agreement the year before, with one provision that bit him in the back. Instead of paying Carol $800 a month, he'd agreed to sign away 30% of his gross income. Now that Clark was in Madison making a good living, Carol wanted her raise as well. That would up Carol's monthly checks from $800 to just over $1,500.

As he punched the gas on the Camry, Clark remembered how they'd tried for seven years to make their marriage work. They'd read books, put up with counseling, even lived apart for a while. Nothing helped. He was sick of her possessive disposition. She was tired of a husband who worked erratic hours and didn't make enough to support her.

The strain between Clark and Carol had been there almost from the start.

"When are we going to have a baby?" Carol would often ask in a singsong voice.

"Let's see how we're doing in a year," was Clark's stock answer.

Clark wanted kids someday—just not right now. After six years in Duluth, he'd still been convinced that his skills would take them to Madison.

If Duluth was Siberia, his home was the gulag. Carol wouldn't let up. If she wasn't nagging Clark about having a baby, she was complaining about how broke they were. The breaking point had come on a Saturday night two years ago, four years after they first set foot in Duluth. Clark came home from work after the early newscast to find that his wife had tossed all his dirty dress shirts out into the snow.

"Clean up your goddamn closet before you go back to work, you bastard!" she yelled into the driveway as he approached the house.

Clark quietly picked up his ruined dress shirts. He decided that he would leave Carol at the next available opportunity.

He found it the next morning in the bathroom as he lifted up the toilet seat.

She's not pregnant, he thought as he looked at the remains in the toilet. And I'm not sticking around.

The divorce cost him. They sold the house, but Carol was awarded most of the profits. Carol could collect alimony until she remarried. After her marriage to Clark, she had no intention of doing that. So Clark went from a guy with a nice living and a nice house to a guy with no money and a run-down apartment in a seedy part of town.

Then fate intervened.

That April, the main sports anchor at WMA-TV in Madison left for ESPN's *SportsCenter*. Clark heard the news the day it happened, when a newspaper connection in Madison tipped him off with the scoop.

He was sitting in his grimy bathtub when the phone rang. On the other end was the news director at WMA, offering him an interview and a promise.

"If you can move within two weeks, we want you," he said.

"I'll be there tomorrow."

The trip was the return of a conquering hero. This was home. Nothing had ever made Clark feel so proud. This was the validation of his long career, eight years of toiling in obscurity.

A raise of $25,000 was also quite a validation. Even clipping off 10 large a year for Carol was a piece of cake with this raise.

On his way to dinner with Randy, Clark worried about the news from Carol's lawyer. The questions ricocheted through his head: I did sign the deal, what can I do? Do I tell Randy about my stupid problems? Should I even be going to dinner with someone on the inside?

He pulled into the gravel parking lot of the Golden Lasso and took a moment to look at the sky. This was what he loved about Madison. Early on an August evening, the sun dipped gently toward the horizon. The wind kept the night crisp.

Randy Munson was already waiting inside. When you have a child with special needs, you learn to be on time whenever you can.

"Clark! Thanks for meeting me." Randy approached with a warm smile. Some coaches flaunted their football status with jewelry, rings, and jackets, but Randy was classier than that. He didn't give one sign that he worked with the football program.

"My pleasure, Randy. Let's get some food. I'm starving."

The two men wasted no time getting a jump on the evening: a whiskey sour for Randy and a Heineken for Clark.

Clark started in on their mutual work.

"So how did practice go today? We didn't make it out for the afternoon workout."

Even with just half a sip of whiskey in his system, Randy couldn't keep it in any longer.

"First, everything I say while sitting here with you is off the record. Fine?"

"Fine."

"OK, then. Flaherty is an idiot." Randy swallowed more whiskey from his tumbler.

Clark's eyes opened as quickly as his ears. He loved sports gossip.

"You like the cigarettes?" Randy asked.

"From Flaherty?"

"Yeah, what a bunch of crap," the coach said. "He picked that up over the summer. Too much stress in this job, he says. Karen told him to quit lighting up during practice when the media are around, and he pretty much told her to kiss it."

Randy shook his head.

"Anyway, Flaherty comes up with this idea for a reverse play. Says it will utilize our receivers and our blocking on the left side of the ball. We run his little idea for nearly an hour. I've got quarterbacks who can't throw the ball to open receivers. I've got running backs who fall over whenever someone gets within three feet of them. Touchdown Tyrone is already wearing Miami Dolphins gear underneath his practice clothes. His head is gone. We're falling apart, Clark. Absolutely falling apart. I should have taken the Baylor job." Randy downed his drink and motioned for another.

Clark sat, stunned by Randy's candor this early in the dinner.

"Why am I telling you this? Because no one else understands. You see, all of the other coaches are Frank's guys. They just stand around and tell him how good his crap smells, how delicious it tastes. There's no accountability out there. Even with our easy schedule, there's no way we make a bowl game at this pace. No way, NO WAY Monroe would have EVER allowed this tomfoolery at practice."

"Have you talked with him about this?"

"No, I'm stuck here. I know Wilcox is out for my job. If I get fired, Frank will just install Wilcox as offensive coordinator and call the plays himself. That's his power trip. I'm on extremely thin ice. Screwed either way."

"Screwed either way?"

"Yeah. If we go, say, 3-9 or 4-8, we'll all get fired. If we make a run at the title, Frank will get a contract extension and more power to do what he wants. I'll probably get fired then."

"Do you really think you'll get fired? After all you've accomplished here? Four Rose Bowls in 11 years?"

Randy shook the ice in his drink around in a circle.

"People don't care about that anymore," he said. "That's old news. The school just cares about money. Money money money money money. That rules college football now. We're all under the gun because our kickers choked last year and we missed out on two million dollars in bowl game money. Why we don't get kickers on scholarship, I'll never know."

Randy finished off his whiskey sour and ordered a cracked-pepper steak with a salad on the side. Even at the embryonic stages of a bender, he wanted to work in a speck of nutrition. Clark had the spicy chicken with green beans. He had to keep his shake up for barhopping later on. Thursdays in Madison are the rowdiest nights of all.

"Clark, I'm sorry to throw all this on you."

"No, really, it's fine."

"I'm just so pissed off right now. I want to provide for my family. With one kid looking at private college and Brett, bless his heart, just trying to live a full life, I'm broke. If I would've taken the Baylor job, we'd be above water. I would probably have been fired after three years, but we'd be rich. I feel like a man trapped inside the football machine. It's a nightmare."

Randy realized that he was treating his dinner companion like a crisis hotline operator. He took the water off the stove to cool for a minute.

"Again, I'm sorry. It's just bottled up."

"Gosh, that makes my problems look small," Clark began. "Today my ex-wife petitioned for 700 more bucks a month in alimony. I agreed to pay her a percentage of my work earnings when we split up. It'll be 1,500 a month. Nothing I can do."

"That's what, 18 grand a year?"

"Yup."

The whiskey nearly shot out of Randy's nostrils after hearing that.

"I tell ya, Clark. You, my friend, are in a pickle. At least for my money, my daughter will get an education."

Clark raised his green bottle of beer for a toast.

"To spending thousands of dollars on something we'll never see."

"Cheers."

After the glasses clanked, Randy started in on something extremely taboo while chopping up his medium-rare sirloin.

"OK. Since I'm a state employee, it's no secret that I make $55,000 a year as offensive coordinator. My wife gets to drive a free Mercury from one of the dealerships. Whenever I appear on Frank's radio show, if, say, he cannot make it, I get 100 bucks. That's about it.

Take out 16 for college next year, 14 for Brett, 10 for taxes. I'm left with, what, 15 grand a year to live on."

"About that."

"I've often wondered what I could do in Las Vegas with what I know about the inside of our program, and most of the Big Ten. I'd make a killing."

"You didn't—"

"No, I didn't gamble, just wrote down some picks each Friday. Dropping money would not get me only fired but thrown in jail. I need to be there for Brett. My little boy is so friendly, but everyone rejects him. At the mall, people look away from his smile. In the neighborhood, no one wants him to play sports. The doctors say Brett should live until he's 40 or 45. There will very well be decades of loneliness for him. I want him to enjoy his childhood now."

"And that's why he's at Wingra Harbor."

"Yes. There's other boys like him there. It's expensive, but no one there will tease him. It hurts me to see him in pain."

Clark grew uneasy as the whiskey sent Randy back to the world of "what if."

"What if I could take my information on the team and put some action on, be it for us or against us? Think about it, Clark. I CALL THE PLAYS. I know what the team's strengths and weaknesses are. If I'm going to be fired anyway, why not?"

"You realize that telling me this could get you in trouble," said Clark. "I won't tell anyone. It's just making me uncomfortable." That statement was one of the hardest things Clark had ever uttered.

Randy stood up to walk to the men's room. Clark wiped fresh sweat off his brow. Did he just hear this? A respected football coach actually talking about betting against his own team, and, even worse, throwing the game from the sidelines? If he uncovered this, that would make the drugged steer scandal in Grand Junction look like a story about a teacher stealing No. 2 pencils.

The cool, calm, guru-like image of Randy Munson had been shattered in Clark's eyes. He was just another plotting man out for an extra buck. The only difference was that instead of wanting money for sin or vice, Randy wanted to take care of his family.

Randy returned to the table with the color drained from his face.

"I'm a little sick after that steak. Do me a favor, Clark."

"Sure."

"Forget what I said tonight about…"

"That?"

Randy nodded. "That."

"I see you're having a difficult time. Work and life seem to have each of us crying in our beers."

"Thanks. However, I would like to keep in touch," Randy said as he cleared his plate. "You're a good guy and I appreciate the fact that you aren't out to kiss anyone's butt at football practice. That's what makes you different in this town."

"Thanks, coach." All coaches loved it when regular people called them "coach."

To Clark's surprise, Randy picked up the tab, and the men headed out into the night. The cool Madison evening was settling in.

Life was still good for Clark Cattoor, as long as he avoided the mailbox.

7. One Final Blowout

The last week of August has a magical quality on the Wisconsin State campus. Thousands of students return for the school year, and a class of freshmen show up to start a new life. Downtown Madison is abuzz with anticipation. At night the weather cools down, and the bars and house parties heat up.

The team broke camp on August 16. Jake Steffon and Sam Cattanach were two of the few football players who didn't have to stay in tip-top shape. As long as Jake showed up and did his job the three or four times he was called on, that was good enough. That line of thinking encouraged the two to find themselves at plenty of bars, plenty of parties, plenty of decadence.

"I'm never drinking again," Jake said twice a week to Sam. A roll of the eyes from Sam was usually the reply.

"Isn't this more exciting than going to an old barn in the country and drinking Coors, or whatever it was you Fall Crickers used to do?" Sam would tease back.

Though still a walk-on who paid his own way, Jake held off all challengers for the starting position. He would be the pressure point, the one who would determine football games with his right leg. He basked in the attention. Both Eau Claire TV stations came down during training camp and did extensive stories on the starting placekicker. The Madison newspaper ran long, flowery pieces on his rise from tryout winner to difference maker. Jake saw his name appear in the summer onslaught of glossy college football magazines.

A big day beckoned.

First, Frank Flaherty slapped a scholarship on the punter. The coach had three extra scholarships to hand out before the first game. Frank pulled Sam aside after practice and told him the school would pick up the tab. Tuition was waived, and he now had access to the training tables, the Old Country Buffet of college football.

To celebrate Sam's good news, Jake drove the Honey Wagon out to Best Buy to pick up NCAA Football 2004, a video game for his Playstation 2. By the mid-1990s, it was almost an NCAA-mandated rule that all college athletes play these things. Touchdown Tyrone even went so far as to take his on all road trips. Frank Flaherty did not mind, as he figured that unless Tyrone lined up hookers to watch him play, the video games would keep him out of trouble.

Unlike his teammates, Jake had no problem dropping 50 bucks for a video game. He was still delivering pizzas twice a week. Even that aspect of his life had gotten out and was part of a feature on one of the local stations. Jake just needed enough scratch to cover his partying, which was getting fairly expensive.

Jake fired up the game, sat back, and watched with delight.

The starting placekicker for the Wisconsin State team was #17. He was on a video game. Immortalized forever.

That Friday night was another swing swift at Pizza Perfecto. A hundred dollars later, Jake met up with Sam at the apartment. They hopped in the Honey Wagon and headed west to a party hosted by the roughhousing offensive linemen, Bob Verly and Cory Larkman.

Their get-togethers were for the handful of rednecks on campus. The corn-fed boys from Up North would play old Garth Brooks songs and a little Charlie Daniels, and consume cheap beer, like Olympia or Busch Light. The African-American players tended to stay away from Bob and Cory's version of Studio 54. A little too country, they would tease the linemen.

Bob and Cory lived in an absolute hole on South Orchard Street, west of the WSU campus on Lake Monona. Yet their hole had history. Boars offensive linemen had lived there every year since the

1995 Rose Bowl season. Rats, roaches, and raccoons all looked to the house as a mess hall. The rodents set up shop with various offensive linemen.

Jake and Sam made their appearance at the rat hole just after midnight.

"Sam, just think, one week from tonight we'll all be holed up at the lock-in," Jake said. The Friday night before home games, Flaherty had all players, walk-ons included, under watch at a hotel on the west edge of campus.

"Last Friday night of freedom, my friend. Make this the Friday night you'll remember until December, cause there won't be no more," Sam replied.

The turnout did not disappoint.

By Jake's quick count, more than 75 football players crammed into the Casa Cory and Bob for this little get-together. Blacks. Whites. The Puerto Rican backup offensive tackle. It didn't matter. The lure of free brew and easy women was enough for even the black players to tolerate hearing Martina McBride. The lure of rubbing elbows was enough to make the everyday Joes pay five bucks for a bottomless plastic cup.

Bob was in the basement, his left hand on the keg of Leinenkugel's, his right hand free to fill the plastic cups. Cory, decked out in a brown fringe jacket with a suede Western hat, was across the basement, in charge of the music.

"OH, MY, LOOKY WHAT WE GOT HERE FOR YOU!" Cory bellowed into the DJ microphone upon spotting Jake and Sam. "KICKERS! Ladies, you gotta love your kickers. Their job is to get it up fast and go the distance!" A decent set-up from a lineman who was best known around campus for vomiting in a washing machine after a bender freshman year.

In the corner of the basement, Jake spotted a familiar face.

"Sam, isn't that the sports babe from Channel 11?"

"I don't know. I've never seen her with her clothes on."

Jake had seen Rachel Randall at practice a handful of times, microphone in hand. She had never interviewed him, but she did catch his eye the few times she was at practice.

"What are you doing here?" Jake asked Rachel.

"I'm new in town and looking for a way to blow off some steam," Rachel countered. "It's not like I'm an old maid or anything."

"Well, in that case, Jake Steffon. Nice to meet you."

They shook hands.

"Rachel Randall."

"Is that your real name?"

"Yes," Rachel said. "I get that all the time."

The 5'11" blond sportscaster started in right away. No "how's practice going?" kind of question for her.

"Do you guys always get this drunk during the season?" she asked.

"Don't lump me into this category. I'm only on my second drink of the night." Jake was already on top of his female conversation game.

"I'm so excited," said Rachel. "Next Saturday will be my first football game working for the station. That is, if Clark doesn't hog the game himself."

"So you work with Clark. How's he doing? I grew up watching him back in the day."

"You're from Duluth?"

"No. Just outside Eau Claire. Tell him I said hi."

Jake had pegged Rachel as simply a pretty face with a remedial knowledge of sports.

"Clark's a good guy," she said. "I'll tell him you said hi."

"Thanks. Did you come here with anyone?"

"Yeah, my roommate, Lisa. She's here somewhere."

A switch in atmosphere ensued. Out with the country, in with the 1990's good-time music. "Jump Around" was next up, a classic white rap/party song heard nearly 100,000 times within the city limits during the previous decade.

"I came to get down! I came to get down! So get out your seat and jump around! Jump around! Jump! Jump! Jump!" Jake yelled with the other partygoers in the basement. He looked for Sam, but the punter was nowhere in sight.

Back at Bob's Beer Hut, Rachel and Jake stood in line for another.

"So how long have you been in Madison?"

"Just since February. I graduated from Point in December. I worked for a station in Green Bay for a few months."

"When you're out of Point, you're out of town," Jake said, a reference to the tag line for Point Beer, brewed in Stevens Point. Neat logo but a wicked drink.

"Not like I don't hear that often."

"Are you from Stevens Point?"

"Farther north. Eagle River."

"Wow, that's up there." People in Wisconsin tend to judge toughness by how far north someone is from.

"Yeah, we have Eskimos and get around on snowmobiles in the winter."

"Do you really—"

"No, Jake, we're just like everyone else."

The two shared a laugh as Bob eagerly filled up their empty cups with more liquid lightning. DJ Cory then took control.

"All right, we're going to slow it down for you folks. Couples only on the floor, please. Couples only."

Cory broke out another slow classic from the previous decade: "End of the Road," by Boyz II Men.

Rachel did something a professional should never do. "Care to dance?" she asked shyly.

"Sure."

Jake felt the smoothness of Rachel's cheek on his own. She brought with her the scent of tropical perfume. As the music faded, Rachel suddenly sobered up. She pulled her face away and looked him in the eyes.

"Jake. Do me a favor. You didn't see me here at this party. I shouldn't be here because of my job."

"Why? Did I do something wrong?"

"No. People don't take me seriously because I'm young and because I'm a woman. Just please, Jake?"

"OK."

Upstairs, Rachel's roommate, Lisa, was sitting on the lap of one Craig Zellnoff. This was the final Friday night that Craig could go out and get what he called "silly drunk-"just as long as he stayed away from the gyro shop after bar time.

Craig was being his usual drunk, loud self with wide receivers Laverneus Wilson and Touchdown Tyrone Collins. The fact that white-bread Craig and his very urban, very street-smart receivers were at a party together in Madison was testimony to the sport's uncanny ability to break down their differences.

"OK. So here we are, boys, the season is only a week away," Craig slurred. "Now what are you two receivers going to do for me? Tyrone, I know you're one step from leaving for the NFL. You think you've got that IT that the league wants."

Tyrone nodded in Craig's direction.

"Damn straight."

"Just don't drop any of my damn balls this year."

Tyrone laughed uneasily at the jab.

"And, you, Laverneus. Can you even spell, Laverneus? Or have they not taught you that back in English as a Second Language?"

In 30 seconds, Craig had put those walls right back up.

Laverneus fired back.

"Craig, man, why you even have to bring that up?" Laverneus had been chronically ineligible since his start at Madison. He sat out his freshman year with grades but brought those up, thanks to easy classes and switching to sociology.

"Shit, you can hardly speak English," Craig continued. "You're in those idiot courses—"

Now Tyrone was sobering up and getting ready to back up his fellow receiver.

"—you can't even run the right routes half the time. I'm throwing passes to where you should be, and half the time you aren't even ready."

"That's not fair, man. You know that."

"Whatever."

Lisa sensed a fight was about to break out and did the smart thing. She jumped off Craig's lap.

Just in time, too.

Craig stood up. The empty glasses of Tanqueray were doing the talking.

"Why don't you do something about it, you dumb receiver?" Craig chuckled but no one else joined in.

Tyrone barked back. "Did I just hear you call him a 'dumb receiver'?"

Laverneus didn't give Craig the chance to answer. He flew out of his chair and jumped on the starting quarterback. A handful of punches were thrown on both sides before the 30 Boars football players in the living room broke it up.

"Gentlemen. Outside," said a voice from downstairs. DJ Cory was now Bouncer Cory. He spent his fall Saturdays protecting Craig and Laverneus. Now he had to send the two brawlers into the night.

Shit, Rachel thought. She'd witnessed the whole thing. She was, after all, a sports reporter, and this could be her big scoop. But people did not need to know she was at this party. People especially did not need to know she'd shared a slow dance with the team's starting kicker.

"Why do I put myself in these positions?" she moaned to herself.

Cory pulled off the cover-up right there. No phone calls. No police. No journalists. Everyone at the house simply shut up and moved on. If there was one thing Frank Flaherty truly despised, it was tales of his brawling players.

Now that the Boars were coming off bad seasons, it was open season on the football program. Each indiscretion-every shoplifting arrest, every domestic assault—would be seen and read by all.

Cory Larkman had earned Most Valuable Player for his quick damage control even before the season started.

8. Last-Minute Jitters

One of Madison's thousands of joggers ran effortlessly past the corner of Frances and University. The drizzle on this late August afternoon gave this young man in the Wisconsin State crew shirt the quality of a gladiator, a superhero in the Madison rain.

Clark Cattoor saw him from his Camry. That used to be me, he thought.

Clark was still coming to grips with the fact that he now lived in the same city where he'd gone to college. Few things in life make a person feel older than that.

His brief dismay over the march of time dissipated over the thought of tomorrow. The football season opener against Murray State was only hours away.

At four in the afternoon, Clark was driving west to work. He had produced so many football stories leading up to tomorrow that he'd allowed himself a break today. Tonight would bring another stressful evening for Clark and Rachel. The start of high school football had the Channel 11 Sports crews all over southern Wisconsin.

As the jogger ran down University toward that sparkling horizon, Clark sped off to the station.

Three miles south, Randy Munson dragged himself onto the bus for the processional to the hotel.

"Everyone on the bus! Let's go! Let's go!" Frank Flaherty bellowed to the football players assembled in the bowels of the Boars' locker room. Frank believed that football teams focused best when together. He would never allow his own players to sleep in their own beds the night before a home game. More than 100 players boarded three buses for a mile-long trip.

Frank and his dozen assistant coaches rode in the front of the first bus. Saturday would set the tone for the season. If the Boars looked disorganized and won by only 10 or 14 points, the vultures would return. A 42-6 victory would shut everybody up. The control freak in Flaherty enjoyed it when the media kept quiet and stayed away from the hard questions.

Randy had much more floating through his brain on the bus ride. He was going to look into The Plan. Saturday would be field research. Las Vegas had installed the Boars as a 26-point favorite over Murray State. The season was still too young for Randy to feel comfortable putting out heavy action one way or the other. Too many new faces in new places.

Randy decided he would look into what plays put the Boars at a real disadvantage and what plays did not. He controlled the substitution patterns and the play-calling. He was about as close to coloring the product as anyone in the stadium.

He and Clark had spoken a handful of times after practice since that dinner at the Golden Lasso. Talk about The Plan never came up, and the two men acted as if the meeting had never happened. Randy took great comfort in Clark's ability to maintain a secret.

After all, Clark had money troubles himself. Both men were just scraping by. This could provide a way out. Randy just needed to find someone else "inside the huddle," as he said to himself, to execute the thrown plays.

The Murray State game would show him who would respond under pressure and who would choke.

Randy thought the Boars didn't have the talent to win seven games. Craig's head was not always in the game, especially against lesser teams. These hotshot receivers had scattershot brains. His offensive linemen were excellent, but without good skill players, the season would collapse.

Randy figured he might as well pad his bank account before the guillotine fell.

Jake Steffon and Sam Cattanach were cooped up in Room 228. The clear water of the indoor pool sloshed just outside their room.

"Let's hit the pool and the hot tub," Jake suggested.

"I'm on it."

Different rules still applied to the kickers and punters. Most players avoided the pool because they didn't want their muscles to cramp up in the middle of the night. Jake appreciated a swim and a soak to help calm his nerves.

Jake had kicked especially well in this final week of practice. Even his spotty range improved. He was now fairly reliable on field goal kicks from 45 yards out. His aim remained as true as ever.

"I know I won't sleep a wink. I'm going to be up all night watching *SportsCenter*," Jake said over the bubbles.

"I figured that. You look like a wreck."

Sam, too, would spend the evening tossing and turning before dozing off around 3. Three hours of sleep would follow before the 6:15 wake-up call.

The Murray State game was an early kickoff. 11:10 A.M. ESPN ruled college football in many circles, and the Boars were always good for a high rating throughout the state of Wisconsin.

"These early games play with your head quite a bit," Sam remarked. "The wind is always real bad at the start, but after halftime, it dies down."

The last thing Jake needed was another element to worry about. He was 192 pounds of nerves as it was.

"So, what's up with you and that sports chick?" Sam asked.

"Oh, shit," Jake said with a groan. "I knew that was coming."

Sam had kept it quiet to that point.

"She was all over you at the party, and I haven't heard the phone ring for you all week."

"She hasn't called me once. She told me to call her at work on Tuesday afternoon and I forgot. I did see her at practice on Wednesday and we didn't say anything to each other."

"That sucks."

"Yeah, but she's just another girl right now."

The chatter kept Jake's nerves from boiling like the water. He and Sam climbed out of the hot tub and went back into their room. It was almost 9. Room check was 9:30.

Beer always helped Jake sleep, but even he didn't have the guts to bring a bottle into the room tonight. So he rolled over and rolled over. Counted sheep. Pretended he was dead. Sometime around 3 in the morning, he was finally out.

9. Murray State

"Welcome to Madison, Wisconsin. It's a sunny 74 degrees as we get ready for the start of the football season. Wisconsin State will take on the Murray State Racers as the home team looks to return to a bowl game for the first time in three years. Good morning, I'm Simon Smith, and welcome to Mendota Stadium and the Wisconsin State Football Radio Network...."

At 9 in the morning, that familiar voice rang out throughout the state of Wisconsin. More than 85 radio stations carried the call of the game, from Milwaukee to Dubuque, Iowa, from Rockford, Illinois, to Duluth, Minnesota.

Over the next two hours, more than 64,000 people dressed in blue and white marched onto the Wisconsin State campus. Nearly all of them expected an easy win. Those close to the program, like the coaches and writers, weren't so sure.

"Zellnoff Key to Good Start," shouted the *Dane County Tribune's* front page. "Flaherty's Hot Seat Warms Up Today," read the top of the sports section.

Jake Steffon had little time to worry about his day. He opened it right at 11:09 A.M.

"Wisconsin State has won the coin toss and elects to kick off. Murray State will receive. Jake Steffon will kick off for the Boars."

The booming voice over the loudspeaker made Jake's spine tingle. In front of this many people, he couldn't even feel his feet.

Jake marched his nine steps back from the ball, turned right, and marched six more steps along the 25-yard line.

The 12,000 students were yelling "OOH!" in unison and jingling their keys. The sun was bright on the light green turf. Jake could hardly see the football sitting upright on the tee just ten yards away.

OK, Jake, just like in practice, he said to himself.

The steps to the ball rattled off effortlessly. One, two, three, four, five, six, seven, eight, impact.

Jake hit a floater to the right. A Murray State returner was under it at the 7-yard line before a crew of blue made the tackle at the 18.

Jake had passed the first test.

"Good job, Jake. Piece of cake, Jake. Nice kick!" John Wilcox was jumping all over him after that. "See, I told you last night you could do this, Jake! Keep it up!" Jake hadn't even seen Wilcox the day before.

After a stop on defense, Craig Zellnoff was locked on target. He connected on his first four passes to lead the offense to the Murray State 8.

"Right slot Z 46," Randy Munson called out to the quarterback. That was his favorite play inside the 20-yard line.

Craig found Laverneus Wilson, of all people, for the first touchdown of the year. Wilson hauled in the 8-yard touchdown pass and broke out into the Electric Slide, saved exclusively for wedding receptions and touchdown celebrations.

Touchdown Tyrone Collins was the first to congratulate Wilson in the end zone. "Good grab, bitch!"

Craig sprinted down to Wilson, the fight eight days ago the last thing on his mind. He patted the rail-thin receiver on the helmet.

"EXTRA POINT TEAM! EXTRA POINT TEAM!"

Jake Steffon hustled onto the field right behind punter and new holder Sam Cattanach. Jake had to work off someone else's timing on the placements—in this case, Sam's. On the fourth "HUT," the ball would snap.

"Hut, hut, hut, HUT!"

Sam handled a wild snap and buried it in time for Jake to knock the leather between the uprights. 7-0 Boars, just four minutes in.

"You nervous anymore?" Sam said with a chuckle.

"Nah, we're all right," Jake said as they trotted off the field for the kickoff.

Leading 14-0, Wisconsin State's offense stalled on the Murray State 16. Jake Steffon faced his first real challenge as a placekicker: the field goal.

Kicking was the team's biggest question mark. It was even more of a question mark now, with Jake working on just four hours of sleep. A 33-yard field goal would be his first college attempt.

"Hut, hut, hut, HUT!"

Jake knew he sliced it, striking the ball to the left of where he should have. Just like a golfer slicing with a 7-iron. The same physics.

The football was high enough, but fading to the right. Jake's body English and a generous east-to-west breeze kept the ball from zipping to the right and outside the goalposts.

The football settled four inches from striking the right upright. Field goal good. Question mark answered...for now.

"Nice hold, hoss," Jake said to Sam after the officials raised their arms for the field goal. 17-0 Boars, after one quarter.

By the late third quarter, Craig was on the bench, enjoying the 41-7 lead. He'd thrown three touchdown passes, including a 56-yard bomb to Touchdown Tyrone. Games against Murray State would help pad his own account, his statistics. Tyrone Collins already had five catches for 103 yards and a score, not eye-catching but solid. For once, Tyrone was content.

Jake had settled down. Six for six on extra points and two made field goals, from 33 and 39 yards. One of his eight kickoffs made the end zone, but none were terribly short. All in all, an outstanding opener.

The same could not be said for Randy Munson. The offense had performed so well, he couldn't find a weak link for The Plan. Craig was out. A starting quarterback with pro aspirations, no matter how minimal, would not go along with it. The receivers had loose mouths.

In the third quarter, Randy called some variations on what Frank

Flaherty wanted. None of the plays resulted in big losses or turnovers. Randy chalked that up to the fact that Murray State was awful.

Final score: Wisconsin State 48, Murray State 13.

"That was exactly how I expected this team to come out and play."

Frank Flaherty held court in the media room at the northeast wing of the WSU Bubble, an attached corner extension of Mendota Stadium. In front of Frank, eight TV cameras, four radio reporters, and more than 60 newspaper hacks stood, armed with microphones and bad questions.

Seated at a desk with Wisconsin State and National Bank draped behind him on a backdrop, Flaherty was unusually jovial. 48-13 wins tend to do that.

"Craig's play? Three touchdown passes, 300 yards passing, no interceptions. I wish I could bottle it and bring it out next week, like rubbing the lamp for good luck."

He laughed at his own joke. No one else did.

"Anyways, let me just say this. If we play like we did today next week in Hawaii, we're in for a long evening. Let me tell you. Hawaii is not so forgiving."

The obligatory knock, even after a near-perfect showing.

Skip Stevens from the *Dane County Tribune* brought up the supposed Achilles' heel.

"Talk about Jake Steffon's performance today. Perfect on all kicks. Did that surprise you?"

"Yeah, actually, it did. You never know how a kid making his first start will perform. Jake was consistent during training camp, but I've seen dozens of kids fall apart in their first real game action. Jake Steffon just may help me sleep tonight."

Directly below where Flaherty charmed, Jake Steffon was in the middle of his first gang pack mass interview. Jake and six teammates were in the weight room. Four cameras, complete with bright lights, and a dozen reporters, surrounded the kid from Fall Creek, each jamming a microphone toward his mouth.

"I was pretty comfortable out there," Jake commented, rubbing his forehead. "Last year I was a wreck during that extra point. Having

Sam out there holding for me helps me settle down. Punters make great roommates."

The media jackals laughed at that one. A kicker as comedian.

Questions for a kicker are fairly limited unless the kicker just made or missed the big one at the end of a game. After four questions, a chorus of "Thanks, Jake" came from the reporters before they searched out the other players.

Jake, sweating from the TV lights in his brown suit and blue tie, walked outside and into the bright afternoon. His parents were waiting, along with a contingent from Fall Creek out to witness town history.

Touchdown Tyrone Collins was in his usual perch, standing on top of a bench press machine so all the cameras could get an easy shot of his face.

"Yeah, Murray State is the kind of team I live for," Collins said, his black sunglasses helping shield the camera lights. "Teams like this are usually slow, and they get confused easily. I probably shoulda had three scores today, but I'll live with just one."

Unlike nearly every other player at Wisconsin State, Collins was not afraid to throw self-aggrandizing statements into his interviews.

"So, Tyrone, your thoughts on Hawaii next weekend."

The receiver flashed his trademark grin.

" 'Mele Kalikimaka' is the way to say 'Tyrone Collins for Heisman.' You watch. We'll smoke those Samoans."

"Actually, they're Americans too," one writer commented.

"That's true. They're not as dark as I am, so those bitches probably won't be able to stick me. 'Aloha' means 'Three TDs for Touchdown Tyrone!' "

What a gem.

Frank Flaherty may have wanted Touchdown Tyrone to shuffle off to the NFL, but the football writers in Wisconsin hoped he would stay forever. Or, at the very least, get drafted by the Packers.

Craig Zellnoff was the last to leave the interview room.

"Sure, Hawaii will be tough. They always play teams from a glamour conference like the Big Ten like it's for their lives. It won't be easy."

"Thanks, Craig."

10. Basking in Victory

Clark Cattoor was still riding out the adrenaline from covering his first game at WMA-TV. He was allowed access to interview players on a one-on-one basis—no gang interviews for him. The Channel 11 crews could park anywhere they wanted around the stadium. All this special treatment because of the station's Sunday morning program, *The Frank Flaherty Show*. Channel 11 had ponied up the cash to wrestle the rights away for the show for the first time in station history.

Clark's Saturday night partying would be subdued. He would have to wake up at 6:30 Sunday morning, drive to the station, and tape the 30-minute show with Frank Flaherty at 8:30. The tight turnaround time meant that Clark would have to show up Sunday morning prepared beyond belief.

Tomorrow, his first show, was a big deal. Clark had interviewed Frank nearly every day during training camp, but he had never sat down to dinner with the head coach. Their relationship just wasn't at that level.

Clark hoped it would change during the first show. He figured the best way to earn Frank's trust was to get the coach in and out as quickly as possible. Like other coach shows, this one was set up as a softball fest. The host would introduce the coach. The coach would struggle through ten minutes of highlights. The host would interview a third person, usually an assistant coach or a player. Soft feature stories about a player's academic success or charity work would follow. End of show.

Not exactly hard-hitting journalism.

Clark pulled his Camry into the WMA-TV parking lot, the first one there at 6:30. Over the next two hours, he met with a tape editor here and a producer there. By 8:15, he was convinced that his debut show would be flawless.

At 8:23, Frank walked into the studio. Clark stood up from his folding chair.

"Congratulations on the win, Coach!" Clark wasn't familiar enough to call him Frank.

"Thanks, Clark. It actually went much smoother than I thought it would."

Behind Frank was his guest for the show, Craig Zellnoff. The coach usually brought on the starting quarterback for the first week's episode. He liked it when the quarterback set the tone for the season after the opener.

Except for one minor tape malfunction, the first show went without a hitch. Taping ended just after 9. Frank and Craig were out the door within two minutes.

"Good morning, and welcome to *The Frank Flaherty Show*. I'm Clark Cattoor, coming to you from the WMA-TV studios in Madison."

It was 10 A.M. Jake Steffon was sitting on the couch. He was rubbing the Saturday night out of his Sunday morning eyes, munching a bagel in the living room of the Kickers' Castle. Jake had watched this show when he was in high school. Ever since he'd made the roster the previous October, it had, once again, become part of his Sunday morning tradition.

He watched while flipping through the Sunday morning *Dane County Tribune*. The sports section featured five pages of coverage of the Murray State win. Buried in the Game Notes section on page 4 was an item about Jake's outstanding debut: "Kicker Jake Steffon erased concerns about the kicking game Saturday. Steffon, a redshirt freshman from Fall Creek, connected on field goals from 33 and 39 yards and was perfect on extra points. Saturday was his first starting assignment."

"See, they love me already," Jake said to Sam. Sam wanted nothing to do with the newspaper. He was afraid his poor day of punting would be highlighted.

Jake came across the next item on page 4.

"Oh, check this out-"

"No—I don't want to hear it. If it's about me, I don't want to hear it."

Jake couldn't resist.

"Now the concern may shift to the punting unit. Sophomore Sam Cattanach was shaky in his three punts," he read. "His 46-yard effort in the third quarter was negated by two punts off the side of his foot. An 11-yard punt in the fourth quarter caused Flaherty to slam his headset down."

"Don't you have some pizzas to deliver?" Sam said, rolling over and going back to sleep.

That was true. Jake had to go to work in 45 minutes. At least the day would be profitable: NFL season opener, Packers on TV at noon. The eight-hour shift was worth a good $250. He would drive around, listen to the NFL games, and make a bundle of cash. Jake needed some extra spending money. The team was flying out to Hawaii on Tuesday afternoon.

Seconds after Sam rolled over, the video of Jake's first field goal came up. Clark Cattoor and Frank Flaherty were cooing over the kick.

"We thought he might be nervous at the time, but look at it. Right through," Frank said on the air.

"Just inside the right upright for the kid from Fall Creek," said Clark.

"If only you dopes knew what was going through my mind at the time," Jake said to his half-eaten bagel.

He sat on his couch, newspaper in hand, his roommate and best friend asleep, and a thought came to him.

Kicking footballs was still a lonely vocation.

11. The Next Step

Randy Munson had seen The Act before. Frank Flaherty was inside the bowels of Mendota Stadium, acting the tough guy on Tuesday morning.

"Gentlemen. The trip we are about to make will be long. You will be restless when we arrive in Honolulu."

Only 75 players were traveling to Hawaii for Saturday night's game. The players and assistant coaches already sat in the team's film room for this week-long odyssey. The non-traveling players were off for the week and under orders not to cut any classes.

"Anyone here ever been to Hawaii?"

Fifteen hands shot up.

"OK. Good. You won't be in for too much of a culture shock, then. Hawaii does this to teams. Great teams lose in Hawaii. Players and coaches lose their focus. We cannot do that."

Great, Jake Steffon thought, another motivational speech.

"Downtown Honolulu and Waikiki are full of temptations. DON'T FALL INTO IT. I'll touch on those in a second.

"Gentlemen, please review the itinerary that we set out for the trip."

Jake glanced at it. He just wanted to get to the islands.

Frank read through the sheet. He omitted the big words for the benefit of his wide receivers and running backs.

"Tuesday, September 3. Leave Madison by plane for Minneapolis, 12:35 P.M. Arrive Minneapolis, 1:20 P.M. Leave Minneapolis for Honolulu at 2:45 P.M. Arrive Honolulu, 6:52 P.M. Arrive at Waikiki DoubleTree Hotel. Bed check at 8:30 P.M. local time."

"Wednesday, September 4. Practice at Aloha Stadium, 11 A.M. Lunch to follow. Special tour of Pearl Harbor after lunch. Dinner will be at 4:30 P.M. Free time until 9 P.M. bed check."

"Thursday, September 5. Practice at Aloha Stadium, 11 A.M. Lunch to follow. Luau dinner at 4:30 P.M. Study tables from 6 P.M. to 8 P.M. Bed check at 9 P.M."

"Friday, September 6. Walk-through at Aloha Stadium, 11 A.M. Lunch to follow. Dinner at 4:30 P.M. Optional movie run at 6 P.M. Bed check at 9 P.M."

"Saturday, September 7. Bus from hotel to Aloha Stadium at 10 A.M. Game time is 2:30 P.M. Beat Hawaii. Free time following victory. No bed check."

"Sunday, September 8. Bus from hotel to airport at 11 A.M. Depart Honolulu at 1 P.M. Arrive at Minneapolis at 12:35 A.M. Fly charter to Madison. Depart Minneapolis at 1:45 A.M. Arrive Madison at 3:00 A.M. Go to class. Anyone who misses a bed check will be met with serious consequences."

The threat of discipline met plenty of subdued eye-rolling. Every man in that room knew that if you produced on the field, you had no rules.

Touchdown Tyrone knew it. All he talked about over the weekend to anyone who would listen was "my Aloha hos." Missed bed checks would not keep him out of the Aloha spirit for Saturday's game.

Frank looked up and tried to get serious again.

"Remember, gentlemen. You are representatives of the school. Not just yourself. Not just the football team. The school. Wisconsin State. Me. If you go out and spend all night partying in Waikiki, people WILL hear about it and WILL talk about it. That not only reflects poorly on you. It reflects poorly on me.

"We will have thousands of fans following us for the game.

Saturday will be like another home game. The Hawaii fans don't care that much. We'll have 10 or 15 thousand fans on our side. Our fans will be out every night until dawn. They CANNOT see you out on the town. It looks bad.

"You will have free time. We will have fun. You will get some time on the beach. I encourage that. This is not just a business trip. If that was all that I wanted, I would have scheduled a game at New Mexico or Alabama."

Frank paused, sensing the fatigue inside the dark film room.

"I will leave you with one piece of advice. In fact, treat this like the gospel. When in Hawaii, act like your mother is watching your every move. Don't embarrass her. No shady women. No massage parlors. No bars. Behave like gentlemen. Let's go."

As nervous as Frank Flaherty was over the prospect of the upcoming trip, Randy Munson was an absolute wreck. During the Sunday film breakdown of last year's Hawaii team with the other coaches, he found the weak spot that would launch The Plan.

Touchdown Tyrone.

The Hawaii Rainbows had a cornerback who could actually stick to him, a guy named Lance Wallrick. Because Hawaii played in a lesser conference, none of those national football highlight jockeys at ESPN ever paid attention to them.

Randy read all the talk from Tyrone saying how he would go about scoring three touchdowns out there. The Hawaii coaches had to show those clips to their star cornerback. They had to, it was part of Coaching 101. The smart money said Touchdown Tyrone would be knee-deep in drugs and hookers and in no shape to play on Saturday.

The Plan was on.

Randy had a connection at the Gold Sports Book, one of the new on-line sports gambling clearinghouses. He had to handle this delicately and far from the Las Vegas casinos. Any Las Vegas win of $10,000 or more would be reported to the IRS, so large sums there were out of the question. Gold Sports Book was based in the Netherlands Antilles of the Caribbean. All wins were exempt from taxes.

If The Plan ever came out, Randy would face jail time, public humiliation, and the knowledge that he would never be able to get back into coaching. Ever.

He planned on getting fired after the final game anyway. If he did nothing, Brett and the rest of the household would just suffer in the end.

He was just a criminal, looking out for his family.

Two weeks before, on August 23, Randy had called Stephen Crossland, his roommate 20 years earlier at Northern Iowa. Stephen worked as a manager at the King's Crossing, a sports book on the north end of the Vegas strip.

The two had kept in touch through the years, and now Randy was ready to go forward with "Operation Alamo," a reference to the second-tier Alamo Bowl that Wisconsin State figured to get into after the season. Stephen agreed to float Randy up to $30,000 to get started, with Stephen taking a third of the wins and Randy paying any losses.

Stephen came up with a scenario. He would place the wagers in his own account at Gold Sports on Friday morning. He would wait for the call from Randy.

On Monday, September 2, Randy made the first call from his Riviera. The pay phone in the parking lot of the PDQ at the north end of West Towne Mall was his new office phone. He couldn't leave anything to chance here. No paper trail.

"What's the number for Saturday?" Randy asked as he held the receiver to his sweaty ear.

"We've got you as a 13-point favorite."

"Shit. Any possibility that'll get moved up to 16 or 17?" Randy wanted a two-touchdown cushion to work with.

"Yeah, I'd say so. Boars fans tend to come through and bet heavy by the end of the week. We don't see much action from Hawaii." As money poured in on Wisconsin State to win by 14 points or more, the Las Vegas Line would inch up to 14, 15, maybe more by the end of the week.

"Let's plan on nine this weekend against," Randy said. That was his code for $9,000 on Hawaii to win the game or lose it by 12 or less. "I'll check the number with you Friday morning and we'll proceed from there."

"Gotcha down. Catch you Friday."

This bet was a sure thing. Wisconsin State could still win 30-20 or 27-17. Hawaii was a solid if unknown program. The writers would be happy with a trip to the islands. The fans would be happy with a win. And Randy would be happy with a fresh $6,000. The first of many days of happiness all around.

For The Plan to work, Wisconsin State would have to beat the spread a few times this year. They couldn't lose all of them. They'd have to win at least three times out of the remaining 11 games. On those weekends, Randy would hold off any action or bet with the team. Knowing the competence of his players on offense, he was most nervous about that prospect.

Saturday was the ideal game. A favored team, on the road with a week of distraction.

Randy Munson was scared but confident as he finally sold his coaching soul.

12. Aloha to the Boars

Big-time college basketball teams fly just about everywhere at all hours. Teams in the Big Ten spend Wednesday nights in small airports like Bloomington, Indiana, or Happy Valley, Pennsylvania, or Champaign, Illinois. The players return home around three in the morning and are expected to go to class and practice the following day.

Football travel is relatively easy on the body. Wisconsin State played most of its early games at home. The Big Ten road games were usually handled by bus.

With only 20 people, including coaches, and minimal equipment, the basketball team gets chartered flights. The football team has to fly commercial, due to the size of the party.

When the team's 737 touched down at Minneapolis/St. Paul International Airport on Tuesday, more than 120 people—players, coaches, media, school officials there for the free trip to Hawaii—disembarked for the connection.

Frank Flaherty was in charge even here. The assembled group gathered in Gate C23, their arrival gate.

"Gentlemen!" he announced. "We have to get to Gate F9 in 20 minutes. That's not a lot of time. Follow me. If you get lost, F9."

Half football coach, half babysitter. Big-time football at its finest.

The posse of blue-and-white-clad football players, nearly all with headphones blasting, was enough to frighten the thousands of business travelers. Most of the suits just yielded as the Sea of Blue passed through each concourse. A few fans yelled from the sidelines.

"Go get 'em, Boars!"

"Kill Hawaii!"

"You da man, Coach Flaherty!"

As expected, a few players took some liberties about arriving at Gate F9 on time. Touchdown Tyrone Collins was the ringleader. Most of the Florida players were always broke. Tyrone was the exception. Due to his "friend," football super-agent Jerry Copperzweig, Tyrone had brought more than $1,800 for the trip. He was ready for some serious mischief on the islands.

Tyrone and a few other players from the Florida clique stopped by the World News newsstand in the main concourse. Tyrone purchased a stack of adult magazines for the eight-hour flight to Honolulu.

"What kind you like, Dante?" Tyrone asked backup safety Dante Lamarr. "Asians? Nurses? Black tail? White girls?"

"All of them, T," Dante said with a chuckle. "As long as you're paying."

Tyrone bought a dozen different magazines to, as he said, "keep the flight interesting." He also added a Wall Street Journal for a total bill of $96.55.

"Gotta keep an eye on my Benjamins, ya know," Tyrone told the shocked clerk. "Keep the change."

He then distributed the bounty to his friends, like Santa Claus handing out candy canes.

Jake had saved up most of his summer money from Pizza Perfecto, and brought more than $1,500 with him for the week in Hawaii. On Packer Sunday, he'd cleared $259 for an 11-hour shift. Green Bay demolished the Vikings, causing pizza customers to tip wildly throughout the afternoon. He stayed late and drove the Honey Wagon as other drivers called in sick. More money for me, he reasoned.

Jake was going to show Sam Cattanach a good time this week. Sam had endured a horrific game against Murray State. The coaches, especially Wilcox and Flaherty, were on him hard during Monday's practice. Sam was clearly a better punter than his numbers demonstrated. Because the offense was so effective, Sam was never able to get into a rhythm.

Jake and Sam did not wear headphones. They enjoyed the outside world. Especially Jake, for this was his first road trip as a college football player.

"Check that out. Pathetic," Jake said to Sam as they watched Tyrone's shopping spree. "At least I'll save my money and get you the real thing out in Hawaii."

"You don't need to pay for me to get some lovin'. I can do it on my own."

"Not according to the coaches."

"Low blow, asshole." That was Sam's last word in any light argument. At least he knew Jake had his back.

"Don't sweat it. You'll taste that crisp island air and you'll be kicking the ball 50 or 60 yards. The coaches will find someone else to make a scapegoat. It's just your week to be the bitch."

"Thanks, man."

The team had reserved a block of the plane, rather than individual seats. On the massive 747, with eight seats per row, the Boars' football party took up 16 of the back rows, from 21 to 36. The coaches sat in the first two rows; the players and journalists sat wherever they wanted to.

Clark Cattoor spotted an empty seat next to Randy Munson in Row 22.

"Randy, great to see you."

"Where you been, stranger?" Randy broke out his genuine grin.

"Working my tail off. This week won't be a picnic either, even if it's Hawaii."

"How can you say that? We're all living the dream, Clark. Say, what are you going to do about the show Sunday morning?"

"Frank and I are taping it from a TV station out in Honolulu. Our affiliate has agreed to cut all the video. We'll just ad lib the whole thing and fill it with the stories I'm doing out here all week."

"I see."

"I'm just happy to go to Hawaii and collect my frequent flyer miles. I need this trip to go to Phoenix for free."

"Phoenix?"

"My aunt's down there. I love her, but not for 500 bucks round trip."

Randy got a chuckle out of that. He also appreciated brutal honesty. The chatter then turned to his family.

"How's Brett doing?" asked Clark.

"Great, actually. Two weeks ago we took him up to Green Bay to watch the Packers practice in the morning. The team gave us a pass inside the fence to watch from the sidelines. During stretching, Brett Favre came over to meet Little Brett. I fought back the tears as I took the picture. The Two Bretts, I called the photo when we got it back. I even had it blown up, and I put it in his room. He just stares at the picture and smiles.

"Favre was great. He didn't have to be but he was. Brett was talking to him about how good they were going to be this year and this and that, and Favre just stood there, smiled, asked some more questions, and even signed a football for him. What a nice guy."

"That's a heartwarming story. So things are going well?"

"It's still a struggle. Brett just started third grade at Wingra Harbor. His teachers have already told us that this year will be the most difficult. Either he'll get the material and learn or he'll stay at his current level for a few years. Every night, Lisa and I work with him, teaching him basic multiplication and some reading. I just hope it all sinks in."

"What about Melissa? Decide on a school yet?"

"It's so hard to say with her," Randy said with a sigh. "One week it's Marquette, then it's Vanderbilt, then it's Georgetown. I'm holding out hope that she'll go to State, just 'cause it's free for me. But I know she's got the brains to do well in private school."

"Maybe she can get some scholarships."

"Even with that, we're still lookin' at 18 or 19 grand a year. I just don't want her to get stuck with student loans like I did."

"State won't happen, huh?"

"Probably not."

Randy changed the subject.

"Are things getting any better from the divorce?" he asked.
Clark laughed sarcastically.

"Hell, no. I'm still shelling out over 20 grand a year, between
what she gets now plus having my attorney try and stop her. It's
almost driving me to spend my weekends at the casino."

After the obligatory half hour on the tarmac at Minneapolis, the
jet headed west for the land of Aloha.

Three rows behind Randy and Clark, Jake and Sam were ready
for the islands. Sam's parents had taken him to Hawaii when he was
just nine. He remembered seeing Pearl Harbor and the beach, but
little else. With that scant experience, Sam was an authority on
Honolulu. Jake had hardly left Wisconsin, so to him Sam was like
Lewis and Clark wrapped into one.

"You were smart to wear shorts getting on the plane. Smart
move," Sam commented. "People look at you in the airport like you're
nuts, but screw 'em. They're going to Fargo while we're going to
Honolulu."

"We're going to have a blast. Cost will be no object," Jake said.
Sam needed cheering up. Not only was he a punter on the hot seat,
but his girlfriend of two years had broken up with him earlier in the
summer. His dry spell had crept into September.

"I gotta get it on my own. Paying is cheating," Sam said.

"Kickers rarely have groupies. That's the one thing I've learned
since last year," Jake said.

Rosa Parks meant little to Touchdown Tyrone Collins. He
always sat in the back of the bus or, in this case, the plane. The
coaches would rarely venture back there to bust up his racy magazine-
viewing sessions or high-stakes card games.

"All right, fools. Let's play some cards," Tyrone said over the
shuffle of a Bally's Casino deck. He'd picked it up during last year's
trip to Las Vegas.

"Texas Hold 'Em. Just like Rounders."

The others chipped in with $1 bills or the occasional $5. Tyrone
did not let on that he had $1,700 with him. He made sure to break
out a stack of Lincolns and Washingtons from his stash.

Eight hours later, the weary players cheered the descent into Honolulu. Tyrone may have been the most exhausted. After all the magazines and seven hours of poker, Tyrone was officially a grinder. Seven hours scored him a whopping total of $52, just over half the cost of his in-flight entertainment.

"Sheeit, guys. I'll just take this money and use it to pay for yo' drinks later in the week, you broke crackahs."

The flight touched down ahead of schedule, just after 6:30 P.M. Hawaii time. 10:30 Madison time. As the players waited impatiently for their luggage, a caravan of buses pulled up to the arrival counter.

After an hour of Oahu gridlock, the team arrived at the DoubleTree hotel just "steps from the beach"—about a thousand steps, for world-famous Waikiki Beach was still twenty minutes away on foot.

As he settled into his room for the early bed check, Jake was already scouting the nightlife scene. Bars galore. Women everywhere. Aloha shirts for sale on each corner. $1,500 to burn.

13. Bad Case of the Kicks

"Get up! Breakfast is downstairs in the Aloha Room! Be in the lobby, ready to go at 9:15. Gentlemen, bring your cameras with you if you want to take pictures of Pearl Harbor. We'll tour there after lunch. DO NOT BRING YOUR MUSIC TO PEARL HARBOR. You can listen to your headphones on the bus, but NO HEADPHONES. Show some respect for our veterans."

The alarm clock read two minutes after seven.

The night before, Frank Flaherty had recorded that message to be played on the telephones of each Wisconsin State player.

Jake Steffon never heard it.

Always an early riser, Jake actually did something unheard-of among the jocks. He woke at five in the morning and watched the sun come up on the beach. By himself.

The uncompromising peace of sunrise did wonders for his jet lag. Jake felt like a new man instead of one who'd spent the previous day cooped up on airplanes. At seven, Jake was the only player munching on a breakfast of muffins, apples, and eggs in the Aloha Room. Just Jake and the coaches.

The convoy left for Aloha Stadium right after nine. To Flaherty's surprise, all 75 players were accounted for. Bed checks had gone without a hitch the night before, according to John Wilcox, the coach in charge of knocking on doors.

Maybe this crew will actually behave like adults, the coach allowed himself to dream. The buses headed west on the H1 Highway across Honolulu.

Wednesday's practice was wonderfully routine. Touchdown Tyrone Collins made his allotment of amazing catches from the various quarterbacks.

That concerned Randy Munson.

The offensive coordinator wondered if Collins had actually spent Tuesday night in his room. Randy himself had gone out along Kuhio Avenue and enjoyed some of the Waikiki nightlife. Frank allowed his coaches free rein, as long as they pleased him while on the clock.

For The Plan to work in its inaugural test, Collins could not have a breakout game. A game with ten or twelve catches, three scores and 200 yards would most likely cause Wisconsin State to win by 14 or more. That would bury him. Being out $9,000 was enough to cause threats in the middle of the night and a certain reluctance to start your own car.

On the other side, if a star like Collins or Craig Zellnoff was injured this week, the game would be taken off the board. No bets would be allowed due to the injury.

Randy would have to take it easy on his star players, the very players he was trying to quietly harness on Saturday.

On the other end of the field, Sam Cattanach had just shanked another kick off the side of his foot. The ball bounced to a harmless stop on the Aloha Stadium turf, right next to Wilcox. The problem was that Wilcox was 20 yards from Sam, not 50.

"New state. Same shitty punter!" Wilcox yelled while pacing towards Sam. "You're better than this, but I don't know anymore. Why in the hell did we put you on scholarship? Answer me!"

Sam simply stared at the ground. His job wasn't on the line for this game. The team didn't have any other punters on the trip. Jake was the only other kicker, and he was a terrible punter.

Jake walked over and patted Sam on the head.

"Your show, bud. Just boot it like the old days. Focus."

"Thanks."

Jake leaned in.

"Show that asshole that you're the shit."

Sam nodded and uncorked a high kick that nearly pierced the few clouds on this warm, Hawaiian afternoon.

For whatever reason, Sam's 60-yard boot kicked off Wilcox even more.

"Gee, you get a little talking-to and you're a damn All-American? We shouldn't waste a scholarship on you, but maybe we should on a damn shrink! Do that again—this time without Jake licking your ear!"

The pressure was back on Sam, seconds after his best punt in weeks.

He sliced the next one for a whopping 22 yards.

"See, goddamn punters! We need a punter here! Cattanach, you'd better hope the offense scores every goddamn possession Saturday. You don't need to litter ESPN with the crap you call punting. Hell, we may just go for it on fourth down every damn time."

Sam wanted to choke Wilcox until the coach's beet-red face turned purple.

Frank Flaherty ran over to Wilcox. Now it was Wilcox's turn for a whisper.

Jake and Sam watched with delight as the color left Wilcox's face.

"Uh, OK. Field goals. Jake, give me ten field goals from 35 yards."

Just before two, the freshly showered players sat down to a catered spread in the visiting locker room at Aloha Stadium. Frank had ordered 65 pounds of ham and 20 pounds of pineapple to give the meal a native accent. Jake indulged in the pineapple, but Sam was too angry to eat.

"I swear. Sometimes I wonder if this shit is even worth the hassle anymore. Even being a football player gets old after a while."

"Yeah," was all Jake could muster. He was still thrilled with his new life as a field goal kicker for Wisconsin State. How else would he get to Honolulu during the first week of school? Still, Jake knew that Sam needed an ear more than the truth.

Sam then set the tone for the remainder of Wednesday.

"We're going to get roughed up tonight after bed check. You and me. We're the only kickers. They won't do anything even if we get caught. You're still bankrolling tonight, right?" Sam jammed a piece of ham into his mouth.

"Oh, yeah. What we gotta do is get some Hawaiian shirts, a couple of hats, put on our sunglasses. No one will know who we are tonight out on the streets."

The three o'clock tour at Pearl Harbor was reserved for the Wisconsin State football party. The coaches rolled off the buses first, observing their players as they walked off the buses. Frank needed just one minute to blow a gasket.

"WHAT DID I SAY ABOUT THE DAMN HEADPHONES?" Frank barked between puffs on a Winston. "DO I NOT SPEAK YOUR DAMN LANGUAGE? NO HEADPHONES AT PEARL HARBOR."

"Huh?"

All Tyrone Collins could see was Frank yelling at him. He couldn't hear Frank, as he was immersed in Naughty By Nature's "O.P.P." Tyrone liked the old stuff.

"NO HEADPHONES."

"Aw, all right, Coach."

"Show some damn respect for the people who died to give us freedom! Jeez."

Tyrone ran back onto the bus and put his headphones on his seat.

"Don't nobody take my CD player now," Tyrone said to his friends. "I know y'all want it so you can sell it on eBay when I'm an All-Pro."

Tyrone had no use for Frank or his attempts at discipline. He was hours from hitting the streets with a stack of hundreds. He might as well get used to the nightlife in Honolulu. Tyrone planned to get back here every year in the NFL's Pro Bowl.

Back at the DoubleTree, the mass of football players ingested another buffet-style meal in the Aloha Room. Jake was wearing down a toothpick after dinner with Sam on his way up to Room 2322, the kickers' oasis.

"All right, how do we do this?" Jake asked. He was still as green as the grass when it came to eluding the coaches on bed check.

"We need to hang on for 30, 45 minutes in our room. That'll put us at 9, maybe 9:15 or 9:30. Then take the stairs to the garage, not the lobby. We don't want to chance it because the coaches like to sit in the lobby at these places and drink. I already checked it out. Get to the garage, quietly, and head out."

Jake unlocked the door to Room 2322. The balcony in their room faced southeast, toward a view of Fort McMurry across the street. The beachfront hotels were past the fort. To the far left was Kalakaua Avenue, where the actual trouble would start later tonight.

"OK. We have the aloha shirts. You've got green, I've got blue," Jake said. "Hats, check. Turf shoes, in case we have to run, check. Now we wait."

An hour later, Coach Wilcox was back.

BOOM BOOM BOOM.

"Bed check!"

The players had to yell their names.

"Jake Steffon."

"Sam Cattanach."

As long as the players said their own name, Wilcox usually didn't bother to look inside.

The kickers spent the next hour watching University of Hawaii volleyball on television.

"Look at that ass," Sam remarked about one of the volleyball players.

"You're all riled up and ready to go there, shooter."

"You have no idea, man. I need some bad."

"As long as she's not a horse, I'll pitch in for you. A happy punter equals a happy defense."

"We're a long way from northern Wisconsin."

Escape From DoubleTree took place at twenty after nine. In full aloha gear, Jake and Sam threw on their Reeboks and got off their queen-size beds.

Jake walked over to the room safe.

"You're not bringing it all?" Sam asked.

"Do you need $1,500? Are you going to screw five hookers at once? Hell, from what I've heard you say, you'll need about two minutes. I hope she charges by the minute."

Jake left six hundreds in the safe. $877 and change would be their limit.

The kickers tiptoed their way down 23 flights of stairs, opening the door to the garage level like James Bond entering the enemy's missile silo—very slowly.

A look left provided freedom.

"Act like we belong here. Don't turn your face toward the lobby," Sam cautioned. The lobby was just above the garage entrance.

Fifty-seven steps later, they were free with nothing but raising hell on their minds.

Sam emerged minutes into this odyssey as the tour leader. The men stepped east in the cool night to McGillicuddy's, an Irish bar in the South Pacific.

"Let's knock 'em down," Sam said as they entered.

For a Wednesday night, McGillicuddy's was packed. The air was itchy and the music pulsating.

"Can I start a tab?" Jake asked the bartender.

"Got a credit card?" came the reply.

"Just lay this on my tab. We'll even up later." Jake placed a $100 bill in the bartender's palm.

"What can I get ya?"

14. Plotting in Paradise

Clark Cattoor and Randy Munson did not have to go secretly into the night. The sports anchor and the offensive coordinator finalized their evening plans at dinner.

A Japanese karaoke bar would be the night's hot spot.

Clark walked behind Randy into Tibuchi II, a bar with massive windows and a light blue neon sign screaming out the name for the tourists. Clark always fancied himself a world traveler, even though he'd never used a passport.

"Two hot sakes, please," Clark shouted to the bartender.

"Coming up right 'way, sah," said the Japanese man working the bar.

Clark dived into the karaoke songbook, flipping the pages in a rhythmic cadence as he searched for musical gold.

"Oh, nice! They've got 'Thunder Island' by Jay Ferguson."

"I don't think any of the others here even know that song, buddy." Randy chuckled. Clark looked around. They were the only two Anglos in the bar.

An Asian man crooned out the Aloha version of "Can't Help Falling in Love with You" as the drinks arrived.

Randy got up from his bar stool.

"I'll be right back. Gotta make a quick phone call home."

He walked to the pay phones by the bathrooms. After a concoction of numbers on his prepaid phone card, the man at the other end had some welcome news.

"Stephen. It's Randy. Sorry to bug you so late."

"That's all right, it's only 11 here. Not too late."

"Where are we at for Saturday?" Randy started tapping the top of the pay phone.

"Right now, the best price I see is 14 and a half."

That gave Randy an extra jolt of joviality. Even if Wisconsin State won by 14 points, he would cash in. "OK. We're getting there. Do you see it moving to 15 or 16?" Randy was looking for 17 and a half. That would be ideal.

"Yeah, that's a good possibility. Do you want me to hold off until then?"

"Yes, for now."

"Thanks. Bye."

Randy returned to the table amid the sounds of "Walk a Mile in My Shoes," Asian-style.

"Lisa's doing well," Randy said as he sat back down.

"Isn't it, like, one in the morning back home?"

"Yeah, but I told her I wouldn't be free until late."

"You know what the best part of this trip is?" Clark asked.

"What? No one asking for your autograph when you go out?" Randy teased.

"Funny. Actually, no trips to the mailbox. No letters from the ex's attorney, at least for the week. I'm still afraid to check my voice mail, though."

"Freakin' women," Randy said dismissively.

"So, are you pretty confident about Saturday?" Clark now wanted to talk shop.

Randy swallowed the sake.

"I can't read this team," Randy said as he flipped peanuts into his mouth. "One day, they're so sharp. Craig will throw bullets to Tyrone and Laverneus. Jason Brunson will emerge in the backfield. He was so solid against Murray." Brunson was a backup running back for three years. He'd picked up 87 yards and two touchdowns in the opener.

"Is Jason the man now?"

"No. We still have to rely on Craig. Our running backs are still too spotty, too prone to fumbles. I'm worried that the guys aren't taking Hawaii seriously. Have you been reading the papers?"

"A little."

"Hawaii really believes they're going to win Saturday."

"I can't say I'd be surprised if it were a close game."

Randy waved his empty glass. "Another one please," he asked a waitress. "This is no bullshit, Clark, but also not for publication. I thought Flaherty was going to kill Wilcox today at practice."

"During the…"

"Yes, punting. Cattanach has been awful lately, but he is proven. Wilcox ripped him a new asshole today. I think Flaherty did the same thing right after. Talk about an overzealous assistant. He needs to just relax and not try to force shit."

"When is he going to move on and get that head job we're all waiting for?"

"I don't think it's going to happen," Randy explained. "You see, when coaching jobs come up, especially head coaching jobs, there's two camps: Who the media thinks should get it and who really should get it. Wilcox is a creation of the media." Randy was careful not to say "you guys," as so many would to Clark. "I was probably a little in the creation camp when Baylor called, but people in the know understand what I've done here."

"Sure."

"And Wilcox, he's a freaking babysitter for the kickers and kickoff teams," Randy continued. "The only time we notice him is when they screw up, which is too often."

The next round of sake arrived. Clark took the conversation up to Defcon level.

"So, anything come of our chat last month?"

"I knew you'd come around asking about that."

"So?" The drinks steered the chatter at this early stage.

"No. It's just not worth it," Randy said before taking another sip. "But if I wanted to do it, I probably could pull it off."

A voice came from the DJ booth.

"Uh…CLAHK! Your turn! Come up here!"

"It's showtime, Randy!"

A confused bar full of Asian tourists took in Clark's spirited performance of the 1978 classic "Thunder Island."

15. His Punter's Keeper

Five blocks east of the coaches, Jake Steffon was drowning in those new, trendy drinks. Stoli vodka malt liquor. Watching the commercials, it would appear that drinking that stuff would turn your life into an endless party with endless beautiful people.

The atmosphere was not far off at McGillicuddy's.

Sam struck out with every woman he came across. That was not unexpected. White guys with bad breath were so last century in paradise.

"Jake, Jake. It's like 11 o'clock," Sam said with mischief in his eyes. "We gotta get down to business if we're gonna make practice tomorrow."

"You want to start after the ladies now?"

"May as well get them before two or three other dudes have had them tonight."

That logic made no sense to Jake. He was willing to let it slide for his drunken roommate, the struggling punter. "All right, let's head out and find you some lovin'."

As he strolled down Kuhio Avenue on east Waikiki, Sam had his pick of the litter. Some of the ladies were done up like poodles at a dog show. Others were more subdued. They all walked with high heels and without purses.

"Here's 500. Will that cover you?" Jake handed over the cash.

"I think so. What if I want two?"

"Just stick to one, shooter."

Jake laughed as he took in Sam's already glazed eyes.

"I'll be back at McGillicuddy's. See you in, what, ten minutes?"

"You're pretty damn funny, you Fall Creek hick. Thanks for the money. I'll see you when I'm done."

"Give her hell."

The process of professional companionship did not take very long. Sam spotted a busty brunette in a miniskirt hanging out by the Burger King. Not very classy, but very efficient. She locked eyes with her drunken prey and walked toward Sam.

"Hi, I'm Mariah. Good evening."

Sam Cattanach was stuck in the Waikiki office of the Honolulu Police Department, held indefinitely and charged with soliciting prostitution. *I should have made her come to my place*, Sam said over and over to himself as he held his head in his hands.

An overweight officer, obviously a native of the islands, walked over to him. "OK, Mr. Catta-knack."

"It's pronounced Cattan-aw."

"Sorry. Here's how we usually deal with this. You are charged with soliciting prostitution," the officer said firmly. "So is she. She was not working for us. We spotted the two of you outside the Burger King and followed you back. In certain hotel rooms in Waikiki, we have video cameras inside the rooms. Hotel operators are instructed to give these rooms to these women. That's how we clean it up.

"Anyway, the fine for this is usually $752. If you have it, we will set you free but it will stay on your record. Public records do go in the newspaper. That may not be a big deal to you since you are from... Wisconsin. Are you here for the football game? Are you a fan?"

A smart move finally came to Sam. This guy had no idea he was the punter.

"Yeah, I'm just here for the game."

"I figured as much. However, we have not booked you yet. For embarrassing crimes like this one, we will hold off making it official if you pay a surcharge in advance."

"How much?"

"650 dollars plus the 752. That will come to just over 1,400 dollars. If you come up with that, you're not only free to go-as far as we're concerned, this never happened."

"May I use the phone?"

"Local call?"

"Yes."

"It's over there."

"White pages?"

The officer handed the thick phone book to Sam. "Here you go."

After nine rings, a bartender picked up a phone four blocks away.

"McGillicuddy's," he said

"CAN YOU FIND SOMEONE FOR ME?" Sam screamed.

"I'll try!" Sam could hear "Margaritaville" playing in the background.

"JAKE STEFFON. IT'S AN EMERGENCY."

"OK." The bartender turned down the music. "Is there a Blake Teffon here? You have a phone call. Blake Teffon."

Jake was deep in the middle of a chat with a blonde woman who claimed to be from San Diego. She said her name was Ashley.

"Blake Teffon!" the bartender called out a third time.

The kicker looked up. "I think that's for me. Excuse me."

Jake headed for the phone. The music came back.

"HELLO?"

"IT'S SAM. I'M IN SERIOUS SHIT. GET DOWN TO THE WAIKIKI POLICE OFFICE. IT'S ON ALA MOANA BOULEVARD BY THE BIG MALL."

"What happened?"

"I got busted for…" He couldn't say the word "prostitution." "I NEED MONEY TO GET OUT. NOW."

"How much?"

"1,400 BUCKS."

Shit, Jake thought. I could get him almost all the way there.

"Ashley. I gotta go. Something came up."

"I'll be watching for you on Saturday at the game!"

Jake bolted downstairs and hailed a cab to the DoubleTree. He had to get to the rest of his money. He also had to get in touch with someone with cash.

"Wait here. I'll be back in five minutes," he told the cabby. He took the elevator from the garage to the 23rd floor and was inside his room in seconds flat.

Only one option remained. He called Touchdown Tyrone's room at one in the morning.

"Hello?" Tyrone's roommate, safety Henry Suttle, answered in a sleepy voice.

"Hey, it's Jake Steffon. Is Tyrone there?"

"Nah, he's out, man."

"Do you know what his cell phone number is? I need him, it's an emergency."

"Actually, I have it in my wallet. Hang on." A miracle for Jake.

After some fumbling, Henry produced the elusive number.

"Thanks."

Jake opened the safe and counted his cash. He was down to $920 after all the Waikiki-priced drinks and Sam's $500.

Time for one more call.

"Hello."

"Tyrone?" Jake could hardly hear the receiver. Tyrone sounded like he was cruising on the highway.

"Who is this?" Tyrone answered.

"Jake Steffon. We have an emergency. We need your help, bad."

"Uh-oh. Sounds like someone needs some money from me."

"Yeah, I need a huge favor," Jake said. "Sam's in jail and we gotta get him out without anybody knowing. I'm going to pay 900 bucks toward it. I need 500 from you. I'll pay you back when we get home."

"Sheeit. What am I, a goddamn pawnshop?"

"Tyrone. Please, we need your help. We need a punter on Saturday."

Silence hung in the air. Jake heard the sounds of a car stereo.

"Dammit!" Tyrone yelled.

Jake stepped up the offer. "OK. I'll pay you 300 in interest when we get home. I'm good for it."

"I didn't know you had all this money."

"Don't tell anyone. Get down to the Waikiki Police Station as soon as you can. It's on Ala Moana by the hotel."

"All right."

To Jake's surprise, Tyrone Collins made it to the precinct before he did. Tyrone had always said he had an aversion to police stations, so that made his quick trip to Ala Moana Boulevard even more of a shock.

It was two in the morning. Practice was in nine hours.

"Thanks for coming down," Jake said somberly. "Sorry about all this."

"500 bucks, right?"

"Yeah, that's what Sam told me." They walked into the precinct.

"Shit, for half a grand, at least tell me what he's in for."

"You don't want to know."

"Drugs? DUI? Hookers?" Tyrone pressed.

"There you go."

"Hookers?"

Jake nodded his head.

"Ahhhhh! I knew it! I knew it! That almost makes it worth my money. Hookers!" Tyrone peeled off five Benjamins for the placekicker.

"Look, thank you for floating him the cash," Jake said. "But you've got to keep this quiet. The coaches can never find out about it. No one can ever find out about this. I'll give you 800 bucks when we get back home."

"I know you good for it, pizza boy." That brought a small smile from Jake.

"Thanks. Just keep it quiet, please."

"Anything for a kicker."

Jake approached the police officer behind the counter. The officer already knew why he was there.

"Are you here for Sam?"

"Yes."

"Has he told you the circumstances surrounding his crime?"

"I think so. What will free him?"

"$752 for the prostitution charge, $1,402 will keep it off the record. No charge, no fingerprints, no mug shot, no paper trail."

"Here's $1,400." Jake handed over a wad of hundreds.

"I'll be right back with Sam."

Sam looked like he'd done an hour inside a working cement mixer. The color was gone from his face.

"I'm sorry about all this, Jake," Sam apologized.

"Don't sweat it. We'll figure it out later."

Tyrone couldn't hold off.

"At least tell me one thing, was she hot?"

Sam wouldn't even dignify that with a comment.

"Well, not to fear," Tyrone shouted, "Touchdown Tyrone is here. I'll give you a ride back to the hotel." He pointed to his rented burgundy Mustang convertible.

After winding their way through the curvy roads of Waikiki, Jake and Sam jumped out of the Mustang in the DoubleTree's garage.

"You done for the night, Tyrone?"

"My night is just beginning, gentlemen," Tyrone smiled at the kickers. "See you boys at breakfast."

The Mustang sped out of the garage and into the final hours of the night.

Jake slept like a baby—a baby with a hangover and a long trip to a police precinct. Sam, on the other hand, couldn't sleep. He felt the embarrassment of his actions buried in his soul. The fact that he now owed Jake over a thousand dollars made it even worse.

Five hours later, the taped wake-up call rang.

"Get up! Breakfast is downstairs in the Aloha Room! Be in the lobby, ready to go, at 9:15, just like yesterday. Don't eat too much greasy food. This will be a hard practice today. We'll arrive back here for lunch around two. Then you guys will get some beach time afterward. See you downstairs."

This time, Sam wasn't there for the message. He'd been in the shower for a good hour, washing away the booze coming out of his pores and the sins of the evening before. He finally emerged at 7:30.

"I'm never going to drink again. Last night never happened, man."

That woke Jake up. He wanted to just stay in bed the entire day. Both men took silent comfort in the fact that they were kickers. Kickers, even in paradise, were exempt from hard running.

"Sam, just forget about last night. I'm going to."

"Yeah. What Tyrone did was huge, though. If not for him, it would be in the paper today."

"Did they know you're a football player?"

"Nope. They assumed I was a fan."

The benefits of kicking.

Sam Cattanach kicked the tar out of the football during Thursday's practice. He was out for redemption, even if no one knew except Jake and Tyrone.

Jake wasn't spectacular on his kicks at practice, but he made enough to keep the Wilcox Monster at bay for another day.

Touchdown Tyrone, however, was another story.

He hadn't made his way back to the DoubleTree until sunrise. Shelling out Sam's bail money was a mere speed bump in his night. If not for that side trip, he would have caroused uninterrupted all night.

Tyrone dropped his first four passes at practice.

"C'mon, Tyrone. Focus. Watch the ball into your hands," Randy Munson yelled with a tinge of delight. An unfocused Tyrone was what he was banking on. "Where's all the skill we've read about in the newspapers?"

For once, Tyrone said nothing.

If he called more plays for running back Jason Brunson, Tyrone would get bored and become even more ineffective. Randy still had to play both sides to the middle. Win Saturday and keep the suspicion away, yet don't win by too much and still get paid.

The team spent the afternoon on the world-famous Waikiki beach. Most of the players wouldn't swim in the Pacific, but they all enjoyed the sights, sand, and surf.

Even Sam Cattanach was there.

Sam was having a good day. His punting was stellar and he was able to keep his breakfast down. Apparently he'd let the events of Wednesday night slip below the radar.

"Do you think anyone will ever find out about this?" he asked Jake under the Hawaii sun.

"As long as Touchdown Tyrone keeps his damn yap shut, you're in the clear."

"Will he?"

"I don't think he'll talk," Jake said. "Remember, he was also out past bed check. He may not follow the rules, but he wants to have a big game. The pro scouts will be watching."

16. Greed Is Good

"Stephen, where are we at?"

Another pay phone call from Randy Munson.

"I got good news for you. We're now at 15. Gold Sports is offering 15 and a half. Should we finalize it now?"

"No, hold off until tomorrow. I'm trying to squeeze it out until 17."

Stephen scoffed. "You greedy bastard. You should be OK at 15 and a half."

"We'll see where we're at tomorrow," Randy insisted.

"I make no guarantee that it will stay at 15, but I think it should move up. Whether the number is 17 is another story."

"We'll see tomorrow. Thanks."

Click.

Randy didn't say anything about Tyrone's weak practice. Why should he mess that up? If Frank broke tradition and took some disciplinary action against the best player on the team, what good would that do Randy? If Frank suspended Randy, that would probably take the game off the board in Las Vegas. Tyrone had that much of an impact.

After dinner, the Aloha Room turned into the school's official version of study tables.

Only 13 players showed up, and that included both kickers.

Sam Cattanach was still praying that his actions the night before would never surface. Study tables were an easier option after he'd decided, once again, never to take another drink.

"You mean you actually packed your books?" Sam asked Jake as the placekicker produced four paperbacks from his backpack.

"Yeah, I hear this English 208 is nasty. But it's a requirement, so I have to pass it."

"My tutor dropped me this trig book the day before we left," Sam said with some sorrow. College math, especially trigonometry, was a real challenge for the punter.

"I had algebra last year, and that nearly killed me."

"Man, I never thought that after last night, digging my nose inside trigonometry would be the best choice out here in Hawaii."

The kickers were under the covers in time for ER.

"Good morning! You know the drill today. Breakfast downstairs. Be on the bus by 9:30. We have walk-through at the stadium. Just wear sweats today. No running for players. Kickers in full uniform for reps."

Frank's Friday announcement came as no surprise to Sam. He knew from last year that the kickers were the only ones to do any work the day before a game.

The stiff breeze that swept through Aloha Stadium on the eve of the second game of the season wreaked havoc on Jake and Sam.

Jake's field goal attempts floated all over the place. His accuracy was rarely an issue. This was like a cruel trick. Whenever he would take the wind into account and aim a little more to his right, the wind would stop. Whenever he thought the wind had died down, it would start up again.

After missing 15 of 19 kicks, Jake took on a philosophical outlook.

Sam, too, felt the sting of the Hawaiian winds. His punts were flying to the right each time, directly toward the south sideline.

John Wilcox, as always, had an answer.

"OK, you guys. Enough dicking around. What is happening here is that you two are not adapting to the changing currents. Have you been watching the weather at all this week?"

The kickers were silent.

"Have you?"

Seventy-five players standing around. Only the wind had an answer.

"Well, if you'd paid any attention to the weather reports for Saturday, you would know that it will be like this all day long. Now, as the man in charge of the damn kickers, I need to know: CAN YOU COPE WITH THIS?"

More silence.

"Well, CAN YOU?"

"Yes," Jake said.

"Yes," Sam followed.

As John tried to work out the meteorological issues with Jake and Sam, another beacon of light flashed across Randy Munson's head.

Harsh winds equal missed field goals. Bad punts. Surely Hawaii was already taking all of this into account. He couldn't wait to call the mainland.

"Stephen, it's Randy."

"Wow. It's a little early for you to be calling."

"I just wanted to check where we're at."

"We're still at 15. It's only three here, our major action won't come until later tonight. Why so early?"

"The winds are a little strong out here. I want to get a good price before it goes back down."

"I doubt it will go back down. It's like all your fans are laying 100 bucks here on their way out to Honolulu. We'll just keep driving the number up until they stop."

"What's the house at?"

"I'm just clicking on it now…they're at 16."

Randy couldn't disguise his disappointment.

"What were you hoping for? 17? 18? 16 is still a very good number."

"I would feel much better at 17 and a half," Randy offered.

"Now the truth comes out. Let's see. If you give back 15 percent of the potential win, Gold Sports will let you buy a half point."

Wow, Randy thought, a new option in this whole mess. For $1,350, he could make it 16 and a half. That would allow a 30-14 win to pay off. Otherwise, it was a push and a missed opportunity.

"Nah, I'll pass. Let's put 9 against."

"Officially?"

"Officially."

"Gotcha down."

Randy had done it. He was now in violation of the most sacred rule in all of sports.

17. Hawaii

"GENTLEMEN! As you know, It's GAME DAY. NO TURNOVERS.
CRISP EXECUTION. LET'S KICK SOME HAWAIIAN ASS!
Breakfast is downstairs. Bus leaves at ten. If you can't bring 110
percent today, don't even get out of bed! See you downstairs."

What an idiot, Jake said aloud after hearing Frank Flaherty's
wake-up message at seven. He was still roughed up from the nasty
winds the day before.

The ride to the stadium had a far different tone than the trips all
week. The three huge buses were filled with players and coaches who
looked, felt, and acted like they were occupying soldiers. No mercy.
No holding back.

Thousands of Wisconsin State fans beat the buses to the parking
lot at Aloha Stadium. The smell of bratwurst, sausage, and Miller
High Life turned Honolulu into Little Waupaca.

"Sheeit, I just can't escape that smell. Sausage-eatin' white folk.
All Wisconsin is," Touchdown Tyrone Collins said as he stepped off
his bus. Still, Tyrone was famous, which explained why a little girl
approached him and asked for an autograph.

"Pleeeezze, Mr. Collins," she said.

"Sho. Anything for a fan." Tyrone may have been rough around
the edges, but he always loved his fans. "What's yo' name, little girl?"

"Molly."

Tyrone kneeled to get to face level with the girl.

"How old are you, Molly?"

"Nine."

"Well, I'll see you in nine years, Molly. By then I'll be three years from the Hall of Fame. Don't forget my name now, ya hear?"

Molly's terrified father overheard the exchange.

"Uh, let's go, sweetheart. Mr. Collins has a game to get ready for."

Touchdown Tyrone Collins said all week that he would score three touchdowns against "those Samoans."

At halftime, he still had 30 minutes to pick up three scores.

Hawaii 13, Wisconsin State 3.

Frank Flaherty raged in the locker room during the halftime break.

"ARE YOU SHITTING ME? We're losing to THESE guys by ten points at the half? Did you hear your own fans? They're booing your ass out of the stadium. Men, I WISH I COULD LEAVE YOU HERE IN HAWAII, you seem to love it so goddamn much. WHAT DID WE TALK ABOUT YESTERDAY? Focus. WHAT HAVE WE TALKED ABOUT ALL WEEK? Focus."

Frank spotted Randy Munson and did something he rarely did in front of other players. He let him have it.

"RANDY, WHAT KIND OF PLAYS ARE YOU CALLING? A draw on 3rd-and-13? A quarterback rollout on 3rd-and-6? Get it together. NOW."

Randy could see Frank was close to stripping him of play-calling duties and doing it himself.

Randy was actually calling smart plays. It wasn't like he was trying to throw the game or anything.

Wisconsin State had simply played into Hawaii's hands. The Warriors knew that Wisconsin State was a slow team that could get beat on the outside. Hawaii cornerback Lance Wallrick not only held Tyrone Collins to just two catches for 11 yards, he also kept Tyrone from talking trash for most of the half.

That was a record.

Jake Steffon curled in a 24-yarder for Wisconsin State's only score of the half.

Craig Zellnoff completed seven of his first eight passes in the first quarter before the drive stalled at the Hawaii 7. The ill-fated rollout on 3rd-and-6 from the 8 ended in just a one-yard gain.

The only bright spot was Sam Cattanach. The wind stayed fairly calm for the punter. Because of Wisconsin State's abysmal offense, Cattanach was called on five times in the half. Each kick netted more than 40 yards.

Sam was the only reason Wisconsin State was still in the game. Hawaii quarterback Tommy Wofford had a field day running the run-and-shoot offense with five receivers.

Wisconsin State received the kickoff in the second half. Randy Munson knew the team needed a touchdown to establish a tone for the half. Trailing 13-3, Munson was already in the clear with The Plan. He had 15 points to play with. To Randy, the score was 28-3 Hawaii. He just needed a comeback win, not a blowout.

After a lousy first half, linemen Cory Larkman and Bob Verly finally plugged holes to buy Craig Zellnoff some time. Jason Brunson ran hard on the plastic turf, which was even firmer than the green concrete back in Madison.

Craig capped off a masterful drive with a 12-yard touchdown pass to Laverneus Wilson. 13-10 Hawaii with 10:42 left in the third quarter.

"There you go, bitch. Good toss. We back now. We back," Wilson said to Craig in the post-score celebration huddle.

"Way to hang onto it." The fight two weeks before was now ancient history in their minds. Quick touchdowns had a way of wiping out anything that lingered in the past.

Wofford then turned back into a WAC quarterback. He fired a laser right to Wisconsin State safety Bob Linten. Wisconsin State took over at the Hawaii 22.

"It's Touchdown time! It's Touchdown time!" Tyrone yelled as he took the field with the offense.

"Slot Z, 72 right look out," Randy signaled to his quarterback.

Craig nodded and ran to the huddle.

"Slot Z, 72 right look out on 3."

"Oh shit…it's money time!" Tyrone crowed.

Everyone in Aloha Stadium knew it was going to Tyrone on this play.

"Hut…hut…HUT."

The thought of an easy score in front of pro scouts sent Tyrone off the line like a world-class sprinter. Even Wallrick was caught flat-footed as Touchdown Tyrone blew past him. Craig uncorked a perfect spiral just over Tyrone's left shoulder. Just in stride for six. Touchdown, Wisconsin State.

Flaherty pranced on the sidelines like he was Vince Lombardi.

"EXTRA POINT TEAM…EXTRA POINT TEAM."

Jake Steffon tacked on the extra point, barely. The right-to-left wind in the third quarter was still messing with his head and his kicks.

17-13, Wisconsin State.

Now Randy had to play it on both sides. He had $9,000 riding that Wisconsin State would either lose or win by 15 or less. With a four-point lead, he was still in good shape. Even a touchdown wouldn't bury his bet. What worried him was that Hawaii would throw a dumb interception or fumble the ball at the end and set up a late Wisconsin State score.

Randy had to be cautious on offense.

The game took on a different complexion as the defense stiffened again. This time, linebacker Boo Jackson tackled Wofford in the end zone for a safety. Now it was 19-13, Wisconsin State, with 1:08 left in the third.

Still, Randy said to himself, a touchdown won't kill you. Just run the clock when you get the ball back, score a touchdown, and win this thing 26-13. You'll still be in the clear.

Craig put together a third consecutive scoring drive. With 12:44 left in the game, the lanky quarterback hit Touchdown Tyrone with a crossing pattern over the middle. Wallrick, so consistent in the first half, fell down on the play. Collins ran like a deer through the Hawaii defense, arriving in the end zone after a 48-yard dance to destiny. Now Collins had two touchdowns amid seven catches and 107 yards.

"GET ME THAT THIRD ONE, COACH. GET ME THAT

THIRD ONE!" Tyrone yelled at Frank as he ran off the field.

As Steffon's kick made the score 26-13, Randy's face suddenly lost a shade of color.

Realistically, he knew he was still on the good side. Yet if Wisconsin State scored even a field goal, he was done, finished, off to the Sports Book Wanted List of broken kneecaps and overt threats.

Wofford drove Hawaii the length of the field, but threw another interception. Wisconsin State had the ball on their own 6. 8:41 left.

Perfect, Randy thought. Just run it between the tackles. No deep passes. It's what the right call is. For the team and for me.

The only problem was that the Hawaii defense was out of gas.

Brunson ran simple running plays for 13, 7, and 12 yards. Wisconsin State crossed midfield with ease.

With 3:44 left, Wisconsin State faced a 3rd-and-5 from the Hawaii 29. Randy doubted Frank would call for a field goal. Too much risk there in case of a miss or a block. Hawaii could get back into the game if they blocked the kick.

"Fade-Z, Slot 74. Left deep." Randy called. That was a play that never worked for the Boars.

Craig then found himself with three green-clad Hawaii defenders in his face. He shook them off and found a wide-open Tyrone Collins in the back of the end zone.

Tyrone dropped it.

In front of the pro scouts.

"Mele Kalikimaka" was also the way to say "dropped pass in the end zone with no one around him."

4th-and-5.

"FIELD GOAL TEAM. FIELD GOAL TEAM."

"What the—" Randy yelled as he paced toward Frank. The gambler drunk on greed was now talking. "What the hell are we kicking a field goal for? We don't need to let them back into the game. We're up 13 points."

"Not now, Randy. Our field goal team needs work. I need to see if we can hit from this far out."

"This is NOT a smart move. What if they block it? Call a time-out."

"No. We're kickin' it."

Jake trotted out for a 46-yarder, the longest attempt of his brief college career. Sam, coming off a superb day punting, offered a few words of encouragement. Jake and Sam always set up in position away from the other nine men in the huddle.

"Let's do it, Jake. Breath deep and kick 'er through."

Jake looked up from the turf and saw the wind flags on the goalposts fall to the sides. No more gusts.

"Ready."

Jake hit the football true, just as he practiced each day dozens of times on the field and hundreds of times in his mind. His right foot struck the ball one-third the way up, right on the seam. It felt perfect.

Clark Cattoor dropped the pen in his mouth up in the press box.

"Wow. Look at that sail," he said under his breath.

Jake, meanwhile, stayed focused on the ground.

"I THINK YOU GOT IT, MAN," Sam barked.

Jake finally looked up. The ball was heading right down the middle. He felt he'd given the kick enough power to make it. He unconsciously raised his arms to the sky.

The officials did the same thing.

"You know there are pro scouts here, roomie," Sam said before letting out a devilish laugh and slapping Jake's silver helmet.

29-13, Wisconsin State.

"Shit," Randy Munson said. Now he needed a Hawaii score. Any Hawaii score.

Tommy Wofford was now Randy's hero and last hope. Wofford led Hawaii down the field against the relaxed Wisconsin State defense. First the Hawaii 47. Then the Wisconsin State 39. Then the 27. Then the 18. As the offensive coach, Randy was helpless with the Boars defense on the field.

All football coaches had seen this before. The junk touchdown at the end of a game. Far too often, Las Vegas point spreads were decided by junk touchdowns.

Wofford and Hawaii faced 4th and 2 from the Wisconsin State 10. Randy knew Hawaii wouldn't kick it. They were after touchdowns at this point. Please, he prayed, let this quarterback find his way into the end zone.

Instead, Wofford's prayer was a wounded duck that landed on

the turf at the 5-yard line.

Craig took a knee to end the game. 29-13, Wisconsin State.

"I'm proud of the way our guys handled adversity. That Hawaii team across the hall is a darn good one. They had us down 13-3 at the half. We were concerned."

Frank Flaherty was holding court, this time in front of a much smaller crowd. Only three cameras and about 15 writers were in the media room at Aloha Stadium. The papers in Janesville, Oshkosh, and Richland Center just couldn't afford a junket to Hawaii.

"I have to give credit to Randy Munson," Frank continued. "He called a whale of a game in the second half. We struck at the right time, played it safe at the right time. I cannot stress enough how important his game management was to our comeback."

Randy sure didn't feel the same way. While he'd violated the highest rule of sports, Frank had violated a major rule of football: Never kick a field goal when you're up 13 that late in a game. Especially when your offensive coordinator has nine large on the outcome.

Randy was even more upset that he didn't buy that half point from Stephen the day before.

"I don't know. I saw the ball. Then I saw the sun and it must have just fallen out of my eyesight."

That was how Touchdown Tyrone Collins explained away what should have been his third touchdown pass.

Skip Stevens wasn't buying it.

"But the sun was at your end. You weren't looking back into it."

"Why you gotta bring that up like that, man? You see, I was running into the sun, then I turned around and the burn of it was still in my head, man."

"Uh-huh. I see."

"Anyways, you didn't see the real Touchdown Tyrone today. Who we got next week?"

"Northern Illinois."

"Sheeit. What's that I smell?"

Skip shrugged his shoulders.

"Y'all smell something?"

Skip knew the drill here.

"I smell something," Tyrone barked out. "I smell a 200-yard, 15-catch, three-touchdown day against Northern Illinois. It sho smells good to me."

"You seem pretty loose today, Tyrone."

At that moment, Sam and Jake walked past Tyrone.

"Yeah, we all pretty loose this week. Especially Sam 'my man' Cattanach. That boy had himself an active week here in Waikiki."

Sam's face turned whiter than the writer's notebook.

"With all that studyin' and shit. Look, my boy Sam stays in all week, stays off the beach and then punts like he's an All-American and shit. See, we all loose. Feel the love."

Sam acted like nothing was the matter.

18. Bet It All Against

The only member of the Wisconsin State football party not enjoying himself was Randy Munson. His heart pounding twice a second, Randy ducked next to a pay phone just outside the locker room. No one raised an eyebrow. Randy always called his son Brett right after a game.

"Randy, Randy, Randy. I figured you'd be calling," said the voice on the other end.

"Save it, Stephen. What do we do now?" Randy asked quietly, hunched and facing a wall.

"I dunno. What DO we do now?"

"Well, I don't have the money."

"OK. I figured as much, but we've got a few avenues here."

"Such as?"

"Next week. NIU at home. I'm sure you didn't want to make this a weekly habit, but we may have to this year."

"OK."

"It's still real early, but we can go two ways about this. You can go either spread or odds."

Randy knew what Stephen meant. A thrown game was being offered up. "You do odds against Northern?"

"Oh yeah," Stephen said, his voice crackling in the receiver. "I'm guessing you'll be around a 20-, 21-point favorite. That will mean that you'll be roughly a 560, maybe a 580 odds favorite. That means if you play NIU for the win, for every 100 you pony up, you'll clear 580. That'll make up for nine grand in a hurry."

"So if I tack on three grand and win, I'll clear about 17?"

"About that," Stephen explained. "After my cut, you'll take home 13 or so. That should put you up four grand. You'll be on your way back. But if you lose this week, I'll have to cut you off until you pay up. I can float you for one game, but not two."

Randy looked back at the locker room door. A few fans in blue milled about. Randy focused on the receiver in his left hand.

"How bad would a loss to NIU look?" Randy sounded like an insomniac calling in to the all-night sports talk show.

"You remember how Northern almost beat you guys last year in Madison? It could happen this time. It's just that no one ever plays the MAC teams out here. We never see any action on them."

"Write me down for three on NIU for odds."

"You sure?"

"Yeah. Do it."

Frank Flaherty stood at the front of the pack an hour later. The buses were belching gray exhaust, trekking east to Waikiki for one final night in paradise.

"Gentlemen," Frank announced to the players on the lead bus. "You guys are free to roam the streets tonight. All I ask is that no one gets arrested. No one embarrasses themselves. We've had a great trip so far on that front. Behave like gentlemen. Be smart out there. No curfew. Just be on the bus by 10:45 tomorrow morning. I recommend you eat breakfast beforehand. Tomorrow will be a long day of travel. Trust me on this one."

Jake and Sam looked up from their seats in the middle of the first bus.

"Did you hear the coach, man, no embarrassing yourself tonight, Sam?" Jake said.

"Whatever."

"You'd better take it easy tonight. Stay in the room. I'll go out for you."

"Asshole." The punter's defense mechanism was on overdrive.

"Just do me one favor, Sam. Leave your cash at home."

Even that produced a wry grin from Sam.

Paradise ended the moment they stepped onto the plane the next morning at Honolulu International Airport.

Jake Steffon dozed off in the South Pacific and woke up in Minneapolis. He and the other groggy players dragged their WSU gear and roller bags to a special gate for a charter flight back to Madison. It was one in the morning on Monday. Jake had lost an entire day.

A familiar voice approached.

"Sheeit, Jake, or should I call you KFC? Ya know, the Kid from Fall Creek?" Touchdown Tyrone Collins asked.

"KFC. I like that." Jake genuinely did. The Kid from Fall Creek tag was getting more and more play in the papers.

"You got my bills from this week?"

"C'mon, TD, can it at least wait until Madison? I can't do much now. I left my cash card at home."

"Oh, you know how I gotta have my money to roll back, right?"

"What do I owe you again, Tyrone?"

"I tell you what," Tyrone said, flashing his teeth. "If you take care of me today when we get back, I'll forget some of the interest. How 'bout 600 instead of 800?"

Jake shrugged. "That's fine."

"I gotta look out for my kicker, ya know. Someday I'll be makin' millions on Sundays while you still delivering pizzas, listenin' to me on the radio, beeatch!"

Tyrone laughed at the ceiling before walking away.

Jake was touched that Tyrone even knew what he did for a living.

The charter plane touched the ground at Dane County-Truax Field just after 2:30 A.M. on Monday. Class beckoned for the players.

Randy Munson endured the loneliest drive home. After the weary traveling party scattered, Randy dragged himself into the driver's seat of his 1995 Buick Riviera.

Now I'm screwed, he thought.

Maybe it was the sleep talking, maybe it was the fact that he now owed some anonymous thug nearly ten grand.

He would be on the hook Saturday. Seriously on the hook. Randy had to force an upset loss to Northern Illinois just to get the heat off.

Randy understood that once his offense was to blame for a loss to NIU, the media storm would hit him in the gut. Repeatedly. He would find himself cooked over a slow roller in the local press, like a pig with an apple in its mouth. Frank Flaherty might take away the play-calling duties. Frank could even fire him right then and there.

As Randy pulled onto Mineral Point Boulevard, a warming thought came over him. At least the school would have to pay his contract for the remainder of the year. He had nearly half the house paid off, and the Madison real estate market was booming.

Randy told himself Lisa and the kids just might be okay, even if something bad happened to him. Life insurance, yeah, Randy whispered, move up that life insurance to a half million when you get a chance. Just in case NIU didn't win Saturday and those thugs gunned him down on the sideline.

19. The Big Payday

"Yeah, that jet lag will mess with your head. I know it sure has mine."

Frank Flaherty was in the midst of his weekly Monday press conference in the bowels of Mendota Stadium.

Clark Cattoor fired a question.

"Frank, any ill effects of the long travel with your team?"

"Not really, Clark. Our kids are strong guys. What I am concerned about is their focus for Northern Illinois. I am certain all of our players will not forget last year anytime soon. They had us on the ropes. If not for some quick thinking by Craig Zellnoff, we probably would have lost that game." Craig had faked out three defenders on 4th-and-goal from the 9, careening his way in for the go-ahead score with 44 seconds left.

Everyone back at the station assumed that Clark's trip to Hawaii was a paid vacation. Far from it. He'd turned in a long story each day for the viewers in Madison, covered a game 5,000 miles away, and taped *The Frank Flaherty Show* at 6 A.M. Sunday in a Honolulu TV studio.

After the press conference, Clark made a beeline for his Camry. Gotta get home. Gotta get some sleep. Gotta go out tonight. Beer was cheapest in downtown Madison on Monday nights—32-ounce taps for a dollar at the Kitty Corner.

Only he wouldn't sleep all day.

"What the—?!"

Clark's mail arrived just after two. A letter from Carol's attorney was, naturally, the first one to see the light of day. Inside was a copy of a ruling from Colorado Circuit Court Judge Roy S. Lackwire.

"CLARK STEPHEN CATTOOR, you are hereby ordered to pay a total sum of $1,496 each month to your former spouse, CAROL MICHELLE CATTOOR."

Clark made nearly $60,000 a year. Take out ten for taxes, ten for housing, six for his weasel agent and, now, almost $18,000 for his ex-wife.

Clark's attorney, Josh Steindorf, was the next to hear his voice.

"Josh, man, what the hell is this about? Why can't we fight this?"

"I figured you'd get in touch," said the attorney. "There's nothing we can do. You signed that document giving her 30 percent of your gross income. She's just getting what she's entitled to. You can have it deducted from your paycheck."

"How much?" Clark panted.

"Roughly 700 bucks each paycheck."

"Holy shit."

"Yeah, that could make for one hell of a nest egg for her one day."

Clark sighed. "I used to clear about 1,300 each paycheck. Now I'm looking at 900 every two weeks?"

"I know, Clark, I know."

After three boring lectures and too much walking after too little sleep, Jake arrived at the locker room stall of a certain number 1.

"Here, Tyrone. Thanks again." He handed a thick envelope to Touchdown Tyrone Collins. Inside it, Bennies for Tyrone.

"I knew you were good for it, kicker."

"One promise, Tyrone?"

"Yeah."

"Not a word about this to anyone."

"Sheeit, kicker," Tyrone said before turning away. "Do I look like a man who would go telling the world?"

Jake tried to give the star receiver a serious look. "Thanks. See you out there."

Frank Flaherty had little energy for this practice. He didn't expect his team to either. The final 90 minutes of each practice were closed to the media. Flaherty was obsessed about injury reports and inside scoops getting out to the other media. In the era of the Internet, he would log on each morning and read the newspapers in the next opponent's hometown. Don't ever believe a coach who says, "We don't read what you guys write." They all do.

"Guys, we're just going to stretch a bit and get some blood moving around. We'll go short today, maybe 45 minutes. We'll be out of here by 4:30."

That was a bonus for Jake. He was working at Pizza Perfecto in three hours. The Packers were on Monday Night Football against Detroit, and the boss had offered him a crack at a quick 200 bucks to work the 5:30-to-close shift.

20. Exes Are Expensive

Clark did go out on Monday night. He knew he'd be broke by the next pay period. May as well go out and make a fool of himself tonight. He watched Rachel glide through her 10 o'clock sportscast from the Kitty Corner while finishing off another tall cup of MGD. Cheap beer for a cheap guy. He could leave only a dollar tip for the entire night.

By the next morning, Clark was determined to follow through on the one idea that stood out in the sea of booze and underage girls.

Call Randy Munson. See if his little plan still had some wings.

Clark stumbled out of bed, holding his brain from the inevitable earthquake each step on the kitchen tile provided.

I can't believe I'm going to do this, he thought. It could mean my career. It could mean everything.

He dialed the numbers.

"Randy, it's Clark."

"How goes it, man?" Randy moved from his kitchen toward the living room, out of Lisa's earshot.

"Can you meet me for lunch today? I've got something to discuss with you."

Randy's heart pounded. Did Clark know about the botched game in Hawaii? Randy figured, hell, Clark is on my side. He wouldn't go all willy-nilly on the air with it. He would talk to me about it first.

"Uh...sure, where and when?"

"Chaps out by the Beltline. 11 work for you?"

"I'll be there."

Randy clicked off his cordless phone. Randy looked at Brett, asleep on the sofa, and Lisa beside him. The little boy had run a fever and had been up crying for much of the evening.

That's my team, Randy reminded himself.

Randy arrived first and chose a quiet table in the corner. Chaps featured high ceilings and plenty of room, perfect for working out The Plan or, in this case, trying to deny it ever existed.

"Hi, Randy."

"Clark. Good to see you." The men shook hands and ordered drinks. An iced tea for Randy, Diet Dr. Pepper for Clark.

"All right. I'll get down to it," Clark started. "You figured that it must be important for me to call you for lunch on such short notice."

A lump grew in Randy's throat.

"Uh, yeah."

"Well, I'm having some money issues right now. Carol got the increase in her alimony, from nine grand a year to almost 18. Damn judge."

"Whoa."

"Yeah. It'll start coming out of my next check."

"I see." Randy sipped his tea. He knew right then he might be in the clear on the Hawaii episode, but he could trace the next question.

"Remember what you talked about at the Lasso?"

Randy curled his mouth in a half smile. "How could I forget?"

"Is that still on?"

Randy broke eye contact with Clark. Time for truth or consequences. He decided to give the sportscaster a taste of each.

"Look. Something could happen this weekend."

"What do you mean by something?" Clark whispered.

Randy focused on Clark's blue eyes.

"I need to know this right now," he said. "If you're in, stay in. If you're out, stay out. Either way, don't say a word."

"OK."

"No, Clark. Look at me. Nothing was said today between the

two of us."

"I didn't hear anything."

"Good. If you're smart, put odds on Northern this weekend. Not the point spread, the odds. I don't think we'll win."

"The odds?" Clark asked with more than a hint of surprise. "What would that pay?"

"About 6 to 1, maybe more by the weekend. I go through a certain guy who goes through another guy. You'll have to find your own way on this."

"You 'go'?"

Randy caught himself.

"Am going. This will be the first one."

"Why odds? Why not the point spread? What's it at, 19, 20?"

Randy leaned in.

"Here's why. If we lose Saturday, the line for the next week will be so low at Kansas that we'll cover that easily. I don't think losing to Northern would be that much of a surprise. Remember last year?"

Clark turned down the volume to an audible whisper.

"You've got this figured out."

"Like you wouldn't believe," Randy said confidently.

An awkward silence descended as the plotters dove into the free chips and salsa.

"I'll come right out and say it," Randy said after swallowing a clump of the turtle-colored salsa. "I need your silence on this. We're the only two in Madison who know this. I'm probably going to get let go in December, no matter what happens. The gates are closing in on me here. To ensure your silence, I will call you each Thursday, at the station, around four or four-thirty, with some information. I'll tell you for or against. Always assume we're talking about the spread. No odds. I'm just after odds here for a quick score to start off."

"Each Thursday."

"Yup. Except this Thursday. You know where I stand. But no one can ever know about this. Otherwise, I'm off to jail."

"Foul. I got that one."

Clark Cattoor was running himself back into shape at the best indoor pickup basketball game in Madison, in the old Wisconsin State track and field building, right next to Mendota Stadium. The Court, as people on campus referred to it.

No NBA All-Stars were chugging up and down the six rubber basketball courts on this Friday. It was all old men, a few ex-athletes, some professors, some bankers, a handful of bartenders and two journalists.

Clark was running the floor with Aaron Schutz, the sports editor at the *Dane County Tribune*. Clark and Aaron had worked side by side ten years earlier. Back then, Aaron had just hooked on with the *Tribune* and Clark was still writing about girls' soccer games for fifty bucks a story.

Clark drained the game-winning shot at a quarter to one.

"Cash money!" he bellowed to the dozen spectators.

"Nice hit, C.C." Aaron offered.

Clark and Aaron walked a hundred yards, the sportscaster a foot taller than the newspaper hack. The oasis of water fountains was their final destination. A line of similarly out-of-shape men was already waiting.

"I got a tip for you, man, just credit the paper if you find anything," Aaron said while holding onto the bottom of his shorts for dear life.

"Sure thing, Schutzie."

"There's word of a gambling ring inside the football program."

Clark swallowed hard. "Here?"

"Yeah," Aaron said. "I guess there's talk now from Florida about Collins. I got a guy in Miami that says he's in so far with some agent that that's the only way he'll get out of debt."

"Really?" Clark tried his best to sound surprised.

"We don't have enough to run anything yet, but we're making a few calls. I'd be surprised if we didn't run a story by the Kansas game."

A tall, athletic woman approached. The two journalists immediately stopped talking.

"May I run with you?" she asked Clark. Karen Strassel, the Wisconsin State athletic director, had once been a player. Quite a player. This was nearly two decades before the WNBA came along, so Karen had zoomed into coaching women's basketball after a remarkable playing career at North Dakota.

"Good to see you, Karen," Clark said. "Back to take us out-of-shape men to task?"

"You bet." Karen flashed her high-wattage smile.

"You know, Aaron, Karen here still holds the D-2 record for career points scored. What was it, 2,700?"

"2,786," Karen replied. "Would've been well over three thousand if we'd had a three-point line back in the day. It's a crime, I tell ya. Not as much of a crime as the Olympic boycott." As a junior at North Dakota, Karen had landed a spot on the 1980 women's basketball Olympic team. Winning an Olympic gold medal was the benchmark of the sport then.

"That still burns you, doesn't it?" Clark asked.

"You have no idea."

Clark looked at the assembled players on the court. "Karen, you should run for the other team. That should balance it out."

Karen nodded. She walked over to the other team, full of bald, overweight men her age.

"She's a skin," one of her new teammates said to Clark and Aaron.

Karen smirked again. "That's no problem. Give me a second." With that, she peeled off her XL blue T-shirt with WISCONSIN STATE WOMEN'S BASKETBALL printed on it to reveal a black sports bra. "I'm ready." The guys' eyes strayed from the bra itself to Karen's muscled abdomen. A six-pack at age 44.

"What's the wait? Let's go, guys."

Clark's team won the pick-up game, but Karen Strassel was good for seven baskets, far more than her four out-of-shape teammates combined.

With 24 hours until the Northern Illinois game, Clark drove home. He felt too dirty to shower in public after Aaron's revelation.

He logged onto one of the hundreds of off-shore sports gambling websites. "Best odds on the Internet," one page screamed. Another site claimed "Quickest payouts in the world." Clark practically needed a machete to slice through all the pop-up ads.

One website stared out at him. Cool Breeze Sports, some outfit based in St. Martaan, offered a 25% start-up bonus, $500 minimum.

"We are in business," Clark mumbled.

Clark broke out the numbers on his MasterCard and transferred $2,000 to a new account. He code named it his initials and birth year, "CC71." Just a few innocent wagers that no one would ever find. He clicked around and uncovered the Northern Illinois-Wisconsin State game.

WISCONSIN STATE (-19.5, -650) vs. Northern Illinois, 9/13/03, 2 P.M.

If he played a grand on Northern Illinois, he would take home $6,500 if they won. Do that three times this year and he'd have all the money to pay off Carol. If he won all his "plays" this year, he could just pay Carol in cash. Cut her a check and say "See ya next year."

The screen prompted him to confirm his first trip into the dark underbelly of sports. $1,250 on Northern to win big money. $8,125 was the final tally on the screen if Wisconsin State lost. Clark decided his sign-up bonus of 250 bucks would best be spent on what Randy had described as a sure thing.

21. Northern Illinois

Randy Munson's pregame custom was a three-mile jog at 6 A.M. The exercise helped him cement the game plan and commit the first 20 planned plays to memory.

This Saturday, Randy laced up his New Balances and felt the weight of his actions on his shoulders. He would be the reason Wisconsin State would lose.

He stepped past the players' rooms for a brief run in the drizzle, around the professors' houses and foothills just off the WSU campus.

At least it'll be easier in the rain, Randy thought. Tyrone will be neutralized on the wet turf, and Craig always struggles with a wet ball. He remembered the last home game in the rain, a loss to Iowa two years before.

The rain would not only slow up the Boars. It would wash away the evidence.

Clark sat next to Aaron Schutz in the press box at Mendota Stadium. Ever since Clark's return to Madison, the two had made it a ritual to sit in adjacent seats, crack wise about the plays below, and relive the old days.

"We didn't find anything on the gambling yet," Aaron said an hour before kickoff.

"Did you think you would?"

"Not yet." Aaron picked up a brat and shoved the end into his mouth. "We made a few calls, but no avenues have checked out."

"Is anyone else involved?" Clark asked before stuffing a jelly donut into his mouth.

"Hard to say. I still think in football only a coach or quarterback can pull it off. There's just too many guys out there."

"You remember Northwestern—"

"Yeah, basketball is so much easier." Aaron had investigated the 1995 basketball point-shaving scandal.

"Well, I certainly haven't heard anything yet on this," Clark offered as he watched raindrops slide down the glass of the press box windows.

An hour later, Randy Munson chomped the gum harder than normal. The flimsy piece of spearmint rolled around his mouth like an olive pit in a blender. He had to make this work.

"Right Heavy 28 Toss," he said, motioning to Craig Zellnoff on Wisconsin State's first possession. Craig took the handoff and slipped backward on 3rd and 4, forcing a punt.

That woke up Frank Flaherty on the sidelines.

"Goddammit, Randy, get Zellnoff in a damn shotgun," the head coach barked. "He looks like he's on ice skates out there, for God's sake."

Randy had to stay under the radar with Frank. Wisconsin State could lose to Northern Illinois because of the turf alone. Randy just had to make it look normal.

Nothing was normal about this game. NIU's Jerry McDonald drove the Huskies all the way to a touchdown on their opening drive. McDonald repeated the feat early in the second quarter. Wisconsin State was in a 14-0 hole.

"What are these idiots doing out here?" Aaron asked Clark. "I already had my damn story written, assuming a 20-point win."

"I'm shocked," Clark countered. "I really am. I thought this team was for real last week in Hawaii."

"At least Collins hasn't dropped anything yet. It's like Flaherty isn't even getting him the ball out there."

Clark paused before responding. He would have to choose each word carefully as long as Aaron was checking out this scoop.

"Maybe it's just the turf. You know rain always neutralizes speed."

Jake trotted onto the field and put Wisconsin State on the board late in the second quarter with a 33-yard field goal. Jake was basking in the limelight of a perfect season. No missed goals. No missed extra points. A few of his kickoffs even flew all the way to the end zone.

"HUT!" Sam Cattanach barked out the snap call.

Thud.

Not the proper pow that perfect kicks bring, but a thud. This kick was a dying quail, veering to the right ever so slightly.

"Shit, I hooked it," Jake said, moving to the left as he watched the ball.

"I think you got it, man." Sam fired back.

Clank.

The ball smacked the right upright and bounced harmlessly inside the end zone. Wisconsin State was still scoreless.

"Shit, shit, shit," Jake muttered as he ran back to the sidelines where John Wilcox stood, arms folded.

The normally rabid Wisconsin State student section did something unprecedented at halftime. A handful of the 13,000 students threw their marshmallows at the home team.

Wisconsin State's dismal first half resulted not only in a 17-0 deficit but the wrath of everyone wearing blue inside Mendota Stadium.

Frank Flaherty heard the chants as he walked toward the locker room.

"YOU SUCK, FLAHERTY!" screamed a blue-painted face.

"CAN'T WAIT FOR YOU TO GET FIRED!" a red-headed female yelled into his face.

Frank ran off the field behind his burly offensive lineman. The more camouflage on this day, the better.

Frank resisted the urge to play tough guy during the six-minute talk in the locker room.

"What we need more than anything else is your attention," the head coach said calmly. "I'm assuming they got your attention with that first half. We need it now.

"We as coaches have failed you so far. It is now up to us- coaches and players—to fix this fast. Craig?"

"Yeah, coach?" The quarterback stood at attention.

"Hit the damn receivers in the numbers. Don't just chuck it up there and expect them to make the grab.

"Bob, Cory?"

Bob Verly and Cory Larkman looked up from opposite sides of the room. Frank lit a Winston and took a slow drag.

"Create some goddamn holes. This is Northern Illinois we're playing."

Bob nodded. Cory looked off without making eye contact with Frank.

"Above all, we coaches need to call a better game."

The entire room knew Frank was singling out Randy.

As Frank had demanded, Craig Zellnoff led Wisconsin State to a touchdown on the opening drive of the second half. Craig hit Tyrone Collins for three catches on the drive. Craig's 3-yard touchdown scamper brought the game back to within reach at 17-7.

The crowd rallied behind the Boars. With one minute left in the third quarter, Tyrone Collins caught a 42-yard bomb from Craig to set Wisconsin State up inside the Northern Illinois 20-yard line. A touchdown would put Wisconsin State within three points.

"Pairs Left 572," Randy signaled in. That play was designed as a deep pass to Laverneus Wilson along the right sideline.

Craig was enraged at the call.

"TIME-OUT!" he screamed at the line judge before peeling off his helmet and racing toward Randy.

Randy, the offensive guru, comforted the quarterback.

"Look, I'm mad you burned that time-out, but I'll forget about it if you run this play. I've seen the pictures upstairs. You just need to find Wilson deep. Throw it along the sidelines."

Frank Flaherty popped in.

"What the—"

"Coach, I got it under control." Randy stared down Frank.

"OK. I'll trust you here."

"Good."

Craig shrugged and ran back into the huddle.

Facing 1st-and-10, Wisconsin State's call should have been a run. That was the most logical play given the situation.

The play worked just as Randy had predicted. Craig spotted two defenders strapping Wilson along the right sideline.

Just throw it, Randy thought.

Craig unleashed a laser toward Wilson.

As the brown leather sailed through the air, Randy saw with his own ex-quarterback's eye that The Plan would work perfectly.

NIU safety Dewey Haymark crossed the field for the interception. Northern Illinois ball.

Craig turned to the bench and threw down his helmet.

"What a shitty call!" Craig barked to anyone within 50 feet.

Frank Flaherty heard his quarterback's assessment and agreed.

Wisconsin State never recovered. The visiting Huskies drained the clock for the rest of the game. They watched with amusement as the heavily favored home team came apart like a stale gingerbread house. Jake missed another field goal to open the fourth quarter. Down 17-7 with just six minutes left, Craig forced an interception into double coverage. Game over. Northern ran out the clock for a 17-7 victory.

Craig's third and final interception caused a groan among Frank's friends in the press box.

"It's like they were in slow motion out there," said *Dane County Tribune* columnist Nick Jackovich to both Clark and Aaron.

"They just choked. Northern ALWAYS plays them tough," Aaron countered.

Clark sat silent and nodded. Northern's win may have made his Sunday morning television show with Frank Flaherty as enjoyable as pulling alligator's teeth, but Clark had pulled in $8,000 thanks to Frank's dysfunctional coaching staff.

Aaron leaned in to Clark.

"I may not have anything on it yet, but if ever there was a thrown game, this was it."

Jim Tillman looked like a man who just discovered his daughter in an ad for the latest edition of *Girls Gone Wild*. The PR flack usually announced the arrival of the head coach as if Frank were the Queen of England. Today he mumbled "Coach Frank Flaherty" to the assembled journalists.

Frank slowly walked to his table among the TV lights and the three dozen microphones.

Aaron opened. "What angers you most about the loss?"

Frank's eyes shot through the back of Aaron's head.

"You know what ticks me off most? It's not that we assumed we would win because we're Wisconsin State. It's not that we assumed we would win because they're Northern Illinois. What ticks me off most about this loss is that our coaching staff did a horrible job of calling the game. I know I should take the blame for it. I will. It's just that I will have more input in the coming weeks."

Clark smirked while thinking about the money as he watched from behind his cameraman.

The players' media room was a morgue. Craig Zellnoff faced the music with a long face.

"I just didn't get it done. When the game was on the line, I didn't make the plays. I made the wrong decisions."

The only other player in the room was Touchdown Tyrone Collins. Win or lose, the media jackals could always count on Touchdown Tyrone.

"You guys saw it out there. What did I finish with? How many catches? How many?"

"Uh, seven," some TV reporter from La Crosse offered.

"How many yards? Anyone know?"

Another reporter looked at his stat sheet for the answer.

"113."

"Thank you," Tyrone said, nudging his Terminator sunglasses to make a point. "See, they gotta get me the ball more. It doesn't matter how many guys are guarding me. Hell, put me in the backfield. Just hand it off to me 20 times a game."

That got a few chuckles.

"Hey, I'm just trying to tell you fellas that it's not the end of the world. They was a bettah team than y'all said all week. Now you guys look as dumb as we look."

Tyrone Collins, poet and media critic.

Two minutes before the six o'clock news, Rachel Randall picked up the phone in the WMA-TV sports office.

"Channel 11 Sports."

"Yeah, is Rachel there?"

"This is."

"Hi. Jake Steffon."

"Well, hi. I didn't expect to hear from you. What's up?" asked Rachel, as if she were completely oblivious to the fact that Jake had been a major reason for program's most embarrassing loss in a decade.

Jake did not waste the moment. "What time are you out of there?"

"11 or so. We're on late tonight."

"Wanna stop by? We're having a little get-together tonight. Just a few friends since we lost. The big bash will have to wait a few weeks."

"What's your address?" Rachel wrote it down. Someplace west of campus. "Maybe I'll stop by. Not 100 percent, but I'll try."

As the designated scapegoat for the Wisconsin State football program, at least Randy Munson was well paid. He pulled his Riviera into a PDQ convenience store at the corner of Verona and Raymond. The PDQ was on his way home, and the pay phone in the east side of the parking lot had become his headquarters.

Randy wanted to see just where his balance stood.

"Stephen. Randy here."

"Welcome back to the plus side."

"What was the final tally?"

"Well, we locked you in at 6 to 1 on Northern. Three gets you 18. I take my cut from that and you're looking at five up."

Randy tingled at the thought of a quick $5,000. "Any thoughts on next week? At Kansas."

"They beat one of those Southwest Missouri, Southeast Missouri teams by ten today. Not sure who, but they didn't post an impressive win."

"But they did win?"

"Yeah. This is just a guess, but I'd say you guys would be a five or maybe a six-point favorite."

"No shit? That's it?"

"Yeah. Are you gonna play with?"

"I think so. I say we take our five and double it. I'll play the spread and for."

"For?"

"Oh, yeah, we'll destroy Kansas next week. Especially if the number is less than ten."

"The number won't be out till tomorrow afternoon. I may start it out early and start it a touch lower than the others would. Maybe the on-line shops will follow suit."

"Very good. If the number is less than seven, place my five on it."

"For the spread?"

"Yup, we'll cover next week. Tell you what, I'm so confident if it's less than five, can you float me the nine from before again?" Randy asked confidently.

"I dunno. If it falls through, you'll have to make it back up the next week for me."

"Don't worry about that," Randy said. "If we hit big here, I may just walk away with what I got."

"Sure. I'll do it 'cause I know you'll make it right."

"Make it 14 for. Will that raise any red flags?"

"Used to in the old days, but not on the Internet. The gaming board and the feds have no control over that. I gotcha down on 14 for."

Randy felt a moment of self-righteousness. This could land him in jail. Yet gambling on his team was, in a sick way, the very definition of school spirit. Something Wisconsin State football was sorely lacking this weekend.

Jake set up the Kickers' Quarters for a low-key soiree. Backup fullback Teddy Hammersley was the only other player present. Sam had invited Teddy because he, like Sam, was from Neillsville and because he was a freshman. Madison could be an intimidating place.

As Jake took in "Weekend Update" on Saturday Night Live, he lifted another bottle of Leinenkugel's. Teddy leaned in.

"So, uh, are classes going OK?" There was only so much small talk you could make with a kicker who had blown two short field goals in a humiliating loss.

"I guess. The workload hasn't gotten too deep yet. Even if it does, the coaches will help us out."

It was no secret that Jake was now in full-blown slacker mode. He was getting just as lazy as the best football players.

"Zoology 101 is a bitch," he added. "If you can avoid it, do. I have to take the damn thing to fill out my science requirements. Hate it. Absolutely hate it. And to have it at 8:50 in the morning-"

"Ouch."

"Yeah. Our first test is coming up in two weeks. I gotta start crackin' the textbook. I'm lost out there."

Sam returned with a refill for Jake, Teddy, and a friend of Teddy's.

"Here, man. Load up, you could use it."

"Thanks, Sunshine." Jake was amused. Wisconsin State's lack of competence on offense meant that Sam's name had been called often. He'd responded with no shanks on eight punts. A banner day for the punter.

"Tell you what, Sam, maybe you could go to the NFL Draft next year and pay me back from our little incident in—" Jake stopped. He decided to hint at Sam's prostitution bust whenever possible, but not spill it. If people back in Neillsville ever found out....

The doorbell rang. "Game on for Little Jakey," Sam taunted at the expected arrival of Rachel Randall.

"Just get the door, Twinkle Toes."

Rachel walked in, still wearing her anchor hair and full makeup. "Hi, Sam. Good to see you. Jake told me to stop by."

"We know. Come this way."

Jake was more than a few beers ahead of her at this point in the evening. His eyes were a shade glassy and his dark green silk shirt was frayed at the collar.

"Rachel. Thanks for coming. Sit down. Want a beer? Don't cost nuttin." His rural Wisconsin charm was not lost on Rachel.

"Haven't heard that one in a while." Rachel smiled.

"Well, you can tell me. We really shit the bed today, didn't we?"

"Coach Flaherty didn't sound too happy afterward."

"Did he single me out?" Jake sat on the couch and motioned for Rachel to sit next to him.

"Not from what I saw on the tape, but I was at the station all day."

"He should," Jake said between sips. "I was awful."

"You had company today in that department," Rachel said reassuringly.

"So, what's it like to work for Clark Cattoor?"

"A pain in the ass," said Rachel. "He thinks he's the state version of Fabio. Don't laugh. He keeps three mirrors in his office alone along with combs, gels, and makeup. At least I keep mine in the bathroom. I think he goes out five or six nights a week. He's just a partier. Although that ex-wife he's always whining about would probably drive me to drink, too."

Ten minutes of dancing around the next step ensued. Jake then focused his eyes with Rachel's for that one moment where a flirting friendship moves to something a little more intimate.

"I'm really glad you came over," Jake said. "I know we didn't get a chance to finish our chat last time."

"No problem. I still should keep that quiet."

"I will," Jake promised. "It's just that I've had such a crappy day out there, but I need someone to be here for me."

Rachel leaned in on the old couch. The living room was empty except for Teddy, who was passed out on the easy chair.

"I like being here with you," Rachel said.

Even a drunk like Jake could see the green light Rachel was flashing.

"May I show you the rest of our place?"

Rachel struggled with the unsaid assumption but gave in. It was late. She was still new to town. This could be fun.

"Sure. I'd love to see it."

The kicker and the reporter only made it to Jake's bedroom for the tour. Rachel Randall didn't see any other rooms for nine hours.

22. Program Under Siege

"Can we make this quick?" Frank Flaherty muttered upon arrival at WMA-TV on Sunday morning. The show paid well but was unbearable to everyone involved after a loss.

"As painless as we can, coach," said the sportscaster who'd made $8,000 betting against Frank's team, thanks to one of Frank's own coaches.

Clark handed Frank his weekly coffee. Black. Just like Frank's mood today.

"I didn't sleep a damn wink last night," Frank said in a rare moment of spontaneous conversation. "Damn neighbor's dog barking all night outside. I nearly walked across the street and kicked the hell out of it. Then I thought of the bad press."

"Yeah, that would have made a good story."

"You know how these animal rights types are here in Madison. They would have roasted me."

"Telling a dog to shut up is not like microwaving a parrot or anything," Clark said, trying to diffuse the tension. He listened to his earpiece for a moment. "Coach, we'll be ready in about three minutes."

"Do I have to do the highlights?" Frank asked.

"Feel free to rip who you need to rip. You could always use the show as motivation for your players."

"Screw that. All our players are probably hung over right now anyways. They should feel some pain. Too many of our guys think they can play in the NFL, but most of them will be in for a rude wake-up call."

"Is that so?"

"I know NFL talent," Frank said. "I've seen NFL talent. I've coached NFL talent. We don't have it."

"What about Tyrone Collins?"

"He's the only one."

Frank was up to his usual form for his show: a few stutters during the highlight portion and less-than-honest analysis afterward.

"How do you bounce back from this loss?" Clark asked.

"Well, Clark, we just need to focus on who's ahead of us now. Don't pay attention to the newspapers, the television, the rankings. None of that stuff matters. Saturday is now a must-win for us. We need to finish 3-1 before Big Ten play starts."

Frank shadowboxed his way through Clark's minefield of questions. As he unclipped his microphone at the end, he offered Clark a scoop for future use.

"One thing I have to do is shake up the play calling," he said as he squeezed into a leather jacket. "Randy just killed us in the last game. I'll give him the first half against Kansas, but that's it. I tell you this so you can do whatever you want with it. Report it, don't report it, whatever. Randy doesn't even know about this."

Frank shifted his eyes and lowered his nicotine-charred voice.

"And it didn't come from me."

Clark slowly nodded as Frank left to salvage his weekend.

He's onto us, I know he's onto us, Clark told the smart half of his brain.

Randy Munson entered the fourth level of hell on Monday morning. He saw it coming as he pulled his Riviera into the parking lot at Mendota Stadium. The sign on his parking space, "R. Munson," was the only thing in town with his name on it not followed by criticism.

He prepared to meet his fate in the team's darkened video conference room with Frank, John Wilcox, and the rest of the coaching staff. The Northern Illinois disaster was replayed and slowly broken down from four different camera angles.

Frank was in front of the video screen with a stick pointer, like David Brinkley on election night in 1964.

"See. What kind of a call is this on 3rd-and-8?" Frank asked sarcastically. "Guys upstairs, you have to overrule a call that is so blatantly incorrect."

The two offensive assistants nodded. At least Frank wasn't holding them responsible.

Randy was about to get cut apart like a leg of lamb. The day before, one of the newspaper columnists had written that "Randy Munson could mess up a bowl of cereal." Randy's family, especially his older son Scott, were anguished by the column. Lisa knew Randy would probably get let go in December. She was just hoping it would be a firing without cause, so the program would pay the rest of his contract.

Randy had taken great pains to hide The Plan not only from everyone outside his house but also his family. His contact with Stephen had been through pay phones. As far as Randy knew, Stephen didn't even have his home phone number. Since Stephen was a professional, Randy believed he would never call unless their account was in serious debt. No paper trail.

"Randy, what do you have to say for yourself?" Frank was now questioning the fourth-quarter interception that Craig Zellnoff threw into double coverage.

"I figured Zellnoff had the arm to get it in there," Randy said weakly. "Sometimes you have to trust your big guns when the game is on the line—"

"DON'T GIVE ME THAT SHIT!" Frank barked. "Zellnoff can't complete that pass on his best day."

"I thought—"

"YOU THOUGHT WHAT?" Frank stepped toward his offensive coordinator.

"I thought he could fit it in there."

"Randy, I'm going to do something I've never done in my career."

The entire room woke up.

"Randy, you will have one half at Kansas to turn it around," Frank said. "If it doesn't work out, if we're down at halftime, I'll call the damn plays and we'll figure out what to do about the big picture when we get back."

"Coach, shouldn't we do this behind closed doors?"

"We all saw what happened out there."

John Wilcox chimed in. "It's just that we're concerned, Randy. The offense isn't where it should—"

"SHUT UP!" Frank boomed at John. "IF ANYBODY SHOULD BE A GODDAMN WALLFLOWER TODAY WITH RANDY, IT SHOULD BE YOU. Your kicker missed two field goals. If he makes them, we probably win because we don't have to play like a pack of desperate housewives!"

The special teams guru slunk back into his black swivel chair.

"Let that be a lesson to all of you. This season is in panic mode, gentlemen." Frank was now a shade more reasoned. "If we don't go to a bowl game, we all get canned. All of us. We all have bills to pay, most of us have families to feed. We need to work through this without ego and without distraction."

Frank waved his arms toward the ceiling.

"Let those assholes in the media say what they want. Let those stupid fans call me an idiot and a bastard when I run off the field. I just know we need a huge win this week to get back into the good graces of the athletic department before we play Indiana. They're gonna fire all our asses if we screw this up."

"C'mon, Steffon! Are you done believing your own bullshit?"

John Wilcox had found his target for the Monday afternoon practice. Jake sliced another short field goal. Another kick wide right in the windless WSU Bubble attached to Mendota stadium. The Bubble was another part of the college football arms race, an 80-yard indoor practice facility complete with artificial turf.

"Do we have to open field goal tryouts again, dammit?" the coach yelled. "Maybe we should. You know why? I think Jake Steffon is just happy to be here. I'm not sure if he has the mental toughness to help us out. Prove me wrong. PROVE ME WRONG!"

Jake said nothing. Just ride the storm out, he thought, just ride it out. With Sam punting at such a high clip, Jake was now half kicker, half whipping boy.

After Jake barely hooked in a 30-yarder, Sam stood up from his crouch.

"Jake, man, just stroke it right in there with good distance. Just like with Rachel the other night."

That got a chuckle. The noise coming from Jake's room that night had kept the punter tossing and turning.

Jake hadn't called Rachel since. He was trying to observe the 48-Hour Rule after first close contact. That meant he could call her as soon as tonight during the late *SportsCenter*.

Wilcox made a hand signal to Frank. Frank nodded, tossed down his clipboard, and blew his whistle four times, the sign that something important was about to occur.

"GENTLEMEN! BREAK IT DOWN. Everyone at the 50." Never mind that the WSU Bubble only had a 40-yard line because of its 80-yard length; Frank was never one to put facts ahead of symbolism.

More than 100 gladiators, in full pads, ran to the STATE imprinted at midfield.

"We have proven that we are still not a team ready to take charge. Northern exposed our weaknesses. For us, it's mostly up here." Frank pointed to his head. "Jake Steffon. Where are you?"

Jake raised his eyebrows and his hand.

"Give me a 45-yard field goal, left hash. No rush. Just a snap, a hold, and a kick. All by yourself out there. If you miss, everybody runs 25 lengths of the field except you. If you make it, you run ten lengths for what happened Saturday and the others go home."

"Yes, sir." Jake was turning into a boozing playboy on the weekends, but he still had enough Fall Creek manners left.

Frank broke out his stopwatch.

"You have 30 seconds to get this play off," Frank said. "Better get moving."

Sam ran out to the 35-yard line and placed the first two fingers of his left hand on the hard turf. Jake zoomed in on Sam's fingers, where the ball would magically appear seconds later.

"HUT!" Sam barked to the snapper.

Stutter step left, half step right, drive step left, impact.

Placekicking is like golf. Sometimes the swing just comes together. Jake hit this one true. The ball's flight almost pierced the protective netting on the roof before settling down just inside the right goalpost.

Jake won himself some running and kept everyone else from serious cardio work.

"Nice kick, roomie. Now get going on those lengths." Sam tapped Jake's helmet.

"Asshole Flaherty," Jake muttered as he glared at the head coach. He was becoming more and more like one of the guys.

Sam wasn't the only one who had Jake on his Christmas card list.

"Sheeit, kickah," said Tyrone Collins. "You saved our asses. Touchdown Tyrone won't forget that."

"Thanks, Tyrone."

Frank picked up his clipboard and put on his wraparound sunglasses.

"All right, gentlemen. We're done here. Nice kick, Jake, now start running. Ten lengths in under 20 seconds each. You guys make study tables tonight. You know who you are. We don't need any academic bullshit problems right now. Dismissed."

23. Too Involved

"You guys set to order?"

"Go ahead," Jake said to Rachel. She ordered a walleye dinner. A true Wisconsin girl. Jake opted for the broasted chicken, another staple of the upper Midwest.

This was the first night Jake was with Rachel in a public place. She didn't disappoint. Her blond hair was pulled back smartly, revealing a set of diamond earrings.

"So, what got you into this business?" Jake asked.

Rachel chuckled. "A lot of people ask me that. Where do you want to end up? Why do you love sports?" She played with her straw, stirring between the ice cubes of her Sprite. "I don't know. I just caught the TV bug in college. That's how I got out of Stevens Point in three years. I went to school each summer and worked at a station in Wausau for credit."

Jake let her boast a little, admiring the way her lips moved with each syllable.

"I was fortunate to graduate with a four-point-oh," Rachel said matter-of-factly. "Granted, it was Stevens Point and not Madison or Northwestern, but a few stations noticed that. Channel 11 was the first. Normally you have to work in Wausau or Eau Claire for a year or two, but WMA took a chance."

"So, do you like it here in Madison? Do you want to stay?" Jake asked, picking up another roll.

Rachel said the city was great, but working for Clark wore her down. He was too wishy-washy and condescending, an unappealing combination.

"I won't stay here more than two years," Rachel said. "Hopefully I can get to Milwaukee or Minneapolis. Maybe even ESPN. I know my stuff. Far too often female sportscasters are accused of just being eye candy."

Jake laughed inside at that. He was certainly enjoying the view.

"But I do know my sports," she concluded.

"Are you going to Kansas?"

Rachel rolled her blue eyes. "Not a chance. Clark's going down. I think he feels like he has to because of the *Flaherty Show* on Sunday morning. I think he's taking all the games to make up for having to spend all that time in Duluth. Ever been to Duluth?"

"No."

"It's even colder than Fall Creek."

"Or Eagle River."

Rachel laughed. "Yes, even Eagle River. You should come on up when the season's done. I think you might like it."

As Jake stared at the fish, regretting that he'd ordered chicken, he realized that Rachel had taken the conversation up a few levels. Meeting the parents? Here they were at the Hermit in Verona on a Tuesday night. Rachel said they would have to keep everything out of the public view.

"We'll see," was all Jake could offer.

"Oh, crap," Rachel said. Jake's hair stood up for a second. What was it? Did he say something wrong? A bone in the fish? "My beeper. Excuse me."

She fished out a black box the size of a 9-volt battery. "It's work. Excuse me for a second."

Rachel and her tight black dress returned to the table after the kicker had chewed through two pieces of chicken. "I'm sorry about that. That was Clark."

"What did he want?"

"He said something's come up this weekend, and he wants me to fly to Lawrence. That stinks. I wasn't planning on leaving town."

Jake's imagination started flowing. He wanted to sneak Rachel into his hotel room Friday night. "What day are you coming in?"

"Saturday morning," Rachel said with a sigh. "I need to stick around for high school football Friday night."

That fantasy squashed, Jake came back to the present. He would stay a gentleman on this cloudless September night, walking Rachel to her apartment after dinner, declining her invitation to come inside, kissing her just once on those supple lips.

24. Preparing for Oz

"Channel 11 Sports," Clark said in his broadcast voice. Authoritative and strong, his Heston-reading-the-Bible imitation.

"Clark. Randy. Play it 'for' Saturday."

"For?" Clark repeated.

"Trust me on this one. Not against, for. I gotta go. We're leaving in a few minutes."

Wisconsin State was just a five-point favorite. Certainly Randy could devise a plan to win by a touchdown or more against bumbling Kansas.

Randy's call reminded Clark to hand over the official media itinerary for the trip to Rachel. Clark felt he needed to be near his computer this weekend. The gamble against Northern Illinois had worked perfectly, but he didn't want to be 600 miles from his home base for the Kansas game. He could cancel his wager any time before Saturday's kickoff.

He told Rachel that she would now fly out to Lawrence on Thursday. Thunderstorms were in the forecast for Friday and Saturday throughout Iowa. He could live without her covering the Friday night high school games in Baraboo and Sauk City.

With the new travel regulations since September 11, stations found it easier to rent small Cessna charters than fight lost luggage, delays, and damage to expensive cameras on the big birds. The real benefit was the guarantee that the footage would be back in Madison by early evening. That allowed plenty of turnaround time for the video to make air at ten o'clock most Saturdays.

"It's going to be about a four-hour flight, five if the weather is windy," Clark said. "I think you'll refuel somewhere in southern Iowa."

He handed Rachel an envelope.

"Just be at Morey Airport by four and enjoy the trip."

Unlike the ten-hour trip to Honolulu, the Boars' odyssey to Lawrence, Kansas, took only a couple of hours. The school chartered a DC-9 to carry the traveling party of 100.

In seats 22C and 22D, Jake Steffon and Sam Cattanach were looking for a traveling party of their own. One of Sam's buddies from Neillsville was a student at Kansas. Sam promised Jake that his friend would show them the nightlife in Lawrence, one of the college jewels of the Midwest.

"Do the women even have teeth in Kansas?" Jake started in.

"Where are you from again? Fall Creek?"

"Do they, really?"

"I was down there last year for a week during the summer, and let me tell you, it was everywhere. All hot and stuff outside. Gotta dress to the weather. Those girls are definitely not bashful about showing it off."

Jake broke into a grin.

"There's this street downtown, the locals call it Mass Ave," Sam said. "It's like State Street."

"Hear hear to that. You bring any books?"

"Just my cartography texts," Sam said. "I'll probably catch up on that Friday morning before the walk-through."

"I'm getting a little concerned about Econ class. It's still kicking my ass. We've got a midterm coming up on the first. I'm not ready."

"So, how much money are you bringin' this time?" Sam said with a sly grin.

"Not enough to get you laid and not enough to bail you out."

"Well, KU is a different economy. It may only take 10 bucks' worth of beer for me."

"For what, action or bail?" Jake had $300 with him, strictly for nightlife and knickknacks. He'd cleared about half of that on Monday night at Pizza Perfecto. "Just promise me one thing."

"What?"

"This friend. What's his name?"

"Karl."

"From Neillsville, right?"

"Yeah. He was a wrestler."

"Oh, great." Jake readied himself for a night of *Vision Quest* references.

"What about him?"

"He cannot do two things. He cannot get us arrested and he cannot get us whales."

"Why are you so hung up on this? I've been to Lawrence. It's everywhere down there. You'll have to fight 'em off with a stick."

Randy Munson spent the travel time in the players' section. He had a long chat with Touchdown Tyrone Collins on the Kansas game and the player's NFL future.

"You really should be able to burn these guys, Tyrone," Randy said while sipping his plastic cup of ginger ale. "All week we spotted big holes and gaps that I want you to see the whole game. Look, we're gonna go no-huddle offense, pass pass pass for the first half. Just to exploit it."

"Yeah, I like that kind of talk," the receiver cooed.

"You need to get yourself in the frame of mind to catch nine, 10, 11 balls in the first half. Some deep throws, but mostly those five-yard slants. They're terrible tacklers. You can fly through them even without some blocks. We saw this on the film. They barely beat Southwest Missouri last week."

"And we a hell of a lot better than some team from Missouri," Tyrone commented.

"We are. Just be ready."

Tyrone appeared to appreciate the extra dose of confidence.

"Thanks, Coach. I'm glad you got trust in me."

"We need to have it this week. You're going to be the real focus here."

Collins broke out the flashy smile. "It's gonna be TDT time."

Randy had never noticed Tyrone's two gold teeth before. "I think it will be, Tyrone. I think it will be."

"Is this Karl?" Sam said into the phone in room 253 of the Holiday Inn in north Lawrence. Sam figured Karl was good for driving them the two miles to Massachusetts Avenue.

"What's up? How's the pride of Neillsville?" Karl Warnke asked.

"My friend Jake and I are after a tour of your fair city. Feel like coming by for a lift tonight? We're at the Holiday Inn on Iowa Street."

"I'd love to help the opposition get trashed before a game. Anything to help the hapless Jayhawks. They're pathetic this year."

"That's what it looks like."

"But it's not like KU has lost to Northern Illinois or anything."

"Hey, remember, I had a good game though."

"How late can you stay out?"

Sam looked at Jake, who was fiddling with the remote control. "Jake, how late do you want to be out?"

"As long as it takes to get my game on," Jake replied.

"Uh, Karl, could be all night."

"Cool. I don't have class on Friday." Something all three men had in common. Football players at Wisconsin State chose, en masse, classes that met Monday, Tuesday, and Thursday or just Tuesday and Thursday.

"Tell you what. I saw a Total gas station just south on Iowa Street. At 6th and Iowa, I think. Can you meet us there? We don't need to be seen leaving in a car."

"I know where that is. Just look for the purple Hyundai."

"I knew we'd be traveling in style. 8:45 work for you?"

"See you then. 8:45 at the Total."

"Karl, a favor. Bring a football. Do you have one?"

"I can dig one up."

"Excellent. See you then."

"Channel 11 Sports." Clark Cattoor as Moses again.

"Clark, what's up? Schutzie here."

"Schutzie? How are things at Madison's source for news?"

"Not bad, not bad. I'm still working that football thing we talked about. I found something you may be interested in."

Clark felt his ears perk up. "Talk to me."

"I think it may involve Collins. It's not any point-shaving stuff. I have a buddy from Miami who's telling me that Collins has already signed with Jerry Copperzweig—"

"The agent?"

"Yeah. He has a stronghold on players from down there. He undercuts the others on commission, plus usually gives them cash up front. I still can't run anything on it, but I think we're getting very close."

"Are there any conflicts of interest with the paper for you?"

"Oh, of course. Management would prefer that we hold off any of this until after the season," Aaron grumbled. "If they make a bowl game, the paper makes a mint off those commemorative issues."

Clark knew that side of the business well. The paper's special edition a few years back featured Wisconsin State's first Rose Bowl. Clark had a framed copy in his own living room.

"Are you just going to sit on it?"

"I have to for now," Aaron said. "If it comes out, say, in two weeks, the NCAA will strip Collins of his eligibility and his school records. All of that, wiped out. Wisconsin State will have to forfeit all of the wins on his watch. It'll be massive, the story of the year."

"I guess you don't put out any commemorative issues for illegal players."

"Uh, nope."

"Nothing on the point-shaving yet?"

"I'm still trying to tie Collins into it. He's just had too many big games to do anything poorly. Even last week, he had seven catches for 113. No big drops. It's just that the play calling sucked. Awful. Munson should get fired for that loss."

"I think that's a given after the season."

"It's too bad, because Randy's a good guy, and I know he feels that he had a shot at his own program and he's probably blown it forever."

"Yeah, I've heard that too," Clark said casually.

"To sum it up, I think we'll have something in two weeks, maybe three. I'll give you a heads-up call the day we run something to get you a start. It'll be nuts around here when it comes out."

"Thanks, Schutzie. Take care. Say hi to Beth for me."

"I will, Clark. I will."

Clark's shelf life on The Plan had about two weeks. The walls were closing in. He wasn't as concerned about getting caught as he was about making money. Greed had set its calculating, heartless claws into Clark Cattoor.

25. A Chance Meeting

Jake thumbed through a Maxim magazine inside a gas station in the middle of Lawrence, Kansas. He and Sam Cattanach were in their "covert drinking" clothes. Baseball caps, nothing blue, not one hint of Wisconsin State football. Jake and Sam were built like average students and always played that to their advantage.

"He's here," Sam said.

Jake closed the latest article on Christina Aguilera's new tongue piercing and walked behind Sam to meet the mysterious Karl Warnke.

"Good to meet you." Karl extended his muscular right arm. Jake could see Karl was a former wrestler, his beefy neck the base for a head of short black hair.

"Thanks for taking us out," Jake said.

"My pleasure. Like I told Sam, anything to help the hapless Hawks."

After many turns, Karl pulled up to a parking spot on 10th Street, just off Massachusetts Avenue.

"Oh, say it ain't so, Karl," Sam said. "Tell me it's not Sunny Shore time."

"You know me too well."

"Jake, you'll get a kick out of this place."

At 9:30 on a Thursday night, the Sunny Shore tavern was decorated like an ode to life on the beach. In the middle of the Plains.

The window displays were covered in sand and sailing flags. Oars covered the ceiling. The door handle was carved in the shape of a canoe.

Elvis Presley's rendition of "Polk Salad Annie" boomed through the air as Karl opened the door. Drunk underage patrons were plentiful. Girls were dancing on the bar.

"What's the special?" Jake yelled to a man behind the bar. The bartender was maybe 50 or 55, and certainly looked out of place.

"50-cent draws," the bartender replied. "Three-dollar pitchers."

"What the hell is a draw?" Jake asked Sam.

"A tap beer in Kansas."

"Oh."

"Just make it a pitcher of MGD for us," Sam yelled. "Three glasses with that."

Jake handed the bartender a five. "Keep it."

The bartender smiled. "This is my bar. I've run it for 17 years. Keep the two bucks for now but make sure you spend it here, not those pretty-boy bars down the street."

"Thanks."

The cheap beer turned the opening stages of a bender into a living, breathing night out on the town.

Fifteen minutes later, Jake spent the two bucks plus another for a second pitcher of The Beer That Ate Milwaukee.

Karl relished his role of tour guide.

"Guys, we have an entire five-block strip of bars awaiting us."

Sam turned his attention away from a redhead dancing to "Cheeseburger in Paradise" to mutter, "Let's roll. Bottoms up."

The kickers cured their thirst for adventure with visits to Mass Ave establishments Quentin's, Free State Brewing, and, finally, dancing at the Groove. By a quarter to midnight, the Groove's wooden dance floor was full of woozy college students, the perfect place for two out-of-town football players with 36 hours to kill.

Sam hoisted a bottle of Sam Adams and danced like a punter. Jake was much smoother on the floor, although the plastic glass for his martini took some of the luster off his appearance.

"Oh my starry-eyed surprise!" Jake sang along as he sidled up to a brown-haired number with long legs and a longer smile. "I just want to dance all night, dance all night to this DJ!"

Different town. Same outfits. Heaven for Jake.

Karl soon came into view in Jake's hazy world.

"Hey, man, we got ONE FINAL STOP on the tour!"

"Huh?" Jake squinted.

"LET'S GO. I GOT ONE MORE PLACE TO TAKE YOU."

"Ah, man, check out this booty!" Jake slurred.

"She's in here every night," Karl yelled. "You don't want that. Your wee-wee'll fall off."

"Not with me, she's not."

Sam saw the commotion and stepped in.

"Let's go, you drunk placekicker. This next place is why we brought a football."

Jake turned into a team player and sang along with the music. "All right, I'm gonna mount my horse and ride on to the next town! Next town!"

The Last Chance is an old-fashioned tavern, more of a saloon. It sits atop a hill next to a sandwich shop. Memorial Stadium is about 100 feet below and 700 feet west of the hill, in what is almost a canyon. The only thing missing from the Last Chance is two swinging doors.

"Ah, yes, the oasis of drink," Sam said as Karl pulled the Hyundai up the steep hill on 12th Street. The transmission whined, shook, and nearly fell out onto the asphalt. "We'll finish it off here for the next hour, then see if we have any kicking in our future at the stadium." Sam and Karl broke out laughing.

Jake tried to comprehend it all.

"So, like, we're gonna have more beer," he mumbled. "Then go to the stadium and kick gield foals?"

Sam stepped up his laughter. "Gield foals? Did you just say 'gield foals'?"

"Yuck foo."

"What we'll do is finish off the festivities here," Karl said. "If you're gonna hook up, go. If you strike out, we'll go down to the stadium. The southeast gates are always unlocked at night. We'll mess around, toss a few, kick a few, and then call it a night."

The Last Chance was like a bar in the Wild West, only this western frontier was populated with frat boys and lovely sorority girls. The drunkenness quotient of the Last Chance clientele hovered at about 85 percent. Karl, Sam, and Jake pushed that to 86 percent upon walking through the doors.

"No pitchers after 12:30, guys. Sorry," the crew-cut bartender said.

"Just make it three draws of Miller Lite," Sam said.

"And uh martini. Can you make uh martini here?" Jake chimed in.

"Comin' right up."

"Jesus, Jake, who are you, Dean Martin? Those martinis are so out of fashion." Classic punter-kicker ribbing.

"Hey, don't you owe me some money? Pay up, bitch!" Jake ribbed back. That always shut Sam up in a hurry.

With martini in hand, Jake sought a new conquest. With gin bravado and breath that could paralyze an elephant, Jake dropped the regular student approach and turned into a football player. He found that always worked best when time was tight.

"What's yo name?"

"Kimberly." This raven-haired beauty was six feet of lady. Kimberly did not possess the drunken southern accent that Jake had somehow acquired around ten o'clock, but she was just as blitzed. "What's yours?"

"Jake."

"What you doin' here?"

"I'm from outta town. Here to check out the nightlife. I'm from Wisconsin."

"Say, aren't they—"

"Yeah, I'm the kicker," Jake said confidently.

"You play soccer?"

That sobered Jake up real quick.

"Uh, no. Football." It was a wonder they could hear each other.

"Oh, that's right. The football team's playing this weekend. They suck, you know."

Some knucklehead popped in "Summer Nights" on the jukebox. Jake and Kimberly's conversation soon developed into a fairly good

John Travolta and Olivia Newton-John musical.

Sam tapped Karl on the shoulder.

"Ah shit. Here he goes," Sam shouted, pointing at his roommate.

"Is he like this all the time?"

"Ever since he made the team last year. He's rich, too, since he works as a pizza man during the season."

"I wondered how he was pickin' up all those drinks tonight," Karl said. "And what time is practice tomorrow?"

"Uh…at one, I think."

"Ah, you guys will be fine."

Jake was more than fine. He and his lady of the hour were seeing eye to eye, at least when their eyes were not shut because of the booze. Jake moved in for the kill, a light kiss on the lips that he hoped would lead to something greater, even if the 70 or 80 people in the bar stared at his sloppy kissing.

Kimberly took the bait and produced some tongue.

The speakers belted it out. Tell me more, tell me more.

The pulse of the music was rhythmic to the intoxicated dancers. Jake's brain felt numb, and his legs were weightless. I better cut off the drinking so I can perform, Jake said to himself. Man, I just hope it's not too late.

After another period of tongue hockey, Kimberly came up for air and leaned in.

"You wanna tell your friends you'll see them later?" she moaned.

"Yeah, just give me a few minutes out here. It'll make later feel better."

"Ooh," Kimberly said with a lusty purr.

The bawdy chorus of "Closer" sent the room into a hormone-laden frenzy. The wood floor shook with each beat.

Jake decided to toy with Sam a little more. He could see the punter watching from the bar, a wallflower in Jake's latest tale of erotica. He moved his face in to meet Kimberly's for another unbalanced attempt at a kiss, the kind a Labrador gives a toddler. He moved his hands slowly up the back of Kimberly's legs, planting them right on the back of her Lees.

Jake opened his eyes long enough to shoot a glare over to Sam and Karl. He smiled that "I'm gonna score while you two jokers kick a football tonight" look toward the bar. Jake kept his hands planted on Kimberly's rump except for the occasional touch of a bra strap.

The land of milk and honey would not last for Jake Steffon much longer.

"YOU ASSHOLE! HOW COULD YOU!" Jake's trip to Electric Ladyland was interrupted by the splash of an amaretto sour thrown on his face. His right cheek met the broad side of a black leather purse a second later.

Rachel Randall.

"Oh. My. God." Sam yelled at Karl amid the loud music and oblivious patrons.

"What?" Karl was lost.

"They hooked up last week back home."

"What is she doing—"

"Hold on for a second," Sam demanded. "Let's let this play out!"

Kimberly suddenly found the moment not right for love. "Who are you, bitch? This is my man! Get your own, bitch-face."

Rachel turned to the wobbly kicker. "WHAT IS ALL THIS? YOU THINK I'M ANOTHER NOTCH FOR YOUR WALL?"

In his highly intoxicated condition, Jake took the path that would present the best chance for a bedroom encounter this night.

"Excuse me. DO I KNOW YOU? I'm from out of town," he said unconvincingly to Rachel.

"OH, DON'T GIVE ME THAT SHIT, JAKE STEFFON."

That was it for Kimberly.

"You two work it out. Nice meeting you, asshole." Kimberly walked toward the bar, leaving Jake with the look a woman gives someone who asks her age.

Sam saw it as an opportunity. He walked over to Kimberly.

"Hey, uh, you all right?" Sam asked with a sly smile. "Can I buy you a drink?"

"Aren't you with that asshole? All men are assholes."

"Who? Him? Never seen him in my life. I've been going to school here three years and I've never seen him." Karl tried to hold in his grin. Both Jake and Sam had balls the size of cast iron pans under pressure. A guy had to admire that.

Kimberly did not buy Sam's new alias. "Rusty! Get me a damn

cab and get me the hell out of here. Pronto, please."

"Will do," the bartender replied.

Kimberly walked out the front door and out of Jake's boozy life forever.

With Kimberly gone, Jake tried to patch things up with Rachel. He still wanted to uncover a way to best meet the original purpose of the evening and return to that land of milk and honey.

"So, uh, what brings you here?" Jake modestly opened.

Rachel was still in hyper-speed mode. "WELL, ASSHOLE. CLARK SENT ME TO COVER THE GAME. WE JUST GOT IN AN HOUR AGO OFF A GODDAMN CESSNA." Her voice slowly lowered in volume as Jake flashed his "I'm sorry" eyes. "AND JARED STOLL went to KU, so we're just going out and blowing off some steam."

Jared Stoll nodded from the bar. Jake nodded back. Jared worked as a TV sports guy at one of Rachel's competitors. He'd interviewed Jake once before.

"And I come off a long, hard day of travel to go have a beer," Rachel said, her sprayed hair fraying with each syllable. "And Jared says 'Let's go to this place on the hill. I know the bartenders there,' and I say 'OK.' Little do I know that the guy I slept with just five nights ago is making out with someone he just met."

"Five days ago, you were someone I just met."

"You know what. YOU'RE AN ASSHOLE," she said, pointing her right index finger into his chest. "Just like all the other football players I've met. ALL ASSHOLES."

Rachel threw her purse over a shoulder and motioned to Jared. "Let's go."

Jared shrugged and smiled at the guys. "Gotta do what the lady says, ya know."

"Don't you go asshole on me, too." Rachel led with Jared following.

"Unbefreakinglievable," Jake assessed. "Get me another beer. It don't matter if I'm full of whiskey tonight. No woman, no cry."

The thought of kicking field goals at Memorial Stadium took shape for Jake. Karl made it happen, leading the trio onto the plastic grass of the Kansas football field. Jake relieved himself on the KU logo at the 50.

"Get over here and knock through this extra point," Sam said in a loud whisper from the 10-yard line near the south end zone.

Jake zipped up and ran over. The world was spinning.

"Take all the time you need," Sam said. "I'll just hold it here. Consider it a little extra field work."

Jake sloppily booted the ball. Good kickers are good kickers even when liquored up. Not much power, but right down the middle. Karl retrieved the ball from the track behind the goalposts.

Sam suddenly sobered up.

"Enough of this bullshit. It's 2 A.M. We're two hours past curfew. Let's get out of here. Wilcox is gonna have our ass when we get back."

"Who cares? We're the only kickers this trip. What are they gonna do?"

Karl dropped off the kickers at the back of the Holiday Inn. Sam had already scoped out the closest rear exit to room 253. All they would have to do is unlock the glass door, walk up a flight of stairs, and down a red carpet hallway about four or five rooms. No big deal.

"Just follow me, don't talk, and tiptoe," Sam alerted Jake.

Sam stuck his plastic key card in the dead bolt. The green light on the door was the start for their final race of the night.

The coast was clear.

"We're safe. I think we're safe," Jake said.

"Not yet, cowboy. We're still not out of the woods."

Sam approached room 253 and slowly turned the door. He walked inside the room in front of Jake.

"Well, well, well, if it isn't our kicker and our punter!"

John Wilcox was sitting on Jake's bed, watching the end of the late *SportsCenter*. Sam looked down. Jake looked up.

"No, no, no, guys, welcome back! Sit on down and watch *SportsCenter* with me." Wilcox was dripping with sarcasm and a little drink himself.

"Uh, coach," Sam started.

"You know what? Save it. I knocked on the door at midnight. No answer. I even gave you boys the benefit of one o'clock. You boys had a good week of practice. But no, you have to go out and get shitty on a road trip."

"I'm not drunk. Test me," Sam snapped.

"What about him?"

Jake fell face first onto his bed, his head landing next to John's feet.

"I'm gonna say this once so you drunks better listen. I won't tell Coach Flaherty about this, but I'm gonna run your asses tomorrow at practice. No walk-through for you guys. You'd better start puking now, because if you do it on the field tomorrow, the coaches will figure it out."

John got up and starting for the door.

"Oh, and just to show that I care for my players, here's a bottle of aspirin to get you started. Happy vomiting. Good night."

At the same hour, Clark Cattoor cruised the Cool Breeze Sports on-line sports book. His account sat at just over $8,300 after the Northern Illinois game.

Instead of tackling the bars this Thursday night, chasing the same young college girls Jake and Sam were checking out three states away, Clark reveled in the comfort of home. George Benson's "Give Me the Night" played in the living room.

When Clark had worked in Duluth, he'd felt that if he made $45,000 a year, his life would be perfect. No problems. No worries. Now the relative poverty he'd faced seemed so much easier than the web he had slowly worked himself into.

Clark came across the page. "WISCONSIN STATE-KANSAS, Saturday 2 P.M. ET. Regional TV." With his $8,300 in credits, Clark bet the whole pot on the local team. The receipt slowly churned out of the printer.

"Wisconsin State (-5.5) at KANSAS. $8,322 to win $7,855."

Don't lead me wrong, Randy, don't lead me wrong.

26. Kansas

Simon Smith signaled the start of another football Saturday through radios across Wisconsin.

"Live from Lawrence, Kansas, this is Boars football. Wisconsin State will meet the Kansas Jayhawks. Wisconsin State comes into the day with a 2-1 record. Last week's 17-7 loss to Northern Illinois knocked the team out of the polls. Today they'll try to get back in with a win over 1-2 Kansas before the start of the Big Ten season.

"I'm Simon Smith, joining my partner Buck Benson..."

On the field below, Randy Munson was supremely confident. Craig Zellnoff had been sharp for much of the week. Touchdown Tyrone was extra cocky as he ran pregame drills. Tyrone was playing for the NFL scouts now, not for the school. He was pursuing an NFL degree, and Randy respected that.

Randy had bought a larger number from Stephen and the Gold Sports book. He had to give up six points on Wisconsin State.

He could have given up 26.

As he'd promised Tyrone on the airplane, Randy ran a no-huddle offense through the first half. Craig to Wilson 16 yards. Craig to Tyrone 22 yards. Craig to Burns 7 yards. Even Teddy Hammersley caught a 13-yard pass on that first drive. Tyrone then closed out the drive with a 21-yard score off a reverse run.

When he broke the goal line, Tyrone flashed a Heisman pose for the cameras. "Sheeit, I can do it all!" the lanky receiver barked to the empty stands at the north end zone. The small pack of Kansas fans were not impressed. One student held up a sign: "17 Days Until Basketball Season."

Wisconsin State led at halftime 28-6, thanks to Tyrone's reverse score and Craig's three touchdown passes, two of them to Tyrone. The offense was flawless and frictionless.

"All right, guys, I know we're up three scores and you probably want to kick back. I'm telling you now: Don't do it. Let's make it 40 and then let our young guys get some time," Frank said under the Memorial Stadium stands.

Safety Donnell Hardy intercepted a Kansas pass and returned the second play of the second half for a touchdown. Jake's extra point made the score Wisconsin State 35, Kansas 6.

The next Wisconsin State drive stalled, forcing a field goal attempt from 44 yards out. Left hash.

John Wilcox offered Jake some encouragement.

"Don't even think about missing this one," John said, his eyes glaring, his spiked hair glistening in the sun. "You wouldn't want to become an ordinary student again, would you?"

Out of earshot, Sam said to his kicker, "What an asshole. Don't sweat it. They need you here. Show them just how much."

Jake was doing fine today. He'd gone to bed at seven the night before to square his sleeping account.

Stutter step left. Half step right. Full step left. Impact.

A slicer.

The football was inching to the right ever so slightly. Jake had factored that into his angle, as his extra points had been slicing to the right all day. The ball sailed just inside the right goalpost. Crisis averted.

Wilcox could go to hell.

Wisconsin State's 45-12 victory sent them to a respectable 3-1 record. The Boars certainly wanted a 4-0 mark to pad their record for bowl season, but 3-1 was still doable for a bowl game and to save everyone's job.

"I would call it a perfect game. About as close as you'll ever find," Frank Flaherty told the pack of a dozen reporters under the bleachers. "I gotta give credit to Coach Munson for his game plan. He saw that our quarterback and our receivers could really take advantage of their youth on defense. We gave him the game ball."

Touchdown Tyrone Collins was basking in the glow of his 14-catch, 178-yard, four-touchdown game.

"Do you think you have a shot at the Heisman after that game?" asked Skip Stevens.

"Look at the numbers, man. If I keep this up, they should give me the trophy by Halloween. Oh wait, maybe not. Those Heisman guys always choke in the NFL. Ha!"

Tyrone looked into Rachel Randall's camera and uttered his new phrase.

"TDT equals Heisman for me!"

Randy Munson's coaching stock had risen from the ashes. Not to mention he now a stake in over 22 grand.

"Masterful game plan by the oft-criticized Randy Munson," wrote columnist Vic Lerou.

"He's sharp on his offense. They clicked on all cylinders. This team could make a run in the Big Ten," declared Skip Stevens on the postgame show.

Before stepping on the plane for Madison, Randy called home to have Lisa and the kids pick him up at the airport. He usually caught a ride on the team bus, but this time he wanted to head straight home after landing.

At just after seven in the evening, the DC-9 touched down at the Dane County Airport.

"Daddy!" Brett cried. The eight-year-old's face was flushed with love as he hobbled toward his father. Randy rubbed Brett's reddish hair.

"What did you bring me, Daddy?"

Always the first question after a road trip. Randy produced an embroidered Kansas City Royals sweatshirt, size medium.

"The Royals?" Brett said. "They're terrible."

"They were better than the Brewers this year."

"You always say that when you get me the other teams, Daddy."

Randy Munson lived like a king this weekend, but he knew his kingdom was as real as a storefront on a Western movie set.

"Channel 11 Sports." Not Moses this time, but Rachel Randall.
"Uh, Rachel?" the voice asked.
"Uh, yes." Rachel replied, assuming a stalker was on the line.
"Jake Steffon." Sort of a stalker.
"Oh. Hi."
"Look, I just want to apolo—"
"You know what? Just save it." Rachel looked around the sports office. Some annoying intern had left on a Taco Bell run, so she was alone and free to launch into the kicker. "I decided that what happened was a mistake."
"You're not going to tell anybody about this, are you?"
"Look. I have more to lose with this than you do, OK? My career is on the line if this comes out. If you want to do me a favor, just forget it. You and Sam know what happened, but that's it, OK? If you say anything, I just may remember how drunk you got during the season. You're 20, remember?"
"What about that other guy?"
"What about him? We're just friends," Rachel said.
"No, no. Will he tell anyone?"
"I hope not. I asked him to keep this quiet, as a favor to me. I think he will."
"Good. Well, I guess this is it."
"Yes it is. Let's not get all sentimental about it, OK?"
"OK, bye."
"Bye."
Jake heard the other line ring. He picked it up.
"Thanks for calling Pizza Perfecto. This is Jake. How can I help you?" Studying for his upcoming Econ test would have been the smartest play this Sunday. Rachel's quick exit was more of a shock than even he'd anticipated.
But the lure of a quick and easy $200 was too much. Jake spent the afternoon and early evening driving around downtown Madison, climbing apartment stairs and delivering pizzas. The Packers were on at noon. The Vikings at 3:15. Madison's high concentration of

students from Minnesota made this day a must to work.

"That'll be $26.25," Jake said over three green pepper and onion pizzas and a bag of garlic bread at a bungalow on Spaight Street.

"Here's $31. Keep it."

The job was as easy as that. Drive around and collect cash. To his surprise, the media spotlight on his own life was minimal. Only the WSU student newspaper, the *Daily Boar*, printed a story on the placekicker who delivered pizza, pasta, and subs twice a week.

Even though he'd cut back on his hours at work, he was still living quite comfortably. Sam had paid him half the balance from the Hawaii fiasco. His Honey Wagon was still running, although a new timing belt would soon be in the cards.

Each shift he spent the final hour scrubbing dishes. Pizza pans, cheese graters, sauce ladles. The chicken wing grease catchers were the worst. With each dirty dish, his thoughts turned to the NFL, not to his studies.

Jake had to get out of this place.

27. The Questions Surface

One morning each September in Madison, usually toward the end of the month, signals the coming of winter. The students who tossed footballs on the Wisconsin State campus put away their toys. The leisurely pace of the summer grinds to a halt as academic survival takes precedence.

Clark Cattoor had experienced enough Septembers at Wisconsin State to appreciate this day. It was a Tuesday morning, around ten. The sun sparkled on the concrete and in the windows of the buildings, but no warmth came from it. Winter was on its way. Clark loved that feeling.

He plodded along, a 32-year-old jogging on a 19-year-old's campus. Clark was now up to running twice a week before playing basketball at The Court.

"One Vision" by Queen pumped through his headphones. Clark found the theme song always kept him inspired for a few extra blocks. A decade before, he'd run these same streets under the night sky, listening to the same songs, often in shorts and often in below-zero weather.

His route was always the same, going back to his days living just off the state capitol on West Gorham Street. He would park his car in the public lot near Gilman and Henry, run two blocks down Gilman, and would make the 45-degree right turn onto State Street, a pedestrian street filled with taverns, restaurants, and other shops.

Clark enjoyed eyeing the homeless people, the skate punks, and especially the young college girls.

Soaking in a gray heavyweight T-shirt and black shiny basketball shorts, Clark strolled into the Court after his run. He wished his cocky strut could signal the start of the real pickup games.

Aaron Schutz was already warming up on the courts. Aaron was a mere 5'3", so his game was distributing the ball to the other guys. He was in it strictly for the exercise.

"What's up, Clark? I missed you in Lawrence."

"I bet you did," Clark said as he stretched his legs. "Who could you go drinkin' with?"

"I found a few people. Say, I wanted to talk with you about a couple of things that have come up."

"What is it?"

Clark looked down at his left sock, pulling it up. The sock had been sagging on him for the last seven blocks.

"Clark, I think we're going to move forward with this thing going on with Collins."

"Really?"

"Yeah, it's pretty apparent that Copperzweig is hooking him up with some benefits. There's no way he can afford that apartment by the capitol, no way he can afford that SUV."

"Yeah, it's pretty loud. I've heard him driving that thing." Clark chuckled.

"Anyway, we're still a ways from seeing this in print. I still have no direct proof that Collins is getting paid directly from Copperzweig. No one in Miami knows anything about it. I want to see if you can help me out."

Clark closed his eyes as he bent his left leg. "Talk to me."

Aaron shifted his gaze directly to Clark's face.

"You actually see Flaherty outside the press conference setting."

"Yeah."

"Ask him on Sunday when you tape the show if he's heard anything weird with Collins. He may have an answer for you. If nothing else, he may be looking to get rid of him before the NCAA slaps the team on probation."

Clark's body language said "over my dead body." He came up with a more polished response.

"You really want me to do this?"

"I think it would be a good starting point for the story."

Clark looked back at the ground.

"I don't think it's my place," Clark pointed out. "Especially in that venue. His show is not journalism. It's PR. We all know that. It's not the time or place to bring that up."

Aaron broke into a smile.

"I figured you might say that, but I wanted to come to you because you don't mind mixing it up."

Clark was on the edge of snapping. He remembered that people were watching. He could not just go off on Aaron in a gym full of 40 people.

"Another thing, Clark. You need to know about this."

"What?"

"Something happened in Lawrence with Rachel."

"Like what?"

"The details are still sketchy, but I guess she hit Jake Steffon with a purse at a bar on Thursday night."

"Who told you this?"

"We off the record here? Jared Stoll," Aaron said. "He was with her. I guess the scene was just wild. Steffon was kissing some girl and Rachel went nuts. Called him an asshole and all that."

"Holy shit."

"I don't know if you guys have a policy against screwing football players, but I figured you should know about this. You're lucky it didn't happen in Madison or else it would be all over the papers."

"I'm shocked, but thanks."

"Yeah, let's run the courts."

Randy Munson pulled into his favorite PDQ parking lot for his favorite pay phone in Madison.

"Stephen. Randy here."

"Hey, man, good day to you, sir. What's shakin' out there?"

"Not much. Rain. I miss the desert sometimes. How's it going out there?"

"Great, except for the book. We took a beating on the Monday night game. The Cowboys opened as a 6-point favorite, the number jumped to 9, and settled at 8. 27-20 final. We were slaughtered by the 'middlers.' Lost about 60 grand."

"Ouch." Randy tried to sound concerned.

"So, are you through or are we going to press our luck a few more times this year?"

"That's what I called about. I'm not sure. Where's the number at for Saturday?"

Stephen paused before responding. "Indiana's loss to Kentucky hurts you big for this weekend. Our current number is you guys minus 9 points."

"Nine? Do you think that will go up?"

"Oh, I'm sure it'll move to 11 before it settles. Get in on this quick if you want it at nine. Let me look at the Gold Sports number. Yup. That's at nine and a half right now."

"Give me a second."

Randy was ahead just over $17,000 after the Kansas game, even more than he'd been counting on when he hatched The Plan. That money could take care of Brett's schooling for nearly two years. That could pay off the Riviera. That cash would make a nice down payment for a house wherever that next job might be.

It still wasn't enough.

"Stephen. Let's roll two more times."

"I knew you would. They all do."

Randy was put off by that last comment, but he let it slide.

"Here's what I'm looking at. We're 17 up. Let it go Saturday 'for.' "

"Easy there. You want to put that much on one game?"

"Why not?" Randy was chomping on his spearmint gum even harder now.

"Here's why not," Stephen explained. "If you don't cover, you'll be crawling right back to me the following week against Northwestern. I'm already getting a little uneasy at the frequency of our action."

What a time to start playing the role of the guardian angel, Randy thought.

"In addition, I'm concerned about the size," Stephen continued. "If someone came up to my shop and bet 17 grand on a college football game, a minor game like this one, I'd probably be forced to mark it down for the feds. They take taxes on wins that large, you know. Now I'm not saying it'll happen with these on-line books, but numbers like this are very suspicious."

"I see."

"I may be wrong. I'm still unsure of their jurisdictions. It's not like a sports book operating out of Makao or Ibiza or wherever the hell it is can call the FBI. I'm just saying look out."

"Can we do it, though?" Randy said with more than a trace of irritation.

"If you want to make it happen, let's make it happen."

"17 for Saturday at 9 and a half."

"Is this the last one?"

"Here's the plan. Let's say we win by 20, 30 points," Randy plotted aloud. "That moves up our stock against Northwestern, right?"

"Sure would."

"What would the Northwestern odds be then?"

Stephen blew out a mouthful of air.

"I'd say four or five to one," Stephen guessed. "Six if Northwestern loses big this week. They still haven't won a game this year."

"Then we would play all of it on Northwestern for odds."

"And that would be it, right?"

"That would be it. We would let the 34 ride. What would that be, 200 grand payout at six to one?"

"Make that 140 for you. I gotta take my cut."

"Sure, sure."

"We can make this work."

28. The Hacks Start Digging

Clark was striking his computer keyboard with precision. When Clark got into writing a story, he worked the keyboard like a seasoned newspaper hack. Even though he knew looks were much of the game in TV sports journalism, he fancied himself a stud writer.

"Rachel, could you find me the raw of the Kansas game?"

Rachel handed over the two tapes of unedited footage she'd shot in Lawrence.

"Thanks."

"Sure."

"Say, something's come up. I need to speak with you."

Rachel looked at Clark with the glare of guilt. Her eyes already said she was in the wrong.

"I heard a story about you and Jake Steffon in Lawrence," Clark said slowly. "Some kind of altercation. What happened?"

"Please let me explain," Rachel started.

"Fine. Explain."

In a melodramatic voice, Rachel took Clark through the evening, from the landing in Lawrence to spotting Jake "slobbering" all over some woman.

"Why did that make you so mad?"

"Because we..."

"Yes."

Rachel could not get out the words.

"Because we...got together the week before."

Silence filled the sports department. Female sports reporters sleeping with football players broke one of the cardinal rules of the industry. Nothing illegal, but certainly very poor form.

That was almost as bad as gambling on the very team you covered.

Clark started first.

"You're a grown-up," Clark said in a fatherly tone. "I'm not going to tell you that you should have done this or that, but now I have to do some damage control."

"Who told you?" Rachel said, blowing her nose.

"It doesn't matter," Clark said with a dismissive wave. "What matters now is that this is making its way through the press box circles. The next time you're at Mendota Stadium or around any of those newspaper guys, they'll talk about you and Jake."

Rachel asked a tough question, her first since starting at the station.

"Will I get fired for this?"

"That I don't know," Clark replied. "That's not my call. I can keep this quiet, which I will for now. I don't want to deal with this circus. So do me a favor."

"Yes, anything."

"You didn't tell me about this, OK? I didn't hear it. Let's leave it that way."

Clark already had a much larger fire to put out. After the early show, he was to meet Randy Munson at the Green Bench on South Park Street. The Green Bench was dark and mysterious, the perfect setting for two criminals plotting the next big score.

"Randy, how's your family?" Clark asked over jalapeño poppers during happy hour.

"Lisa's OK. She still has no idea about The Plan. Melissa decided to go to UW-Eau Claire for now."

"Good school. Excellent music program."

"That's what she's into. I'm real happy with that. I just hope she doesn't feel like she couldn't go to Northwestern or North Carolina because her parents are always clipping coupons."

"I wouldn't exactly steer her toward Northwestern. That's 30 grand a year."

"Oh, I didn't. Scott just turned 15. He's a real sharp kid, but now all he thinks about are girls and hoops. I think he may start at Memorial this year." Basketball practice was just three weeks away.

"How about Brett?"

"He's doing OK," Randy said as he tossed a deep-fried popper into his mouth. "His teachers say he's more temperamental than last year, but that he also seems a bit smarter. I want him to be happy. Just seeing the love he has when I walk into a room still melts my heart."

Clark ordered the potato soup and started in with his agenda.

"We need to be a bit concerned. One of my newspaper colleagues has been sniffing around the program a bit. He thinks Collins has been getting paid by an agent."

Randy added another Sweet & Low to his iced tea.

"That's no surprise. Collins has been courting them for about a year now."

Clark lowered his voice.

"But Randy, this same writer thinks there's an element of throwing games on this year's team."

"How could he say that? We've only blown one game. We covered the rest."

"Let's just say he still has questions about the Northern Illinois game."

"Look," Randy whispered as he leaned across the table. "That NIU loss was awful on my family. Yes, I played a big part in it. I did something horrible. The press called me a buffoon for a week. I know this. But I don't think anyone will find anything on that game. There's no paper trail."

Clark opened the next big topic on his agenda.

"So, are you done for the year on the numbers?"

Randy put down his salad fork.

"No, and especially not now if this is true."

"Why not?"

"If this comes out about Collins, he'll be kicked out of school." Randy looked around to see if any loose ears were nearby and open.

"Clark, if he's out, I lose control over what happens. He's that much of a factor. The spread changes or gets taken down if he just gets hurt. If he gets kicked out next week, the books will take us off the board for a few weeks. I can't lose that chance."

"Right."

"Look, I'm already making plans to get out of town after this year. Ideally, I could hook on at a small school as the main guy."

Clark took a bite of his broiled walleye. He'd given up red meat during the summer, to recapture the physique of his youth.

"So, what's the word for this weekend?"

"Oh, we'll cover. Indiana is just as bad as Kansas. Another basketball school waiting for the season to start."

"Even on the road? Ten's a high number."

"It's up to ten now? I still think that's a steal." Randy sounded convincing.

"Will you ever go against the team again?"

Randy stabbed the air with his fork. A dripping piece of Swiss steak dangled from the end.

"Yes. Northwestern next week. We'll win so big this weekend that the odds will be through the roof for Northwestern to win. Game is at home. Northwestern is awful, yet, like NIU, they always seem to play us tough."

"Don't you think people will talk after that?"

"I'm sure they will," Randy said matter-of-factly. "Two home losses to bad teams. They'll talk. But they'll talk about Frank's lack of game management or my stupid play-calling. They can say what they want. We'll go riding into the sunset with a bag full of greenbacks."

"So for this week and against odds next?"

"Yes, unless you hear from me otherwise. If those both work out, then I'm done. I'll have enough where I'll never do it again."

29. Indiana

After landing at the Bloomington airport, the Wisconsin State football team rolled into Memorial Stadium in their three-bus convoy. An unusual sense of urgency filled the buses. Frank Flaherty had beat it into the players' heads that Indiana was not a terrible team. That was a lie. Frank told the players they could easily lose, even if they played well. That was a lie. Frank said that the stadium would be so loud that they would have to be, as he put it, "really dialed in."

The players saw that was indeed a lie when the buses arrived. Only 20,000 Hoosiers fans were expected for the game, and the campus was dead at this early hour on Saturday morning. A few thousand Wisconsin State fans had made the eight-hour trek to Bloomington to cheer the Boars.

"Yeah, FRANK FLAHERTY!" yelled a Wisconsin State fan wearing what appeared to be a stuffed boar on his head. Frank waved at the crazy fan.

The players walked like rock stars from their buses to the visiting locker room.

Randy Munson wanted his crew to humiliate Indiana. That was his primary focus.

Clark sat in the empty press box above the field, flipping through the program. He still had time to get some action on the game. Randy had sounded so certain Wisconsin State would cover what was now a ten-and-a-half-point spread. Indiana was terrible, Clark told himself. How could I go wrong? The window for making big money was closing. Tyrone Collins was going to get kicked out of school soon. Today might be the last day, the final chance to cash in before The Plan cracked.

Black clouds hovered over the stadium. It was 10:15 A.M. Eastern time, still nearly two hours before the early 12:10 start to accommodate ESPN. That gave him a bad feeling. Indiana played on thick, lush grass, and the rain would only slow Wisconsin State down.

Clark weighed all the options: I'm up 15 grand, I can't pull the trigger on this one. I just can't do it. The fear of discovery and of losing kept him from walking over to the pay phone in the corner of the press box to press his luck one more time.

Jim Tillman startled Clark.

"Here you go," Jim said, leaving a pregame press packet in front of him. "Anything else I can get for you, Clark?"

"Uh, no. I'm good. Thanks, Jim."

Clark sat, reassured, as the rains came. He could only wonder how much Randy Munson was sweating the change in weather.

"It's still rainin', Coach." Randy announced to Frank as the head coach was about to address the team.

"Thanks." Frank took off his navy baseball cap. "GENTLEMEN, this is the Big Ten opener. What that means is that we're all equal. Right now, we have the same record as those guys. Ohio State has the same record as Northwestern."

Most of the players looked down and rolled their eyes. They heard this every year.

"Don't be fooled by the fact that Indiana has struggled. You all know they love to jump up and bite our ass. They live for this stuff. You older guys remember this." Indiana had upset Wisconsin State two years before in Bloomington.

"Zellnoff? What was that like, to lose to IU? In fact, I believe you started that last game down here."

Craig Zellnoff lifted his head.

"It sucked, coach."

"Thanks, Craig. See, it sucked. Now, with the rain, they're probably expecting us to power the ball and stay away from throwing it. Coach Munson doesn't think we should do that. He says we stay in the no-huddle, passing offense that worked so well at Kansas. I'm going to defer to his judgment."

A smile came over the face of Touchdown Tyrone Collins. Whatever speed he lost on wet grass he would gain in confidence.

Frank put his hat back on.

"THIS IS IT. 4-1 IS THERE FOR YOU. YOU JUST NEED TO GO OUT AND GRAB IT. NOW LET'S GO."

The 75 traveling players moved into a neat, single-file line to open the Big Ten season.

For the second straight game, Craig Zellnoff was a surgeon with the football. Running Randy's no-huddle offense, Craig led Wisconsin State on drives of 67, 82, and 55 to open the first quarter. Touchdown Tyrone Collins hauled in eight passes for 71 yards and two scores in the first.

The Boars led 21-3 after one.

After nailing his third extra point in less than an hour, Jake ran off the field and caught up with Sam.

"Why the hell do we even bring you for these shitty teams? I'd trade a punter for another defensive back," Jake needled his punter.

"At least you need a holder. Who else does such a professional job?"

This game was a laugher through halftime, when Frank decided to pull Craig with a 31-3 lead. Jake ended the first half scoring with a 35-yard line drive that still counted, if not for style points.

Randy ran off the field concerned with Frank's choice to switch quarterbacks. He decided to catch up with the head coach on the way to the locker room.

"Can we keep Craig for just one more drive in the second half? Alex isn't ready for a full half yet." Alex Sistos was the backup quarterback. He had taken a few snaps against Murray State and Kansas, but still had not gotten rid of a quarterback's worst enemy, the dreaded happy feet.

"You're right, Randy. One drive." Frank remembered Indiana's comeback from a deep hole two years before. That loss had almost scored him a pink slip.

Randy watched Frank address the team in the tiny locker room at halftime, but he didn't hear him. With only a nine-point spread to cover, Randy knew this game was in the bag. Wisconsin State would cover three of the four games since he'd put The Plan into practice. He was sure neither the NCAA nor the FBI would ever find out. Teams that do this sort of stuff are far too obvious about it. Not Wisconsin State football. He was proud of the way he'd conducted himself during all of this. The money was almost square in his pocket.

Craig took the second half kickoff for Wisconsin State's sixth score of the afternoon. The senior floated a beautiful ball up for Tyrone Collins. Two Indiana defenders were draped all over him. Collins used his 37-inch vertical leap to pull down the ball with his left hand. The defenders were facedown on the wet grass with Collins holding the ball up to the crowd.

It would make for a great front-page picture on the Sunday morning *Dane County Tribune*.

"TDT FOR HEISMAN!" He yelled to the half-empty bleachers. The 4,000 Wisconsin State fans yelled it back to him.

Score: 38-3 Wisconsin State. Not even Alex Sistos could screw it up. The freshman from Slinger tossed two interceptions but did lead two scoring drives. Jake punched a 40-yard field goal through, and Teddy Hammersley even scored on a 4-yard plunge in the fourth quarter to make the final score 48-16. The good folks knocking back Blatz at Lon's Roadhouse at the corner of Highways 10 and 73 in Neillsville got a thrill from that.

Wisconsin State was now 4-1 and 1-0 in the Big Ten. Frank Flaherty just might save his job after all.

Randy took another view, naturally a dim one. He couldn't feel the water in his damp shoes because The Plan had worked to perfection. Yet he had a bad feeling in his gut. Someone outside of Clark and Stephen knew about this. That pipsqueak reporter from the *Tribune* might. Anyone could, really. He just had to stay the course and stay discreet.

Clark decided to be the media jerk. He asked the one question Frank Flaherty would blow up at.

"So, Frank, is this team Rose Bowl material?"

Frank loosened his neck from side to side. The blue satin windbreaker emitted a screeching noise with each move of Frank's body.

"I would say no, we're not there yet," the coach said, tapping his left index finger on the podium. "Look at the other teams in this conference. Ohio State, did they win today, Jim?"

Jim Tillman took a step in front of the media pack. "Yes, 45-7."

"Ohio State, Michigan, Iowa. They're all superior teams to us right now. I do like where we're headed. Two excellent games in a row. Both big road wins. We might be ready to take the next step.

"All I know is that we're now preparing for Northwestern. We have to beat those guys before we worry about anyone on top."

Clark knew this team was a paper tiger. Northwestern's 45-7 loss to Ohio State made next week the perfect trap game for Wisconsin State. The Boars would be looking ahead to the next two weeks, home against Purdue and at Minnesota.

Talk of drink and debauchery topped the Saturday night social agenda on the plane back to Madison. Offensive tackle Bob Verly announced an impromptu fest at his apartment. He declared the special vodka humidifier would return for one night and one night only. Bob said a bottle of vodka in the humidifier would slowly get everyone in the room drunk.

"You kickers comin' by? It's gonna be a good time. I'll even let Collins in without charging him," Verly said to Jake and Sam.

Jake looked up from his Econ notes.

"I can't make it tonight, man," he whined. "My ass is grass on Wednesday if I'm not ready for this test. I'm treading water in that class right now."

Bob looked at Sam. "How about you?"

"You know I'm in. It's a great day for Neillsville. Hammertime got a touchdown, I only had to punt twice."

Jake was refocused on the world of supply-and-demand, Keynesian models and supply-side theory.

"Jake, man, you really should think about dropping by. Women will be everywhere. They always grab onto us after wins. We're heroes at home tonight."

Jake laughed and looked back to Bob.

"This humidifier, can it really get people drunk? Maybe I will come over and check it out."

Randy tossed his blue overnight bag into the trunk of his Riviera. He could see the sun slipping under the state capitol to the southwest of the airport.

I've done it, he thought. I've pulled off The Plan—$32,000 after Stephen took his cut. Not too shabby, and I only got my hands dirty once, he rationalized. Randy had made himself believe that betting with Wisconsin State was fine. He knew deep down the NCAA would look on it differently.

They would never find out.

He steered the Riviera down East Washington and turned left onto Blair Street. He looked out toward Lake Monona and remembered when his life was simpler. Ten years earlier, he, Lisa, and the two kids would walk up and down Law Park along Lake Monona. They'd stroll the path, laughing and playing as people zoomed past them, jogging or in-line skating. The Frank Lloyd Wright Convention Center covered much of the lake-walk skyline now.

Brett's arrival in 1995 had put a strain on their marriage. Randy and Lisa got precious little sleep in Brett's first three years. Brett screamed for much of each night, and Lisa usually cried. Hardly anyone in the house got any sleep for that stretch.

The sun was a memory as Randy pulled up to his pay phone at the PDQ.

"Stephen. Randy."

"Good show out there today, old chap! You guys are hot."

"Yeah, what are we up to now?"

"Let's see," Stephen said. "17 got you 32 today."

"Not bad. I think next week will be the last one. I see they lost big." Randy remembered not to say "Northwestern" over the phone.

"Yeah, are you guys just playing awful teams this year? You haven't played anyone with a winning record yet."

Randy cut to the chase.

"What do you think the odds will be for next week?"

"Nothing's on the board yet, but I'd guess 6 to 1, maybe 7 to 1. You guys will probably be a 22-, 23-point favorite."

"7 to 1, huh?"

"Probably."

"If it's 6 to 1 or higher, let's take the 32 and let it roll."

"Are you serious?"

"Sure. That will net, what, 220 thousand?"

"Let's see," Stephen said, and Randy could hear him punching a calculator. "$226,100 is the exact figure. Around 180 for you after the house cut."

"That's a nice profit for a little bit of work for you. Have you heard anything about this?"

"Not out here, man. There's been no unusual business going on with your action. Any action has stayed strictly with the on-line sports books, not us."

"Yes, let's plan on that. Take the whole thing on Northwestern for odds."

"Will do."

"I need one favor, though."

"What is it?"

"Will you spook one kid this week?" Randy asked. "The kicker."

"Sure. What's his number?"

Randy dug under his coaching clipboard for the team contact list, and gave Stephen the phone number of one Jake Steffon.

"Got it. What should I say?"

"Just let him know that any game-winning kicks could prove harmful to his future," Randy said. "Consider it a little extra insurance for our cause. He probably gets calls like this all the time. Another one can't hurt. It could very well come down to him."

"Will do."

Randy felt a swift release of tension as he entered the final stage, the final decision of The Plan. If he won next Saturday, he would just make The Plan go away.

He and Stephen had already worked out the payments and the delivery. Stephen would fly to St. Martaan and take the 80 percent cash option. Normally, sports books sent the full amount in a check for US dollars. As an insider in the sports gambling business, Stephen told him that most shops would pay a discounted amount in cash for clients who wanted to avoid taxes. Like the secret special in a Las Vegas coffee shop, it wasn't on the menu. You had to ask for it.

Stephen planned to wire the money himself from a bank in St. Martaan to a private Swiss account. Randy was still unsure just how he would get the money back to the States. His best option might be to leave his take in his own Swiss account. He swore not to tell Lisa or anyone unless he absolutely needed to break the piggy bank.

As Randy drove the final two miles to his house, he forgot about the money and the problems this particular money might bring one day.

"DADDY!" Brett screamed when the triumphant coach walked in the front door.

30. Parties and Pranks

Sam Cattanach was one of the few starters not sore from the Indiana win. For the past two weeks, Sam had hardly seen the field. He even chose not to take a shower after the game in Bloomington. He simply threw on his gray cotton dress shirt, knotted up a blue paisley tie, threw on some tan pants, and hopped on the bus. His jet-black hair was still in place.

"C'mon, Jake. Quit being a girlie man and come out with me," Sam said with a hint of annoyance.

Jake was now plopped on the infamous green couch at the Kickers' Quarters.

"Not a chance, man."

Sam found another angle of attack.

"I'm pretty sure Rachel Randall won't be there. You won't have to taste any purse tonight."

"I'm only going to taste my Sundrop tonight." Jake smiled back. Like many of the other rural players from northern Wisconsin, he had an unusual allegiance to the locally brewed Mello Yello knockoff. Jake drank the sugary stuff as if it were water.

"Suit yourself, man. When you get bored and start strokin' it here, just think, you could have had someone else doing it for you. Man, we are 4 and 1. People love us. You remember last year, right?"

That got Jake's full attention.

Sam continued.

"When we lost that sixth game of the year. Remember? The Michigan loss. We were almost like Regular Joes on campus. Like those sorry dudes trying to pick up whales at two in the morning during last call. Man, take advantage of the situation." Sam paused for dramatic effect. "So you comin'?"

"Uh...no."

Sam threw his hands up. "I'm off to Verly's. Gotta see this vodka humidifier for myself."

"See ya."

Sam slammed the apartment door.

Jake laughed off the punter and returned to the world of Econ. A world where he was absolutely clueless. He was angry at himself for even taking the class.

Jake decided that partying and women were a lot more attractive than interest models and this Volcker guy.

He laid his mass of test papers on top of the old brown trunk that served as living room table, breakfast table, Playstation 2 home, and bar counter.

A trip to his room followed, where he searched furiously for a heavy wool, western-print shirt he enjoyed wearing with his Indiana Jones western hat. If he was going to hang out in a room with a humidifier that pumped out vodka-perfumed air, he might as well look the fool he would eventually become.

Clark didn't say a single word to Randy on the way back to Madison. Clark scored a seat on the charter plane when two equipment managers couldn't travel because of raging cases of mononucleosis. Frank Flaherty was adamant that anyone flying with his players be free of contagious disease.

Clark and Randy eyed each other on the plane, but agreed to keep a healthy distance from The Plan. They acted like a couple having an affair. Meeting in empty restaurants. Calling on pay phones.

Clark kicked himself on the trip back for not betting with Wisconsin State on this game. He could easily have turned his 15 grand into 28 with a simple phone call. He wasn't terribly upset because he still knew the big score was coming against Northwestern.

Yet he could have won today and just cashed out. No more worries.

After cutting a two-minute story on Wisconsin State's "dominant road prowess," as he termed it in the piece, Clark set the videotape on Rachel's desk for the late news and drove home. He looked forward to an evening on his own couch. No smoky bars. No trashy women. No lame pick-up lines to dream up. Just him, his Lay-Z-Boy, and some leftover kung pao chicken.

"Oh shit. Not again," he muttered as he thumbed through the Saturday mail. Inside the pile was another letter from Carol's attorney, Marlin L. Sanders. What, is that bastard going to make it an even 50 percent now?

Inside the envelope, three simple sentences in Carol's classy handwriting.

"Clark, I have some news for you that might make your day. I'm getting married—to Marlin. In four months, you won't have to pay me a dime. Carol."

"Her goddamn attorney!" Clark screamed at the creased paper. Then sweet reality sank in, pushing the jealousy away. Clark calculated that he'd probably donated eight or nine grand to the upcoming wedding of his ex-wife and the person who was having the courts garnish his wages.

The WMA-TV studio lights were unusually hot on Clark Cattoor the next morning.

"Northwestern now comes to town. First home game in three weeks. You're coming off two impressive road wins. How do you keep it together?" Clark asked Frank.

"Well, Clark, what you want to do is keep the players focused…"

More award-winning journalism.

Clark tuned out ten words into Frank's answer. He remembered Aaron Schutz was still sticking his nose around the program for dirt. A loss next Saturday would keep Aaron working the story. A loss next Saturday would also be the big score.

Aaron had asked again after the Indiana game if Clark would ask Frank about point-shaving or agent rumors regarding Touchdown Tyrone Collins.

Screw Aaron, Clark thought. I'll just tell him Frank denied everything.

"…and that's what we need to do. One game at a time. We can't worry about Minnesota or Michigan right now," Frank finished up his coaching clichés.

After walking Frank to the front door, Clark retreated to the sports office. Carol's surprise letter had sent him into a dilemma. He was leaning toward just keeping the $15,000 and getting out of this entirely. If Aaron uncovered anything about the Northwestern game, Clark thought his own hands might be clean. But $100,000? That's real money. That's nest egg money.

Randy had all but guaranteed Saturday for him. Beat Indiana. Lose to Northwestern. He'd been right on all three plays so far. Why would Randy be wrong now?

Wisconsin State cracked the top 25 in Monday's poll, checking in at number 24. Even with their 4-1 record, none of the college football experts gave them any credit. Their schedule was too easy, they all grumbled.

The upcoming weeks would not get any harder. Northwestern was awful; Purdue and Minnesota were below average. Frank knew his team should be 7-1 before the final games against four nationally ranked teams: Michigan, Ohio State, Illinois, and Michigan State. Seven wins would get Wisconsin State into a bowl game and, likely, save the jobs of Frank and his staff.

While Frank beamed at practice, Randy was torn. He was locked in for the entire $32,300 at 7 to 1. A Northwestern victory would gross Randy the princely sum of $226,100. Stephen would take nearly a fifth of that for his cut. The rest would be for Randy, sitting silent in an account in the Caribbean, awaiting future pick-up.

Frank Flaherty blew his whistle four times. The end of practice.

"Gentlemen, we're finally playing like a Top 25 team. Ignore all that crap from the writers. Stay off the sports sites on the Internet. That will only make your head big. We still haven't played the best out there. Saturday is another test. Stay focused, men. Focused! You're dismissed."

Jake Steffon stirred yellow and green powder from the Pasta Roni package in a small pot. Even with his overflowing wallet, the kicker still subsisted on boxed noodles and sauce.

The phone rang.

"Hello?" Brokaw was on TV in the background, blabbering about the economy. Jake tossed a pinch of oregano into the pot to give the meal some kick.

"Make sure Wisconsin State loses on Saturday, and we won't have any problems," the voice growled. "If you win the game at the end, let's just say I'd hate to be you."

Click.

Jake dropped the phone.

This was nothing new for Jake and Sam. Their phone number was published in the student directory. Intoxicated college kids often called at all hours of the night. The week before, Indiana fans had bugged them with taunts. Jake could ignore the prank calls. But this had a different tone. The caller didn't ask whether it was Jake or Sam. He seemed to simply know.

"Who was it?" Sam called from the living room.

"I dunno."

The headline in the Thursday morning *Dane County Tribune* read "Top 25? Maybe, But Not Due To Schedule." Aaron Schutz wrote that Wisconsin State was finally coming around, even if the Northern Illinois loss scarred the season.

From his desk, Clark Cattoor worked through the column. Each afternoon turned into a cross-examination of the newspapers' news and sports sections. This Thursday was another day free of any football investigation from Aaron. The coast just might be clear for the big score.

The phone rang.

"Channel 11 Sports!" Clark's voice rang out.

"Clark, Randy."

"Oh, hi." Clark fidgeted with a ballpoint pen.

"As we said, play the against on odds. You won't be disappointed."

Rachel was on the other side of the sports office.

"Thanks for calling," Clark said. "We'll have those highlights on tonight at 10!"

Click. Clark turned around. "That was someone from Sun Prairie," he announced. "A parent of one of the players. They can't wait to see the highlights of tonight from Middleton. Don't disappoint."

"Oh."

As Clark returned to the printed words of Aaron Schutz, greed took him for one final ride. He'd make his final wager from his home computer just after the 6 P.M. newscast.

31. Northwestern

Every fall, an October football game in Madison signals the true start of winter. The T-shirts of September give way to the sweatshirts of October and, eventually, the heavy coats and thick boots of November.

Clark walked, brown leather briefcase in hand, from a parking spot in the lot at The Court, next to Mendota Stadium. He passed the long line of people picking up tickets at the Will Call window. He peeked at the WSU Fieldhouse, the old, tan lady of campus basking in the late morning Saturday sunshine. Definitely sweatshirt weather. The northern gusts from the two downtown lakes were just starting up.

Clark closed his eyes for a second. He flashed back ten years, almost to the day. 1993. Purdue at Wisconsin State. Homecoming. Same eye-squinting sunshine. Same blustery weather. Snowflakes could fall with each passing cloud.

He'd hardly slept the night before. This would be the game that would either make him six figures or get him fired from Channel 11. He might even be thrown in jail. He'd clicked onto his Internet sports book and sent his entire account of $15,532.50 on Wisconsin State for a 7-to-1 payout. The wager was so large that he had to call the 800 number to verify it. If Wisconsin State lost, his account would swell to a robust $108,724. Tax-free.

He loved being on TV so much he was still unsure which was worse, no tube time or an extended stay at the correctional facilities in Waupun or Stanley, as a guest of the State of Wisconsin.

Randy Munson was just changing into his coaching clothes in the cramped locker room. He felt like he was the most nervous person in the state on this crisp Saturday—$32,000 on the line to clear more than $160,000 after everything was done. Or so he hoped.

Randy had total confidence that he could lead the Wisconsin State offense to a loss against Northwestern. He also felt troubled over directing that anonymous phone call to Jake two days before. The smell of money had turned Randy into a control freak. Would Jake tell the world about the phone call? The kid had built up so much good press; the journalists ate out of his hand. Randy looked at himself in the mirror and knew he'd made a mistake regarding Jake.

He just had to hope the offense did its part. Randy needed Craig Zellnoff to miss his receivers. Randy needed Touchdown Tyrone Collins to start believing the hype on the field instead of playing like a man out for a payday from the NFL draft in April.

"Doubles Right 90 Hitch," Randy called out to Craig on 3rd-and-7 in the first quarter. Craig nodded yes.

Make him move to his left, Randy thought. Northwestern is strong on that side, and Craig's terrible at throwing against his body.

Craig responded with another incompletion.

"PUNT TEAM!" Frank barked, his arms folded.

Sam Cattanach led the way onto the Mendota Stadium turf for the first of six punts in the first half.

Northwestern scored 10 points in the first quarter, and Craig started pressing. The quick-strike offense from the past two weeks was history.

Wisconsin State trailed 13-0 as the final seconds ticked off the clock in the first half.

"FLAHERTY! YOU SUCK!" The yells came down from the student section. That was one of the milder taunts.

"ROSE BOWL BYE BYE! Da-da da-da-da! ROSE BOWL BYE BYE! Da-da da-da-da!" the students crowed in unison. Frank ran off the field, ducking the thrown marshmallows and raw bologna usually reserved for the other team's head coach.

Randy was an hour and a half from the big score. Then Frank assembled the assistant coaches just off the locker room.

"RANDY! You're off the offense," Frank announced. "John Wilcox, where are you?"

"Back here, coach." John shot his hand up over the defensive line coach.

"Wilcox, you call the plays. Randy, help relay."

"But, coach—"

The veins bulged in Frank's neck.

"Don't 'but coach' me. We need a spark, dammit. If we lose here, WE'RE ALL FIRED. TOMORROW. We won't even make it to Monday. Do you want that?"

"No, coach. Course not," Randy said, looking at the carpet.

"Jiminy Christmas!" Frank threw his arms to the ceiling. "We need some damn competent play-calling on offense!"

The only thing Randy could do was signal in the wrong signs. In coaching circles, that was a grave offense. Just like throwing a game.

Frank walked into the locker room with the assistants behind him. United front all the way for the players.

"Gentlemen, you are ALL better than what we just saw. NORTHWESTERN IS NOT GOOD. BUT YOU ARE WORSE. Do you actually believe all the rankings bullshit? DO YOU? Well, don't. Here's what's gonna happen to start out the second half. We get the ball first, right?" Frank looked at John Wilcox.

"Yes, coach—"

"OK, we're just down two scores. I need some inspired blocking out there. Give Craig time to find a receiver. I'm not going to launch into you guys too much because we can do better. Let's just focus. NEVER LOSE THAT GLEAM, GENTLEMEN!"

John Wilcox was calling plays for the first time in years. Craig Zellnoff led Wisconsin State on an 8-play, 76-yard drive to open the second half. Touchdown Tyrone Collins hauled in his third catch of the day for Wisconsin State's first score. 13-7 Northwestern.

In the press box, Clark worked his eighth cup of Pepsi. Beads of sweat formed on his temples when he saw John Wilcox pacing up and down the near sideline with the offense on the field. Those bastards made the damn change. Clark's day had been going along perfectly at halftime. He was one agonizing half from the score. Now Clark had to sweat through the next 24 minutes as Northwestern led by only six.

Northwestern did not roll over. Wildcats quarterback Len Kiltmore led Northwestern on a seven-minute drive the other way. Wisconsin State's defense finally held on 3rd-and-goal from their own 7-yard line.

On the sidelines, John Wilcox called for Collins.

"GET IN THERE FOR JACKSON! We need you for the field goal block. Start in the middle."

Tyrone Collins had never played a down on special teams in his three years in Madison. Frank did not want to expose the star to injury on punt returns.

Northwestern kicker Cal Hamstell tried to punch a 24-yard field goal through. Collins used his skyscraping vertical leap to perfection. His extended right arm just grazed the nose of the football, knocking the kick off-target and wide right.

"TOUCHDOWN TYRONE FOR HEISMAN!" Collins yelled while flailing his arms toward the sea of blue fans in the north end zone.

The 12,000 Wisconsin State students erupted in their own chant.

"TOUCHDOWN TYRONE! Da-da da-da-da! TOUCHDOWN TYRONE! Da-da da-da-da!"

Aaron Schutz leaned over to Clark in the press box.

"Can't say he's throwing this game. The dude can do it all," Aaron said with his pen still in his mouth.

Clark laughed nervously. He knew he was screwed. They would lose everything and wind up in jail. If only he'd quit after the Kansas game.

John Wilcox's offensive wizardry soon faded as Wisconsin State was forced to punt early in the fourth quarter. One more Northwestern score would put this game out of reach.

Frank Flaherty cracked the whip on his defense during the

second half and they responded with one more stop.

Wisconsin State took the ball back at their own 31. 7:14 left in the fourth quarter.

Randy Munson signaled in the next play from John Wilcox, saying to himself, "Just hang on, baby, hang on."

Wilcox called for a harmless hook to Tyrone Collins on the right side.

Craig Zellnoff took the snap and three hard steps back. The quarterback fired a rope to Collins for a 6-yard gain on the far side of the field.

Randy looked down at his offensive chart for the next play. He heard a roar from the east side of the stadium. A Northwestern defender had fallen down trying to tackle Collins. Randy's vision was blocked by scores of his players running and jumping out onto the field for a better view.

Randy ran 10 yards past the sideline, onto the white "3" that marked the Wisconsin State 30, in time to catch a glimpse of Collins high-stepping a touchdown into the end zone.

"Un-be-freaking-lievable," Clark said up in the press box.

Collins spiked the football and jumped into the student section as if it were a mosh pit.

13-13.

The score happened so quickly, and the atmosphere on the field was so hectic, that Jake Steffon still had to tie his right shoe and run onto the field with Sam. Jake had completely forgotten about the threatening phone call.

Snap down, ball up. Extra point, shaky but good.

14-13 Wisconsin State. Less than seven minutes left.

"Damn Jake." Randy pulled his headset off in frustration.

Northwestern was without a win but not without spirit. Kiltmore found one more packet of magic in the final minutes. He led the Wildcats to the Wisconsin State 11 with 1:28 left when the drive conked out. Wisconsin State burned time-outs in preparation for a final comeback if Northwestern scored.

Kicker Cal Hamstell fired a 28-yard field goal even over Tyrone Collins' extended right arm to give Northwestern a 16-14 lead with 1:23 left.

Randy was far too enthusiastic for a coach whose team now trailed by two to a winless opponent.

"We can get this back, guys. GET IT BACK!" Randy said, smiling and clapping.

Craig Zellnoff felt the urgency. Being a Chicago guy, he hated Northwestern. He couldn't lose to them his senior year. He scrambled for a 17-yard gain to start the drive, and hit Laverneus Wilson for a 7-yard pickup. Tyrone caught a slant for 13 yards. The clock ticked: 0:36, 0:35, 0:34.

Craig took off on his feet one more time. He darted past a defender across the Northwestern 30 and tripped at the 25. First down Wisconsin State from the 25. The clock went back to rolling down: 0:22, 0:21, 0:20.

Craig spiked the ball into the turf to stop the clock. Wisconsin State had no more time-outs left. The clock read 0:14.

"FIELD GOAL TEAM! FIELD GOAL TEAM!" Frank called out.

Randy ran out to the head coach. "We can run one more play, coach. Craig can spike it again." Randy knew a Northwestern sack would end the game. Had to play the percentages.

"No, Randy. We just can't risk it. If they sack us, we're done."

The referee blew his whistle and flipped on his microphone.

"TIME-OUT NORTHWESTERN," echoed throughout a nervous Mendota Stadium.

Jake had been on the field just three times. One kickoff to start the game and two extra points. The time-out forced him over to the sideline with the coaches.

"Hey, Jake," Randy yelled, breaking the unspoken coaches' code: Never talk to a kicker about to try a game-winning field goal. Randy's shout to Jake stuck out like a fart in church.

Randy ignored the dozen coaching eyes focused on him.

"Jake!" Randy put his first two fingers up to his own eyes. "Focus! You can make this, man." Jake locked eyes with Randy, nodded and ran back to the field.

Jake had never kicked a game-winning field goal. Not in college. Not even in high school. His coaches back at Fall Creek hadn't volunteered that information to the Boars coaching staff.

"Your time, Jake," Sam encouraged. The punter was on his left knee facing west from the 32-yard line. Sam's first two fingers also had a purpose. His left hand marked the spot where the ball would land for the kick.

Randy pegged Jake for a 50/50 shot here. 42 yards for the game. No way this greenhorn would make it with all this pressure.

Thirty yards away from the sidelines, Jake finally remembered that bizarre phone call on Thursday. He wondered: If he made this kick, would someone hurt him? Put a pillow over his face in bed and shoot him? He looked to the top of the stadium for a sniper. Get your head back on the kick, man. Just make the damn thing like you do in practice.

Clark stood alone on the sidelines for the game's final four minutes. With 100 grand on the line, some solitude in a stadium with 63,577 nervous people was somehow calming.

Jake started jumping up and down to calm his nerves. He had dreamed of this moment for years. A game-winning field goal for the Boars. He'd made hundreds of these in his backyard in Fall Creek.

I'm going to make this damn kick, Jake thought. Just like in practice.

"Ready?" Sam called.

Jake nodded.

"Hut, hut, HUT!"

Perfect snap. Perfect hold. Perfect kick.

For the first 35 yards.

Jake had hit the ball a little lower than he hoped, resulting in a high kick. Normally that would be ideal, but with 42 yards to clear, Jake could see the end-over-end kick floating in the wind. To the right. A slice.

"Shit," Jake said into the silent stadium.

"That's floatin', that's floatin!" one Northwestern defender yelled.

The football slowly tailed to the right.

Come down, just come down, just come down, Jake said as he shuffled to the right, hoping for some body English along the way.

The football floated on the lake wind, careening to the right.

Jake cringed as the football edged in front of the right goalpost. He fell to his knees with his silver helmet into the turf.

No good. Wide right.

Northwestern 16, Wisconsin State 14.

The Northwestern players exploded onto the field with their helmets off and their smiles on. Jake was stuck in the turf, unable and unwilling to pick his head up and walk out. He'd let down his team, his school, his state.

He'd never dreamed of this in his backyard.

Frank shook hands with the Northwestern head coach and ran under the student section to the locker room.

Clark said nothing. He'd just made enough money to buy two large Hummers or a small house. But Clark couldn't celebrate. He had to take on the dour expression Madison journalists wore when Wisconsin State lost.

Randy Munson walked off the field slowly. As an assistant coach, he could leave the field without too much attention from the students. Randy glowed inside. He had pulled off The Plan.

"We had it. I mean, WE HAD IT," Frank Flaherty said to the 80 reporters in front of him in the press room. "We were there. So many chances to win and we just couldn't do it."

Aaron Schutz stepped up.

"Coach, we saw John Wilcox signaling in plays. Is he working with the offense?"

Frank managed a smile.

"I was waiting for that one. He is technically working with the offense. Today he was just signaling in plays for the offense. Randy was still calling the shots." Frank was only too happy to put Randy out there as a responsible party in the loss.

Clark fired away next.

"What did you say to Jake afterward?"

Frank sighed.

"That was tough. I still think the wind messed with it more than anything else. The guys in the box said it looked good until the end. Tough break for him. He's always great under pressure in practice. That's why I have faith in him."

The questions kept coming.

"Was there any talk on the sidelines about one more play before the field goal?"

"Yes. But we just couldn't risk a sack. That would have buried us. I thought the good in that call outweighed the risks." Frank could not just come out and say that Randy was pushing for one more play, the correct call in that spot.

"Does this harm your chances at a Rose Bowl?"

"Of course it does. Now we have to go and beat Purdue and Minnesota."

After giving the media jackals their afternoon snack, Frank ran into Randy outside the shower.

"Look, Randy. I'm sorry about what happened out there. We probably would have won if I hadn't messed with the offense."

Randy acted shocked by the apology.

"Frank, I would have probably replaced me too at halftime. Don't sweat it. I just wish I could have done more."

"Me too. Go out and get a good meal tonight with the family. Don't read the paper tomorrow. They're gonna kill us."

"I know." Spoken like a veteran of Madison football wars.

With his hair still wet from the shower, Randy pushed his arms into a black leather jacket and walked into the late afternoon. A glum crowd of parents and girlfriends stood outside the WSU Bubble locker room, awaiting the trickle of downtrodden football players.

If only they knew. If they only knew.

"Stephen. Randy." Back at the PDQ pay phone.

"Well, well, well. You pulled it off. I'm impressed. We're done with this, right?"

Randy breathed a sigh of relief. "Oh yeah, we're done."

"Well, you're not going to see any of it for a few weeks, maybe even past Christmas. You know that, right?"

"Yes, that's fine. As long as it arrives."

"I have some vacation coming up around Thanksgiving," Stephen said. "I'll fly down there that week to collect. Just give me an account number before then and you'll see it before you know it."

"I'll call you Thursday of the week of the Michigan State game with that information."

"Very good."

Randy still wasn't sure if his wife knew about The Plan. He'd been so secretive with his phone calls from the PDQ that he constantly worried she thought something was up.

Lisa never confronted Randy about anything. Having a boy as dependent as Brett tended to make a parent overlook the little nuances of life. Randy would simply keep The Plan under wraps. Maybe for a year. Maybe two. Maybe even until he retired.

Clark was overjoyed and ready for a bender after the last phase of The Plan.

State Street had a subdued quality after the loss. The bar crawl on a Saturday night during the season is normally a scene right out of Mardi Gras, but this was more like a Tuesday night in December. Losing to Northwestern does that.

Clark and a few of his colleagues from the TV station were on their bar march from the Irish Pub to State Street Brats, past the Red Shed.

First, though, a stop at Jackal's on University Avenue, a karaoke pit like no other in all of Madison.

In his short tenure at Channel 11, Clark had developed a reputation as the unofficial station flake. His karaoke exploits were the stuff of legend.

He opened the glass door to Jackal's.

"What's up, Clark?" the bartender said.

"Wow. They know you here. Not sure I'd be too proud of that," remarked ace WMA-TV news reporter Harvey Walsh.

"I need to get one of my publicity photos on the wall here."

"This block just hasn't been the same since they closed the Black Bear," said cameraman Tony Wollman.

"Screw that biker joint. Man, it's time to get down. More whiskey sours, Jack," Clark yelled to the bartender. "I got 'em, fellas. Put away your wallets."

"First time I've ever seen a sports guy pay first," Harvey said.

"CLARK! Your turn." The DJ shouted out after a young redhead finished another lame version of "You're The One That I Want."

"That's right, no waiting for the King!" Clark said to his co-workers.

The opening chorus for "Bridge Over Troubled Water" began, to a howl from the rest of the WMA-TV party.

Holding his tumbler of more vodka than ice, Clark hobbled into the chorus.

"Like a bridge over troubled water, I will lay me down...."

32. What Next?

Clark Cattoor's booze-filled celebration turned Sunday morning into a smoking hole.

"OH SHIT," he yelled at his alarm clock after waking up from the haze. 7:43 A.M.

He had 15 minutes until the start of this week's must-see edition of *The Frank Flaherty Show*.

Clark rolled out of bed, wearing only black jockeys, like Travolta in *Saturday Night Fever*. The underwear was marinated in cigarette smoke.

His bedroom moved from side to side as the hangover crashed inside his head, the waves sloshing against the shore of his brain.

He still had no idea how he'd gotten home. Did he drive? Take a cab? Clark ran out to the front window and looked out into the street. Good, the Camry sat in the driveway. What about his keys?

What about his hair?

"I'm sorry. Sorry about this, Coach," Clark muttered. Frank glared as Clark walked across the studio toward the seat next to his.

"Great," the coach said gruffly. "Just wonderful. I have to wait for the cross-examination of my most embarrassing loss ever."

Clark let that comment slide as he sat down and attached the clip-on microphone. He simply had to wing it.

The show open appeared on the screen. Boars scoring. Boars

tackling. Boars picking up huge yards. In other words, the intro would not be indicative of this show's content.

Red light on.

"Welcome to *The Frank Flaherty Show*. I'm Clark Cattoor. This week's show is coming off a shocker as the Northwestern Wildcats came into Madison and pulled out a 16-14 win. Wisconsin State head coach Frank Flaherty joins us now. Frank, you've had an evening to mull it over…"

The coach glared at the sportscaster under the hot studio lights. "Well, Clark, let's just say that today feels like an extension of Saturday. I didn't get any sleep after such an uninspired performance. I apologize to our fans all across the state…"

The show usually started with extended highlights from the previous day's game. Instead, for six painful minutes, Frank carried on about how awful the Boars had played and how ashamed the entire team felt.

Then the painful highlights overpowered even Frank's words about Wisconsin State football.

The front door slammed shut at the Kickers' Quarters.

"I DON'T WANT TO SEE IT!" Jake cried from his room. On Sunday mornings Sam liked to cook Spanish omelets and devour the thick Sunday edition of the *Dane County Tribune*.

As Sam unrolled the plastic covering on the newspaper, he saw the evidence that Jake wanted no part of. Front page. 1A.

"FLOATING AWAY."

That headline blared out above a half-page, full-color picture of Jake, taken from behind, on his knees after the kick, his head buried in the turf. Sam was in the background, also looking down, with his hands on his hips.

The caption read, " 'Jake Steffon (17) reacts after missing a potential game-winning field goal in Wisconsin State's 16-14 loss to Northwestern. Story, 1C.' "

Despite his threats to destroy all 150,000 copies of today's newspaper in southern Wisconsin, Jake wandered out of his room and plopped down on the infamous green couch.

"OK, let me see it," he said.

"You sure? It's not the kind of stuff your parents will cut out and put in the scrapbook."

"Give me the damn paper NOW!"

"OK. Here." Sam handed over the front section first, followed by the sports section.

Jake examined his first picture on the front page of any newspaper since a cameo in the *Fall Creek Cricket* monthly three years before.

"I still can't believe I missed that. Can't believe it one bit," Jake said, biting into a raisin bagel. "Your hold was perfect, man, perfect. The kick felt dead-on. I just sliced it too much."

"Next week, you'll hit the game winner. Just think about the next game."

"Thanks, man." Jake appreciated what Sam had done for him over the previous 24 hours. After the loss, Sam bought a rotisserie chicken and a box of mashed potatoes and made dinner while the two watched anything on television except ESPN College Football Saturday. Jake was in no hurry to see his miss replayed over and over.

Now he looked up from the newspaper that recounted, in gruesome detail, the worst moment in his 20 years.

"This means I've gotta stay in this week, right?" he said half-jokingly.

"Pretty much, man. You better dress like a regular student for a week."

At least for a couple of weeks, Jake would put away the "WISCONSIN STATE FOOTBALL 17" sweatshirt that worked as a chick magnet all season.

"I did catch the news last night. Rachel sure hung you out to dry on the air. She said you choked on the field goal." Sam chuckled.

Jake figured he had that coming from her. "Yeah, she's a real damn professional. You know what, though? Let's watch Flaherty's show. That should be a riot today. I could probably even stomach seeing my kick on TV after watching Coach squirm for a few minutes. I need something to cheer me up before work."

It was another NFL Sunday, and he wanted to be known as a pizza man, not the guy who cost Wisconsin State a shot at a Big Ten title.

33. Take the Bullet

The glum mood of Saturday lingered on campus until Monday morning. Damp clouds covered the sky from the stadium to the capitol.

"Sonofabitch!" Randy yelled at the orange-clad construction workers standing in the coaches' parking spots just north of the stadium. He'd forgotten about the memo sent out the week before that the parking spots would be off-limits from Monday until Thursday.

Parking on campus was always a disaster. Randy drove across the railroad tracks and found a spot five blocks south of Mendota Stadium. One-hour street parking. He'd have to move his car a couple of times to avoid the Madison parking police. He was already 15 minutes late for the morning meeting, a meeting he wanted to be a lifetime late for.

The coaching staff sat motionless in the football video conference room, trying to break down Purdue for the next week. Randy sneaked in and took his customary seat.

When the video specialist switched tapes, Frank stood up and turned the lights back on.

"Gentlemen, let me just say that Saturday was my fault," Frank said calmly. "Totally mine. I still don't think the writers know about the halftime switch on offense. I intend to keep it that way. Randy—"

Randy broke away from his dreams of cash. Pure cold cash. No money troubles. "Yes, coach?"

"As I mentioned to Randy right after the game Saturday, I should not have messed with the offense. I'm sorry."

Randy nodded.

"That aside, we need to regroup and do it fast. If we lose this weekend, any hopes of a title are gone. The alums will be calling for my head, which means they'll be calling for yours. Just remember how desperate we really are."

Randy endured two more hours of breaking down Purdue's defense on the projection TV. He'd once worked out the math and realized he'd spent roughly five months of his life in film rooms, watching football. The whole process was the worst part of coaching, after recruiting. Randy's mind kept shifting: from the money to Purdue to the money to Brett's health-care needs to the money.

Frank stood up at 11:20 to end the dreadful morning session.

"Break for lunch. See you back here at 1:30."

Randy gathered his offensive notebook and leather briefcase. After three hours in the video room, he was looking forward to lunch at the Greasy Granny, just across the street from Mendota Stadium.

He felt a tap on his left shoulder as he walked across the lot.

"Randy." It was John Wilcox. John couldn't simply call his name. He had to invade his personal space.

"Yes, John," Randy said.

"I've got to talk to you. Something very serious may be going down."

Randy froze but tried to keep it light. "Finally get that gig?" John was always clamoring for whatever coaching job was open on any given day.

"No, no. Nothing like that."

"I'm going to lunch over at the Granny. Wanna come with?"

"Sure."

John waited until Randy ordered his usual: patty melt, Swiss cheese, grilled onions, and thousand island dressing on the side. Randy was still a double-dipper with the secret sauce.

"All right," John said slowly. "I'm hearing in the media circles an investigation about the football program."

Randy wasn't surprised. Wisconsin State fought off small probes every year.

"Who's involved?"

"Apparently, something with Collins."

Randy rolled his eyes. "Let me guess. An agent?"

"Yes, but there's more to it."

"Like what?" Randy took a swig from his iced tea.

"I guess there's talk out there that this guy, Copperzweig, is having Collins play a part in our losses."

Randy felt the sweat form around his temples. "Well, let's see. Against Northern, he didn't have any drops that I remember. Last week, he had one drop, but that didn't necessarily cost us."

"Did you notice that Tyrone wasn't as open against Northwestern as he usually can get?"

"Not really," Randy said dismissively.

"I think Tyrone knows how to put up the numbers to keep any red flags away, but he could have done more."

"Do you REALLY believe that?"

Silence fell as the waitress brought Randy's patty melt and John's egg salad with ranch.

John floated the question he'd wanted to ask for three days.

"Randy, are you pissed off about Saturday?"

"Which part?"

"Me taking over the play calling at halftime."

Randy lied. "Not really. I would have done the same thing if I was runnin' the show."

John forced a smile. "I'm glad. I did feel uncomfortable calling the plays."

"It's not as easy as it looks, is it?"

"No."

Randy drowned a french fry in the sauce. "But you did get us the lead. Gotta give you credit there."

John put down his napkin.

"Here's where I'm torn," John said. "I really think we should tell Frank what's going on with Collins."

Randy had already played out the scenarios in his head. If Tyrone was discovered with an agent, they would all be fired, even if the NCAA didn't lay down any formal edicts. The Wisconsin State athletic department would lead the purge, probably citing the generic "institutional lack of control" on Frank and his staff. Karen Strassel was looking for a reason to show Frank the door. No bowl games in two years. Alumni donations were way down. The program hadn't been in this bad shape for a dozen years.

Randy wasn't that concerned about the first scenario because he planned on getting canned anyway. He was more worried about the writers and their constant snooping. Someone would talk about Randy's poor play-calling during the Northern Illinois and Northwestern games. Someone would. Be it a player, trainer, or another assistant coach. If the on-line sports books heard about a Wisconsin State football scandal, they would probably turn in the large wager records against Wisconsin State to the NCAA or the federal government.

This simply could not come out. Randy had to buy himself some time to mull it over.

"No. Don't tell Frank. Tyrone's my player. Let me talk to him today."

"We have a responsibility—"

Randy held up his right hand. "No, that's where you're wrong. Think about it. You tell Frank. Frank calls a press conference about this. The NCAA will be breathing down all of our necks. Strassel will fire all of us the day after the Michigan State game. Do you want that on your resume? Fired at, what, 25, 26 years old?"

"No, of course not."

"I know you like to talk with the media types, hang out and what not." Randy pointed his butter knife at John for emphasis. "The best assistant coaches are the ones who keep the secrets, keep their mouths shut, and keep taking the bullets. You remember that."

"OK. I won't say anything."

"So, who told you all this?" Randy figured John wouldn't give up his source easily.

He was wrong.

"Aaron Schutz from the *Tribune*."

"Schutzie's a pretty fair shooter. I respect him as a writer. He's not a smoke blower like some of them are." Randy really did think highly of Aaron's work. The two had had a decent relationship since Aaron picked up the Wisconsin State football beat seven years before. "What did he tell you about Collins?"

John paused and swallowed. "He said they're still a ways away from putting anything out in print. Said they don't have a smoking gun on Collins yet. He just found it odd that a poor kid from Miami dresses like a celebrity and drives that SUV all over campus."

"You're not talking to Aaron about this, right? He came to you, I assume?"

"Oh yeah. Wouldn't dream of spilling this to him."

"You sure about that? I know you love to see your name in print around here."

John took offense. "Randy, I wouldn't go that far—"

In a flash, Randy saw a warped plan develop in front of his eyes. John just might be the only link to the media who could bring it all down. Randy turned from provocateur to peacemaker.

"I'm sorry, John. I was out of line."

John shrugged. "Thank you."

"Tell you what. Are you free tonight?"

"Sure." John was free every night.

"Meet me at the Bluefin in McFarland, tonight at 6. Go over Sigglekow on 51 and you're there. It's on the right, about a half mile past Culver's. I'll buy dinner. We'll hash this out. I don't want to talk about this in town. Too many people around, ya know what I'm sayin'?"

John smiled and appeared flattered to have a coaching veteran like Randy take him out for dinner.

"John, let's have a good practice today."

Clark made a cameo appearance at the start of Monday's football practice. He was a primary witness as Frank Flaherty took in 20 minutes of interrogation from the journalists.

He decided to get fresh footage of the Boars—"The Monday After," as he would refer to it on the air in about four hours.

Aaron Schutz walked over.

"What's up, buddy? Missed you at basketball today." Aaron waved an imaginary jump shot at Clark.

"Had some stuff to take care of. Anything new with you?"

"Not really. The wife and I are still working on that house out in Lodi. Have to put in carpeting this weekend. Glad I'm going to Green Bay on Sunday, so she's stuck doing most of it."

"That drive must be hell, though." Lodi was a good 35 minutes from the newspaper.

"Yeah, but I never have to drive it during rush hour."

Clark watched Randy encourage Craig Zellnoff on a passing drill. This drill demonstrated Randy's offensive genius to Clark. Craig threw seamless spirals to Touchdown Tyrone Collins, Laverneus Wilson, and the rest of the receivers like it was target practice. Craig's accuracy could be mind-boggling at times.

"Anything new on Collins?" Clark asked.

"No. I think it's died down. I spoke with Wilcox last week and he had nothing to say. I figured if he's not concerned, there really may be nothing there."

Clark tried to reinforce that notion. "I haven't heard anything. Frank told me nothing. You don't sound too concerned," Clark said hopefully.

Aaron said what Clark'd been waiting for all season. "Clark, I think I'm done pursuing it. There's just nothing there, and if there is, no one in this town will say anything."

A hundred and seventy feet away, Randy was wondering what everyone else in the WSU Bubble was thinking about. John Wilcox was the only one Aaron had gotten to. Randy knew that John was the only coach on the staff who would squeal to the media.

"Nice pass, Craig! Right in there. Like a machine. Your right arm is a machine!" he called out to his quarterback.

He looked behind his left shoulder as John Wilcox instructed Jake about footwork.

"Solid boot, Steffon! Solid boot," John called out. His voice echoed across the curved metal dome, back to Randy.

Aaron, Clark, and the rest of the sports journalists left The Bubble soon after. Frank opened the first 30 minutes of practice for film crews, photographers, and media.

The final 90 minutes took on a more urgent tone. A loss to

Purdue would be fatal to any Rose Bowl hopes. The Big Ten championship was on ice. Losing to Northwestern in any year usually killed dreams of Pasadena.

Frank blew his whistle four times.

"All right, guys, take a knee!" More than 120 players shrunk two feet in unison.

"I was very pleased with today's practice. You guys could have easily come out here and sulked and dogged it, but you didn't. I saw good work out there. We're doing everything we can to get that edge on Purdue. I know Coach Munson has found a few holes in their defense."

Randy nodded slowly from his perch just behind Frank.

"We will have a winning game plan for you by this time tomorrow. Fellas, get in here and break it down." Frank then walked away while the team chanted, "ROSE BOWL…BELIEVE IT!" before scattering.

Randy flipped on the TV at home just long enough to see Clark Cattoor's smiling face.

"Today brought 'The Monday After' for the Wisconsin State football team," Clark said dramatically on the Channel 11 airwaves. "Saturday's 16-14 loss to Northwestern was devastating. Now head coach Frank Flaherty must forget about the disastrous loss and look towards Purdue…."

Disastrous my ass, Randy said to himself. You made almost as much off it as I did, you lucky bastard.

Randy had to lie to Lisa.

"I have that kid in Sun Prairie I have to visit tonight."

"The running back? The one Illinois's now after?"

"Yeah, he's been talking about going to Illinois or even Northern. We can't lose him to Northern." Randy was always impressed by the interest Lisa took in his job.

"When will you be back?"

"Probably around 10. Hopefully earlier."

"OK. Give Brett a hug before you go." Lisa rarely had to remind Randy to do that. Randy walked up the stairs, along the burgundy carpet, until he reached Brett's room.

"Brett, Daddy's got to take off and go land a football player for the team."

Brett was reorganizing his baseball cards, this time by the last names of the players. He looked up at his smiling father. "OK, Daddy. You get yourself a running back who doesn't drop the ball!" he said with a fresh layer of excitement.

Randy tingled. "We'll try, Brett, we'll try. The running backs that don't drop the ball are hard to find. This one could be the one."

He hugged his son, adjusting Brett's thick eyeglasses.

"Bye, Daddy!"

"Bye, Brett. I'll be back in a few hours."

The Bluefin's Monday fish fry welcomed Randy and John, just off Highway 51 in McFarland. When Randy had moved to Madison in 1991, McFarland was its own little town of 4,000. Now McFarland was a full-fledged suburb of Madison. It even boasted a Pick 'n' Save, a sign of true suburbia in the 21st century.

The Bluefin also served a strong Friday fish fry, like every other chow house in Wisconsin. Randy was a fan of the Monday option, seeing as most of his fall Fridays were spent in hotel rooms. He was an even bigger fan of the Bluefin's seating options. Randy and John sat in a large, secluded corner booth. No one except the waitress knew they were even there.

"What I love about it is the food. The color never varies past yellow and light brown," Randy said as he ordered all-you-can-eat cod, fries, and biscuits for eight bucks. "All the food is the same color tonight. All greasy and bad for you. I love that."

"You can't do that too often or else you'll be a damn blimp," John countered.

"Assistant coaches can be fat. Head coaches can't. ADs don't like hiring fat guys."

Both laughed at that. Randy eased the conversation along.

"So, how goes the head coaching chase?"

John opened up. "It's hard to say. I haven't gotten any nibbles for a while, but nothing attractive is out there right now." That was true. Coaches were rarely fired before November. "I'd still like to see if I can land a WAC or a Mountain West school."

"Maybe Hawaii?" Randy offered.

"That would be nice. What a great week that was. Football and sand."

The waitress returned. "Drinks tonight, gentlemen?"

Randy set the tone for the evening.

"Double scotch, no ice."

John absorbed that and countered.

"Uh…I'll have a whiskey sour."

Randy refocused his eyes as the waitress left.

"John, we have to discuss this matter of the stuff about Collins."

John responded with a shrug and another bite of fish dripping with tartar sauce.

"What do you know? Tell me everything." Randy held the upper hand.

John sighed and let loose. "Well, today before practice, Jake was stretching and he told me that someone called his apartment last week and told him to miss that field goal."

The upper hand had just changed hands.

Randy sat up. "No shit?"

"No shit," John continued. "I stayed after practice today and watched that kick again. Watched it two dozen times. I don't think he missed it on purpose. The wind was too heavy at the end. Trust me. The kick was on. It just hung up too long."

Randy stared down at the remaining flakes of fish on his plate with the inner panic that a man feels the second he discovers his wallet is lost. The room got hotter and smaller by the second.

"What else?" was all he could offer.

"Jake said he gets those calls all the time," John said. "Why he told me about this one, I'll never know."

Randy suddenly recognized it. The moment was here. The Plan was about to be exposed by John. He just felt it.

He started talking and hoped he would remember his story later.

"John, you have just entered into the middle of a serious situation," Randy said somberly as John's whiskey arrived. "What I am about to tell you could get you fired or even jailed someday. However, if you listen to me and do not tell a soul, it will be worth your while."

Randy could tell that John wanted to spring out of his seat and jump on the upcoming nugget of information, like a poker player with two pocket aces waiting for the next card.

"I can't tell you too much, but from what I know, there's a gambling ring inside the program," Randy said. "As far as I know, it's over, the score was already made. There's nothing on the horizon. I've heard the gambling ring has been broken."

John's eyes bugged just as Randy thought they would. "So, that's it, no more?"

"Look, I don't know where it originated, but there is a covenant of silence surrounding this. I could report it to Frank, but I haven't," Randy said. "If it's big enough, it'll come out. I don't need to help push it."

John sipped the final ounce of his drink and started in.

"Why should I stay quiet about this?" John demanded.

"The same reasons I told you at lunch," Randy said forcefully. "You don't want this on your record unless someone uncovers it. Besides, do you really think Frank gives a damn about either of us? Sure, he kept me on and brought you here, but he's on the decline. Karen will surely clip him next month. We'll follow Frank out the door.

"Let's say we're all gone and Frank lands at, oh, I don't know, Ball State. Do you want to be an assistant coach at Ball State?" Randy asked rhetorically. "Of course not. You're a comer, a mover. Deal with this year and hook on at another big school closer to home."

John was clearly shaken. "Well, what do I get out of this for staying quiet?"

Randy knew this was the most important question of the meal.

"You'll keep your reputation as an assistant who can be trusted," he said. "The second you betray that trust is the day you become untouchable to others.

"Frank has said nothing but great things about you. I'll bet even if we all get sacked you'll land on your feet. You're still distant enough from the product."

John shook the ice cubes in his glass. "OK, boss, I'll keep quiet. Will this be discovered?"

Randy regained the upper hand for the last time. "Not unless one of the coaches talks or someone gets to Collins or Steffon."

34. Purdue

Tuesday afternoon in Madison was another glorious October showcase of color and light. It was the kind of day when the school takes those promotional pictures of people walking the campus, snapping happy people for next year's official catalog for high school students. Once the first snowfall hits each November, the school puts away the cameras until late March.

Randy Munson rolled his Riviera in for the coaches' meeting at two o'clock. Orange tape filled Stall 24, his space in the stadium parking lot.

Stall 23 featured a big hole from the digging earlier that morning. Its normal tenant, John Wilcox, was minutes from missing his first practice ever.

"Where's Wilcox?" Frank asked in the video conference room. "Anyone seen him?"

No one had an answer. Randy could think only the worst: John Wilcox driving to the NCAA headquarters in Indianapolis to turn in the program. Just stay cool in the pocket.

Frank scratched his temple. "Well, we'll go on without him."

Yes we will, Randy thought. This money was getting to be too much trouble.

Frank continued. "I hope you guys enjoyed the morning off.

Look, we've all been under the gun since Saturday. I did some extra film work last night here and I think we'll have some angles on Purdue this week that they haven't seen."

A gravelly voice filled the room.

"Sorry I'm late. Damn parking," John Wilcox said.

Randy looked at his offensive play notes for the week, but he couldn't read them. The sentences looked like random letters thrown together on an eye chart. As long as John stayed quiet. As long as John stayed quiet.

Clark had spoken with Aaron Schutz, but Aaron wasn't letting on any of his inside information. Clark didn't push it. He understood the kind of relationship journalists enjoy. Clark and Aaron could be the best of friends, but the one with the scoop usually kept quiet.

Clark had a busy weekend ahead. High school football was in full swing the next day, and the pivotal game against Purdue didn't make the weekend any easier.

And there was the money.

The Northwestern game added $108,724 to Clark's Internet gambling account. He had a remedial knowledge of how to hide the money. His sports book also had a discounted cash option. He could receive nearly $87,000 in cash via FedEx. No records. No information to the IRS. Just a simple delivery from the islands to his house. Once the loot was in his arms, he could hide it under a mattress. The process was like buying drugs—it wasn't the actual drug usage that drew the attention, it was the delivery.

Clark opted via a pay phone for the cash option. He asked for $25,000 of his $86,979.20 to arrive by FedEx box in three days. A Monday delivery by 10:30 A.M. worked perfectly. Flaherty held his weekly press conference at noon each Monday. A simple plan had become the perfect plan.

Purdue football was in the midst of a football revival. The Boilermakers had been a dominant program in the 1960s, but experienced true gridiron malaise over the following two decades. As bad as Wisconsin State had been decades before, they could always give Purdue a decent game.

In 2000, Purdue's sharp passing game had fooled Frank and his assistants. The head coach had beaten Purdue only once in his four years at Wisconsin State.

"Men, I cannot tell you how much we have stunk it up when we play these guys," Flaherty told his players in the locker room before the game. He went over a few specifics about Purdue's quick receivers, and ended with a generic, "Let's get after it!"

Randy stood to his boss's immediate left. He looked down at his offensive game plan, attached to his wooden clipboard. He'd survived the entire week without questions from the other coaches or the press. He made it a point not to make eye contact with Jake.

Wisconsin State should simply have run back into the locker room.

The Boilermakers scored a touchdown on the first drive of the game. Craig Zellnoff fumbled on the second play of Wisconsin State's opening drive. Purdue linebacker Jaleel Simpson clocked Craig from behind, stripped the ball, and recovered it on the Wisconsin State 12-yard line. Purdue running back Jevon Jamros ran the touchdown in on the very next play. 14-0 Purdue.

"Shit," Randy barked as mascot Purdue Pete, complete with yellow foam hammer, danced on the Mendota Stadium turf. In an odd way, Randy was comforted by the fact that this game was the first in weeks where he just had to coach, not manipulate.

"Don't go stretch just yet, Randy. Give it one more drive," Frank yelled from 20 yards away. Stretch was an offense that was strictly set up for passing. "We can still beat them down with running."

Wisconsin State would not on this early afternoon, the coldest day the team had faced this season.

"Sheeit, man, that ball feels like a box of rocks on my hands," said Touchdown Tyrone Collins to Craig after a rare dropped pass.

Aaron Schutz leaned over to Clark in the press box, high above Mendota Stadium.

"See, Collins just doesn't have the numbers today," Aaron said. "If ever there was a game to throw, it's this one."

Early in the second quarter, Purdue led 24-0 after another touchdown. The crowd broke out their personal flasks of firewater to endure the next two hours.

"Base! Let's just go base for the rest of the way. We don't need to give Minnesota anything to watch for." Frank was waving the unofficial white flag among football coaches.

He was also starting to wave the flag for his own job. Frank knew what was at stake. A loss would drop his squad to 4-3, 1-2 in the Big Ten. That would likely spiral Wisconsin State to another winter without a bowl game. They'd have to win three of their final five games to finish 7-5 and make the postseason. That still might not be enough to stay on the payroll.

Jake Steffon was the lone bright spot. His week of inner torment ended as he put Wisconsin State's only points of the first half on the board. A 43-yard field goal from the left hash mark. Perfect snap. Decent hold by Sam. Perfect kick. Like a nice swing at the golf range. Nearly down the middle.

"Good kick, Jake. You're makin' poppa proud!" John Wilcox said as the kicker walked off the field.

More marshmallows, bologna, and hot dog buns fell on the coaches as they ran off the field.

Randy entered the locker room with a spike of excitement. Not because his team was in a 24-3 hole, but because he'd found his own holes in the Purdue defense. He caught up to Frank.

"Coach, I got something here for the second half."

"Oh, really?" Frank said dismissively.

"Yeah, we can burn them deep off Collins. They aren't even playing him tight."

"Shit, Randy," Frank said, on the verge of an explosion. "If you think you're so brilliant, YOU talk to them at halftime. They sure as shit aren't playing for me."

Randy had been a coach long enough not to take Frank's words to heart.

"All right. Let's try this. I think we can work well on this."

"Fine."

Football halftimes serve no one very well. In cold weather, fans have to walk around the stadium to keep from freezing, buying overpriced hot chocolate or bratwurst. The 15 minutes of halftime don't allow much time for adjustments in the locker room. The teams are finally ready to listen with 12 minutes left. By seven minutes, the teams are taping ankles or relieving themselves before returning to the field.

Randy had five minutes to let his big ideas sink in before the second half.

"All right guys, Coach Flaherty is allowing me a few minutes to plant this seed. He'll talk to you guys on defense in a second.

"We've found something to expose their defense. Collins? Where are you?"

All 115 people in the locker room looked for #1.

"Shitter."

Frank's face turned into a tomato. "I don't care if he's got shit on his pants. GET HIM IN HERE NOW!"

Collins walked in, pants up. No skid marks to show.

"Yeah, coach?"

Randy deftly handled the brief aside.

"Tyrone, they're not doubling you anymore in their basic coverage. You see that, right?"

"They ain't respectin' Tyrone Collins. They—"

"Tyrone," Randy interrupted. "They don't respect you because of the three drops you had."

Tyrone shrugged.

"Do you think you can get outside on your guy deep?"

"Sure."

"OK. Here's what we'll do. First play will be a slant to the sidelines. Second play will be the deep ball. I figure they'll be ripe for it to start the half."

Randy looked from Tyrone to the rest of his team. For the first time in five years, this felt like his team.

"All right, guys, Purdue is in there laughing at you. They're talking about how the quarterback fell apart like a teddy bear on that sack. They're talking about how the defense just doesn't care anymore because the offense can't do anything anyway. They're talking about how Wisconsin State always chokes whenever they play us."

Randy locked eyes with nearly every Wisconsin State football player as he came to the apex of his own Gettysburg Address.

"Guys, the character of a football team is forged in a situation like this. You guys had an awful first half. Get that out of your head. WIPE IT OUT. Remember Hawaii? Remember Kansas? Remember Indiana? All huge second halves. Look, we're down 21. That sounds like a lot, but really it isn't. Here's what we need. One touchdown to open the second half and TWO STOPS ON DEFENSE because I know the offense will find ways to score."

Randy shifted his eyes.

"YOU GUYS ON DEFENSE—CAN YOU GIVE ME TWO STOPS?"

Their "YES" was loud enough to send a parked Chevy six city blocks.

"OFFENSE. Let's burn them to open up. You heard the defense. They'll do it for you. YOU just need to take the game back. Get out there and save the season. On three, yell SAVE THE SEASON."

Craig Zellnoff led the team onto the field for the second half.

Frank patted Randy on the back as the players ran out.

"Helluva talk, Randy. You've still got what it takes to be the head guy somewhere."

Clark had just polished off his third press box bratwurst of the game when he saw the start of a rally.

"Holy crap."

Touchdown Tyrone Collins had just opened the second half with a 73-yard gain down the far sideline. He burned the Purdue cornerback on 2nd and 9. Only free safety Ralph Hedge kept the play from becoming a 76-yard gain and a touchdown. Hedge knocked Collins out at the Purdue 3.

"Game time is ON TIME!" Collins said to Hedge as he walked to the Wisconsin State huddle, arms raised in a V.

Clark looked around. No reaction from Aaron, who was munching on the brownies a few rows back. Teddy Hammersley scored on the next play for Wisconsin State. 24-10 Purdue.

The defense pulled the stop that Randy had asked for. One first down for Purdue, but the Boilermakers still punted.

Wisconsin State drove 42 yards to the Purdue 37 in just four plays. 1st and 10.

"Right 66 Z Corner." Randy motioned in to Craig Zellnoff.

Tyrone time.

"I think they're going to Tyrone," said Aaron, fully recovered from the brownie break.

"It would be the ideal time," Clark countered.

Craig faked left to freeze the defense. The Purdue safety bought it. Craig then uncorked a ball that looked like one a Greek god would toss.

"Oh, shit. The sun." Randy saw Tyrone's face turn back toward the rays. No problem. Tyrone hugged the far sideline for his second big catch in five minutes. Jake booted through the extra point. 24-17 Purdue.

"Collins for Heisman!" Collins yelled at Randy as he walked off the field. "Pay to the order of Touchdown Tyrone Collins!"

Randy jumped up to Tyrone and slapped him on the helmet.

"Now that is what I'm talkin' about, bitch!"

Of course, the cameras caught the exchange.

"There he is, Randy Munson, the elder statesman of the Wisconsin State coaching staff, like a kid who just got his first bike for Christmas after seeing the catch by All-American receiver Tyrone Collins," said ABC's Brent Musberger.

Musberger and the commentator then talked about Randy's stellar coaching background, mentioning that he'd turned down the Baylor job a few years back.

"I have no doubt Randy Munson's name will pop up again as a head coach this off-season. You can't fake that kind of love for your players."

"No question, Brent, no question."

The Wisconsin State momentum slowed as Purdue forced a five-minute drive to eat up the rest of the third quarter. Wisconsin State held Purdue just past midfield, as the Boilermakers had to punt again.

Randy's formula was working perfectly. Two touchdowns. Now two stops on defense.

"Craig, don't worry about time here," Randy said into Craig's ear. "Let's soften them up with runs and then find Tyrone one more time."

Runners Teddy Hammersley and Jason Brunson became a potent combination for Wisconsin State. Teddy would pound for three yards and Jason would run around the Purdue defense for another six yards.

Wisconsin State was down to the Purdue 29, 1st and 10 with 9:45 left in the 4th quarter.

"Slot Left 90 Fade," Craig said in the huddle. He looked up at Collins. Nothing but bug eyes and grinning teeth.

"Sheeit, it's TDT time!"

"That's right it is. On three...BREAK!"

The clock ran between plays, but Craig took his sweet time. He always enjoyed the tight camera shot of his face barking out meaningless commands before the snap of the ball. Even mediocre quarterbacks love face time.

Craig faked a hand-off to Jason and hid the football on his right hip. Jason sold the fake even more, acting as if he had fumbled the ball to throw off Purdue's deep defenders.

Both of the players assigned to Collins stopped and watched the fake fumble long enough for Touchdown Tyrone to blow by them.

Craig simply played catch with Collins for their second touchdown of the half. 64,322 fans in blue screamed at the top of their collective lungs.

"LET IT FLOW. LET IT RIP," John Wilcox yelled to Jake before the kicker punched through the all-important extra point to tie the game at 24.

One more stop. That was all Wisconsin State needed. One more stop and Wisconsin State would score at the end to win it. Linebacker Carlton Harrell played the hero. He sacked the Purdue quarterback on 3rd-and-3 to force another punt.

Wisconsin State took the ball at its own 11 with just 4:31 left.

"Take it slow, gentleman. Be strong on your blocks and your routes," Randy told the offense during the TV time-out.

"Where would this rank in the Flaherty Era? Biggest comeback ever?" Clark asked Aaron high above the turf.

"Oh, without question," Aaron fired back. "To be down 21 in a Big Ten game and come back? That would be enough to save Flaherty for another week."

"Hell, if they pull this out, *The Flaherty Show* will finally stop feeling like a visit to the morgue."

Wisconsin State wasn't heading for a morgue anytime soon. Craig scrambled for seven yards for a first down. Laverneus Wilson picked up another first down with a catch. The clock ticked away. 2:36, 2:35, 2:34.

"Roll it down to two. Down to TWO!" Randy called to Craig, pointing to the play clock. Craig already knew to milk as much time as possible between plays. Bleed the clock out.

Jake was pacing. The ABC cameras followed him around the sideline. Brent Musberger went through Jake's story between plays. The improbable walk-on from Fall Creek, Wisconsin, population 897. That number changed in each story about Fall Creek. The kid who'd missed the game-winning field goal the week before. Jake was kicking footballs into a net on the sidelines, with Sam holding and retrieving the kicks.

Wisconsin State was sitting pretty at the Purdue 38 with just 31 seconds left. 2nd-and-13 after a running play went nowhere. Wisconsin State called a time-out. Wisconsin State had one time-out left. A 55-yard field goal was too far for Jake. Wisconsin State needed about 10 more yards for a realistic kick, 20 more to feel good about the kick.

"Trips Right 80 Slant," Randy called to Craig. That play allowed Craig the freedom to bail out and run if no one was open. That was important. A sack would probably kill the drive and eventually force overtime.

Craig looked for his first option, Tyrone Collins. Randy saw the opening for Collins from the sideline. "Throw it!" he yelled.

Craig took a little off what would usually be a bullet. Touchdown Tyrone Collins jumped up at the 19-yard line. A catch would mean Wisconsin State could line up for a field goal and the win.

The ball smacked the receiver's large mitts. Both hands were on the football.

"Crap," Randy said under the crowd. He had seen these hands before.

Tyrone Collins tried to run with the ball before catching it, his one fatal flaw. The ball flew out of his hands, into the air like a balloon and into the surprised arms of Purdue cornerback Troy Jarrod. Jarrod was running in full stride just to make a tackle. He had an army of blockers in front of him.

"It's over," Clark said in the press box. "They're not going to catch him."

Jarrod had passed Bob Verly and Cory Larkman by the time the linemen even realized what had happened. Only Craig Zellnoff was in the picture. Three defensive linemen took out the quarterback at midfield.

Jarrod was streaking for the touchdown. The clock ticked down...0:13, 0:12, 0:11. Jarrod crossed the Wisconsin State 40, the 35, the 30. Then he looked up at the clock. His sprint slowed to a trot.

6 seconds...5 seconds...

Jarrod stopped at the Wisconsin State 2-yard line, to the shock and dismay of the sellout crowd. No one in blue was chasing him. They'd given up seconds before.

Three, two, one, 00:00.

Jarrod walked into the end zone for the final play of the game. 30-24 Purdue. His actions triggered a brawl. White pants fighting gold pants. Blue shirts wrestling with white shirts.

"That was completely unnecessary, Brent! He didn't need to showboat like that," yelled the color commentator.

"No, I disagree. That was the smart play. Jarrod clearly saw Wisconsin State had given up. Why not? Game is over."

Randy put away his disgust at the botched play long enough to pull his players off the pile.

"In the locker room NOW, DAMMIT!"

Jake was the first player to show some emotion.

"DAMMIT!" He pounded the silver helmet into his locker. He not only wanted the victory, but he also desperately wanted to clear his name.

Frank pushed through the locker room door.

"I'm going to have Coach Munson say a few words to you guys."

Randy walked forward, for once without his clipboard. He'd thrown the clipboard onto the ground during the final play of the game and left it on the Mendota Stadium turf.

"Thanks, Coach. Let me just say that I'm tremendously proud of you guys. All of you. You came in here down 24-3 and we nearly won the damn thing. Should have won the damn thing."

Randy looked at Tyrone. The Collins swagger was replaced with sweat and tears.

"Tyrone, as you can see, as we all can see, one play will make the difference. You had the best half I've ever seen a receiver have, and we've sent six receivers to the NFL on my watch here at Wisconsin State. Keep your chin up."

Collins' day of 11 catches for 176 yards and two touchdowns would attract more attention for his Heisman Trophy chase. But Tyrone Collins was more focused on the one that got away.

"Ya know, Clark, I'm actually not all that pissed." Frank was in a decent mood on Sunday morning back in Madison. The show taping was a few minutes away. Clark brought the head coach his Sunday morning caffeine hit, coffee with two creams, no sugar.

"That's good. I thought you'd be encouraged by the second half."

"I was. What a game by Collins. What a game. I just wish he could have hauled in that last catch."

"Did you have any problem with Jarrod's antics at the end?"

"No. Not at all. That was actually a very smart play. He was aware of his surroundings and the situation. I wish we had guys like that. No, I'm not ticked by that at all. At least we didn't have to wait around for a kickoff with five seconds left. That waiting for the clock to tick down during a loss is the worst."

Clark knew how much waiting hurt. Here he was, on the set of *The Frank Flaherty Show,* and all he could think about was the $25,000 that would be delivered to his door tomorrow morning. Cash he'd won by betting against Frank's team. Cash he'd won on games that would probably bring about Frank's firing in a few weeks.

35. Beach Towels in a Box

Clark rolled out of bed at an unbelievably early hour on Monday. Eight in the morning. He fired up the range and cranked out an omelet with turkey, black olives, and red peppers. He'd hold off on the Alaskan lobster tails until he had the cash in his hand and his ex-wife paid off. Clark fought boredom by catching the morning repeats of the previous night's *SportsCenter*.

Sure enough, FedEx delivered a package just before 10 A.M. Clark signed for it and closed the door.

"Jim's Beach and Surf Shop—St. Martaan" was the return address. The box didn't rattle, and weighed only a pound or two. Clark had never seen $25,000 in cash. He thought the package would weigh as much as a brick.

He couldn't have been more wrong.

Carefully, he cut open one end of the flat, rectangular box and found two turquoise and purple beach towels. Inside the second beach towel was the booty: 25 $1,000 bills, taped to a terry cloth towel that resembled a Caribbean sunset. They'd survived whatever X-ray precautions FedEx had in place. Cool Breeze Sports in St. Martaan had been true to its word.

"Axe Could Fall on Flaherty with Loss" screamed the Wednesday sports section of the *Dane County Tribune*. Randy rolled his eyes at the headline as he passed Frank in the hallway of the football office.

"I know I mentioned this on the show on Sunday, but you did a hell of a job at Purdue," Frank said.

"Thank you, Frank. I actually caught that. I was touched." Randy had tuned in to gauge Frank's mood the day after.

"Look, I know we're all under some real stress and that we may be all coaching apart and elsewhere next year, but it's great having a real veteran on this staff." Frank looked around and lowered his voice. "Sometimes I wonder if the others are in over their heads here."

Randy had often wondered that same thing about Frank. "I appreciate that, Frank. I can't say it was easy, but all of our jobs are to win here. I just wish we could have pulled out Saturday. I mean, we had it RIGHT THERE." Randy held up his hands for emphasis.

"Yeah, if we lose Saturday, I think we're done," Frank said. "On Sunday, Karen called me at the house. She wants a meeting with me today about our progress." A meeting with Karen rarely meant anything good for a Wisconsin State coach. It was the professional equivalent of "going for a drive" with the Godfather.

"Clark, what do you make of all this talk about Flaherty getting canned if they lose?" News director Lou Proctor wondered back into the Commonwealth of Sports at WMA.

"Geesh, I dunno," Clark said, turning from his computer to face his boss. "It's not like Wisconsin State to can a coach in the middle of the season. The day after the end of the season, yes, but not in the middle."

"That's what I thought, too. Maybe it's just the *Tribune* trying to sell some papers."

"Well, if they do lose at Minnesota, they're done. No way this team takes three games from Michigan, Ohio State, Illinois, and Michigan State," Clark reasoned. "It's already assumed that they'll all get canned if they don't make a bowl game again. They need seven wins to get there."

Lou walked back to his fiefdom of news. Clark's phone rang.

"Channel 11 Sports!"

"Clark, hi." The unmistakable voice of his ex-wife.

"Hi Carol. What's up?" Clark always sounded like he was in a hurry when she called.

"Did you get my letter?"

The day after Clark's loot arrived, wrapped in beach towels, Carol had mailed a letter outlining the final payments before her marriage to that "slime-bucket hack attorney," as Clark referred to Marlin. A final total of $7,651 would free him forever from financial obligation.

Clark felt the bravado of his big win ooze through his limbs.

"I can pay you that today, if you'd like."

Silence on the other end. Clark seized on the quiet.

"I'm good for it, Carol."

"I don't understand—"

"Carol, I've been saving my money for months. I can cover that." That was partially true. Clark had just under $9,000 in the bank for this moment. A sliver of his newfound $25,000 would go to pay his other bills.

"Oh."

"How does an even eight grand sound? You and Marlin can buy a La-Z-Boy or something with the extra 400 bucks."

"Well, uh—"

Clark went for the pin.

"I'll take that as a yes, Carol. You'll see it soon."

"Well, thank you."

"Who loves you, baby!" Clark bellowed out as if he were Telly Savalas.

Click.

Clark Cattoor, back in his role as Dane County's Master of the Universe.

36. Minnesota

The biannual trip to Minnesota always brought particular challenges for the Wisconsin State coaching staff. Not only were the Gophers a decent team this year, but the distractions of the trip were always suffocating.

Nearly three dozen of the players hailed from Minnesota. Most of those were from the metro area of Minneapolis-St. Paul. All had family and friends requesting tickets. All wanted free time to visit moms and dads, girlfriends and buddies from the neighborhood.

Frank set aside Friday night, from 5 to 9, as free time. Many players chose to roam the downtown streets. The team stayed at the Marriott, just four blocks from the stadium, the forgettable Metrodome in Minneapolis.

All 75 traveling players received a sheet of instructions as they climbed aboard their luxury coaches for the four-hour ride from Madison. With three different buses and all the distractions, this would probably be the last time everyone would be together until Saturday afternoon. The game would start later than usual, 6 P.M. to accommodate ESPN.

Jake went down the sheet, which read like the Treaty of Versailles.

"Sam, check out number three."

"3. As usual, no females (not even your mom) are allowed in

your hotel room at any time."

"Damn, Sam, I was hoping your mom would show me a good time."

"Asshole."

Sam's parents were still up in the air as to whether they could make the two-hour drive west from Neillsville to Minneapolis. The Steffons, however, had not seen their son since late summer. Fall Creek was just 100 miles from the hotel.

The Flaherty Declaration also set out the usual: No alcohol, tobacco, or other drug use at any time. The urban setting of the road trip also brought another ban.

9. NO GENTLEMEN'S CLUBS WHATSOEVER. YOU GUYS KNOW WHERE THEY ARE. STAY OUT OF THEM.

That second sentence was true. Everyone knew Tails and Buckskin's in downtown Minneapolis.

Touchdown Tyrone Collins had even bought a city map back in Madison to plot the exact distance from Tails to the Marriott. He had no family coming to visit him. Tyrone planned to take advantage of whatever Happy Hour specials awaited on Friday.

"Sheeit, that number 9 rule has got to go." Tyrone looked at his roommate, Laverneus Wilson. "What the hell am I goin' to do for fo' hours?"

The trek from Madison to Minneapolis is not for the faint of heart. The only source of visual entertainment is watching the mile markers tick down. Once a traveler arrives in Tomah, the land of cranberries, the miles count down from 144. Once the road hits 0, downtown Minneapolis is only thirty minutes away.

Jake Steffon and Sam Cattanach were the only two players actually enjoying the trip. This was their world. Rural schools like Fall Creek and Neillsville often traveled 90 or 100 miles just to play another school. As the towns rattled by—Black River Falls, Osseo, Augusta, Elk Mound, Spring Valley—either Jake or Sam had a football story to share. Their western Wisconsin bond always kept stress to a minimum. They were survivors.

A collective yell boomed through the bus as the Minnesota natives welcomed the two-mile bridge on westbound I-94 just outside Hudson, Wisconsin. Now they were home.

The last 30 miles felt like five minutes. The caravan zoomed through St. Paul's rush-hour traffic and rolled up to the Marriott just before 4:30. Jake stumbled off the bus.

"JAKE!" Carl Steffon was all decked out in his "Wisconsin State Dad" sweatshirt. Nancy was a bit more subdued, wearing a blue sweater and earrings.

"Mom! Dad!" Jake hugged his parents.

Sam threw his bag over his shoulder and walked over to the Steffons. Carl shook the punter's hand.

"Sam, we spoke with your folks a couple of hours ago. They wanted me to pass along the message that your dad couldn't get away from work today. They'll be here tomorrow for the game, though."

Nancy worked her mom magic.

"However, we're going to take Jake out for a decent meal, and you're welcome to come along. Mongolian Beef House!"

Sam smiled. "I will graciously decline. You haven't seen Jake since August." Sam looked at Jake. "I'll keep the room warm for you."

Carl did not protest. "Very well, Sam. It's good seeing you."

After the iced teas arrived at the Mongolian Beef House, Nancy opened the inquisition.

"Are you all right down there? Getting your studies in?"

Jake put down his glass. He had a lot to get off his chest.

"I'm just realizing how much of a machine playing football at a big school really is. It's humbling and empowering at the same time."

"How so?" Carl asked.

"The coaches have all this power, but we're the reasons they're so rich and powerful. They walk around campus like dictators. Sometimes it's just not fun."

That statement shocked both Carl and Nancy Steffon. Football not fun?

"It's a job now," Jake said, fidgeting with a straw. "I'm hearing that I'll be on scholarship next year, but I don't know if Flaherty will even be around after the off-season to sign off on it. Who knows what'll happen? A new coach could just bring in his guys."

"Jake, you've proven yourself to be a good kicker," Carl said. "You're not perfect, but you're good enough to start on a Big Ten team."

Jake nodded. "I know that, Dad. It's just not everything I thought it would be." He picked at his peanut shrimp and bamboo shoots. "I'm thinking about transferring to a smaller program."

Carl dropped his fork.

"WHAT? Are you serious?"

Jake looked at his mother.

"Actually, I've been thinking about it for a few weeks. And it's not just because of the game two weeks ago. The only reason I would stay here is to see if I can kick in the NFL."

My God, Jake thought, I sound like a whiner. "But, then, I'm still real fortunate in a lot of ways," he added. "On a campus of 27,000 people, I'm somebody, and that's kind of neat, too."

Only two Big Ten schools still played on hard artificial turf—Wisconsin State and Minnesota. Each time Wisconsin State and Minnesota played at the Metrodome, every Boars fan in the state of Minnesota found a way to get in the door. For many years, the game at Minnesota had been like another home game for Wisconsin State.

Randy Munson went to sleep on Friday night knowing his offense would torch Minnesota. As he paced the Metrodome turf the next afternoon, an hour before kickoff, he saw the determination in his players' eyes. Wisconsin State's Minnesota faction was eager to win in front of friendly eyes.

He walked around to his stars, patting them on the helmet and reminding them of a small tidbit or tip to take into the game.

"Craig, when you see 27 guarding any of our receivers, throw it toward the sideline."

"Verly, Lark, watch for 90 on the left side."

"Teddy, you'll see an extra hole each time we run right. Hit that right away. It'll stay open."

On and on it went for Randy and his offensive players. Frank Flaherty had gone to endless lengths to praise Randy's second-half game-plan against Purdue.

Randy paced the pregame field like a jaguar, a coach whose power had been restored.

Minnesota entered the game 5-2, but Wisconsin State really did have more talent. Randy and Frank cajoled it out of the abyss in front of the ESPN cameras.

Craig Zellnoff opened the game with a touchdown scramble from 11 yards. Jake Steffon knocked through a 38-yard field goal. 10-0 Wisconsin State, after the first quarter.

"Pairs Right 532 Z Go," Randy signaled in.

Touchdown Tyrone Collins caught the hand signals from the sideline.

"Sheeit, it's TDT for Heisman time again, ain't it?"

In a play specifically designed for the quick turf, Tyrone faked a block on his defender before sprinting from the far side of the field. Running back Jason Brunson tossed Tyrone the ball, and Craig threw a block that amazed the milk-fed linemen from Wausau.

"He's gone!" Clark said to Aaron in the Metrodome press box.

"I don't know why they haven't tried that more often."

Tyrone was high-stepping by the Minnesota 40-yard line. The final numbers on the play: 68 yards. One touchdown. One outstanding block by a quarterback. Tyrone struck the pose in the end zone.

"TDT for Heisman!" he screamed.

"EXTRA POINT TEAM! EXTRA POINT TEAM!" John Wilcox yelled out.

"Great block, Craig, real tight. Just like we talked about." Randy gave Craig a hero's welcome on the sideline.

"Oh, shit, coach, what happened to Collins?"

Out of the corner of his eye, Tyrone saw Goldy Gopher, the Minnesota mascot, mocking his Heisman stance.

Tyrone Collins then did something unheard of in 107 years of Big Ten football.

He tackled the mascot on the hard rubber floor behind the end zone. Then he sat on the fallen Goldy's gigantic face and rubbed his behind into Goldy's massive plastic teeth.

That ignited a donnybrook as the Minnesota players took some exception to TDT's perverted end-zone celebration. Within 90 seconds the refs had tossed TDT and five other Wisconsin State players. Six Gophers also were sent to the locker room without supper.

"That flat-tailed bastard was makin' fun of me!" Tyrone protested to the line judge.

Randy Munson was amused by the incident.

"It's OK. It's the defense's game now, anyway. We'll be fine."

Wisconsin State was indeed fine. The Gophers were unable to crawl out of the 17-0 hole. Randy took the throttle off the offense in the second half, churning out first downs and speeding up the game. Jason scored from two yards out, and Jake booted a 27-yard field goal for Wisconsin State's final points as they won 27-10.

For now, the season was saved. With a 5-3 record and a 2-2 mark in the Big Ten, Wisconsin State needed just two more wins to clinch a bowl game. That was the benchmark to save everyone's job.

Winning two games would be much more difficult 48 hours later.

37. One Angry Millionaire

"AGENT: I'VE PAID COLLINS SINCE '01."

The Monday morning edition of the *Dane County Tribune* had a coup on its hands.

Aaron Schutz's name was on the story. Clark was after the real details. He called Aaron's cell phone.

"Aaron, what the hell is going on down there? I just read the piece."

"Well, the smoking gun finally came out on Saturday. I ran into Copperzweig right after the game, down in the tunnel where the players come out. He was in town to watch the Vikings game on Sunday. He told me that Collins isn't coming back next year—"

"Big surprise."

"Right, but he also did something weird. He told me that Collins had decided earlier in the week that he was looking to leave school before the end of the season."

"Why?"

"Apparently someone in his family planted the bug in his ear about getting injured. Collins does have an insurance policy against injury for two mil. But how far will $2 million go if you stand to make $20 million in the NFL?"

"Good point."

"I think Collins decided he had placed himself in a high enough standing with the pro scouts that he could skip out on the rest of the games."

Clark moved in for the big question.

"So Copperzweig actually said he paid Collins?"

"Yes, that was the most shocking part of it. He guaranteed that Collins will never play college football ever again."

"You'll be at Flaherty's press conference, right?"

"Wouldn't miss it for the world. Every knucklehead from Milwaukee to Eau Claire will be there. Kinda takes the glow off the Gopher win, doesn't it?"

"Yeah, no kidding. Thanks, Aaron. You guys did a solid job on this one."

"I'm sure Flaherty will love to see me there."

"Wow. Lots of people want to talk about Michigan," Frank deadpanned as he walked to the microphone. A writer from Janesville laughed. That was it.

Frank sat down, with cameras and microphones in front of him and the huge signs for Big Flavor sports drink behind him.

"In the last two hours, we in the football department have taken corrective action along the NCAA guidelines."

Clark looked around. Aaron Schutz had the respect of the media jackals. Aaron sat in the front row for what could be Frank's show trial before his professional execution.

Frank continued. "Tyrone Collins will be held out of practice and game action for an indefinite period of time until two full investigations are completed. One will be done internally by the athletic department, and the other will be by the NCAA. I'll tell you now there's no way he'll be available for the Michigan game. The Ohio State game, maybe. We simply don't know how long the process will take.

"Let me just say one thing before we open this up: There's been lots of loose talk about Tyrone from the time he got here. Don't think I haven't heard it. People see a kid with the skills he has and people are jealous. That's just the way it is in athletics. People are always looking for a way to tear star players down."

Frank looked right at Aaron Schutz. "I hope that's not the case here.

"I'll tell you now, I really can't say much more about the Collins situation. It's in the hands of the department and the NCAA. I ask that you leave Tyrone alone. Please don't try to contact him because he can't say anything about this anyway. I know some of you probably will, but I have to ask. Thanks. OK. Fire away."

Sixty journalists wanted to ask the same question. Jared Stoll stepped up to the plate.

"Frank, do you think this incident involving Tyrone Collins hurts your own job security within the program?"

On the videotape, once the words "job security" were uttered, Frank's eyes started to narrow and the lines on his forehead began to develop. Chilling pixels on the screen.

"What kind of question is that?" Frank said forcefully. "That's such a loaded question. But you know what, I'll give you an answer because I know everyone here will run it tonight and tomorrow." He pointed at the dozen cameras present.

"Of course this hurts. If you read the papers, I'm always getting fired or getting an extension based upon the latest game. I'm used to that. That's part of the job. I accept that. But to ask if something that has just surfaced today affects whether I'm still the coach here is just bush league. It really is. I plan to be at Wisconsin State for many years to come."

Frank leaned toward Aaron Schutz and uttered the sound bite that would play on *SportsCenter* later that night and on every newscast from Minneapolis to Chicago.

"It'll take more than one wide receiver, one agent, and one damn sportswriter to send me packing."

Randy Munson was in his office, dissecting the Michigan defense and how to beat it without Tyrone Collins in the mix. He knew that would be a nasty task for his short-handed offense. Wisconsin State hadn't won at Michigan since its last Rose Bowl season.

"What a bunch of crap!" Frank burst through the door.

"How did it go, boss?" Randy said without breaking eye contact with the Michigan players, frozen on the TV screen.

"They've made up their minds about me because of this whole Collins mess. I tried to go out there like a tough guy, but I'm afraid bad shit is on the way."

38. No TLC Without TDT

"Channel 11 Sports!"

"Clark, it's Schutzie."

"What's up?"

"Too much, man, too much. I got something you might be interested in. I know a guy who has two classes with Tyrone Collins on Mondays and Wednesdays. English 208 and some Mass Comm lecture. Apparently, TDT was AWOL today in both classes."

"Is that unusual?"

"Apparently, he's only missed twice so far," Aaron reported. "I'm thinking he's left campus. I called him four times with no response."

"Maybe he's letting the machine get everything."

"Could be, but it's not like Collins to avoid the phone. He loves to talk. Why would he hang out in Madison? I'm betting he's back in Miami with his boys."

"I'll look into that."

"Just figured you might want the morsel."

"Thanks, Aaron. See you at noon hoops tomorrow."

Clark made a special appearance on the 5 P.M. newscast. The show opened with the usual music followed by Frank Flaherty's now-famous sound bite.

Under the video of Tyrone Collins shaking his rump on Goldy Gopher's face, news anchor Matthew Mallory announced, "Frank

Flaherty defends his program after his star receiver is tossed off the team!"

After teasing stories about the latest with North Korea and the economy, Matthew introduced Clark with the latest on the Tyrone Collins saga.

Wearing his charcoal suit and a black and gray tie, Clark leapt into his story.

"Matt, this morning the *Dane County Tribune* reported that Wisconsin State star receiver Tyrone Collins had signed with Florida-based agent Jerry Copperzweig. On top of that, the story stated that Copperzweig had paid Collins, which would be a violation of NCAA rules. Amid these odd turns in the team's season, head coach Frank Flaherty found himself defending his program."

The tape of the story rolled.

Clark left the set and returned to the sports office. Rachel Randall was typing away on her story about the undefeated boys' soccer team at Brodhead High School.

"Clark, check it out. *SportsCenter* is all over it."

Clark looked up at the eye-level TV. Even ESPN, the worldwide leader in sports, loved the sound bite.

"It'll take more than one wide receiver, one agent, and one damn sportswriter to send me packing."

"Yeah, Coach Frank is in deep," Jake said an hour later at the Kickers' Quarters.

"Holy shit! I can't believe he said that!" Sam said after the latest ESPN replay of the sound bite.

Jake and Sam watched Frank explain to the team that Tyrone Collins would be out for at least the Michigan game.

"We have to find a way to pick up all our games to win Saturday," the coach said at least three times.

Jake was already feeling better. He'd made it through the past two games without a miss. He was now 10 for 13 on field goals, good for second place in accuracy in the Big Ten. That stat alone was quite impressive for a walk-on in his first year as a starter. Even Jake was landing some interest from the pro scouts, according to John Wilcox.

Yet Frank hadn't come to Jake during the season to tell him he'd be back the next year on a scholarship.

He was getting recognized more and more in the football fishbowl that is Madison. More guys nodded at him on campus. More girls stared at him as he walked to class.

"Hell, I'm so confident right now, watch this," Jake said to the punter. He picked up the telephone and dialed a number from his black book.

Rachel Randall.

Jake knew she'd be at the station. A perfect opportunity to leave a voice message.

"Rachel, hi, Jake Steffon here. I just wanted to call and see what you're up to. I'm sorry we got off on a bad footing a few weeks back. I should be home tonight. Give me a call if you get a second."

Click.

"Wow. That's ballsy, man," Sam said.

"You watch. She'll call."

Randy's wife, Lisa, knew exactly what kind of day he'd had just from reading the newspaper and watching the news. She stopped by a supermarket to pick up the ingredients for his favorite dish, coconut shrimp. Just before seven, she brought out the plate of sugar- and coconut-covered shrimp. Randy dove into his plate and was already on his third shrimp when Lisa looked around.

"Randy, I think Melissa has some good news for us."

Melissa smiled. "I've decided where I want to go to college." The table turned quiet. "I want to go to Minnesota."

Randy slowly chewed his sweet shrimp. "Minnesota is a good school, and I'll be happy to send you there. Are you sure that's it, though? This is a big decision. What about Eau Claire?"

"What about Northwestern?" she fired back.

"Good point," Randy said. Better to write a little bit larger check for Minnesota than take out another mortgage for Northwestern. Not that Randy had not made enough money off that school as it was. The irony was delicious.

"I'm sure about this one," Melissa said.

Randy couldn't resist. "You sure you don't want to go to WSU?"

"Daddy, no offense, but I have to get out of Madison for a few years."

Randy chugged his iced tea and broke out laughing.

"No, you just have to get away from me for a few years."

Scott piped up. "Uh, Dad, I'll still go to Wisconsin State in three years."

"I'm not so sure we'll be here by that point. Been reading the paper, son?"

Lisa understood Randy's anguish. Randy had told Lisa earlier in the day that the discovery about Tyrone taking money from an agent would be just cause for firing Frank. All the coaches would probably have to walk the plank at the end of the year. Families and friendships would break apart as each coach tried to get back on his feet.

For a football coach's wife, Lisa had been extremely lucky. They hadn't moved in 12 years. Scott and Brett had spent nearly all their lives in Madison. Melissa had been there since first grade. In this nomadic line of work, the Munsons were becoming lifers.

As Randy quietly prepared her for the inevitable, Lisa began working on projects around the house. The basement needed fresh paint. The kitchen needed new white cabinets, not the old orange ones. The Munsons had to get the house ready for sale.

Yet these final four weeks also brought a chance for Randy to resurrect his career. Frank made sure to mention Randy's role in the Purdue comeback and the win over Minnesota. Randy still hadn't received any interest yet from other schools, but the season was still early. Those calls usually came in November, when schools wanted to get their prospective coaches in the mix by Thanksgiving.

If Randy could come up with a way to win two of these final four games without his best offensive player, his own stock could skyrocket. He might even be able to land a head coaching job.

As long as Craig Zellnoff played well and John Wilcox kept his mouth shut, Randy still had a future worth dreaming about.

Thursday's practice was not worth dreaming about. The team was still not sharp without Tyrone Collins.

"Damn it, Laverneus! Six yards, then cut to the right for two yards. Cut hard. None of this lazy shit!" Randy barked to his new top receiver. Laverneus Wilson was no Tyrone Collins, that much was clear.

After another failed route, Randy did something out of character. He dressed down a player in public.

"My God! I knew that with Collins out, we'd each have to pick it up. Now, I'm considering scrapping the whole goddamn game plan because you"—Randy stuck his index finger in Wilson's chest—can't run the right damn pattern out here. Maybe I should just call Michigan right now and tell them we're going to run the ball every single damn play. Hell, I'm gonna tell them we're going to run the off tackle to the left EVERY SINGLE DAMN PLAY! Now get it right!"

On the sidelines, Clark was taken aback.

"These guys look terrible."

Aaron shook his head. "At least we see why a guy like Copperzweig threw all that money at Collins. He's going to make a mint in the pros. Collins proves his worth every day to this football program by his absence."

Jim Tillman walked over to the journalists.

"OK, fellas, we're at 30 minutes. Time to finish up your shots and go. Thanks for coming."

Once the last hack with a zoom lens left the WSU Bubble, Frank Flaherty made Randy's tirade feel like a warm cuddle from Mom.

"WHAT IN THE HELL IS GOING ON OUT HERE? We're playing like a goddamn girls' powder puff team! What are you, a BUNCH OF LADIES? We went in and WON AT MINNESOTA. Hell, we're still in the hunt for the Big Ten title! You guys are looking around for Collins to bail our asses out. Well, guess what!"

The players looked at the turf.

"Tyrone Collins is not walking through that door! He will never walk through that door again! He's gone. And if all of you keep playing like this, every damn one of you will have to watch him on TV on Sundays, cause no one here is worthy of playing in the Big Ten, much less the NFL."

That last part got everyone's attention.

"Randy, run 'em down. Everyone. Offense, defense, special teams. Everyone has gotta run."

The players and coaches were still ticked off the day after when they walked onto the charter airplane at the Dane County Airport. Instead of the eight-hour bus ride to Ann Arbor, the school had splurged for an hour-long flight over Lake Michigan.

Frank sat up front with Randy. Any hope for the Michigan game was muted after the week of sorry practices.

"At least I hear TCU may open up next week. You like Texas?" Frank asked Randy.

"Sure."

"I've said this before, but I really mean it. If the worst happens here, I'll fight tooth and nail to help you land that head job somewhere. You have the most roots planted here of any of the coaches, and I recognize that."

Randy was genuinely touched by the gesture.

39. Michigan

Randy Munson had the brains to beat Michigan but no one to execute it. Michigan Stadium holds more than 100,000 people. It's the largest college football stadium in the world, and its regular fans expect the maize-and-blue to win each home game. This week, even Randy and Frank expected it, too.

Randy stressed to his offensive line that they needed to block harder and sharper than ever before. He stayed up until midnight counseling Craig Zellnoff on what to do when Michigan charged him and there was no Collins to throw to.

"Shrink the game! Treasure the time!" Randy reminded the quarterback before the first possession. Wisconsin State received the kickoff. Craig ran for three yards. Jason Brunson scrambled for two. Craig hit Laverneus Wilson for a first down.

"There you go, Zellnoff! Thread it right in there!" Randy cajoled. This was what he enjoyed most, using his smarts to lead an overmatched team to victory. If Wisconsin State didn't make any mistakes, they might have a chance. Even then, Michigan would have to seriously screw it up for Wisconsin State to leave with a smile.

Craig led Wisconsin State to a blood-dripping drive. Seventeen plays and 10 minutes into the first quarter, he fell just short of a first down at the Michigan 15. 4th-and-1.

"FIELD GOAL TEAM!" Frank called out behind Randy. "FIELD

GOAL TEAM!"

"Yup, field goal team. That's the right call," Randy said over the headset. He was in agreement that his offense couldn't risk going for a touchdown here.

Jake was still in awe of the Big House, the nickname for Michigan Stadium. He had only seen the place on TV before. He'd spent an extra half hour on the field before kickoff, just walking around and taking in the history.

Just another kick, Jake, just another kick.

"Ready?" Sam asked from his holding position.

Jake nodded.

Snap down, ball up, 32-yard field goal for Jake Steffon. 3-0 Wisconsin State.

That ended Randy Munson's brilliant game plan.

The coaching staff had worried all season about Jake's short kickoffs. Frank had often said in the film meetings that Jake's kickoffs would cost Wisconsin State at least two touchdowns this year.

Frank was right.

Michigan's Anthony Thompson returned the kick from the Michigan 11, through an army of white-clad Wisconsin State players in dark blue pants. Thompson scooted in for a Michigan touchdown.

Frank's face matched those hideous blue pants. He charged toward John Wilcox.

"I SWEAR, WILCOX, YOU MAY NOT EVEN MAKE IT BACK TO MADISON!" Frank screamed. "I MAY LEAVE YOU HERE IN GODDAMN MICHIGAN!"

Ten feet away, Randy tried to calm his team. Craig was too nervous at having to play from behind without Touchdown Tyrone Collins. Passes sailed wide. Randy kept trying to reel Craig in, but the quarterback was shaken by Michigan's quick strike.

Wisconsin State trailed 14-3 at the half—not an insurmountable margin, but they couldn't make any mistakes in the second half.

"For god's sake, just calm the hell down out there!" Frank screamed in the locker room. "We're running around with our mouths yapping like ducks' butts!"

Flaherty's Prophecy met the second phase seven minutes later. Jake uncorked another short kickoff. Michigan's Herman Williams caught it at the Michigan 8, found some space in the middle of the field, and was off for another Michigan touchdown.

Jake knew he wasn't in football shape. As Williams ran past him along the sideline, Jake heaved himself into the air for a last-second dive.

All Jake heard was the collective roar of 107,000 fans while he ate a chunk of the white-painted grass on the sideline. 21-3 Michigan.

Frank paced quickly toward a terrified John Wilcox but dialed down what he wanted to say.

"John," Frank said under the cheers, "you need to put some extra work in this week on your kickoff team."

Randy walked over to the embarrassed coach.

"Randy, I—" John said apologetically.

Randy held up his hands. "Save it, John. This league has a way of humbling even the best. We'll make up that score."

Wisconsin State would not make up the touchdown. Randy knew it. He was forced to take more chances on offense. That simply played into the hands of the more talented team on the field.

Michigan bled the clock dry in the second half. Trailing 35-3 in the final minutes, Craig threw a junk score to Laverneus Wilson to move Wisconsin State closer to double digits, and then ran in a two-point conversion. Final score: Michigan 35, Wisconsin State 11. The Boars were 5-4.

"I ought to fire his ass," Frank said as he and Randy walked off the field. "That Wilcox is more trouble than he's worth."

"What do you want me to say?" Frank asked the dozen reporters in a trailer underneath the stadium. "Our performance was sub-par, our execution not where it needs to be."

Clark Catoor heard this as coming from a coach who wanted to state the obvious, and save his hide. Frank wasn't going to blame his own coaching for the pathetic showing on national television. Not at all.

"We just need to figure out a way to succeed with the hand we are currently playing. That's the major challenge."

Randy took a small interest in an item he'd read earlier in one of the Detroit papers: Las Vegas had taken the Wisconsin State-

Michigan game off the board due to Tyrone's absence. The receiver really was that much of a factor.

Randy was itching to phone Stephen once the plane landed in Madison, just to see if Wisconsin State would be off the board for the rest of the season. Don't do it, Randy, don't do it, he kept reminding himself. He fought his gambling demons on the shuttle to the airport. On the plane. In the Riviera on the way home. You made your money. You're done with it. Hell, it's not like you really need the cash now, he kept telling himself.

Finally, Randy stopped at a gas station on East Washington and made a phone call. To Lisa.

"Oh, honey, I've been trying to get hold of you!" Lisa said excitedly.

"Really? What's up? I figured no one wanted to talk with me after today."

"Well, San Diego College called today. The AD wants to talk to you as soon as possible. Keep it hush-hush. They're getting rid of their head coach. They're interested."

"No kidding?"

"A gentleman named Ed Hartsberg said to call him tonight, even if it's late."

"Yeah, I know Ed a little bit. I didn't know they'd have an opening down there this year, though." The door out of Madison suddenly kicked wide open. Lisa had to ask the important question.

"So, how much would that job pay?"

"Probably 250, 300 thousand."

"Hmm. I could like San Diego."

40. A Last Life Raft

Clark woke up early Sunday morning. As he examined his face in the mirror, he noticed the first signs of gray hair. A little light around the temples. A few more wrinkles in the forehead.

"Ah, who cares," Clark mumbled. He'd read in *Men's Health* that divorced men tend to talk to themselves more.

Clark walked barefoot into his kitchen. He set an iron pan on the range and twisted the knob to medium-high. French toast and sausage would help him prepare to tape *The Frank Flaherty Show* later that morning.

The microwave clock read 6:49. The paper should be here. Clark unlocked the front door and found the Sunday edition of the *Dane County Tribune* on his porch. He always tried to dissect the sports section before heading into the show taping.

Today, though, he didn't make it past the front-page headline.

"COLLINS: FLAHERTY KNEW ABOUT CASH." Reporter Jason Gitter took Aaron's story one step further. Gitter had flown to Miami and tracked down Touchdown Tyrone Collins, knocking on the door of TDT's mother's house. The star receiver welcomed the writer like a long-lost friend.

Not surprisingly, Tyrone was frank in the article. Tyrone said for the record that he had received cash payments from Jerry Copperzweig for all three seasons at Wisconsin State. He also said that Frank did not look out for his players as much as he did their statistics. One quote stuck with Clark.

"They simply run a program up there where they herd us all out like sheep. The best sheep get the nicest stalls while the rest of us are sent out to the electric shocker, like veal."

Quite a ringing endorsement for Frank Flaherty.

"Yep," Clark said aloud, "this taping will be a real joy."

"CAN YOU BELIEVE THIS SHIT?" Frank said as Clark opened the front door at WMA-TV.

"Yeah, coach, I caught it this morning."

Frank handed Clark his overcoat.

"LIES! LIES! LIES!"

"Really?"

"After all the shit I went through to keep that kid eligible, to keep his damn meal ticket punched, he goes out and does this to me? I tell ya, Clark, if the alums don't kill me, these damn kids will!"

Clark tried to find something positive in Frank's darkening mood.

"Uh, Frank, you look great. We'll start taping in 10 minutes."

Frank understood Clark's attempt at shifting gears.

"Thanks, Clark. I'll be ready to give you a great show by then."

Randy read Gitter's exclusive from the comfort of bed. Lisa had brought him his favorite breakfast, eggs Benedict with toasted blueberry bagels on the side. After years of struggle, Lisa and Randy knew their second chance was on the horizon.

Randy had called Ed Hartsberg late Saturday night. Hartsberg told him that the San Diego College job would not officially open until the week after Thanksgiving. Most college football programs didn't fire coaches mid-season. Rather, schools told coaches that they would resign effective at the end of the season. San Diego College fell into that group of sensitive football factories.

"I've done some checking up on you and you're our guy right now. Can you come out this week?" Ed asked.

"I'm not sure about that," Randy admitted. "We're fighting for a bowl bid these final three weeks. The only time I might be able to do it would be Saturday night right after the Ohio State game. I could spend Sunday out there and be back here Monday morning. I know that's not ideal for meeting the proper people, but I don't want to walk away from the job I'm doing here."

"No problem, Randy," the athletic director said. "We can work around that. Even if you can't come out here right away, we'll leave the job open until the end of the year."

But Randy knew that if a better candidate came along before then, he'd be toast. Coaches always got fired in the final three weeks of the year. Randy had to pounce on it.

The last warm weather of October reached Madison on Monday morning. Bright red and orange leaves hung onto their branches for a last day or two. The sun peeked over the tree-lined sidewalks on Nakoma Road as Randy drove to work.

Randy had rehearsed exactly what he would say to Frank. He usually felt comfortable enough with his boss to call him at home about anything. Yet after the beating Frank had taken in the Sunday paper, Randy figured his bombshell would have to wait.

He pulled into the stadium parking lot. Frank's new Cadillac gleamed in the sunshine. Randy exhaled slowly, grabbed his keys and his briefcase, and made The Walk.

Frank was the only person in the office. The head coach often tortured himself after losses with long hours. He was like an NFL coach in that regard. Frank ate Chinese takeout and often slept on his office couch during the season.

"Frank, got a minute?"

Frank looked up from an avalanche of printouts on Ohio State's offense. "Randy, hi. Sure do. What is it?"

"Well, Frank, I got a phone call over the weekend from San Diego College. They want me to interview for the head coaching job." Randy waited to gauge Frank's reaction.

Frank smiled. "Good. I'm glad they followed through. They called me on Friday for a recommendation. I didn't want to get your hopes up on the plane over to Ann Arbor." Frank always enjoyed playing God to his assistants.

Randy masked his disappointment. "Well, thank you for the kind word."

"Not a problem."

"There is one pickle, though."

"Let me guess. They want you out there right away?"

"At least to interview."

"OK." Frank fidgeted with a pen that had once belonged to Alabama coaching legend Bear Bryant. He'd bought it on eBay two years earlier. "Look, here's the deal. I want you to stay. I need your experience to get us these wins. But the reality is that we're all going to get fired. Even if we win two games, Strassel will can all of us. This whole crap with Collins put that over the top with her, from what my sources are telling me."

Randy looked at his feet.

"So, Randy, what I'm saying is go, interview down there, land the offer, and get off the reservation before they burn down our teepees. This is your chance. Don't blow it."

"When should I go to San Diego?"

"Go this week if you can. We'll work around practice this week. Look, you gave me four years of exceptional work. The last thing I want to do is keep you and your family from getting what's yours."

"But what about—"

"Randy, if we lose on Saturday, all of us will get shit-canned. That's all there is to it. I think we can still pull it off, but why take that chance with your family? Go. We'll tell the damn media that you have herpes or something."

Randy couldn't help but wonder. He wondered why exactly San Diego College was showing this much interest in an assistant coach who was probably days from the unemployment line.

"Should I call them back and say I can go tonight?"

"Damn straight, Randy," Frank said as he fiddled with his lighter. "Don't wait around for them to get cold on you or for Karen to clip all of us. She will if we lose, you know."

"All right. I'll call them right now."

Randy walked into his office and dialed. Just punching the 619 area code made him feel warmer.

"Randy, thanks for calling me back," said the rich baritone voice of Ed Hartsberg. "I thought you might like to know it's 78 degrees here. Sunny, just like every other day. I can see the yachts in the harbor as we speak."

Randy played along with the San Diego College athletic director. "Yeah, well, I see an old Malibu outside my window, and snowflakes starting to fall from the heavens."

Ed let out one of those laughs that reminded Randy of his grandpa.

"Well, Randy, I shoot from the hip here, and, uh, I'll lay it out on the line for you right now," Ed said, as if the entire sentence were just one long word. "We like you. We like your background and what you've done over the past 12 years. When your team played us out here a few years back, I remember walking away real impressed with the team organization, especially on offense. That's what we're looking for."

Randy braced himself for the "but" statement.

"But—"

Randy had done this dance a time or two.

"We have concerns about this story regarding this, uh, wide receiver who got himself mixed up with an agent. Collins, is it?"

"Yes." Randy saw his dream job fading.

"I'll ask you straight out. I just need a yes or no from you. Did you have any knowledge of the agent?"

Randy paused a full second so he did not sound too casual.

"No."

"I ask because I need to know. You see, it makes no sense for us to pursue a coach from a program that's being investigated. Unless, of course, the coach had no knowledge of any wrongdoing. You said no. That's good enough for me."

That bullet dodged, Randy returned to his agenda.

"Well, Ed, I have permission to fly out and meet with you this week. Frank Flaherty has allowed me to meet anytime you see fit."

Now Ed paused. Both men understood the value of proper pausing during this poker game.

"Yes, I think we can make that work. You can come out this week?"

"Yes, sir." Randy liked to throw in a "sir" once or twice during any interview.

"Tell you what, I'll have my secretary book everything for you. Do you have any airline preference?"

"No, but Northwest usually works best for us. Shortest routes."

"Can you fly out later today?"

"I'd be happy to. Will a Wednesday morning return work?"

"Excellent. We'll spend Tuesday going around the campus. I look forward to that, Randy."

Randy called Lisa and told her not to worry about dinner tonight. He just needed her to throw the essentials into his suitcase. Ed's assistant phoned back with the flight information. Randy had just two hours to return home and then drive back across town to the airport.

Randy Munson was riding the waves of his professional dream. He didn't even feel the potholes on Mineral Point Road as he steered the Riviera toward home. He thought of The Plan again.

Should I call Stephen and check on the money? he asked himself aloud. Should I just tell Stephen to keep it and just forget I was even part of this? Only if I take the San Diego job. If I do that, I'll make so much money I won't even worry about the cash from The Plan.

Randy drove right on by his PDQ pay phone. No stop. He didn't have time for bookies. He had a dream job and a dream paycheck to go chase.

41. New Relationships

For a guy in his early thirties, Clark still ate like a 19-year-old. His trips to the grocery store usually produced the same basic foods: frozen chimichangas, tortillas, chicken, barbecue sauce, pasta, Apple Jacks, cheese, milk, and blueberry muffin mix.

But he was on a mission this time as he pushed his cart through the supermarket.

Clark had to cook for a date tonight.

This was such a rare occurrence that he'd taken this Monday night off work and had Rachel Randall fill in. Clark had met a woman named Sheila Hayes over the weekend, not at a meat market bar on a Saturday night, but at Barnes & Noble on Sunday afternoon.

Sheila had walked up with a grin and said, "Aren't you—"

Clark never tired of being recognized in public. They went from there. Sheila impressed Clark with talk of the football game the day before. Clark suggested dinner on Monday, penne pasta with lobster smothered in "a rich clam sauce." Sheila said that sounded fine.

"Excuse me, where would I find clam sauce?" Clark asked a teenage stock boy.

At home with the date minutes away, Clark blasted "Reminiscing" by the Little River Band as he looked at himself in the bathroom mirror, making sure his trademark gelled hair was all in place.

"Friday night, it was late, I was walkin' you home, we got down to the gate, and I was dreaming of the night," he sang along.

He kept a hideous paisley shirt in his closet for occasions such as this. White and dark green, 1993 all the way around. A shirt that he loved having a woman take off. No, he said aloud, go with the nice shirt tonight. Screw that greasy kid stuff. He reached for the Tommy Bahama. Gold rayon. It cost him $110.

He could afford a few extra $110 shirts these days. Clark had only broken one of the $1,000 bills. He'd driven just outside town to the casino on the southeast edge of Madison. The cashier had broken it into hundreds for him. The rest of the big bills sat in a Mason jar at the bottom of his bedroom closet.

Clark updated his music to the next decade in anticipation of Sheila's arrival. LRB was out. Seal was in.

Sheila rang the doorbell two minutes early, just before seven. She said she was hoping to watch the first half of the Chiefs-Raiders Monday night game. What a catch. Clark reminded himself that Carol also liked to watch football at the beginning of their relationship.

"Great, you found it!" Clark said as he accepted her burgundy overcoat.

"Not a problem," Sheila said, and smiled at him. She shook a few snowflakes out of her shoulder-length brown hair. Her 5'10" frame moved gracefully from the entrance to the living room. The curve of her face broadcast a sense of approval as she appraised the bachelor pad. "Smells great in here. You do have the clam sauce. I can tell."

Of course it smells great in here, Clark wanted to say. I'm cooking lobster and bathed in Eternity. A combination women could not resist.

As Seal cried out "Bring It On," Clark performed his master-of-ceremonies role proficiently. He did not overcook the lobster. The expensive pasta tasted like expensive pasta. He even found ten minutes to cook the frozen garlic bread.

"So, what did you think when I approached you yesterday?" Sheila asked.

Clark's face turned red. How do I answer this? Say you appeared as an angel in white? The woman of my dreams? No, too corny. Play it cool.

"Oh, you certainly caught my eye," Clark admitted. "Your smile made me feel at ease." Smooth, buddy, smooth.

They talked about their jobs. In mere minutes, Clark knew that Sheila was 29, had never been married, and worked downtown as a lobbyist for the Taxpayers' Coalition. She'd lived in Madison all her adult life.

"We're essentially a group that wants to fire music teachers in public schools and keep roads from getting fixed," Sheila deadpanned. "Now you haven't been here that long, have you?"

It was Clark's turn for revelation. "I've only been back in Madison six months now," he said. "Before that, I worked in Duluth, Eau Claire, and Grand Junction, Colorado, a little town over by Utah."

"The skiing's pretty good out there, I hear."

Clark was impressed. "Yes, Park City is just two hours west, and Vail and Steamboat Springs are nearby."

"You say 'back in Madison'?"

"Yes, I graduated from Wisconsin State in 1995."

Sheila's blue eyes lit up. "I went to school here, too, but I graduated a couple of years later, in the spring of '98."

She put down her pasta spoon. "So, were you, like, a dance club freak back in the day?"

Clark shifted his eyes from side to side. "Let's just say I enjoyed my share of Long Island iced teas on Thursday nights. Never on Kiddie Night, though."

Sheila pointed her salad fork at Clark. "I thought I might have seen you there once or twice."

Clark lightened the moment. "Well, maybe we should put our money together and buy the place!" The bar had long since changed themes, from a dance club to a live music bar to a country joint to a lounge.

As Clark sipped his white Zinfandel, he wondered if women got any better than this one. She likes sports, she's outgoing, she's funny. It was like those women in the Just For Men hair commercials.

It got even better.

"Hey, the game's about to start," Sheila offered when their plates held only the remains of a fabulous meal. "I hate the Raiders. I don't root against the Raiders as much as I root for them to suffer career-ending injuries." What a lovely cynic.

They snuggled on the couch to the romantic voice of John Madden and Monday Night Football. Clark decided to take this one slow. Sheila just might be a keeper.

"Welcome to San Diego."

Randy Munson heard those welcoming words in the San Diego International Airport. Not from a cab driver or airline pilot, but from a chauffeur named Max. San Diego College had sent a limo and driver. This was another taste of the Big Time, a rare second chance for Randy after he'd blown off the Baylor job years before.

"Raiders winning?" Randy asked the driver.

"Yes, 17-10 late in the third," the driver replied.

Randy walked past one of those airport sports bars. He saw the image of Oakland wide receiver Johnny Leech on the big-screen TV. Leech had gone from a bench warmer at Wisconsin State in the mid-1990s to an NFL starter, under Randy's guidance.

"Mr. Munson, how many bags did you check?" asked the chauffeur.

"None. I carried everything on." Randy said. He was a fanatic about not checking bags, and only brought enough clothes for two days. His black suit hung in a garment bag over his left shoulder.

"Great," Max said. "A man with no time to waste. Here's the plan: I will take you to the Embassy Suites near campus. Your rental car is waiting in the parking lot there. I also have maps, guidebooks, and apartment and home listings for you to use during your stay here."

Randy was astounded. He was a veteran of coaching interviews, but he'd never enjoyed a limo and a rental car without even signing his name to anything. "The car, already taken care of?"

"Signed, sealed, and delivered." Max's cliché was actually true. "We're only about 10 minutes from the hotel. It'll be a quick drive."

As they stepped outside, Randy took in the breezy San Diego evening. The lyrics from a rock song he'd once heard zoomed through his skull.

I just want to see some palm trees. I am going to try to shake away this disease.

All through his flight from Minneapolis to San Diego, walking through the San Diego airport, even now, Randy just wanted The Plan to go away. This monster he'd created was now appearing in the shadows to eat his career whole. What if this ever comes out? I'll get fired, he reminded himself. Jail?

What good would it do now to turn myself in? he wondered as he looked out the window of the stretch Cadillac. The palm trees and stucco condos blew past him. All he could think about was the mess his life had become in the past seven weeks. All because of his endless longing for the mighty dollar.

OK, enough of this crap, let's get practical, Randy thought. He decided that once San Diego College offered him the job and once he'd accepted it, Randy would call Stephen out in Vegas and tell him to keep all of it. Do whatever he wanted with the money. That might be enough to keep him quiet forever.

"We're here, Mr. Munson."

That shook Randy from his introspection.

"Thanks for the lift, Max."

Max pulled up next to a black, late-model Toyota Camry, stopped the limo, and walked around to let Randy out.

"Here's your key for the Camry." Max produced a plastic hotel key. "And your room is 236."

Randy, impressed with the extra step that the school had taken, pulled out a $20 bill.

Max raised his hand.

"No thank you, Mr. Munson. That, too, has been taken care of. Good luck tomorrow, and if you need anything while you're in town, here's my card. Call me."

Either San Diego College must really want me, Randy thought, or their football program is in bad shape.

Randy was not a superstitious man by nature, but he had to have the closer breakfast. The same meal he'd eaten on South Park Street in 1991, hours before landing the job at Wisconsin State.

"I'll have the blueberry pancakes and a toasted English muffin. Cream cheese on the side, please."

It was eight in the morning. The sun peeked through the blinds at Shenanigan's, one of those nondescript hotel restaurants.

Randy wiped his hand with his napkin. Already clammy. He wiped just above his sideburns and over his temples. He loosened his light blue tie. Just slow down, shooter. You'll be all right.

In his first coaching interview back in 1985—for the job of offensive assistant at the University of South Dakota—Randy had brought computer printouts and charts he created on his brand-new Macintosh. The USD brass was so impressed they offered him the job during the interview. The technology had changed, but Randy had not. He had an armful of charts and statistics in his briefcase. He'd also gone to the trouble of writing a 20-page, 14-point plan to turn around San Diego College. He figured this might be his final chance at the big bucks before he was relegated to the underpaid underworld of assistant coaching for the rest of his life.

He polished off the third blueberry pancake, wiped his sweat points one more time, buttoned his shirt, grabbed his briefcase, and left for the Camry and the future.

He parked in a visitor's slot right adjacent to the building marked "WARRIOR ATHLETICS." The space was right next to the athletic director's parking spot. A silver Mercedes 560 sat innocently in the morning sun.

Randy walked through the door to meet his destiny.

"Randy! Great to finally meet you." Ed threw out his right hand. What an imposing man: 6'5", a shade taller than Randy and about 70 pounds heavier. Randy figured Ed for an offensive lineman about 30 years before.

"I'm happy to be here. Thank you for taking great care of everything with the trip."

Ed shrugged. "What can I say? This is stressful enough for you. You shouldn't have to worry about the particulars."

He led Randy into his spacious office, one fit for an athletic director at a major school. Ed did have an ocean view, although Randy had to squint to see it. Still, an ocean view is an ocean view.

The two hit it off immediately. Ed appeared impressed with Randy's preparation for the interview and his vision for the future of San Diego College football.

Twenty minutes after sitting down, Ed dropped the bomb.

"Well, you certainly look like you have quite a plan to get us back to winning the Mountain West. Here's where I'm at.

"I'm the only person who directs the hiring process," Ed went on calmly. "I made that clear when I signed on six years ago. I would be the one to hire and fire. The school has been great with me in that respect. We don't have to meet with any presidents or regents or any crap like that. It is my decision. But as you know, we still have a football coach."

San Diego College was 1-7, and it was generally assumed that the coach, Pat McGinntry, would get fired once the season was over.

"It's just not working out with Pat. That's why you're here. This is a real delicate spot for me. Pat is a local guy and the media loves him. I'll take a beating over this, especially if the damn hacks find out I'm interviewing candidates while he's still coaching."

Ed stood up, left his black leather chair, and walked toward the window.

"You'll notice I didn't have a secretary today. That's because I gave her the day off to keep this from getting out. Writers have been sniffing around for weeks. Names have popped up left and right. I must have absolute confidentiality during this process from you."

"That's not a problem. I understand how touchy these things can get."

"Good. If it comes out before we let Pat go, I'll be forced to deny everything," Ed said. "Pat's attorney and I are in buyout talks right now. We could have an agreement this week. If that's the case, then I'll make my announcement."

Ed returned to his chair.

"Here's why this is so important, Randy. This area is ripe for a good college football team. The Chargers are about to leave town because they didn't get a new stadium. We're fine with sharing the stadium with them until then. That's no problem. We've always had the talent. I believe if you go down the rosters, you'll see more Warriors in the NFL than even Boars."

"That's true, 17 to 12," Randy interrupted.

"So it hasn't been because of a lack of talent, but because of the coaching. Look around today. Drive around town. Why wouldn't a top-level college football player want to spend four years here? You've been recruiting good players to frozen Madison for years. Wouldn't it be easier to bring the best here?"

Randy smiled. "I must confess that you have a point there."

An easy silence sat between the two men. Randy had said all he wanted to. Anything more might only hurt at this point.

"All right, Randy. I'll ask it right out. Are you still interested?"

"Very much so."

"Good, because you're the guy right now for me," Ed said. "Coach Flaherty and I worked together back at Michigan State. Betcha didn't know that."

Randy did know that. Frank hadn't told him, but Randy saw that both men had been lowly assistant coaches at Michigan State in 1986.

"Frank said nothing but great things about you, how your offensive mind was able to take advantage of the situation. I did have some real concerns about a couple of the losses this year, to Northern Illinois and Northwestern."

Randy tried not to look pained.

"Frank took complete blame for those when I asked him. He said he took control of those games and he shouldn't have. Typical Frank." Ed chuckled and looked down at a sheet of paper. "However, he said the wins over Hawaii, Kansas, Indiana, and Minnesota, plus the comeback at Purdue, were nothing short of masterful."

Ed took the talk to a higher level.

"If you're still interested, I'm looking for a three-year deal. No outs or anything. Just work for us for three years. Then we'll each see if we want to continue."

C'mon, Randy was about to explode, what are the damn numbers? This was shaving days off the end of his life with each second. Ed got to the goods.

"First year, 125, then 135, and then 145 for a base salary. Of course, there are perks with being the head coach."

Randy was satisfied. Not pleased, but satisfied. Maybe the bonuses would help out.

"Such as?"

"Well, let's see." Ed returned to the sheet on his desk. "A free sedan from one of the local dealerships. A weekly radio show. One hour on 650 AM for 14 weeks will pay you an extra $11,000. There's also a TV show on Channel 8. It airs Sunday morning. That pays an extra $17,000. That'll push you up to 153."

Randy cracked a small smile. They could still live well on this.

"Oh, but I'm not done." Ed smiled back. "We have a school-wide shoe deal with Converse. It's directly proportional to how many athletes are wearing their shoes, so football gets the most. You'll stand to make another $44,000 next year from Converse just for doing a few ads around town."

"Any performance bonuses?"

"Of course. You know the game too well, Randy. Bonuses, let's see." Ed shuffled sheets on his desk. "A winning season nets you an extra $5,000. A bowl game will be worth an extra $15,000. If you win the Mountain West and land a bid in the Holiday Bowl, that's an extra 10 grand on top of the $20,000. There's lot of potential there. Finally, if San Diego College finishes in the AP Top 10 at the end of any season, that's worth $45,000. Top 5 will get you $80,000."

Randy cracked a smile as Ed kept up his pitch.

"It's a simple idea. Those bonus figures are something, aren't they? Remember, though, we've never finished that high. If we finish in the Top 5, that 80 grand will seem like chicken feed."

Another easy silence. Ed broke it.

"So, what do you think?"

"Is this an offer?" Randy grinned.

"Well, uh, yes. It is an offer. We just have to keep it quiet."

"I assume I'll be able to name my own staff?" Randy asked. All he could think about was paying back John Wilcox for his silence.

"Of course. It's your sandbox. You play in it with who you want."

There. Wilcox would be offensive coordinator.

"I will verbally accept it right here. I'd just like to look over a contract before I fully commit to it."

Ed nodded. "I respect that. As long as you agree to the terms, we'll be all right here. However, I don't want to let the contract get out there because Pat is still our coach."

For the first time all day, Randy was disappointed.

"Oh."

"Look, Randy. Once we get Pat out of the way, we'll move

forward and sign you to this deal. I'm a man of my word. If I put this deal together, it will still exist when I'm in a position to formally offer it. Tell you what, go take that car and drive around the city a little bit. When's your flight back?"

"Tomorrow at 5:30 in the morning."

"OK. Go call your wife, tell her it's 80 degrees here today, tell her what you'll be making next year as the head coach of San Diego College. You do that and I'll handle this end of it. Enjoy the rest of the day. Take in the sun. Go walk on the beach. It'll be good for you."

That put Randy at ease.

"Great. Here's my cell phone number if anything comes up." Randy wrote the number on the back of his business card.

The two men shook hands as Ed showed Randy the way out. Randy glanced at his watch. Not even noon. He pulled the Camry out of the parking lot with his first destination being a quiet place to call his wife.

"Sweetie, guess what?" Randy said.

"What?" Lisa played along.

"They offered me the job!"

"Oh my God!"

The scream warmed Randy's heart. "Want to know what the pay is?"

"Let me guess. 200?"

"About that, after all the bonuses and side deals. So, do you want to move to San Diego?"

"Yes, and we'd better move soon."

Randy felt his heart skip a beat.

"Move soon?"

"We just got the paper. They're saying the NCAA is looking into point-shaving allegations."

Randy felt it skip a few more beats. "Who's involved?"

"It just talks about Tyrone Collins and his agent from Miami."

Lisa read the story verbatim over the phone to her frightened husband.

42. Defiance

Clark Cattoor rolled into WMA-TV at ten that Tuesday morning. Aaron had called him at home at nine to tip him off.

"Clark, man, we've got the smoking gun here," Aaron had said with genuine excitement. "There's a guy who just split from Copperzweig who is spilling all. It will be on the Internet in a few minutes."

Clark had enjoyed a wonderful evening with Sheila. She left his place just after midnight, but not after getting her hair a little messy and her clothes a little wrinkled. Clark took it as slow as he could. At least he tried to.

He wanted to be the hero today at WMA-TV. He knew Lou Proctor would be asking for the world. Yet before he started blowing the trumpets, Clark had to see the story himself on the Internet.

"SOURCE: AGENT HAD COLLINS FIX GAMES." Clark scanned through the piece.

"A former associate of football agent Jerry Copperzweig told the *Dane County Tribune* on Monday night that Wisconsin State wide receiver Tyrone Collins agreed to help throw at least two games this season. Manny Colquist, a former employee of Copperzweig's Miami-based firm, said that Collins was instrumental in the home losses to Northern Illinois and Northwestern. Wisconsin State lost both games and was a heavy favorite going into each."

" 'There's no question that what Collins did was help fix the results in Copperzweig's favor'," said Colquist. " 'There was an understanding that they (Wisconsin State) were not to cover the spread in either game.'

"Collins and Copperzweig had no comment after repeated phone calls."

Clark scanned the story for any mention of Randy Munson. Nothing, not a thing. He doubted their windfall would withstand the scrutiny. Tyrone Collins was the only reason Wisconsin State was even in the games. He had seven catches for 113 yards in the 17-7 loss to Northern Illinois. In the 16-14 defeat to Northwestern, Collins was the only guy on the field doing anything. He'd caught two touchdown passes and blocked a field goal. Hardly a case where a star player was dogging it.

Clark returned to the story and dug in for all of the details.

At that moment, Lou Proctor walked into the sports office.

"Did you see the Trib today?" Lou asked.

"Yes, I'm reading it right now."

"You're close with the writer, right?"

"We've been friends since college." Play dumb, Clark, play dumb. "But I didn't know anything about this."

Lou looked down at Clark with an appraising stare. "OK. We need a comment from Flaherty about this. He won't want to talk, but you tell him that he needs to say something about this. Otherwise, all this loose talk will send him out the door."

Clark said the one thing a sports reporter should never say to Lou Proctor. "Maybe news should handle this. I think I'm too close to it."

"Excuse me?"

Clark wished he could hit a delete button and wipe out the previous four seconds.

"Let me get this straight: You're TOO close to this story? What are you, gambling on the games, too?" Lou asked with his crooked half-smile.

Clark stared blankly into the corner. Did Lou know something? he wondered.

"You sports guys need to remember that you're journalists first,"

Lou snapped. "That's what we pay you for. Not to run your stupid high school softball highlights, but to get after the meat of stories like this. Clark, this is a once-in-a-decade story. You should embrace this."

Randy made sure to cover his tracks in dealing with Stephen Crossland. Sitting in a San Diego parking lot with his left ear on his new favorite pay phone, Randy pressed his luck one more time.

"Stephen, it's Randy."

"Man, I was hoping you'd call today. What the hell is going on down there?"

"So you've heard?" Randy asked.

"Hell, yes, I've heard," Stephen said. "The FBI has already contacted us regarding our book activity for those two games. I saw it. Nothing unusual from here, so we should be OK. I can't say the same for the other shops in town."

"Can we still talk from here? Want to call me back?"

"No, we're fine here, just don't get too specific."

"Uh, fine."

Stephen stunned Randy with his next question.

"So, how's San Diego treating you?" Stephen said, laughing.

"Excuse me?"

"You heard me, how's San Diego?"

No answer from Randy. How did he know?

"You may as well tell me. Our information is better than anything on ESPN."

"OK, well, it was fine," Randy said. "It went well."

"Yeah, the word on the street is that you're the guy."

"That's what I wanted to talk to you about."

"OK."

Randy told Stephen he was tossing all the cash from The Plan away. Had to clean it up.

"Look, with what we've been through, it's getting too hot with this. I don't want the money. Give most of my cut to someone else."

For once, Stephen did not have an answer.

"Stephen, you still there?"

"Uh, yeah. So let me get this straight. You don't want anything?"

"No, nothing. Just gimme a slice of it for someone here who

stayed quiet. Enjoy it and let's break off contact right now. Will you do that for me?"

"Yeah, I can do that," Stephen said. "I don't anticipate anything will come of it because it was overseas action. The trail ends with me. If asked, I put the action on without any inside knowledge. We never spoke. I never knew you. So, you want me to mail the package to this person or do you want to do it?"

Randy sensed an opening. "Would you do that?"

"Sure. It would probably keep you in the clear. Who is it?"

"John Wilcox. Got a pen? Here's his address."

Randy arrived back in Madison just in time to watch Frank's latest press conference with Lisa.

"Let me say first that the rumors of me leaving as head coach at Wisconsin State are not true," Frank said on the screen. He knew this would wind up on ESPN, so he was going to make it good. "That is the rampant speculation in the, uh, media circles, and it is bogus. It is false. I plan to stay here through the end of my contract and, hopefully, longer.

"I have and have had no prior knowledge of the allegations of point-shaving and agent payments. But I do know this. Agents like Jerry Copperzweig are rogues and parasites to the spirit of college football—"

"It sounds like he's practiced in the mirror," said Lisa.

"I'm sure he has. This is too good to be off the cuff."

A newspaper photographer lit the room with strobe flashes.

"—and many kids from disadvantaged backgrounds fall prey to these agents. These people are ruining college football. They talk to these players and convince them that they're NFL material. Let me also say this: I'm not as worried about whether Tyrone Collins took the money or not as I am worried about Tyrone Collins, the person. For three years, that kid gave so much of his heart to this school, so much of his time to you guys, and now to have his name thrown around like he's a criminal breaks my heart. I refuse to believe he did this."

Frank paused for dramatic effect.

"Look at the numbers of the two games in question," he said, looking directly into the TV cameras. "Against Northern Illinois and Northwestern, Tyrone Collins was the ONLY reason we even had a shot."

Frank turned toward the newspaper writers.

"I'll open this up to questions, but I may not be able to answer many of them."

Aaron Schutz fired first.

"Frank, have you been asked to resign?"

Frank launched two green-eyed lasers through the back of Aaron's head.

"Aaron, I don't even want to dignify that with a response. Even if I wanted to, I couldn't answer that question."

In the comfort of home, Lisa turned to Randy. "Do you think Karen asked him to quit?"

Randy shrugged. "I wouldn't be surprised. She's been looking for a reason to get rid of us and hire that clown from South Carolina for two years. I guess I'm surprised Frank is still coaching after the payments surfaced."

Frank handled the reporters' questions for eight more minutes, which seemed to last an hour to Randy on his couch, and left the press conference with another delicious sound bite for the media.

"Look, this has been my dream job since the day it opened. For five years, I've smiled every day that I drive to work, even today. I won't go away easily. If they want to get rid of me, they'll have to tie me up, strap sandbags to my feet, and throw me off the docks into Lake Monona."

He was openly challenging Karen Strassel.

Frank left the room, and Jim Tillman made an announcement.

"Coach Flaherty has decided to close practice to the media until further notice. Thank you for your cooperation."

Randy made sure to greet his boss two hours later at the start of practice.

"Frank, good to see you. I caught the press conference earlier today."

Frank managed a smile. "So this is what happens when I allow the damn writers and the cameras in? All they want to do is screw me."

"Yeah, they bite us far too often," Randy said. "Anyway, I'm still in a holding pattern in San Diego. Ed said the job is mine, but I have to wait until they send Pat on his way. Should I trust him? I'm getting nervous."

The players trickled out into The Bubble to begin stretching.

"I don't think he would screw you. He has a family, too."

"Good."

Frank looked Randy in the eye. Something was bothering him.

"Randy, I haven't talked with anyone about this yet, but after the press conference today, Karen and I sat down."

"Yes?"

"She asked me if I thought I was the right coach for the job. I told her I thought so. She didn't say anything." Frank turned from the ground to the door as his players filed in. "This could get real ugly over the next two weeks, especially if we lose Saturday. If we lose, I think they'll make a change right after the game. In other words, get yourself signed in to San Diego as soon as possible."

43. Ohio State

Sam Cattanach was trying to keep his roommate from throwing it all away. Jake Steffon had spent the two hours between the press conference and football practice making phone calls and sending e-mails.

In the span of 90 minutes, Jake had landed verbal scholarship offers from four schools in the Midwest. Minnesota-Duluth offered a half-scholarship for the following season. Northern Iowa, Western Illinois, and Illinois State also offered scholarships, sight unseen. The head coaches for those programs kept a special eye on the Big Ten schools. Players unhappy with their situations were often looking at these smaller programs. By transferring to those schools, a player could suit up right away and not have to sit out a year.

During the season, Jake had enjoyed the benefits of being a football player along with the frustrations. He could waltz into any bar on campus and have guys buy him drinks and have women flash an eyelash in his direction.

Yet every Thursday, Friday, and Saturday evening, every freshman with a couple of beers flowing through his bloodstream seemed to feel a need to call Wisconsin State's placekicker and give him a piece of his mind.

The Northwestern loss was devastating not only for Jake but also for his phone line. After 20 hostile calls, he simply turned off the ringer. His answering machine took 75 messages that night, all of them filled with angry words except for one from his mother.

As Frank Flaherty put on a brave face on television, Jake still stung from that one phone call before the Northwestern game. Maybe it was a stupid Northwestern fan calling him up. Maybe it was another drunk college student. Maybe it really was a gambler out to rattle him. Now he wondered if he had a connection to the point-shaving allegations, even on a subconscious level.

"I've had it here," Jake simply said to Sam. "Between all the crap and Wilcox, I've had it here."

"Don't do it, Jake. Do you really want to spend three years at any of those cow schools?"

"I don't know. It's not everything it's cracked up to be. I'm just sick of all the damn pressure, man. It's really getting to me."

Sam grabbed Jake's arm.

"Look, man, we're living like kings here. You're at a Big Ten school. Even if you don't go to the NFL, you'll still get a good degree. Next year you'll be on scholarship. That's 12 grand right there your parents won't have to fork over. Don't throw it all away."

Sam used the one thing he knew would get Jake back in good spirits.

"Let's go kick some footballs today. You have to work tonight, right?"

"Yeah, till 11."

"OK. When you get home, you pick the bar, we'll get blasted, my treat. You'll feel better."

Randy Munson was in no mood to feel better. As he scanned the players stretching at practice, he rehashed just how his life had disintegrated in 72 hours. He masked the restlessness through work.

"There you go, Craig! Make Wilson your go-to guy. Work with his patterns. His timing," Randy said to his quarterback.

Across the turf, John Wilcox was cracking the whip on Jake.

"C'mon, Jake, you're only as good as your last kick," he snapped after Jake sailed a knuckleball well off the mark. "Gotta focus. Head down, leg up."

Sam walked up to Jake out of earshot of their taskmaster.

"Remember. Drinks. On me. Tonight. Just get through practice."

A simple premise, one that was like spinach to Popeye. Jake regained the pep in his step and punched through enough solid kicks to get Wilcox off his back. He tapped Sam on the helmet after another perfect kick.

"Yeah, thanks. Make mine a double."

The November game with Ohio State marked the start of the Wisconsin winter.

Snow started dropping out of the gray sky at noon. Fresh off the team bus from the hotel, Jake Steffon and Sam Cattanach walked through the tailgaters around Mendota Stadium. The Ohio State-Wisconsin State game was a 2:30 start to accommodate the networks. Ohio State marched in ranked #4 in the country.

"I feel the magic, man, I just FEEL IT!" Jake shouted to the skies.

"You know what this is like? The '94 game," Sam remembered.

Jake's eyes lit up. "You are SO right on that." They'd been just 10 that day, when Wisconsin State knocked out Ohio State in the Madison snow on national television. The Boars then went on to their first Rose Bowl.

Aaron Schultz and Clark Cattoor loaded up on the free brats and hot dogs far above Mendota Stadium's artificial turf. Clark had had a decent week, all things considered. He'd survived the week of chasing the point-shaving allegations in his own newsroom. Sheila had agreed to meet up with him after the game at the Blue Moon for drinks and darts. He'd decided to keep the remainder of his gambling loot in the Caribbean until this point-shaving stuff blew over.

"What a freakin' week," Aaron observed, pouring relish onto his bratwurst.

"Practice was closed to you guys also, right?" Clark asked.

"Yup. None of us from Wednesday on. It'll be interesting to see if Flaherty plays this 'us-against-the-world' bit afterward."

"Hell, I'd be surprised if they stayed within three touchdowns today."

"Oh, I'm not sure about that. I'd be shocked if the Boars lose today."

"Really?"

"Yeah, this is a coach's dream." Aaron amended his comment. "Make that an about-to-get-canned coach's dream. If he wins this, he can essentially throw the middle finger at the school and all of us. Flaherty will have them ready."

The snowflakes continued to fall from the heavens. In just two hours, the field turned from bright green to the color of wintergreen gum.

The snow flew around Randy as he watched his boss deliver his most impassioned pregame speech in four years at Madison.

"We've been through hell this week, absolute hell!" Frank screamed at his players. "Now you have the chance to tell all the naysayers to go to hell!"

He told the players that a loss would probably mean he and his staff would get fired the next day.

"But don't play this game for us," Frank warned. "Play it for yourselves. A new coach will bring in new players. You guys who are freshmen, sophomores, juniors, play your hearts out today." Frank made eye contact with each player. "If we're not going to be with you next year, every man in this room owes it to himself not to give anything less than everything today."

Randy pulled Craig Zellnoff aside before the game and told the quarterback he believed Craig could make his mark with a victory against Ohio State. And Craig oozed confidence on the opening drive, leading Wisconsin State on a 66-yard odyssey. He scrambled, hit receivers, called running plays when the defense allowed. He was finally acting like a mature quarterback. Craig had nothing to lose at this point, his career nothing more than a prolonged display of mediocrity.

The drive stalled at the Ohio State 12.

"FIELD GOAL TEAM! FIELD GOAL TEAM!" John Wilcox yelled. Jake and Sam trotted onto the field.

"Damn snow," Jake said to his holder.

"Just watch my fingers, watch the fingers."

Snap down. Ball up. Steffon booted the field goal through for a 3-0 Wisconsin State lead.

"Maybe they won't roll over." Clark said from above.

Randy cajoled his quarterback on the sidelines. "C'mon, Craig, that drive was perfect until the end. Gotta stay patient back there. Don't throw it away until the last possible second. You're sharp out there. Stay out on the edge." Randy always liked his quarterbacks to be on that edge, not content and relaxed.

A roar came from the crowd. Randy whipped around to see what had happened. Ohio State fumbled and linebacker Jackson Wheeler fell on it for Wisconsin State.

"Your show, baby, your show." Randy patted Craig on the helmet, and raised his index and pinkie fingers to Craig's face mask. "On the edge."

Craig responded with a 46-yard touchdown strike to Laverneus Wilson on the very next play. 10-0 Wisconsin State.

The Mendota Stadium crowd hadn't been this loud since the last Rose Bowl season. That night, Randy had thought Wisconsin State would never slip from its lofty perch.

Frank walked over to Randy.

"They'd be nuts not to hire you in San Diego if we pull this off!" he yelled.

Randy slapped Frank on the shoulder. "Don't jinx it, man," he yelled over the crowd.

Wisconsin State's defense suffocated the Ohio State attack. Defensive lineman Jack Thompson forced two fumbles and bagged three sacks. ABC's Brent Musberger was ready to crown him the next Reggie White after his performance.

Jake patrolled the sidelines. If nothing else, he was going to treat this game like a national audition, in case anyone was looking for a kicker. Sam's open tab on Wednesday night had soothed his anguish over his future for a few hours, but he still had no intention of returning. Jake had even told his mother that he was making calls and looking to leave.

"FIELD GOAL TEAM!" John Wilcox called out right before the half.

Six seconds left. Ball on the 34. That's a 51-yarder. Jake could hardly boot those in practice.

Sam walked out to kneel at his spot on the 41. "Make this and you can just walk to the NFL right now, Steffon! Screw those pansy-ass schools you're looking at."

Jake felt his blood boil at Sam's last comment. If Sam was sharp on anything, it was playing with Jake's mind. The kicker was so ticked after that he could not help but find The Zone, as athletes often describe that high level of concentration. He looked north to the two yellow sticks in the air 51 yards away. The snowflakes distracted his vision.

"HUT!" Sam barked out.

Two steps and one kick later, Jake smashed the ball into the snowy sky.

"YOU GOT IT, BABY!" Sam yelled. Kickers and punters could often tell just by the sound on impact whether a kick would have the distance.

"Come back, come back." Jake walked to the right towards the Ohio State sideline. Jake squinted and lost track of the ball. "Where is it? Where is it?"

The north end zone fans told Jake through their sheer volume that the ball had traveled at least 55 yards and was straight enough.

John Wilcox sprinted over from the sidelines and nearly tackled his placekicker into the turf.

13-0 Wisconsin State at the half. ABC's Musberger unleashed a rich monologue filled with hyperbole for the Midwest viewing audience.

"And there goes Frank Flaherty, the polarizing symbol of Wisconsin State football," Musberger intoned from the booth. "As Flaherty runs off the field, he is, essentially, running away from the vultures calling for his head. In the last three weeks, his All-American receiver left, and he continues to fight off allegations of wrongdoing. Well, Wisconsin State is doing plenty right today. They lead fourth-ranked Ohio State 13-0 at halftime. We'll send it back to the halftime studios in New York City right after this…."

"Unbelievable," muttered Clark.

"Well, look at it this way," said Aaron. "Maybe Ohio State has someone throwing the game."

"Ah, they'll find a way to screw it up," Clark retorted as only a media cynic could.

Frank was possessed in the locker room. Trying to hold onto a million-dollar-a-year job brings out the fight in any man.

"Men, don't lose the gleam! DON'T LOSE THE GLEAM! We have this team right where we want them! They're sleeping out there while you're making plays."

Frank walked over and pointed into Craig Zellnoff's chest.

"You made three plays this half. Don't be happy with that. It's not over yet."

Jake had seen this tango before from his coach. He and Sam didn't have to stay as intense as the position players. Jake just had to do his job three or four times each game. He glanced back and accidentally made eye contact with Frank.

Frank zeroed in.

"Jake, nice kick there. But ARE YOU READY IF THE GAME COMES DOWN TO YOU?" A horrible display of non-confidence by the head coach. Not even John Wilcox would do that to Jake.

Jake smirked and gave his coach a sarcastic answer. "Yes. Bring it on!"

"All right, then. I got faith in you if it gets to that point. In fact, all of us do. You, just like every man in this room, have proven that you are a Big Ten-caliber football player. We all are."

For once, Clark was right. This game was not over. Ohio State backup quarterback Shea Hanson led the second half opening drive for a touchdown to pull the Buckeyes to 13-7.

"Here comes the shitstorm," Clark said to Aaron.

On the sidelines, Randy finally broke out the speech that he'd saved all year for Craig Zellnoff. Randy whipped off his sunglasses and looked his quarterback in the eye.

"Craig! Hey, listen to me! Forget about that," Randy said. "We've worked tirelessly for four years to turn you from the best quarterback in freaking Naperville into the best in the Big Ten. This is YOUR final chance to prove it. Win here. Win today. You'll be a hero forever. Be confident out there. TRUST OUR PLAYS. We know what we're doing. Think tall. You'll play tall."

Craig responded by staying sharp on his passes and his handoffs.

He fired three completions to Laverneus Wilson and made a short shovel pass to Jason Brunson to bring the drive inside the Ohio State 20. Teddy Hammersley barreled down on the next play to the 7.

Randy watched the clock tick down. 3:55. 3:54. 3:53. This third quarter was taking forever. "Twins Right Sprint Right X Snag!" He yelled to Craig.

"This is where the magic happens! This is where the magic happens!" Randy said over his headset to the coaches upstairs.

Craig nearly slid on the snowy turf in the south end after three steps. He regained his composure and was searching for Wilson in the end zone. Ohio State lineman Darrell Lonsdale was creeping up behind Craig for a sack. Randy was in shock as Cory Larkman left his assigned defender and planted his #63 into the side of the pursuing Lonsdale. The quarterback took the extra two seconds to throw a rope toward the near sideline and into the arms of Laverneus Wilson.

Touchdown Wisconsin State, 19-7.

"EXTRA POINT! EXTRA POINT!" Frank called out.

Jake tossed off his blue WSU windbreaker and followed Sam into the snow.

Snap down, ball up. His aim deceived him.

"OH SHIT." Jake sliced it. "Come back. Come back. Come back."

Jake felt the weight of 64,622 people come down on him in the 1.6 seconds it took for the ball to leave his right foot, hit the right upright, and bounce into the south end zone. He hadn't missed an extra point in a game in years. Not since his junior year at Fall Creek.

"You SUCK, Steffon!" some guy with a sideline pass yelled. The boos rained down with more force than the snowflakes.

"Crap," Frank said to Randy. "These goddamn kickers do nothing but cost me money and jobs!"

John Wilcox just stared at his kicker. John didn't have to say anything. All placekickers are humiliated when they botch an extra point.

"We'll hang on, Frank. He'll be ready next time," reassured Randy. He peeked at his watch. 5:13. These ABC games take forever. It was daylight saving time until later that night so the skies were still a touch gray, not completely black.

Opaque was the apt term for the sky when Ohio State running back Eddie Hamilton scored a touchdown in the south end zone. His touchdown with 6:41 left in the fourth quarter brought Ohio State to within five points at 19-14.

"Damn kickers," Clark muttered to Aaron in the press box.

"Totally," Aaron chimed in. "They'll play like chickens on this next drive."

Wisconsin State did as Aaron said. Three straight running plays. Three straight stops.

"PUNT TEAM!"

"Your show, man. Boot the hell out of it. Save my ass," Jake said to Sam on the sidelines.

Randy was now pacing like a head coach. He glanced at the clock as frequently as a guy who had spotted a cleavage peek. 4:37, 4:36, 4:35.

Sam had the chance to keep his roommate from becoming the goat. An Ohio State touchdown would give them the lead. Rarely had Sam felt the pressure of just getting a punt off without it getting blocked.

Jake would soon have company in the goat's circle.

"They're coming!" Clark said as he watched the play below. Three Ohio State players broke toward Sam and had a free shot at him. One player blocked the kick while the another drove Sam into the turf. The third Buckeye, Stanley Hoffland, picked up the bouncing football at the Wisconsin State 8 and breezed in for the touchdown. 20-19 Ohio State, with 4:21 left in the fourth quarter.

All Sam could do was listen to the horror from the crowd. He still had one Buckeye sitting on his back, but he knew. He knew.

"Un-be-freakin'-lievable," Aaron muttered.

"Wasn't the punter's fault. He was taking on more guys than Elizabeth Taylor," Clark tried to joke.

Aaron ignored him. "And THAT's what they deserve for playing like chickens." The crowd had grown so quiet that the TV volume was audible again in the press box. A stop on a two-point conversion attempt lifted the spirits of the crowd but not the momentum.

"Like Rasputin, these Ohio State Buckeyes WON'T GO AWAY," ABC's Musberger said. "You can shoot them, bury them, poison them, and toss them in the river, but they won't roll over and die! The Buckeyes lead in Madison 20-19."

Aaron laughed at that historical reference.

"Hell, Cattoor, why don't you get his job?"

Randy had thought 20 points would be enough to win it at halftime, but now he resorted to a more primal kind of motivation for Craig Zellnoff.

"All right, we're done calling plays like pussies," he said to Craig. "They know we're desperate, but that doesn't mean you need to get all reckless out there."

This was the drive. Wisconsin State had all three time-outs left, but this was their last chance. Frank and his coaches all knew it.

Laverneus Wilson returned the kickoff to the Wisconsin State 22. 1st-and-10. Jason Brunson ran for five yards. Randy wasn't going to get his team stuck in 2nd-and-10. Craig looked to pass to tight end Mark Rindo, but fired a floater well over his head.

"Damn third down already!" Frank called out.

"Left Zip 22 Draw." Randy motioned to his quarterback.

The boys from Wausau, Cory Larkman and Bob Verly, knew this was called for them. Both Cory and Bob planted their helmets in the charging linebackers, allowing Brunson to run for 11 yards and a first down.

The clock ticked away. 3:42...3:41...3:40. Randy was patient on his headset. He called a 20-yard pass to Wilson over the middle but Craig caught a case of happy feet. He took off up the middle on his slow, bandaged feet and slid on the edge of the blue STATE at midfield. 1st-and-10 from the Wisconsin State 46. With his number 12 dangling off the back of his navy jersey, Craig got up and threw his right arm out with an open hand to signal "first down."

Pacing the sidelines, Jake had one final shot at redemption. He needed to make this kick more than anyone else in the stadium needed the win. It's acceptable to miss one game-winning kick, but if you miss two in a row, then you get the label of a choker. The nation was watching. Miss this and he'd better get a good degree in three years. The NFL does not court chokers.

John Wilcox strolled over to Jake.

"Look. We gotta talk you up," John said. "You're still walking around here like you lost your best friend. CUT IT OUT."

Jake continued to look at the ground while he kicked into a net behind the benches. Sam retrieved the balls and placed them for kicking.

John had had enough.

"Dammit, look at me when I talk to you, Steffon!"

Jake's head snapped to the right.

"Look, I've helped send kickers to the next level. That's what you want, right?"

"Uh-huh," said Jake.

"You have great form," John said. "Just picture the ball sailing through. Each kick. Two steps, half-step, swing it like a golf club. You know you short-kicked that extra point."

"I know."

"All I'm saying is follow through when it's your turn out there. You're too good a kicker not to make it as long as you do that." John slapped Jake's helmet and walked away.

"WILCOX!" Frank called. John walked briskly to Frank, who was hounding Randy with each call.

"Is Steffon ready or do we need a touchdown?" Frank demanded.

John hesitated and looked back at Jake, who was working to regain his form. "Yeah, he'll be ready. Just try to get inside the 20."

Craig Zellnoff ran an option play on his slow feet inside the Ohio State 33-yard line. Randy had the offense bleed out the clock. 1:28…1:27…1:26. Screams erupted from the crowd as they thought the coaches had forgotten that time was running out.

Randy was still the master of the two-minute drill, the last-second victory.

"Let it bleed. We've got our time-outs."

Jake's legs were toasty as he finished off another kick. Sam tried to lighten the mood.

"We got a game to watch, hoss," Sam said nonchalantly. They ran to the sidelines. Craig hit Wilson for a completion to the Ohio State 6 with just :38 left.

"Let's punch it in!" Frank said. "Punch it in! No kickers if we don't need 'em!"

Jason Brunson ran toward the south end zone behind Bob Verly
before falling at the 2.

"Run it down! Down to 10 seconds!" Ohio State could only
watch. They'd burned their time-outs earlier in the drive. Craig
motioned for a time-out with nine seconds left in the game. This was
a 19-yard field goal, a chip shot.

"We gotta send the field goal team out there," Randy said to
Frank.

"PUNCH IT IN! ONE MORE SHOT!" Frank said.

"OK. One more crack. Time-out when the play is over," Randy
allowed.

Randy called for a simple handoff to Teddy Hammersley. He had
the best hands of the running backs and was a tank to tackle.

"Hammer! Just follow Verly. He's your point man."

The ball never made it to Teddy Hammersley.

The weight of the situation finally caught Craig. The ball
squirted out of his hands and onto the turf.

"Oh, my, God," Clark said.

"BALL! BALL!" players on both sides cried.

"SHIT!" Randy Munson said.

Cory Larkman was the beneficiary of incompetence. He had
accidentally missed his block, resulting in the clobbering of a
quarterback. As Craig Zellnoff lay looking at the stars, Larkman was
free to fall on a football seven feet away. His missed block saved the
Boars.

"TIME-OUT! TIME-OUT! TIME-OUT!" Larkman yelled at
the referees. Wisconsin State had the ball on the Ohio State 8 and
three seconds were on the clock.

"FIELD GOAL TEAM! FIELD GOAL TEAM!" Frank yelled.

Jake ran onto the field to meet his destiny. For years, he'd
dreamed of a last-second kick to lift Wisconsin State to victory. He'd
blown that dream with his miss against Northwestern. Since that day,
he had thought of nothing but getting back to that position.

"Our chance. Our night. Just follow through," Sam encouraged
from his knees.

Jake said nothing. He was already in The Zone.

The Wisconsin State players fell to their knees on the sidelines.

"The home team...praying to a higher power against bad snaps and missed kicks," Musberger said to the nation.

"HUT!"

The bad snap deity raised his ugly head. Center Monte Holloway sent a snowy grounder to his holder. Sam plucked the football off the turf, planted it down on his spot. He didn't even have time to spin the laces the way Jake preferred.

Jake booted his destiny and looked up right away.

"Oh SHIT!" Jake said. "Hooked it!"

Sam could not look up. The crowd would tell him whether the kick was good or not. Jake's "hooked it" were the last words he could make out. Jake did hook it, but not enough to float wide left. The ball would have missed from 27 yards, but it was good from 25.

Wisconsin State 22, Ohio State 20.

Sam jumped up and lifted Jake into the sky. John Wilcox was the next person to hug the kicker.

"WE DID IT! WE FREAKIN' DID IT!" Frank said as he hugged Randy before running out to midfield to shake hands with the Ohio State coaches.

As the players burst off the sidelines into their assembled riot on the field, thousands of students jumped over the three-foot fence in the north end zone. They all were after #17. Jake would get a ride off the field. The trombone players from the rowdy Boars band marched onto the turf to party with the players and students.

Randy trailed behind Frank as the head coach soaked in the adulation of the fans. Frank gave the Nixon "V" signs with both hands as he walked under the tunnel, toward the locker room and, eventually, the same journalists who'd left his team for dead earlier in the week.

Randy stopped halfway up the ramp and turned around. The vision of celebrating players and students still brought goose bumps. This was the way it was supposed to be at Wisconsin State. All he could think about was San Diego College. Damn, they better call after this.

As usual, Jim Tillman was the first team representative in the media interview room.

"Um, Coach Flaherty will be here in a minute to answer your questions," Tillman said, grinning. "We would bring out Jake Steffon but I believe he's still doing the chicken dance on the field. We'll try to get him into the players' media room as soon as possible. Thank you."

Frank strutted in seconds later. He walked like a man about to tell his detractors where they could stick their microphones.

"Normally, I like to open with a statement," Frank gleamed. "Today, I'll answer all the questions you want. Bring it on!" Frank looked over the assembled writers. "Tell you what, Aaron Schutz."

Aaron looked up from his notepad.

"Yeah, Aaron, you get the first question today, or do you not have one after that performance?"

Aaron didn't blink an eye.

"Frank, did this win save your job?" Aaron asked.

It was Frank's turn to look down. He shook his head while looking at the various television and radio microphones from across the state.

"Ya know, I said I would answer all of the questions. I lied. I won't answer that one. Next question."

One of Jim Tillman's interns found Jake dancing the polka, in full uniform, helmet in hand, with a couple of girls after the game.

"The media needs you, Jake!"

"Can't it wait until after the song?"

Such was life for the kicker from Fall Creek. Jake had dreamed of this moment for years, and it did not disappoint. So rare in life is a second chance, and Jake made the most of his.

The band ended its impromptu concert. Jake began to walk off the field.

"Do I have to shower or can I just go like this?" Jake asked the staffer.

"That's up to you, Jake."

Jake declined to shower. He hadn't sweated through his padding during a single game this year. The snowy skies kept him from perspiring today, even with the stress at the end.

Jake walked through the tunnel and through the crowd in the

northeast corner of Mendota Stadium. The locker room was across a service drive inside the WSU Bubble, about 30 feet away and one floor below the stadium concourse.

Fans recognized him and began yelling his name and applauding like he was one of the original Mercury astronauts in *The Right Stuff*.

Jake waved to the crowd as if he were the Pope.

"JAKE STEFFON!" Jim Tillman yelled into the players' media room.

Jake walked in with his shoulder pads off but with his blue #17 jersey still on. Cameras from La Crosse to Green Bay, from Milwaukee to Wausau, all jostled closer to the placekicker. Cameramen stood on top of chairs to get a clear shot of his head. Jake had never seen anything like this. The newspaper and radio writers stretched their arms out.

"Talk about the winning kick," said one of the Wausau reporters.

"Man, I was terrified," Jake admitted. "But at least I've been here before. Last time out, I didn't do so hot. I knew I wouldn't miss it if I got another shot at it."

"The extra point had to be devastating," came another probing question from a television reporter.

"Yeah, that was the first time I missed one of those in a game in years. I mean, that's a kicker's worst nightmare."

Skip Stevens fired next.

"Jake, from the sidelines we saw Sam talking to you before the kick. Care to tell us what he said?"

Jake smiled and lied. "Yeah, Sam just told me not to get my kick blocked like his was. If we would have lost, Sam would have run up the stairs to the top of Mendota Stadium and jumped off head first."

The journalists burst out laughing. Jake had delivered the line perfectly. He wanted to zing his roommate for days to come on the airwaves.

Once the media jackals were fat and happy from their sound bites, Frank addressed his team in the locker room. After 60 minutes against Ohio State, most of the players had no energy to even lift off their shoulder pads. It wasn't even 6:30, but most of the Boars were about ready for bed.

Frank knew the temptations of a night like this.

"Gentlemen, I have not had a victory like this in my years here," Frank said, his hat dripping slowly from a combination of melted snow and sweat. "None of you have enjoyed a win like this one. I know you older guys are going to go out on the town tonight and walk around like heroes. Parade up and down State Street. That's fine. You all deserve to. Just please, PLEASE, use some common sense out there."

At the start of each season, Frank posted the coaches' home and cell phone numbers in each player's locker for just an evening like tonight.

"All the coaches will be either at home or have our cell phones on tonight," Frank said. "If ANY of you need a ride or just need to get out of a bad situation, call your position coach first. If you can't reach him, call me. I'll get you. Take the sheet inside your lockers with you tonight. If there's one thing we don't need, it's more bad news in the paper. Are we crystal clear?"

A chorus of low-key "Yeahs" filled the room.

"Zellnoff, this means no throwing anyone through windows tonight, right?"

Craig shrugged and chuckled. "Uh, no, coach. Wouldn't dream of it."

Jake and Sam opened the door to the WSU Bubble to the cheers of the remaining fans outside. Saturday's hero would have to walk through the snow to his apartment, alongside his roommate. Both had been goats an hour before, but now Jake was a big shot, and Sam's blocked punt was all but forgotten.

The question lingered in the air between the two men for about 500 feet before Sam shaped the words.

"So, when are we going out?"

44. Nothing Good Happens After Midnight

The kickers arrived at their apartment just before seven.

Since the start of the season in August, the Saturday messages had become a source of entertainment. Hammered fans and concerned friends and the kickers' parents all exercised their First Amendment rights.

Not that Jake and Sam necessarily discouraged it. Every caller was greeted with the recorded "You've reached Jake and Sam. We're out kicking balls right now. Please leave us a message."

"Holy crap!" Sam said at the blinking machine. "36 messages."

"Oh, this ought to be good," Jake said. He grabbed two beers, a jar of peanuts, and a bag of Sun Chips and sat down on the couch. Jake flipped on ESPN2 to catch the start of the Illinois at Minnesota game.

The answering machine blared out its inventory.

"Message 1. Received at 1:19 P.M.," an automated female voice said before playing the message. " 'Hey, Steffon, you SUCK! You're gonna choke today.' "

That was generally the theme before each game. A few exceptions were in the mix.

"Message 7. Received at 2:33 P.M. 'Hey Sam, it's Mom. Just wanted to let you guys know we're all watching and we're thinking about you. Love you, bye.'" Sam's mom always called at the opening kickoff.

"Message 12. Received at 4:58 P.M. 'Steffon! I can't believe you just missed that extra point, bitch!'" Click. Jake received six calls over the next nine minutes berating his failed extra point.

The machine was still going through its oratory at 7:20.

"Message 20. Received at 5:19 P.M. 'I'll be damned. It's bad enough to have a shitty kicker in this state, but a damn punter who gets his kick blocked? BOTH OF YOU SUCK! You'd better watch yourselves tonight if we lose!'" Click.

"Jake, was that or was that not my fault?" Sam said as he sipped a Killian's Red. "I mean, they had three guys flyin' at me!"

"Not your fault," Jake said, eyes glued to the television.

A total of eight phone calls came in from angry fans after the blocked punt.

"Message 26. Received at 5:37 P.M. 'Oh shit, just what we need. Jake Steffon lining up for a game-winning field goal. Just shoot us all now. You'd better not miss, bitch!'"

"Is it time we sprung for Caller ID?" Jake asked sarcastically as he finished his beer bottle.

"Think so, Jake, think so. Can you get me another?"

Suddenly, the tide turned on the answering machine.

"Message 27. Received at 5:38 P.M. 'You did it! Jake, this is Coach Stammers. All of us back in Fall Creek are proud of you. Bravo! Hang in there. No need to call me back, just wanted to say great job! Take care."

Ten messages congratulated Jake on the winning kick, and one acknowledged that the missed punt was not Sam's fault. In a disturbing way, the answering machine replayed their respective days better than any television broadcast.

Jake and Sam stuck around the apartment through the end of the late game. Since Illinois was the next opponent, Jake taped all the punts and field goals to scout out the coverage.

The chatter turned from the Illinois game to how drunk they

were going to get to whether this would be an easy night to score.

"Hell, if I don't hook up with Miss America tonight, I may as well turn gay," Jake said at one point.

"I'm not even going to dignify that with a comment," Sam retorted.

If there was ever a night where Jake felt he could walk on water, this would be it.

Illinois polished off the Gophers by 9:30, and the kickers were getting ready for what Saturday night had in store. "No driving tonight," Jake said smartly. "We'll take a cab down to Horsepuckey's and go from there."

"You buyin' again, just like in Hawaii?" Sam asked as he got out of the shower.

"Yeah, what the hell? It's not every night you are the BMOC."

Jake and Sam arrived at Horsepuckey's, a bar frequented by wealthy East Coasters and assorted campus pretty boys.

The bouncer recognized Jake and waved them in. Horsepuckey's was packed as people moved very, very slowly from the tables to the pool tables to the bar. "Shakedown Street" blared on the speakers.

"Seven-and-7 and a whiskey sour," Jake said to the bartender.

The bartender shook his head and extended his hand. "This one's on the house. Nice job out there today."

Jake took the gratis drinks, murmured a thank you, left two dollars on the oak bar, and returned to Sam. He had to lean against a wooden post. Fame was his tonight, but not enough to free up a booth.

"The drinks are free," Jake yelled to Sam over the strains of "Heart of Glass." "It's good to be king."

"So would this happen at Western Illinois?" Sam asked. He had a point. "You really should knock off this crap about transferring."

"What if I'd missed?" Jake yelled back.

"No shit. You almost did!" The kickers toasted themselves on Jake's goat-to-greatness status in Madison that night.

The campus bars were wall-to-wall with football fans whose drunkenness clearly surpassed their happiness over the victory. After another round of drinks, free of course, Jake and Sam left Horsepuckey's and wandered west on State Street, away from the

Capitol and closer to the reckless watering holes the underage favor. They ducked into the traditional bars on State Street. Football players usually assembled at the Red Herring at 12:30 after a home victory. Jake didn't want to miss this testosterone-filled ice cream social.

A gigantic bouncer saw the kickers approach the red doors at the Herring.

"Welcome, guys. Enjoy," he said sarcastically.

"STEFFON!" Cory Larkman yelled near the door. "STEFFON IN THE HOUSE!"

In unison, three dozen football players, their ladies for the evening, and far too many fans for the fire marshal to allow turned and saluted Jake. Sam was a mere hanger-on today.

Craig Zellnoff sucked the final drops of what appeared to be a gin and juice. He hugged Jake.

"Great kick, man, we are gods tonight!" said the golden-haired Zellnoff. For four years, he'd been known as the underachieving quarterback whose best pass was throwing that poor drunk through a window. "GIVE THIS MAN A SCHOLARSHIP!"

Jake was so tipsy by this point that the faces were a little fuzzy around the edges, their words fading in and out of comprehension.

"What'll you have, kicker?" asked defensive tackle Sean Griffin.

"Ah, hell, I dunno. Anything with liquor in it," said Jake. He could barely stand up.

"Uh, Sean, I'll have a Foster's, please."

"Who asked you, punter? You nearly screwed the pooch out there today."

The life of a punter.

The festive mood at the Red Herring was accentuated by an impromptu birthday party for Laverneus Wilson. He'd turned 22 the day before and decided to celebrate his birthday and his big game with the guys. Wilson, so shy compared to Touchdown Tyrone Collins, was finally coming out of his shell.

"Man, Jake, what a high I'm ridin' tonight," Wilson said to the kicker.

"You played a helluvagameoutthere," Jake muttered.

"Say, there's a lady spyin' you," Wilson said. "She askin' her friends about you. You'd better turn around."

Jake had an idea who that lady might be. Sam confirmed it.

"Oh shit," Sam said.

Rachel Randall.

"Hey, Jake, nice kick out there today," said Rachel. Jake could smell peach schnapps as she spoke. Maybe with a hint of amaretto. "Congratulations."

Jake was in no mood to pussyfoot around.

"Great to see you, Rachel," Jake opened before asking the real question. "What are you doing later? Wanna get out of here?"

Rachel acted shocked.

"Uh, well, I'm not sure that's a good—"

"That's fine," Jake rambled. "You just gotta say no, right? I mean, who wouldn't want to bring back the kicker who won the game tonight, right?" The little hand on Jake's watch was approaching the 1, and he needed to find a mate for the night.

"Look, Jake, I think we're done. What happened has happened. We have to move on."

Jake was hurt by the rejection but forced out some bravado.

"That's all right, but you'll be thinking about me tonight no matter who you're screwin'," Jake said confidently.

"Uh, Sam, good to see you," Rachel said before rolling her eyes and leaving.

Jake rolled his eyes back to the classic bar tune "Whoomp! There It Is!"

"I still can't believe she busted you in Kansas, dude," Sam said.

"Yeah, of all the damn people." Dozens of other women were vying for a position on any of the football players' bedtime starting teams this evening. If Rachel wouldn't play, someone else would keep Jake warm.

Soon he was trying to, as he put it, "get his love on" with a girl named Carrie. She said she was from Brookfield.

A guy who looked a week past 18 walked up and started gushing.

"Mr. Steffon, that was a great kick today and I just wanted to tell you—"

Jake excused himself to shake the guy's hand.

"Thanks, man, I appreciate that," Jake said without a shred of sincerity.

The fan then stepped across the line.

"And what's your name?" he said to Carrie. "I'm Max." Max stuck out his right hand.

"Carrie. Good to meet you."

"EXCUSE ME!" Jake yelled at Max. "What do you think you're doing here?" The booze had his mind and his mouth.

Max's tone changed from butt kisser to bully.

"I'm just talking to her, man," Max said before raising the ante. "Cool off. Chill out. Jeez, you really are an asshole."

"I'm an asshole?" Jake said. "Why don't you just go back and leave us alone? We're talking here."

Carrie cut her losses as she sensed male bonding through fists. "Whoa. See you guys later," she said, and left.

"Thanks a lot, asshole," Jake said to Max.

"You know what, you're nothing more than a goddamn kicker!" Max said.

Sam was talking to another woman just a few feet away. Hearing the phrase "goddamn kicker" to him was like hearing a racial slur. It made everyone around a little nervous.

He turned and confronted Max.

"Hey man, you got a problem with my friend?" Sam demanded, the most sober of the three.

"Well well well, another damn kicker. Apparently your friend really is an asshole," Max said back to Sam.

Jake had had enough verbal escalation. "All right, outside."

"What are you gonna do, beat me up, you little kicker?" Max flashed his teeth, taunting Jake.

"Jake, just forget it," Sam said, knowing that trouble was now at their door.

Jake landed a fierce right hook straight into Max's nose. Max flew backward. The back of his head hit a chair as he fell onto his back.

"FIGHT! FIGHT!" yelled most of the patrons.

"CALL THE COPS! CALL 'EM NOW!" yelled one of the bartenders.

Jake jumped on top of Max, throwing punches at his face. He landed six good shots before Sam pulled him off. The right side of

Max's head was floating in a small pool of his own blood. His nose had turned into a blood drain. The music stopped.

"What's wrong with you?" Craig Zellnoff yelled at Jake. "Cops are probably on their way. Too many witnesses around, man."

Jake sat on his stool, not saying a word and awaiting his fate. A familiar voice came from behind.

"You shouldn't have done that, Jake. Stupid move."

Rachel Randall.

Jake looked up.

"People WILL hear about this, Jake," Rachel yelled at her former lover. "I hoped it wouldn't end up like this, but it will."

"Don't you say a damn word about this!" Jake exploded off his stool at Rachel. Sam and Craig intercepted the irate kicker before he touched her.

"Yeah, Jake, have them protect you," Rachel rolled her eyes at Jake one final time. "You're gonna need a good lawyer a helluva lot more than strong teammates."

Jake saw his blurry future approaching just to Rachel's left. Three Madison police officers waded through the crowd to the scene.

"You do this?" the lead officer asked Jake, pointing at Max, who was trying to pull himself up from the floor.

"Yeah," Jake said, looking at the red concrete floor.

"Come with us."

Randy's dreamy Saturday night ended with a phone call at three in the morning.

"Randy, it's Frank, sorry to wake you."

Randy flew up to a sitting position beside Lisa, who was still sound asleep.

"What is it?"

"The Madison police just called me," Frank said. "We've got seven guys in custody right now on various charges. Let's see here..." Randy heard the shuffling of paper on the other end.

"Craig Zellnoff was mouthing off to an officer at The Herring," Frank said. "He's in jail. Bob Verly was charged with disorderly conduct. Gary Kastern, Jamal Johnson, and T.J. Lammers were involved in a fight at a house party. Uh, Steve Franks got a DUI, and, oh yeah, Jake Steffon beat a guy up at the Herring."

"Oh shit," Randy said. That woke Lisa up.

"What's wrong, honey?"

Randy motioned for her to stay quiet. "What should we do here?"

"Well, the cops know this is a sticky situation," Frank said. "That's why they called me first. They said they won't publicize it if we can get down there and pick up the guys. I can't fit seven guys in my car but you might be able to help me out."

"Are they at Dane County?"

"Yeah."

"Should I meet you there in, say, 15 minutes?"

"Yeah, park on Carroll Street by the exit. They'll release them to our custody."

"See ya."

Randy hung up the phone and looked at his drowsy wife.

"Gotta go pick up some idiots from jail," he blurted. "Babysitting. That's what this job has become. Goddamn babysitting, I tell ya!"

He knew the deal. A probing reporter could find the information, but the police wouldn't volunteer it. Frank worked tirelessly to maintain that relationship to keep DUIs, bar fights, and domestic assaults out of the paper.

Just what the head coach needed hours after his biggest win.

45. Discovered

"Morning, Clark!" Frank Flaherty beamed as Clark Cattoor held the front door of WMA-TV open for him.

"Good morning, Frank."

"Ah, yes, nothing like a win over a Top 5 team to make the weekend."

"Did you celebrate last night?"

"Oh, man, you have no idea," Frank said.

"I was too wiped out after covering the game to do anything. I just wanted to get some sleep."

"Yeah, well, us old guys usually have enough in us for one good party a year." Frank followed Clark into the studios. "Let's do this, I've been waiting for an easy show like this all year!"

"Your boys stay out of trouble last night?" Clark asked as he pinned a wireless microphone on his lapel.

"Gosh, I hope so." Frank said. "You never know until the day after."

"Isn't that the truth?" Clark said. His own Saturday night had been spent in the bathtub relaxing from the stressful game. He'd pulled into his driveway just before 9 on Saturday and was in bed by 11. Sheila had had a late date planned for the two of them, but Clark called and said he was too exhausted. Sheila suggested she come over and cheer him up. She did. Clark was considerably cheered up as he prepared for the show taping.

"This win, the sixth of the year, puts you in position for a bowl game. Realistically, one more win and you're in," Clark said on the air after the highlights segment.

Frank took the softball question for a ride.

"Well, that's what we aim for," he said. "Each year we aim for a Big Ten title. Then, if that's out of reach, we have to get to a bowl game. It's important for us. It's important for our fans."

Randy Munson was at home nibbling on a blueberry pancake with Scott and Brett and watching *The Frank Flaherty Show* on the small television in the kitchen.

"Daddy, are we going to move to California?" Brett asked. Though his world was far different than most boys', he still got it. Randy made it a point to never talk down to his youngest son.

"I'm not sure. They say they're interested but nothing's come of it yet. I'd like to. It's warm there, you know."

"Yeah, I know, Daddy. I see it's going to be 81 there today." Brett now entertained himself by watching San Diego's weather patterns.

"Is there any time frame for this?" Scott asked.

"It's hard to say," his father replied. "The interview went great. We just have to wait it out."

Another replay of Jake's knuckleball to beat Ohio State popped up on the screen. A shot of Randy hugging Frank on the sidelines followed.

"That's you, Daddy!" Brett said.

Randy smiled. "Yeah, that was a great game."

The phone rang. All the possibilities burned through Randy's mind. Who was it? Each time someone called, he feared the worst. Police? Frank? One of those damn journalists?

"Hello?" Randy said.

"Is this Randy?"

"Yes."

"Randy, Ed Hartsberg."

Randy's heart leaped. California, here I come.

"Hi, Ed. Good Sunday morning to you, sir." Randy gave his sons a thumbs-up sign and motioned for them to leave the kitchen at once.

"Likewise to you," Ed said. "Congratulations on the win

yesterday. I caught the tail end of it after the Oregon-UCLA game ended early. That was a great drive you called at the end. You really turned that momentum around."

"Why, thank you."

"Well, anyways, last night we struck a deal with Pat," Ed continued. "He's going to leave after the season. It's official and signed. I'll put out a press release today."

Randy felt the anxiety flowing down his spine. Would this be the offer?

"So, what's our status?" he asked meekly.

"Tomorrow I'll FedEx a contract for you to examine," Ed said. "Take it to your attorney. I request that you overnight it back to me so we can get this on the road, if you're still interested."

"I am still very much interested," Randy said. He was finally going to meet his own coaching destiny.

"I have the terms we discussed here in front of me," Ed said. "Three years. 125 the first year. Then 135 and 145. All the bonuses we discussed will be in there."

Lisa was still sleeping. My God, she'll love to wake up to this, Randy thought.

"Now Randy, one thing that I am demanding is an ironclad contract," Ed continued. "No outs. If you go 9-2 your first year, I don't want to lose you to a large school, OK?"

"Yes."

"Likewise, if you go 2-9, I'm going to stick by you unless there's some gross misconduct or criminal activity. You don't have any of that in your background, do you?" Ed asked with a laugh.

"Uh, no."

"Good then. The deal, as we discussed, is now on the table," Ed said. "May I send you the contract? It should arrive Tuesday."

"Great! I look forward to leading you guys to the WAC title!"

"Uh, that's 'Mountain West,' Randy."

"Oh my," Randy said, embarrassed. He'd forgotten the Warriors had switched conferences seven years before. "I'm just so excited right now."

"That's OK, Randy. Enjoy the day. Look for the contract on Tuesday morning. Talk to you then."

"Thank you. Bye."

Randy told his boys they were indeed going to San Diego.

"COOL!" Scott said. He wanted to learn to ride a surfboard.

"San Diego? We're going to San Diego?" Brett said, tears of joy running down his face. "Do we get to go to Padres games?"

"Of course," Randy said.

He left his boys and went upstairs to make his wife's morning.

The lyrics of the Johnny Cash song "Sunday Morning Coming Down" rumbled through Jake Steffon's head.

"And the beer I had for breakfast wasn't bad, so I had one more for dessert."

Jake remembered precious little about the night before. He did remember punching that guy at the Red Herring. He also remembered spending three hours at the Dane County Jail with a few of his fellow football heroes.

Frank had been merciless on the ride home from the hole. He'd dropped just about every word in the book on Jake, Bob Verly, and Steve Franks. Frank talked about responsibility and how he'd "told them to stay out of trouble."

Jake was so drunk when he was released that he still didn't know what he was charged with. He thought he heard third-degree assault from the officers as they finished their paperwork.

"Well, good morning sunshine!" Sam said as Jake walked into the living room.

"Hey," Jake muttered weakly. "Do you have any aspirin?"

"Let me get it for you." Sam was in true best-friend mode for his roughed-up roommate. "So, what's gonna happen with you?"

"Ya know, I don't know," Jake said. "Oh shit, was Rachel there last night at the Herring?"

"Oh yes, she was," Sam said slowly, the bearer of bad news. "She said she was going to report it today. Do you remember any of that?"

"OH SHIT!" Jake yelled. "All that and I've got to work today." He squinted to read the numbers off the VCR. 10:41 A.M. "Man, I gotta get moving."

"Are you opening today?" Sam asked. He knew the lingo of the pizza business. Jake usually had to be at Pizza Perfecto by 11 on

Sunday mornings.

"Yeah."

"Are you OK to drive, man?"

"I think so," Jake said, holding his head with both hands. "Shower. I need to shower."

Randy was at the apex of naptime. The NFL game on WMA-TV served as his dreaming music in the master bedroom. Randy and Lisa made love as if they were 20 years younger after he dropped the news on her about San Diego College.

Lisa decided to spend the afternoon at West Towne Mall with Brett in tow. She'd been through a difficult season with Randy. His upcoming raise justified whatever she could rustle up between clearance sales, jewelry discounts, and what was on special at Bath & Body Works.

Melissa and Scott were out with friends. Randy's trademark snore filled the room, in direct competition with the crowd noise coming from the TV.

He felt the sounds of the commercials flow into his ears. DirecTV. Budweiser. Some local electronics store. Then...

"SEVEN BOARS FOOTBALL PLAYERS DETAINED LAST NIGHT. DETAILS AFTER THE GAME." A tease for the upcoming newscast.

No, I couldn't have heard that, Randy told himself. It was strictly a product of the late-night rescue combined with his own paranoia about any of his own recent crimes.

The phone rang.

Shit, Randy thought. So much for naptime.

"Hello?"

"WHAT THE HELL IS THIS ABOUT?" Frank said.

"What is what about?"

"The TV, damn it. Channel 11 just said seven guys were detained and they'll have more. I was just down there at eight for the taping of the show. No one said a goddamn word to me about what happened last night!"

"I don't know what to say, Frank."

"Is Cattoor behind all this? You're tight with him. Is he inside this?"

"Frank, I really don't know."

"Well, damn it, you find out! I'm going to call that bastard Cattoor myself and find out what the hell is going on."

Randy couldn't keep his news to himself.

"Frank, this may not be the time, but San Diego College offered me the job this morning, and I'm going to take it."

Frank's chatter tailed off.

"Well, uh, congratulations," Frank said sincerely. "That's great. I'm sorry to wake you up with all this, but now I'm worried about my own future. We're probably going to have to suspend guys this week."

"Probably."

"Hell, you've got your own stuff to deal with," Frank said. "When will it be official?"

"Hopefully Tuesday."

"Can you stay for the final two weeks or will you take off?" Frank asked.

"I guess that's up to you, really."

"Here's why I ask," Frank said. "Things are going to get really hairy around here if I have to sit seven guys next week. Ya know, Karen will be on my ass for all the bad press. A bowl game may not even save us. Will they pull your deal off the table if I get canned?"

"I don't think so," said Randy. "Hartsberg is sending me a signed contract. I should have it Tuesday."

Silence hung between the two coaches.

"Look, man, sorry to bug you with this," Frank said. "Tell you what I'll do. If I can, I'll hold off suspending anyone until you sign the deal. That way they can't take it off the table."

"That's generous of you," Randy said.

"Between the game and last night, I still owe you big time."

Randy said goodbye, clicked off the phone, and rolled back into the wonderful world of sleep. Wisconsin State's problems would not be his to deal with anymore in 48 hours.

Clark was also in electronic dreamland. He'd led a peaceful afternoon while flipping between *The Good, the Bad, and the Ugly* on TNT and the Packers-Lions late game on Fox.

Green Bay held a 31-14 lead at 5:30. They were going to cruise, so Clark turned on his employer to catch the early Sunday evening newscast.

Rachel Randall appeared with the top story. Her words were dramatic.

"Seven football players spent the night in jail on various charges after their upset victory over Ohio State."

After Rachel went through the roster of players who were arrested, a police mug shot of Jake Steffon filled the screen. His glassy eyes were there for all to see.

"The police said Steffon will likely face the most severe charges," Rachel continued. "This reporter was a witness to an altercation last night at the Red Herring in which Steffon threw the first punch and bloodied the nose of a person who was not a team member. The attack was unprovoked."

Clark was so focused on the report he barely heard his own phone ring.

"Clark, what is this?" demanded Frank.

"Uh, coach, I really don't know," Clark said. "I left when you did this morning. I never talked with Rachel regarding this."

"She NEVER called you about this? I find that hard to believe."

"Never did, Frank."

"Yeah, well, the next time you see her, make sure she has her shit together on this case. What the hell was SHE doing out there last night anyway? Is she trying to screw one of my players?"

Clark nearly spilled it but decided the Rachel-and-Jake card was worthy of a poker game with higher stakes.

"I really don't know what's going on."

"Well, Clark, I'm not sure about you anymore," Frank continued, clearly on the offensive. "I have a hard time believing you didn't know this was going down."

"Sorry you feel that way," Clark said.

"You guys better have your shit together about this or else we'll take our show over to one of the other stations."

Clark felt his anger meter move into the red zone. Diplomacy had gotten him nowhere. He fired back.

"Ya know, Frank, I've about had it up to here with your

bullshit!" Clark yelled into the telephone. "It's not our fault you can't have your goddamn players behave like gentlemen. Hell, after each win, they turn Madison into goddamn Bourbon Street! It's our job to keep an eye out for what's going on, and your players have no respect for the law."

For once, a media hack had put Frank Flaherty in his place.

"And you know what?" Clark continued. "I suggest that YOU have YOUR shit together before you call me at home next time your damn diaper gets a little wet! Good day to you, sir."

Clark clicked the cordless phone off. He'd made his reputation by not being one of the brownnosers. Once again, in the face of fire, Clark Cattoor was nobody's shill.

46. The Waiting Game

Clark was not looking forward to Frank's Monday noon press conference. He wondered if he was now persona non grata in Madison football circles. Frank had done that to previous writers and sports anchors who offended. Clark found himself tempted to call in sick, but a pro in his line of work never called in sick unless a limb was falling off.

"Clark. Good morning," Jim Tillman said as Clark walked into the football media room.

"Hi Jim, how are you?"

"Fine. This is for you. We'll be a little shorthanded this week at Illinois." Jim handed him a press release. Frank Flaherty was the master of spin control.

"FLAHERTY SUSPENDS 6 FOR ILLINOIS GAME." Six of the seven players who were held in custody after Saturday's game would have to sit for the road trip to Illinois. Craig Zellnoff got a free pass since his offense had been strictly verbal. He wasn't booked.

Frank concluded the release with a tough-guy edict at the bottom of the page: "No one, not one player, is above the rules set out by the coaching staff."

Frank walked in with the look of a man who had lost his placekicker and top offensive lineman for a crucial road game.

Clark noticed the gray streaks in Frank's hair, more pronounced than at the start of the season. He avoided eye contact with Frank as he tried to blend in with the other two dozen journalists.

Frank sat down in front of the cameras and microphones. He adjusted his gold wire-rimmed glasses. The specs were a look Frank brought out in times of crisis.

"As you can see from the release, we've decided to suspend six of our players for this weekend's game at Illinois," Frank said, knowing these first sentences were the most likely to appear on the evening news in six hours. "All six regret what happened and they all apologize for their actions. I cannot say too much more than what is on the release for legal reasons. I appreciate your cooperation on this."

And that was it. Not one reporter could penetrate that. Frank made the first strike with the release and then hid behind "legal reasons." He'd often joked to Randy Munson that if coaching football did not work out, he could always hire himself out to beleaguered politicians.

The reporters danced around the issue, asking how difficult the Illinois game would be without the players. Clark knew the real question to ask but was too nervous from his argument with Frank the day before to bring it up. What the hell, Clark figured, Frank already hates me anyway.

"Any more questions?" Jim Tillman asked.

"Yeah," Clark said as he raised his hand. Frank shot him a "don't-screw-this-up-for-all-your-colleagues" look. "Frank, does what happened over the weekend reflect on you, about the program you run and the character issues that, uh, are coming from it?"

Frank looked down at the microphones and chuckled like Gordon Gekko dismissing a poor stock tip. He glanced over at Tillman and shook his head.

"I'm not touching that. See you guys later." Clark stared as the coach stood up, turned right, and returned to his office.

Randy Munson steamed as he watched the press conference from the back of the room. He followed Frank up to the football offices.

"Frank, got a minute?" Randy said as Frank walked into his spacious office.

"Yeah, Randy, I figured you'd be here."

Randy was in no mood for pleasantries. "What the hell, man?

You told me you'd hold off until Wednesday for the suspensions."

"Look, I had to do it today," Frank said. "It was the only way I could keep my job."

Randy did not respond. Frank filled the silence.

"Karen met with me this morning and told me in no uncertain terms that she's all but forgotten about the Ohio State win," Frank went on. "All because of our stupid players and their stupid antics. They went out and turned downtown upside down! Karen said we're all on thin ice because of this."

Randy cooled off after that.

"I see."

"As for you, I don't think it will have an effect on San Diego College," Frank continued. "I mean, you're an offensive coordinator. NONE of this comes down on you. It's all me. You've worked here longer than I have, so that also plays in. I wouldn't sweat it. The offer arrives tomorrow?"

"Yes, I checked the shipping on the Internet an hour ago. It's in the system."

"Randy, I will need one favor from you today, though."

"What is it?"

"I haven't been able to tell any of the players they've been suspended," Frank said. "Will you call Steffon, Verly, Johnson, and Lammers? Tell them they'll have to sit but they are required to practice."

Jake tossed off his blue WISCONSIN STATE FOOTBALL jacket upon arrival from Zoology 101. He'd toned down his usual cocky strut after his arrest. "Nice kick, Steffon!" he heard more than once from random students.

Once home, Jake bit into an apple in the empty apartment. Sam was stuck each Monday in a two-hour lecture about the history of American education. Out of the corner of his eye, Jake saw the flashing red light on the answering machine. He pressed the retrieve button.

"Uh, Jake, this is Coach Munson. I just wanted to let you know that you will have to sit this weekend. We still expect you at practice but you are suspended for the trip to Illinois. See you at the Bubble at the usual time."

"SHIT!" Jake still hadn't told his parents about the fight. He'd sat through class this morning fearing what the newspapers wrote about his arrest. The thought of the humiliation that his mother, a schoolteacher in tiny Fall Creek, was probably enduring made him sick to his stomach.

His telephone had become the sum of all of his fears. Each time it rang from here on out, his parents' anguish rushed through his head. Jake would eventually have to tell them. His mother came home from school around four. No doubt she'd already heard rumors at school. I'll call her after practice, Jake planned.

Jake killed the final hour until practice in grand fashion. He fell asleep on the couch to *Another World*.

47. The Escape Hatch

Dreams of San Diego sunshine trickled into Randy Munson's Tuesday morning. The contract was somewhere in the FedEx world, due to arrive any minute.

Frank had told Randy to stay home on Tuesday until the contract arrived. Randy was excused from all meetings until his own business was taken care of.

Randy took great delight in the anticipation. Two hours earlier, he'd driven Brett to school. Lisa'd cooked up ham, peppers, and sausage and squeezed fresh orange juice. All of the years. All of the struggle. All of it nearly over.

Randy and Lisa ate and said nothing. They each knew a better life was ahead, maybe even in the next minute.

The doorbell.

Randy winked at his wife and stood up. He strolled over the shiny white enamel tile, across the beige living room carpet toward the front door.

"Package for you," said the FedEx guy.

"From San Diego?"

"California. Please sign here."

"Thanks." Randy scribbled his signature as if he were signing the contract right there.

Then he closed the door and sighed. He'd finally made it.

"Open it! I want to see!" Lisa shrieked as she ran toward her husband.

Randy grabbed the kitchen scissors and sat down. Lisa pulled her chair next to his. Randy leafed through the pages of the contract.

"Looks like it's all here."

Indeed it was. The terms were just as Ed Hartsberg had described them. Ed had even tossed in a country-club membership at someplace called Eastlake, down in Chula Vista. Free car.

"We've made it!" Lisa said while scanning the contract sideways.

"Yup. Well, should we take it?" Randy asked.

"Sign it and send it."

Randy Munson threw down his sloppy signature on eight different spots, right next to Ed's dignified John Hancock. Randy had to sign for pay, the car, the bonuses, and the country club. He also had to vouch that he had never committed a crime more severe than a traffic violation and that he would not seek or accept any other football coaching jobs during the next three years.

"Lisa, I'd better call him just to let him know the contract has arrived and that he's got himself a new coach."

Randy eyed the ugly, pea-soup green telephone on the wall and dialed Ed Hartsberg's direct line.

"Hello, this is Ed Hartsberg."

"Hi, Randy Munson calling."

"Randy, how are you?"

"Great, sir. I just received the contract. I signed it and will FedEx it back to you today."

"Why, that's great, Randy. Say, I just saw this last night on ESPN. What's up with those suspended players y'all got there?"

The chill of the question shot down Randy's spine faster than gravity.

"Well, sir, they didn't handle success too well after Saturday's win. We had to take action against them."

"Randy, I'm sorry to see that. You know, that kind of tomfoolery will not be tolerated in my football program. You'll see to that, I'm sure."

"Discipline won't be a problem with me running the ship." Randy tried to sound forceful.

Randy felt Ed buy it and move on.

"Good, good. I'm sure you know the drill these days. I want to introduce you, but I have to interview three more people to make the search official in the eyes of the administration. State rules, you know. Anyway, with a signed contract, you are officially the coach and should be able to sleep at night. Just keep this whole thing under your hat for one more week, and we'll fly you out and introduce you to the media and the fans. All right?"

Randy could live with that. $125,000 could buy plenty of silence from Randy Munson.

"Jake, you embarrassed your mother. She's been crying all day."

Jake Steffon had endured a painful phone conversation with his father the night before. In the end, he'd gotten what he wanted from it. An "I love you" from both parents and a lawyer to handle the case. A friend of the family back in Fall Creek agreed to handle it free of charge for the Steffons. Still, his father's words made him focus squarely on the task at hand, here at Tuesday practice.

He had to connect on a 35-yard field goal to end practice and keep the first team offense from running ten separate 80-yard sprints.

Snap down. Ball through the uprights.

"All right, first team, get out!" Frank boomed from the sidelines.

"Nice job, Rocky," Bob Verly said with a smile toward the placekicker.

"Thanks, disorderly."

The first team ran toward the other end of the dome and the showers.

Jake's physical crime against another person was all over the school newspapers. In just two days, the *Daily Boar* sports editor said he'd received more than 200 emails regarding Jake's football fate. Most were for sitting him for the Illinois game and that was it. Illinois was a heavy favorite anyway, what was the real harm? As long as the six were back for the Michigan State game, most wrote, writing off Illinois was no big deal.

Jake had spent much of the previous night listening, in horrific detail, to what his mother had dealt with the day before. Junior high school kids asking her in class if her son was a criminal. If he was in jail. If he was drunk. If he was on drugs. The snickering in the halls. Nancy Steffon wanted to leave school for the day but stuck it out.

"You need to make things right with her," his father warned.

In the locker room, Sam found a way to break through his roommate's visible funk.

"Hey, man, with a punch like that, at least the Raiders will take a look at you in three years."

Jake already had his Saturday plans figured out. He was going to drive home to Fall Creek and try to make things right.

"Have fun in Illinois, man," Jake told Sam an hour before they left. Sam was the designated backup placekicker for the Illinois trip.

"Don't do anything stupid back here," Sam said.

"I'll try not to."

Jake threw together enough clothes to make it through two nights in Fall Creek. Jeans, shirts, socks, underwear, two turtlenecks. No loud Wisconsin State football gear. Throw in a few textbooks. Twelve-week exams were around the corner.

He anticipated the evening would be difficult. The Fall Creek football team was still alive in the play-offs and they were at home that night against Edgar, one of those Wausau-area teams where the linemen grew up on dairy farms and had bellies the size of award-winning watermelons.

Jake spent the first 50 miles driving up I-94 debating whether he should show up at the game. The Steffon home was just two blocks from the back end of the high school football field. The lights could be seen from his folks' kitchen.

Returning as a football hero had always been a dream to Jake. Yet for the past year, Jake hadn't had the opportunity to attend a Fall Creek game. He was always tied up with big-time college football on fall Fridays.

Somewhere around the Wisconsin Dells exits an hour north of Madison, Jake decided he was better off staying in once he rolled into Fall Creek. No need to cause a disturbance as the shamed, drunk brawler returned home to Mommy and Daddy.

Clark Catoor had a reprieve from traveling on the same airplane as Frank Flaherty. The state budget was in such bad shape, the governor told the school on Monday that they'd have to travel to Champaign, Illinois, by bus. Clark opted for the Saturday morning media flight instead.

He'd had little time to prepare as he sat on the other end of Lou Proctor's mahogany desk at WMA-TV.

The WMA worker bees were punching away on their keyboards. The five o'clock newscast was just over an hour away.

"Ya know, Clark, when I graduated from school a few years ago, it was a different time. 1976. We were proud to come from a school where sports had their place. Our teams were usually lousy, but they were students first, you know what I mean?"

Another back-in-my-day speech from the master, Clark thought. Clark smiled at his boss.

"Now this. I'm embarrassed over this. I am almost to the point of resigning my endowment unless there are serious changes over there." Lou had opened a journalism endowment in 1985 when he was named news director. He contributed $5,000 each year to scholarships for promising journalism students. The nearly $100,000 across 18 years did not go unnoticed by the school. The endowment boasted a modest $47,000 after interest. Lou looked down at Clark.

"I'll cut right to the chase, Clark. We have to get these guys. I want you working with Walsh to uncover why Collins is chirping now. Something smells bad in there and I want us to dominate the coverage."

"OK, I'm on it." Clark returned to the sports office. Back to the toy department.

After nearly three hours on the roads, Jake arrived at 815 First Street in Fall Creek, his boyhood home. As he hurled his bag over his shoulder, he heard the Fall Creek marching band going through the motions. The game was about to start.

"Mom, I'm home!"

Nancy planted a kiss on her son's cheek. Carl nodded and extended his right hand.

"Dad," Jake said cautiously.

"Good to have you home, Jake. Sit down."

Nancy cracked open a Sundrop soda with two ice cubes and delivered the drink to Jake. Carl was clearly running the show.

"So, you gonna go to the game tonight?" Carl asked.

"Nah, I really think I should stay in," Jake offered.

"It really hasn't been that bad," Carl said as he looked at an old green ashtray on the coffee table. Carl had given up smoking when Jake was seven, but he kept the ashtray to help him fight the urge. "Tuesday and Wednesday were hard, but I think people are getting over it. They're a forgiving lot in this town."

Jake looked away from his father and out the living room window.

"I don't know. I'd rather not have to deal with it tonight."

"OK, you're your own man now, Jake. I'll be at the game. You'll know where to find me." Carl always sat right under the press box at the 50. Last row so his back could rest on the wood. Thanks to Jake's recent celebrity in Madison, the locals always left Carl's seat vacant in case he was running a little behind.

"Dinner's just about ready," Nancy said. "Come on in." She'd made Jake's favorite for this rare fall homecoming. Chicken-fried steak with sausage gravy and mashed potatoes. Like any other boy raised in a small town, Jake loved an artery-clogging meal.

Jake dug into the tender steak and felt the tension. He wanted this awful vibe to fade.

After some idle chatter, Nancy brought up the game.

"Maybe you should think about going. Your dad would really be proud even with all that's happened."

Jake sighed and produced a pained expression. "Mom, I'm sorry about this week."

Nancy put down her fork and held up her hand. "I don't want to talk about it. It was a hard week, but I know you're getting through it."

"Look, I'm sorry."

Nancy and Jake kept chewing. Nancy looked at her watch.

"Almost seven. Kickoff should be any minute."

"OK, I'll go. What the heck, right?" Jake smiled and crawled into his weathered brown leather jacket, which he'd left behind the previous summer.

"See you after the game. I may come down after halftime, though," Nancy said as her son jumped off the porch and ran to the field.

48. Illinois

"This is more proof that it really is all about the money."

Aaron Schutz nibbled on a super-fatty, triple-glazed chocolate doughnut high above Memorial Stadium in Champaign, Illinois. Clark watched the diminutive sportswriter eat 46 grams of fat in less than 46 seconds.

Aaron continued between bites.

"Think about it. The school is only out here playing to keep from paying out, what, a quarter of a million, half a million?" Aaron had written earlier in the week that Wisconsin State should forfeit the game because of the suspensions.

Clark finally pitched in. "Any word yet from the casinos? Any heavy action one way or the other on the two losses?" Clark tossed out the questions to find out whether he needed to catch another flight, this time to another country.

"We just started digging around the on-line betting houses," Aaron said. "Ya know, the ones in the Caribbean. Las Vegas had nothing on the games. The ones that are still a concern are the two home losses." Clark felt his bone marrow freeze at the mention of the very games that had landed him his big score. He tried to downplay the subject.

"If there was a fix, why not simply beat those teams by less than the huge spread?"

"Odds. Strictly odds. The same reason people bet long-shot

horses at the track. Someone made a bundle of money on those two games. The odds were 6-1 or 7-1 for Wisconsin State for both. That's a lot of cash."

Clark took a deep breath and examined the sparkling metal benches in the stands. Kickoff was over an hour away, and Clark was already worn out from anxiety.

"Who could have done it?" Clark asked.

"You've got to look at who had bad games," Aaron explained as if he were talking to a seven-year-old. "Collins actually put up great numbers. He scored the only points in both games. I would have to rule him out here, regardless of what that Colquist guy said. Steffon had two horrible games, but I'm probably going to toss him out because he's just a freshman kicker. Hadn't been in that spot before."

"Sure."

"For me, that leaves the coaching staff. Remember all the hell the offense caught after that Northern Illinois game?"

"Sure do. You boys had a field day with that."

"Well, it was awful. Maybe there was a sinister edge to why that was," Aaron concluded.

As Aaron got closer and closer to the truth, Clark felt the collar on his beige cotton dress shirt getting tighter.

"But I've got nothing on them right now," Aaron admitted. "We may never really know the truth, and even if we do, all the main players will be gone. Strassel will probably get rid of this crew if they lose big today anyway."

That roused Clark from his palace of paranoia. "No shit?"

"On top of that, I'm hearing from California that San Diego College hired Randy Munson to be the head coach."

Clark's jaw headed toward the floor.

"I had no id—"

"Nobody here does," Aaron continued. "Munson had no comment an hour ago, but he knows we're onto him. My guy out in California said San Diego will make the announcement early next week."

"Like that last helicopter out of Saigon."

Aaron had always loved that about Clark. The ability to compare football to fallen Asian cities.

"Exactly, Cattoor!"

Despite being 500 miles from where he was supposed to be, Jake was enjoying his Saturday morning. Fall Creek lost its play-off game, but the crowd was unbelievably friendly to one of their own. Former teammates who'd attended one of the area colleges or simply worked on the farms came up and talked about old times. Teachers patted him on the back. Little kids wanted to take pictures with Jake.

"Real people here in Fall Creek, don't you forget that," Carl told his son more than once during the game.

Jake stretched out on the worn-out brown couch in the living room while Carl eased into his favorite corner chair. The Wisconsin State-Illinois game was on cable, and Jake had the bizarre experience of watching his teammates on television, not from the sidelines.

"I keep reading that Flaherty's going to get fired. What do you think?" Carl asked, attempting to bring down whatever walls remained from the week.

"He's an idiot," Jake fired back. "Randy Munson is a good guy, though. I wish he ran the show. He does, at least on offense."

Carl got down to business.

"So what's all this ruckus about you wanting to drop out and go play somewhere else? You got it made, son. You just need some guidance, that's all."

Jake braced for this conversation. Carl kept on.

"You saw it last night. People think you're a hero. You know how many kids would trade their lives to be in your shoes? Do you?"

"Yes."

"Seize it, welcome it, man. Don't be one of those screw-ups who walk around town saying 'what if, what if.'" Jake had never heard his father talk like this. "Promise me this, Jake. Just ride it out this year and think about how much you actually have going for you. Don't do it for me, but do it for yourself."

Jake felt the room getting a touch dusty.

Sam Cattanach booted the opening kickoff into the end zone and then celebrated the first salvo at Illinois.

Frank had also brought along an extra offensive lineman, since the other walk-on kickers weren't ready for game action.

Craig Zellnoff did not benefit from the extra beef. Missing his top two linemen, the senior quarterback spent his final road game tasting the manicured grass of central Illinois. Six sacks in the first half. Three interceptions as he was trying to save his hide from the pursuing Illini.

Illinois led 28-7 at halftime.

Frank saw the disaster in progress and pulled Craig from the game. May as well feed the backups to the lions. Craig watched the game with the same detachment as Jake. The Illini rolled on 42-13. Wisconsin State was now 6-5.

Frank ran up beside Randy after shaking hands with the Illinois head coach.

"It could happen today," Frank said, lighting a cigarette while still on the football field. He let out a long puff. "We could get clipped. Hold on tight. At least you got somewhere to land."

Randy opened the door ahead of Frank and saw head trainer Buddy LaMancha pushing Craig Zellnoff's right shoulder into an uncomfortable angle. Craig grimaced like an old man with month-long constipation.

"AAHHHHHH!" Craig screamed as the pain shot through his side.

"I don't think he'll be ready for next week," the trainer with the bullhorn mustache said to Randy and Frank. "We'll take him in when we get back tonight."

"Shit. Do what you can. We need the win next week, regardless of the cost," Frank barked. Randy knew the head coach would strong-arm both Buddy and Craig later in the week to get the quarterback back on the field. Frank needed a win more than anyone in the state of Wisconsin.

Frank talked to the players about personal responsibility. "Those six guys who are back in Madison watching the game on TV are the reason YOU lost today. It wasn't you. We were out four starters. We couldn't block anybody." Frank looked at Sam. "Hell, we couldn't even kick a damn field goal today.

"Let this be a lesson to all of you," Frank continued. "When we get back in five hours, behave tonight. I don't want to hear

ANYTHING from the police or the papers about you guys. I'm going to make this promise right now: Anyone who goes out tonight and gets in trouble will be gone. Forever. No trial. No question. No more scholarship. Understood? Is that crystal clear?"

Two dozen players belted out a "Yessir!" in unison. Frank walked into the visiting coach's office. Randy had beaten him to the small windowless room.

"Frank, Karen Strassel is outside. She wants to talk to you."

Frank pulled off his navy WSU baseball cap and scratched his balding forehead. All this money and he had no hair on top to show for it. "Great. Just great. Send her in."

Karen walked in with the elegance of a person who was part CEO, part fan. Karen floated effortlessly through the macho world of football. She worked at schools with strong football programs and was used to the usual crap from coaches.

"Frank. Randy. Do you have a couple of minutes?" Karen asked with an insincere smile.

Randy walked toward the office door. "Excuse me."

Karen held up her hand. "No, Randy, you can stay. We're not at a funeral here. Just close the blinds. We don't need any leaks here." Randy followed the order.

"Look, Frank, this was a bad loss, but I kind of expected it," Karen said. "You did the right thing with those suspensions."

Randy felt Karen's gaze as he stood by the closed office door.

"Randy, you're going anyway, so this may not mean that much to you, but next week is everything," Karen said. "We win next week and it all changes. The media will be off our ass. The alums will start giving money again."

Frank nodded. He knew the drill all too well.

Karen tugged at her black trench coat.

"We're going through a lot of shit because of Collins and all the gambling garbage. Just get me a win next week, and that will go a long way toward keeping everything around here the same."

Clark led the media pack out to interrogate Frank after the latest debacle.

"How much did the suspensions keep you from finding a

rhythm?" Clark made it a point to try to break the underlying tension with the head coach. They still had to be friendly enough to tape a television show the morning after this humiliating loss.

"Not that much." Frank at least tried to lie. "We like to think we're pretty deep at each position. The only part where we were really hurting was at kicker. But sometimes you have to do what's right, regardless of the consequences."

Clark and Aaron eyed each other. The bastard's covering his ass, Clark thought. Aaron also sensed it and smiled.

"Frank, we saw Karen Strassel walk into the locker room. Did she have a meeting with you or the players?"

Frank snorted. He only did that when "the damn media" asked a probing question.

"Yes, she did come in and, no, I'm not going to tell you what that was all about." Frank shot those laser eyes through the back of Aaron's head.

"Anyone else?" Jim Tillman said.

Aaron raised his hand again. Jim pretended not to see it.

"What do you want, Schutz?" Frank blurted.

"Frank, we've heard that Randy Munson will be the next coach at San Diego College. Can you confirm this?"

The question caught Frank so off guard that his real answer was obvious to the cameramen. The guys who lugged tripods and boom mikes could spot the wheels spinning on damage control like no one else.

After looking down for a good three seconds, Frank faced Aaron and bit his bottom lip, Clinton-style. "Can't comment on that." He might as well have said, "Yes, he's going down there on Tuesday, will make more money than I, and will be the only person who gets out of this with his career still intact."

Jake hugged his folks good-bye and fired up the Bonneville for the return trip to Madison. Watching the second half of the game had left him depressed. He should have been there. Jake knew his mistake had cost his teammates dearly.

Jake turned south on Highway KK to Foster and Interstate 94. He always left his cell phone on until Osseo. That's where the signal faded until he drove through Wisconsin Dells, 100 miles down the interstate.

The phone rang just as he turned onto I-94.

"Hello?"

"Hey man, it's Sam."

"Where are you calling from?"

"Just outside the stadium. We're about to get on the bus. Look, we can't go out tonight. Flaherty's threatening to pull scholarships if he catches anyone out on the town tonight."

"No shit?"

Sam lowered his voice. "On top of that, he's still pissed at you for what happened."

"Oh, I figured that. I don't know what I'll do now."

"Anyway, I'd love to, but I'm stayin' in tonight when we get back. Our night is off, man."

"All right, I'll find something else."

"Just be careful tonight no matter what you do."

Be careful, Jake told himself.

He first saw the signs that planted the seed of trouble as he approached Wisconsin Dells. With the summer season long gone, only the locals worked the Dells strip. The lure of the Gronk was in Jake's head. One of the bartenders at the Gronk was from Fall Creek, a former high school football teammate named Steve Whelan. They'd been casual friends growing up. Just one drink. Just stop by for one. Just need to get off, turn left, and zip into town.

After 90 miles of monotonous interstate, the signs appeared for the Dells. A water park on the left and the turn to the casino on the right.

Jake kept the Bonneville on I-94 toward Portage. No exit. No monkey to fight off. He was a new man. A better man.

Jake's world now had order. His parents' advice rang in his ears.

As the Dells melted into the rearview mirror, Jake felt a new urge overtake him.

Call Rachel Randall. Give it a shot. Rachel was a smart woman. Jake knew that much. He was lucky to have had her until the morning light just once. Six weeks before, she was talking about a trip to Eagle River to meet the parents. There was always hope.

Jake punched out the 800 number to the Channel 11 Sports office.

"Channel 11 Sports," Rachel answered.

"Rachel, it's Jake Steffon. Is now a bad time?" Jake asked the question with a trace of apology.

"No, I'm hardly doing anything today. No six o'clock show. I'm just waiting for Clark to get back from Illinois with all the stuff." A trace that Rachel must have picked up on.

"Look, I'm sorry I've been such a jerk lately," Jake said. "I spent the weekend at home trying to sort it all out."

Rachel would not give in that easily.

"I imagine you had a hard time watching the game today."

"Like you wouldn't believe," Jake confessed.

"So why are you calling me?"

"Look, I know it's your job," Jake said. "That's what you do. I shouldn't have acted like that in public, and I shouldn't have gotten into a fight. I should have treated you better."

Rachel turned the tables.

"Didn't get any last night in Fall Creek, huh?" she asked.

Jake was thrown off for a second. "Uh, no, you're right. I didn't get any."

Rachel charged back in.

"And you probably think I'll take pity on you?"

"Well, uh, I didn't mean—"

Rachel laughed. "Jake, don't worry. It's OK. You've made my life difficult at times this year. You've made it hell. I had to dish it back to you a little bit."

Jake sensed the door was still open, even if just a crack. "So can you meet me?"

"Tonight?" Rachel asked sarcastically.

The answer hung in the air for Jake. He'd just passed the ski hill at Exit 106. Madison was just thirty minutes down I-94.

"Yeah, come over to my place at 11," Jake said. "I'm trying to turn it around, and I'd love you to be there."

"I don't know," Rachel said slowly. Jake heard her let out a long sigh. "Sure. I'll see you then."

Life as a stand-up guy was already paying off.

49. Sign-Off

"Get up, get up, get up, get up…Wake up, wake up, wake up, wake up…let's make love tonight."

The light flipped on inside Clark's body. Marvin Gaye's "Sexual Healing" was two measures in on the radio when he started his car and backed out of the driveway.

As he drove the three miles from his house to WMA-TV, Clark was on top of his small empire. The birds chirped a little louder today, their song sweeter with each second.

Clark had survived the Sunday taping of *The Frank Flaherty Show*. The coach had been fairly chipper, all things considered.

The blowout loss at Illinois kept the Madison media speculators busy for another Sunday and Monday. Skip Stevens wrote that the school should consider bringing Bob Monroe back from the NFL. Aaron Schutz suggested former Packers coach Mike Holmgren.

All Frank asked before the taping was no questions about the future after the Michigan State game. Clark followed that lead.

Sheila had spent the night at his place and made him feel like Marvin Gaye, Kid Rock, and Burt Reynolds rolled into one. Clark wanted to show her his cash stash, now down to $24,000. But he decided against letting his guard down. He would do that another day.

He pulled up to a four-way stop three blocks from the station. He peeked in the mirror at his new outfit. WMA-TV offered Clark $4,000 in clothes from one of the local men's stores each year. Clark and Sheila had spent almost all of it on Sunday, stocking up on sports jackets, dress shirts, and colorful ties. News people rarely invest in expensive pants, but Clark bought two pair of tan Savane pants. No wrinkles. Hard creases. Low maintenance.

"Damn, that tie is sharp," Clark said to the rearview mirror, catching sight of his dark purple silk tie with a smidgen of silver checkered in. "I'm living the great American life!" he yelled to himself as he pulled into the parking lot.

An easy day was ahead for Clark. He'd sent Rachel Randall and a photographer to Frank Flaherty's press conference the hour before. Clark had had enough of Frank to last a decade. He was ready for the season to wind down, bowl game or no bowl game.

One of the dirty secrets of sports journalism is that most sports anchors root against the local team at the end of the season. Winning teams are fun, but championship teams mean 12-hour days and 70-hour weeks.

"Hi Rachel," Clark said as he tossed his leather briefcase on the chair at his desk.

"Oh hey. Here's the raw." Rachel handed the tape of the press conference to her boss. "Nothing great. No one asked about his future."

Clark popped the tape into a machine to make notes for his sportscast. His phone line rang.

"Clark, this is Lou. Got a second?"

Clark felt the anxiety tickle down his neck. A call from the boss was rarely good.

"Sure. Be right over."

Must be a bowl game planning meeting, or maybe what to do about the Packers. They were 8-1 and looking at a Super Bowl run.

Lou sat behind his desk. Harvey Walsh was off to Lou's right. The station's general manager, David Brooks, stood on the opposite side, arms folded.

Since no one made any attempt at eye contact, Clark knew immediately what this was about.

"Shut the door, sit down," Lou Proctor commanded.

Clark did as he was told, wiped his moist brow, and looked at the burgundy carpet in Lou's office. Harvey closed the blinds to the newsroom.

Lou was in control. "Clark, Harvey has uncovered something that is very disturbing, perhaps criminal, involving you." Lou shuffled through a small stack of papers on his desk.

"Ever heard of Cool Breeze Sports, some outfit in the Caribbean?" Lou's question hung in the air as a fork in the road for Clark. If any other reporter had dug this up, Clark might be able to weasel out of it. Not here. Walsh was a pro with a Rolodex the size of a Wheaties box.

Clark told the truth. "Yes, I have."

"It appears from our investigation that you won a considerable sum of money betting on Wisconsin State football games this year," Lou said. "It says here you bet two games against the school and made serious money. About 85 grand. Is this true?"

"Yes."

Lou untangled his hands. He looked at his reporter.

"Harvey, thanks for the information. We've got it from here."

Harvey walked past Clark, opened the door, and left the office.

"I'm not going to bullshit around," Lou continued. "First, you're gone. You'll have three hours to collect your stuff and get out."

Clark nodded his head slowly. He'd unconsciously prepared for this day. Just in case.

"Here's the deal," Lou said as he loosened his tie. "We're letting you go because of this, but THIS can't ever get out. EVER. Nothing about the gambling. We'll lose ALL of the shows. Flaherty's. The basketball shows. The hockey show. Everything. The school will never have anything to do with us if this comes out. One whiff of this and the shows will go right back across the street."

David Brooks finally broke his silence. A graying man of 47 with a dozen extra pounds around his waist, David pulled an envelope out of his left inside pocket.

"Clark, you have over two years left on your contract here," David said. "We could fire you, we should fire you because of this. But because of the, uh, sensitive nature of this—" David and Lou clearly had a hard time saying the word "gambling"—"we'll pay the final two years of your contract in a lump sum. It's in there."

David handed the envelope to Clark. Clark peeked inside and

stared at the middle line on the check.

PAY TO THE ORDER OF: Clark Cattoor. The numbers in the box on the far right spit out the final bounty: $122,678.

"That's the whole thing, Clark," Lou said. "You're paid through the end of your contract. We took out some taxes and social security, but it's all there."

David produced a second envelope. "To accept that check, you must sign this. It's a document saying you received the payment and promise confidentiality regarding all of this. Also, there's a clause that you will NEVER work for a TV station in the Madison market. EVER."

"Oh, come on, that's a bit harsh," Clark protested.

"Is it? We could take this check back as easily as we're giving it out," Lou said.

"OK, OK." Clark took out a pen and signed the release.

"On top of that," Lou said. "We have to come out with a cover story for the newspaper as to why you're leaving so abruptly. You're from Missouri, right?"

"Yes. St. Louis."

"OK, then, we put out a memo today that you're leaving for family reasons. A sick parent?"

"Sick mother works for me," Clark said with a smirk. He was enjoying this.

"Another thing, Clark," Lou instructed. "I can't tell you where to live, but it would be in your best interest to leave the state. If you're not around Wisconsin, this whole mess won't come out."

Clark nodded in agreement. "I can do that."

"Good. There's over $120,000 in that check," Lou said. "Add in that other money you made and you should be able to get back on your feet fairly quickly.

"We don't want this to ever come out, so we'll never bad-mouth you to other stations. I just ask that you stay quiet, get out of town, and don't use me as a reference if you want to stay in the business."

Clark found an ounce of humor as he folded the check and put it in his pocket.

"I'm assuming Rachel Randall will be the interim sports director," he said.

"Yes. She doesn't know yet. We'll start a national search right away."

Clark stared at Lou and David, pausing for dramatic effect.

"You know she slept with Jake Steffon, the placekicker who got himself suspended after that fight last week, don't you?"

"Excuse me?" Lou said.

"You heard me," Clark said. "She screwed him back in September and then ripped him on the air after she punched him in a bar on a road trip. The Kansas game, I think. You may want to clear that up with her before you give her the raise."

"I think it's time to leave, Clark," Lou said sharply.

"Oh, I'm leaving." Clark smiled.

Clark walked out and returned to the sports office.

"Rachel, something's come up. I have to go home and take care of my mother in Missouri. I'm resigning, effective immediately. Lou will probably tell you something regarding the sports department."

Rachel sat blankly, mouth open and motionless. Clark put his belongings into an empty cardboard box. The picture with Mark McGwire in St. Louis. Old videotapes.

"So, that's it?" Rachel was able to finally muster.

"Yes, that's it." Clark said as he gathered an armful of sports books from the top of his desk.

Rachel's phone rang. "Be right there," Rachel told the caller.

"Was that Lou?" Clark asked.

"Yeah, how did you know?"

"I'm sure they'll want to talk with you. Make sure to get a raise out of all of this. Oh, and Rachel—" Clark was going to let her in on the latest about Randy Munson. San Diego College was introducing him as the new coach tomorrow morning.

"Yes?"

Clark decided to let her figure it out after watching the other stations later that day.

"Oh, nothing." Clark surveyed the sports office for any final remains of his personal collection. "I'm taking off right now. Best of luck to you, Rachel. I really mean that."

"Thanks. I hope your mother gets well."

Clark and Rachel shook hands. Cardboard box in hand, Clark Cattoor shut the door at WMA-TV for the final time.

50. A New Coach's Dream Day

"What should I go with? Green tie?"

Randy was in a clothing dilemma.

"Try this." Lisa handed her husband a sand-colored dress shirt with a green and black patterned tie. "Green and black are their colors, right?"

"Yup, green and black."

Ed Hartsberg had arranged for Randy to fly to San Diego later that night for the Tuesday morning press conference. Randy had spoken with his new boss Monday morning. No mention of Tyrone Collins or the loss at Illinois. The only important morsel Ed told Randy was not to expect much media coverage for the press conference. Warrior football was still not a major priority in San Diego, Ed said. He reminded Randy that part of the reason Randy Munson was the new head coach at San Diego College was to change all that.

"Honey, I'm sorry I can't make it out there. It's just too much with Brett," Lisa said with regret. Ed had offered to fly the entire family out to San Diego for the press conference, but Randy said two long flights in two days would be asking too much of the little boy.

"I know," Randy said with a smile. "That's OK. I'll just smile, straighten my tie, and do my thing."

Frank had given Randy as much time away as he needed to take care of his California affairs. Randy said he'd be back in time for the Thursday morning meeting, possibly Wednesday's practice if everything went smoothly.

"So, what should we open the house at?" Lisa asked. The real estate agent was coming by while Randy was in the air.

"Man, I can't believe we've been in this house nine years," Randy said. "Nine years. It'll be hard to leave." He stared out their bedroom window into the front yard. "Let's not aim too high here. 165, 170 should be the range. We should clear well over 100 grand off the house. Remember, San Diego is expensive."

"That's fine. We'll just make more money when we move back here in four years, right?"

"You're always plotting that next move, huh?" Randy said with a chuckle.

Lisa tossed in two pairs of black dress socks and closed the suitcase. "Get out of here, sexy. Go get that job."

Randy wasn't disappointed by the attendance at his first press conference as head coach. Unlike most coaches, who walk in like the president and stand at a podium, Randy walked out to the assembled sports journalists and introduced himself to each one.

After two dozen handshakes, rounds of small talk and new names that he'd already forgotten, Randy stood next to Ed Hartsberg for the official announcement.

"I am pleased to introduce to you to the man who will take Warrior football to the next level, Randy Munson." A handful of plants from the athletic department clapped on the outskirts of the cramped media room.

Randy delivered his rehearsed monologue.

"Thanks, Ed. It is with great pleasure that I accept this job at San Diego College," Randy opened. "I'm confident we will take San Diego College into its proper place on the national scene."

After more bland remarks, a guy with slicker hair and an even deeper tan than Clark Cattoor stood up near the back.

"Randy, Teddy Willmar from Channel 8. With all that's gone on at Wisconsin State, have you been able to distance yourself from what's come out recently?"

Randy had braced himself for one of these questions.

"Well, it's been a difficult year, the hardest in all my years of coaching. The team" (Randy made it a point to talk about Wisconsin State as "them" and not "we" or "us,") "has battled through horrible adversity. And some of the other issues surrounding the program are in the process of examination. I cannot comment on those."

"Randy, Jack Castillo from Sports Radio 650. Will you coach in Wisconsin State's final game on Saturday?"

Ed had cleared Randy to return and finish out the regular season, so long as he was back in San Diego the following week for scouting and recruiting. Randy wouldn't be able to stay with Wisconsin State for any bowl games.

"I am planning on coaching Saturday," Randy said. "I feel I owe that to those players, especially the seniors who are trying to get back to a bowl game. If Wisconsin State wins Saturday, they're in a bowl. I want to help them achieve that."

That was it. No real probing questions, no self-appointed program gurus, unlike at Wisconsin State.

51. Everything but the Girl

"Why are you telling me all this?" Sheila Hayes asked as she played with her straight black bangs.

"Because I have to leave town," Clark said. He hadn't seen her Monday night, and decided to stay quiet about his termination from WMA-TV. But he couldn't hold off by Tuesday. He'd called her right after rolling out of bed at noon. Told her it was urgent. She ducked out of the accounting firm just after one and drove straight to his place.

Clark spilled it all. He led her into his bedroom and handed her the large bills. He told her about the $200,000 he was sitting on, but no job to go to five days a week.

"I don't know what to say," Sheila said sadly. "What does this do to us?"

"I'd really like to keep this thing together," Clark said, before plunging in. "I love you, Sheila."

He had never said that to her before.

Sheila sighed. "I love you, too."

Clark broke the tension. "I don't even know yet where I'll move. It has to be out of state. I may go back to St. Louis or Kansas City. Maybe out west. I have to go someplace where this will never come up."

"Yeah, I'd say," Sheila said sternly. "Was any of this illegal?"

"No, that's the good part. As long as I pay my taxes, I'm in the clear."

Clark reached over and put his hands in hers.

"Come with me," he said into her eyes.

"Where?"

Clark could see that Sheila wasn't caught up in the romantic moment as he was. She was much more concerned about practicalities.

"I don't know yet, but I'll take care of you until you find something you want to do."

"Well, I'd hope so," Sheila said sarcastically.

Since his divorce, Clark had been obsessed about making enough money to pay the bills. Now he had the remaining two-plus years of his contract paid in full as hush money. More than $61,000 in cash would arrive at his door within 48 hours from the Caribbean. The significance Clark attached to his newfound wealth did not impress Sheila the way he'd hoped it would.

Clark opted for a safer proposal.

"Maybe once I move, we could see if it would work out," Clark said. "I don't want to lose you."

"I just can't do it," Sheila said, as her voice cracked. "I've fallen for you, Clark, but I can't live like this."

"Can't live like this?"

"When will it end? You're already on the run."

Clark shook his head. "I'm not on the run. I just can't work here. I have to leave."

"I just can't leave Wisconsin. I love it here. I love you, but I can't do it." Sheila sniffled. "Maybe it could work, but I have to stay here, at least for now."

Clark noticed the tears as Sheila turned her face away.

"I should go now," Sheila said. She stood up and fetched her purse. "Call me tonight. I want it to work between us, but I have to think about this."

Clark Cattoor had everything but the girl.

"Yeah, Coach Munson!"

Craig Zellnoff high-fived his position coach and guru in the

locker room. Randy had just arrived back in town from San Diego.
The start of Wednesday's practice was minutes away.

"Thanks, Craig. That means a lot."

Jake stood ten feet away at his own locker. He and the other
players had heard about Randy's hiring the day before from Frank.

"At least he's getting out before the shit goes down," Jake said to
Sam. The punter was tying his blue practice pants.

"Don't sweat it, man," Sam said reassuringly. "We're kickers.
We've got nothing to worry about."

Jake was worried about his own future, in football and in life. He
still worked at Pizza Perfecto two nights a week, but the experience of
the past weekend had cast a new light. Jake had battled himself to
stay out of the bars. He'd survived the test.

After the Ohio State game, all five of those smaller schools had
come through with offers. All the head coaches were willing to forgive
the punch and the suspension. Jake realized that good kickers must be
hard to find at the lower levels. A large school like Wisconsin State
had had enough problems with kickers over the past five years.

"HUT!" barked Sam as Jake pounded another 35-yard field goal
through the uprights inside The Bubble. Like a machine, Jake had
produced a stellar week of practice.

"Gimme another!" Jake said to Sam and John Wilcox. "From
45."

The offense marched back ten yards. Jake set up four yards from
Sam's planted left hand.

"HUT!"

Jake blasted a low line drive that shot through the air like a
tennis ball. Unwavering and true.

"Nice kick, Steffon! Real nice." Wilcox said with a tap on his
helmet. "You just may be ready for us on Saturday after all."

"So what was it like ten years ago?"

Karen Strassel had asked Randy to stop by her office for a brief
history lesson of the football program. "What was the feeling like
around here when you guys finally turned the corner?"

Randy sat in Karen's spacious office and thought back, between
glances at his boss. Man, she's got it for someone who is 44, he

thought. He peeked at the family pictures on her desk. Tall Scandinavian husband, two tall Scandinavian kids.

"It was magic. In 1992, we had this one day, it was October, against Iowa, and we won. They were ranked, and we were still having problems scoring points," Randy remembered. "My daughter was just seven then, and she came out onto the field and danced a polka with me after that game. God, that was awesome. I still think about that day. That was even before my son Brett came along. It was a much simpler time for us."

Karen smiled at the story.

"The reason I ask is that I need to find a way to get the football program back to that point," Karen said. "I went through the books from that time. Everyone—car dealers, soda distributors, everyone— was on board writing checks to Wisconsin State. We don't have that anymore. I'm trying to figure out what to do."

Randy couldn't stop the memory train.

"You know, Karen, I look around these offices and think what it was before then. We were a second-rate athletic program. I mean, second-rate."

"Oh, I'm aware of that."

"The football program was awful when I got here. We scored six points almost every game. It was depressing. But in the span of two years, we turned it all the way around. No one expected it.

"After we won that first Rose Bowl, football paid for everything, but something was missing. It's not the lack of bowl games or winning seasons. Something is just not right."

Karen flashed her pearly whites again and cut to the chase.

"Look, I still don't know what I'm going to do about the football team next year," Karen admitted. "I want that charisma from ten years ago. You're the last link to those glory days, and I hate to lose you."

"Thank you."

"But three home losses?"

Randy shrugged. He was also embarrassed by his team's record at home.

"I usually get what I want," Karen said. "That's why I left coaching. Running the building is much more fun than worrying about kids and playing time and recruiting. My God, the recruiting…

Anyway, since you're leaving—next week, right?"

"Right."

"Since you're leaving, I know I can trust you with this," Karen said with a hint of a smile. "Like I said, I don't know what I'm going to do with the coaching staff here. The NCAA has already told me that there's enough to keep us from going to a bowl game next year. They won't make the official announcement on any penalties until after New Year's. They did it as a favor to me to get a coach in here before anything comes down, if I need to." Karen was careful to throw in that final clause.

"Look, Randy, I asked the NCAA about you. They said you're clean. Some large amounts of gambling did go on, but they said nothing has been traced back to the program, so in that regard, the school won't get hit too hard."

Randy felt what was coming next as he watched Karen's lips move with each syllable. He knew she was about to offer him the big job. A million bucks a year.

"I know you've already signed with San Diego, but let's say the top spot is open here in a month. Would you consider coming back?" Karen flashed a million-dollar smile of her own.

Randy sighed and said to himself, ain't that the luck? Pull off one of the great scams in recent college football history, only to find that you were about to make more just staying legit. Randy thought of his wife. Lisa had always dreamed of staying in Madison.

Karen sat down on the corner of her desk and leaned in.

"You're the only one on the coaching staff who doesn't hate my guts," Karen said. Randy agreed with that. He was the one coach who understood that he and Karen had the same goals. Getting talented players, good people, and winning games.

As Karen kept talking, Randy's mind went to John Wilcox. The special teams coach had been delightfully quiet ever since that chat in McFarland. If Randy stayed in Madison, Wilcox couldn't. Karen sounded as if she wanted Randy to stay and everyone else to go. At least in San Diego, he might be able to land Wilcox a position on his staff.

Why, Randy tortured himself, did he ever get into The Plan?

Randy refocused on what Karen Strassel was offering.

"—and the final total will come out to just over a million a year. We could announce it in three weeks. Think about it."

Her winning smile said "Randy, stay here, I'll take care of you." She leaned in close for an answer.

Randy did the first thing he actually felt good about since August.

"Sorry, Karen. I can't do it. I signed a 'no-out' deal with San Diego. I have to honor it."

52. Hey, Mr. Postman

Since Clark's abrupt departure from WMA-TV four days before, he'd lived a closeted life inside his West Side townhouse. The station had alerted the newspaper of his resignation.

The last two lines of the station's internal memo were printed verbatim in Tuesday's *Dane County Tribune*. "Clark has decided to return home to Missouri to care for his family. Our thoughts and prayers are with him."

Clark had understood the risks going into The Plan. He'd made out like a bandit. Randy Munson had risked his freedom for big money, and Clark was merely along for the ride.

Now Clark was alone. Sheila hadn't called him since their talk on Tuesday. Three days had passed, and Sheila had moved on.

Clark walked to his door, barefoot, wearing his WISCONSIN STATE BASKETBALL gear from his own days as a college student.

"FedEx delivery for a…. Clark Cater."

Clark ignored the mispronunciation and looked for the return address. "Jim's Beach and Surf Shop—St. Martaan." Perfect.

"Where do I sign?"

Clark floated to his living room couch and cut open the box.

More beach towels on the outside. Cash on the inside—61 beautiful $1,000 bills, American, Grover Cleveland all the way. Add in nine Benjamins and four Jacksons to even the account. Cool Breeze had overpaid by 80 cents to avoid the coins. A final receipt lay on the inside.

"C. CATTOOR: $61,979.20. Remaining balance: $0."

Clark pushed the big bills into a tiny white cardboard box that he'd used to store baseball cards from the 1980s. Now nearly $86,000 sat inside.

He rustled on a pair of old jeans and slipped into a pair of rabbit slippers, a gift from Carol for Christmas in 1999.

"Can't forget the box," Clark sang to himself, off-key as usual. The old baseball card box was the final package from his townhouse. The other boxes sat motionless in the truck out back, awaiting the move south. He would leave the cash inside and spend the evening, his final fling in Madison, at the karaoke joints downtown.

Clark had no woman, but he did have a song.

Two miles west, Randy Munson was also packing. Frank had given him permission to skip the hotel check-in the night before Saturday's game with Michigan State. Randy was trying to move four people more than 2,000 miles west in the span of a week.

Melissa, who was in the middle of her senior year at Memorial High School, was going to stay at the house for two weeks and then move into her best friend's house. Randy and Lisa were apprehensive at the prospect, but Melissa was 18, had excellent grades, and was quite mature. She'd convinced them that moving in the middle of her senior year would be detrimental to her grades and scholarship chances. She also reminded them that she'd be on her own at college in just a few months.

Randy and Lisa would fly Melissa out to San Diego every two or three weekends. She would live out there during the holidays and the summer.

San Diego College had been quite generous with the move. All the Munsons had to do was pack and unpack. Professional movers would handle the rest, including the transport of two cars.

As Randy opened his garage door, John Wilcox's Toyota pulled up, Night Ranger blasting.

"Hey, boss, congratulations!" John said, rolling down the window. "I just wanted to drop by and offer my congrats. We didn't have much time at the stadium today."

Randy took John's eagerness as a sign that the special teams coach wanted a job in San Diego. New coaches with open staffs are the industry version of the beautiful woman walking along a beach without a boyfriend.

"Thanks, John, I appreciate that."

John shut off his car and removed his sunglasses. "Actually, there's another reason as well."

"Let me guess," Randy said. "You want to be the offensive coordinator?"

John shrugged. "You know me too well, but I'm not always about advancing my career."

"OK, then."

John sighed. "Remember our chat in McFarland last month?"

"How could I forget?"

"I've been quiet, but I'm concerned about what's next," John said.

Now Randy sighed. "What are we gonna do about this?"

"When the cavalry comes for me, and I'm afraid they will, I won't back down," John said. "And I won't name names. If they take away my livelihood, just don't forget about me, please."

Tears began to slide down John's face.

"I did nothing wrong," John quivered.

Randy hugged his coaching rival.

"If the worst happens, I won't forget you, man, I won't forget."

53. Michigan State

"Good afternoon! Welcome to Madison for the season finale. A trip to somewhere warm in December is up for grabs as 6-5 Wisconsin State takes on 8-3 Michigan State. A win continues the season, and a loss sends everyone home early. I'm Simon Smith, and thanks for joining us..."

The pregame show blasted over the speakers inside Mendota Stadium. More than 64,000 fans were enjoying an unseasonably warm, sunny day.

Clark Cattoor heard the radio call. As the commanding officer of a 25-foot rental truck, Clark was riding high in the cab. As Simon described the "picture-perfect November afternoon for football," Clark steered the yellow truck south.

Las Vegas was his final destination. He'd decided to make his trip west a four-day party, stopping to see friends in St. Louis, Kansas City, Denver, and maybe even Grand Junction. He still had some back alimony for Carol. He would just show up unannounced and do it in person. That would bring a laugh, at least to him.

The thought of listening to a football game he should have been covering ate at his soul, but Clark knew listening to football on Saturday and Sunday would make hauling the truck much easier.

Randy Munson surveyed the scene from the hard turf of the

stadium. He was counting the hours until he, Lisa, Scott, and Brett were flying out Sunday morning to San Diego. Lisa had already picked out a dozen houses for them to look at on Monday and Tuesday. Their real estate agent here had already found three qualified buyers for their own home. Houses on the West Side moved fast, as the Munsons had discovered.

"Be quick! Like a swivel. Always looking," Randy said to Craig Zellnoff. He felt a twinge of sadness. Tutoring quarterbacks was what he truly loved to do. He'd brought this kid from average to well above average in three years. Randy would miss him.

Randy had read about Clark's untimely departure from Channel 11 in the *Dane County Tribune*. Something unusual must have happened. He knew Clark wasn't close to his parents. Clark had kept his promise of silence. Randy would keep his.

Craig's silver helmet glistened under the sunshine as he led Wisconsin State to a touchdown on the opening drive. His pass to Laverneus Wilson put Wisconsin State up 7-0. Craig and Wilson had been able to put the "dumb receiver" incident behind them to the tune of seven scores this year. Wilson was even picking up some interest from the NFL. Not Craig Zellnoff. He knew his own career was near its end, likely today if they lost.

Randy pumped his fist into the air after the score. The television people stuck a camera on the San Diego College head coach. Randy considered this game an audition for his future team in California. Each facial gesture was dramatic, each hand motion for the cameras.

"Nice grab, Wilson," Randy said as he slammed his left hand onto Wilson's helmet.

Jake booted the kickoff into the end zone. He, too, had something to prove after being forced to sit out the previous weekend.

The Wisconsin State defense held Michigan State in seven plays. Running back Jason Brunson broke a 22-yard gain for the Boars.

"The holes are as big as elephants out there!" Frank barked to Randy seconds later.

"Empty Right 573 X Shallow," Randy motioned to Craig. The quarterback nodded.

The quarterback looked over the Michigan State line and changed the play. The Spartans knew it was coming and stacked the line.

"Shit. They see it," Randy said under his breath. "Change it, change it." He hoped the quarterback would read his mind and change the play.

Randy bent down and put his hands on his kneecaps. Craig took five steps back, looked for a receiver and was crunched by one of the Michigan State 300-pounders. To his credit, Craig held onto the ball and endured a nine-yard sack.

"Oh, shit!" Frank yelled. The two coaches threw down their headsets and ran out to the motionless quarterback. 64,175 fans in blue fell silent as the trainers ran out to the field.

Randy stuck his head over Craig's, blocking the sun with the bill of his baseball cap.

"Where are you, Craig?" he asked.

"Facing 2nd and damn 19. Maybe 20, cause our line sucks." Craig said with a delirious grin.

Randy laughed. "At least you haven't lost that."

"Watch this, coach." Craig moved his legs to give the fans a reason to breathe easier.

The crowd applauded.

"Uh-oh," said Craig.

"What is it, son?" asked Frank.

Craig's eyes bulged as he looked ready to sneeze. Instead, Craig let out a vicious cough and showered the head coach with blood.

"Holy shit!" said Randy as Frank wiped his quarterback's blood off his white turtleneck.

"He's coughing up blood," one of the three trainers said. "Get him under examination now!"

"Sit up, Craig," a trainer with a deep voice commanded. "Can you get to your feet? We gotta look inside now."

Craig nodded as the trainers helped him to his feet.

Frank was already talking to backup quarterback Alex Sistos. Randy ran toward the summit meeting.

"Just like Indiana. Work within the offense," Randy told the nervous quarterback.

"And here comes the gunslinger from Slinger!" Simon Smith said across the airwaves. "Alex Sistos takes over the offense here in the first quarter with Wisconsin State leading 7-0."

"Shit, they're done," Clark Cattoor said to his radio as he crossed the state line into Illinois.

Sistos fired a completion to Teddy Hammersley on his first play, an easy screen pass to the left side toward Wisconsin State's sideline.

Jason Brunson picked up the first down on 3rd-and-3 with a run up the middle. The smattering of claps from the crowd helped Sistos shake off the nerves.

Michigan State prevented Sistos from a touchdown, but Wisconsin State faced 4th-and-7 from the Spartans' 26-yard line.

"FIELD GOAL TEAM!" Frank called out.

"Go time," Sam said to Jake.

The kicker cracked his neck. With Craig out, Wisconsin State had no margin of error. Each dropped pass, each missed field goal, each mistake would doom their chances at a bowl game.

With the sun at his back and a breeze blowing in his helmet, Jake hammered the 43-yard field goal just inside the right crossbar. The football fluttered and bounced off a tuba player behind the north end zone. 10-0 Wisconsin State.

Craig patted Jake on the helmet as the kicker walked by on the sideline.

"You all right, man?" Jake asked.

"They want me back in there," Craig said. "Need the win."

Jake looked at Craig's hands and saw more blood. Craig smiled and his blood-stained teeth came through.

Jake nodded and walked to his customary spot on the sideline, behind the benches by the kicking nets.

"Unbelievable, man," he said to Sam. "Zellnoff could freakin' die out here. Why isn't he in a hospital?"

"Wins. You know it's all about the cash at this level."

Michigan State scored a touchdown late in the first half to pull within three at 10-7. Alex Sistos ended the half with two interceptions.

"Zellnoff is ready for the second half," trainer Buddy La Macha said in his deep voice to Randy on the way to the locker room.

"Are you sure? He was coughing blood."

"He's ready. Frank knows it."

Randy shook his head and understood. Wisconsin State needed the win. They needed Craig for two more hours, and then he would get a one-way ticket to University Hospital for the night.

Frank was already in the middle of his halftime speech.

"I've been told that Craig is available for the second half," Frank said. "Craig, you'll start the rest of the game."

Craig acknowledged the command.

Randy said nothing. This wasn't his call. He was supposed to just run the offense and run it well.

Michigan State tied the game 10-10 with a 35-yard field goal six minutes into the third quarter.

Craig waddled onto the field. He had talked all week of how emotional his final game in Madison would be. The internal bleeding only added to the drama.

Randy called running plays to start off the drive. This would allow Craig to regain the flow and pace. Jason Brunson and Teddy Hammersley pounded out two first downs on five plays amid the massive holes from the offensive line.

"Pairs Right 572 Y Read," Randy signaled to Craig.

"I just hope he gets some blocking," Randy said over his headset to the coaches in the press box.

Craig rolled back the required seven steps. He heard more than seven footsteps on the hard turf. Two Michigan State defenders in white jerseys and green helmets put their claws within grasp of the quarterback. Craig ducked and saw Laverneus Wilson break open 30 yards downfield. Craig fired the leather right into Wilson's hands. First down at the Michigan State 32. Craig threw his hands toward the cloudless sky. He was now King of the Universe. At least the King of Dane County.

Teddy Hammersley barreled for a first down as the third quarter melted away. Each play ate up 45 seconds. Randy and Frank needed to shrink the game with an injured quarterback.

Wisconsin State drove to the 7-yard line. 3rd-and-goal. 1:15 and ticking in the third quarter.

"Twins Right Spring Right X Curl," Randy motioned to Craig.

"Hut hut HUT!"

Craig rolled to his right, anticipating Wilson to break free in the back of the end zone. Wilson was covered with two guys. Craig faked a toss to freeze the defenders before turning around and running left to the sunny side of the field and the south end zone.

Three defenders gave chase, but Craig had the angle. Five yards from the far sideline, Craig finally turned at the 9 and sprinted toward the goal line.

"Zellnoff inside the 5 and diving for the end zoooonnnneee!" Simon Smith yelled.

Craig jumped from the 3 and was joined in the air by two Michigan State cornerbacks. They clobbered Craig two feet above the ground but the quarterback held onto the ball. His knees landed on the 1 but the ball was on the goal line for a touchdown. 16-10 Wisconsin State.

"He did it!" Randy yelled under the crowd noise.

Craig stood up, spiked the football on one of the defenders, and broke out in the Macarena before the officials flagged him 10 yards for taunting. Craig was about to make the fourth and final turn of the dance when Bob Verly grabbed him and aimed the quarterback in the direction of his own sideline.

Randy hugged him.

"Hey, Craig-a-rena!" Craig sang.

Jake hit the extra point. 17-10 Wisconsin State.

The kickers trotted off the field. Jake stepped to the bench where Craig was inhaling citrus Gatorade.

"Nice run, you OK?" Jake asked.

"Yeah, I'm…"

Jake watched as the senior quarterback fell forward and crumpled on the plastic turf. A score of other players also witnessed the collapse and called for help.

"What is it, what is it?" Randy pushed through the other assistants to get to Craig.

"He's out. Passed out," Jake yelled.

"Give him air! Give him air!" One of the paramedics on the sidelines instructed. "Stretcher and truck NOW!"

Craig opened his eyes and coughed up more blood. Jake caught a few drops on his white football pants. A stretcher landed next to the quarterback.

"Lift him on three! 1-2-3!" Paramedics and players lifted Craig onto the stretcher. Craig was locked in and on the way to University Hospital in less than 60 seconds.

"It appears Craig Zellnoff is on the way to…" Clark heard on the radio, just before the signal finally gave out. He was an hour south of Rockford, and the reception faded with each country mile.

"Crap." Clark was stuck with the Northwestern at Illinois game just down the dial.

Randy blew up.

"Goddamn! He shouldn't have been playing!" he yelled in front of the players as Craig rode off. Crap, what did I just do, he thought. Fifteen or 20 guys heard that. That will get back to Frank.

A hush fell over the team, even with the 17-10 lead. Alex Sistos wasn't sharp enough yet to commandeer a comeback, and they all knew Michigan State would not simply go away.

Michigan State running back Lebron Hill scampered in on an 11-yard touchdown with just under five minutes left. The Spartans kicked the extra point to tie the game 17-17.

Randy pulled Alex aside for a pep chat. The quarterback had thrown three interceptions and hadn't looked past the ground since the last mistake.

"It's your show, man," Randy said. "They don't think you can win it. Otherwise, they would have gone for two there. Prove them wrong. Be sharp. Run the plays. Good footwork."

Alex cracked a small smile and ran to the huddle amid the boos from the fans.

"We just need 45 yards here. Just need 45," Randy said to himself.

Bob Verly plowed a serious block to free Jason Brunson for a 13-yard pickup for a first down at the Wisconsin State 42. Alex took a sack on the next play. 2nd-and-16. 3:41…3:40…3:39.

"Gun Left 532 Divide," Randy said.

Sistos battled the happy feet and the Michigan State defenders. Laverneus Wilson turned right toward the MSU sideline and zoomed free. Sistos uncorked a duck that Wilson jumped high to grab. Wilson came down with the catch and was tackled at the Michigan State 44.

3rd-and-2. 3:02...3:01...3:00.

Teddy Hammersley buried himself in the pile of bodies for a four-yard gain. First down.

Randy called for two simple running plays to the left. He knew Jake liked to kick from the left side or the middle, not the right. Brunson blew through for four yards. Hammersley burst for two. 3rd-and-4 from the 34. 1:15...1:14...1:13.

"Throwin' it, right?" Frank barked as the clock ticked away.

"No, gotta run it. Gotta have the ball last," Randy responded. "Same play...on TWO!" he yelled to Alex.

0:50...0:49...0:48.

"Hut...HUT!" Cory Larkman and Bob Verly dragged their 300-pound frames to the left as Teddy Hammersley ran between the two of them. He saw the end zone yards away and felt no heat on him.

Hammersley broke through the defense and was free to the end zone, except for his size 14 shoes. He tripped over his own feet at the Michigan State 24. He would have scored easily.

"Ooh, Teddy," Jake said from the kicking nets. The last thing he wanted was another game-winning field goal kick. He preferred just to take this one without all the extra stress.

Michigan State burned its last two time-outs to make Jake think about the field goal. 41 yards. Third down. 0:04 on the clock.

Sam broke the ice. Players usually left kickers alone when the game was on the line. Sam acted as the liaison.

"Look at this place," Sam said with a wry grin. "All 'cause of you. Two million bucks on the line for the program here. Who knows how much in Vegas cause we're a one-point favorite. It all comes down to you, man."

Jake shot an angry look at his roommate.

"Why are you—" Jake asked.

"Just to show you how damn much fun this is. Now make the damn kick."

Jake felt the wind blow into his left ear. Just aim it at the left stick, he told himself. Kick it straight. Let the breeze do the rest.

Sam's left hand sat limp on the left hash mark on the near sideline. 41 yards. Jake had hit hundreds of these kicks, maybe even thousands since he'd moved to Madison.

"HUT!"

Snap down. Ball up. The football cleared the Michigan State rush and headed straight for the left stick, as Jake planned. Jake saw the fans behind the goalpost raise their hands up in triumph. It must be slicing right.

The football toppled and trickled just inside the left upright to win the game. 20-17 Wisconsin State.

Jake threw off his helmet and ran across the field. He outran the students and tired teammates who were chasing him.

Sam finally caught Jake and lifted him into the air. Alex Sistos ran up behind the kicker and poured citrus Gatorade on his head. Carl Steffon chased his son down in time for a hug.

From the sidelines, Rachel Randall smiled and ran down Jake for a quick interview on the field. The first of many up-close encounters on this weekend.

Randy hugged Frank for what felt like the last time. Once again, Randy's cunning sense of knowledge and timing had led Wisconsin State to a victory against a team that should have won.

"What a way to go out," Frank said, tears in his eyes.

"You know I can't go with you to El Paso or Hawaii or wherever, right?" Randy said as they sprinted off the field.

"I know that. But thanks for getting us there. You saved my ass."

Randy stopped and turned to watch the field behind them. Players danced with girlfriends. Students strutted to polkas from the band. Boars football as it should be.

"C'mon. I gotta say a blurb to the radio guys and then we'll come back here. The media can wait today!" Frank said.

"I'm right behind ya."

Randy followed Frank into the coach's office in the locker room and sat in as Frank said all the right things to commentator Buck Benson.

"I can't wait to get somewhere warm. It's been a long time, Buck."

"That's it from here, Simon," Buck said into a microphone. "One very happy coach as Wisconsin State wins 20-17. They're off to a bowl game. Where exactly, we'll find out soon enough. Simon, back upstairs to you."

Buck took off his headphones and congratulated the two coaches. "I hope it's San Diego. If the bowl game is there, maybe Frank will bring you back to run the offense."

The three men laughed before Buck walked out.

"Let's go celebrate," Frank said. "We've earned this one. I should check on Zellnoff."

Karen Strassel knocked on the large window next to the office door. Frank motioned her in.

"We did it, Karen!" Frank beamed while chewing a Royal Jamaican cigar, a significant upgrade from the Winston Lights.

Karen looked away from the coaches.

"I'm not going to mess around here," she said. "I declined the bowl bid to El Paso and I'm buying out your contract. This was your last game."

The cigar drooped in Frank's mouth "But…why?" was all he could muster.

"The lack of morals and integrity around the program," Karen said. "Craig Zellnoff is lying in a hospital fighting for his life. I rode over there in the ambulance with him and he said that you" she pointed a finger at Frank" made him get back in there. He has a lacerated kidney. He could die tonight, Frank."

Frank was livid now. "He said he wanted to play! He's a senior"

"I don't care," Karen said. "Craig said that Coach Munson expressed his doubts and was upset that you were even considering it. That's what this program needs. Accountability and responsibility. I was a coach once, too, ya know. A damn good one and I would never have—"

Frank exploded. "Why, Randy, you backstabbing bast—"

"Frank, save it," Karen said. "Randy didn't do anything. Why would he? He's off to San Diego to start his own program, and he's earned it."

"Maybe I should leave—" Randy said, getting up from his chair.

"Yeah, maybe you SHOULD!" Frank yelled.

Karen also stood up. "No, I think you should stay here, Randy. Stay here and take notes on how a football team shouldn't be run." She exhaled, the sound of a woman who was about to write a check for over half a million dollars to send Frank to the coaching pasture. "Your players don't know yet. It's your job to tell them. I'd say let them have their fun, and then tell them when they get in here."

"Karen, you'll have to tell them. I won't do it. That's your job as my boss. I can't tell them I was just fired." Frank looked out into the empty locker room. "This will be the best hour of their time here," he said, thinking of the dancing players back on the field. "You can ruin it, but I won't."

Karen walked upstairs to the media room. She sat down in the coach's seat. The Madison sports journalists quickly understood that something major was about to go down.

"I have decided to end the tenure of Frank Flaherty as head football coach," Karen read from a statement as the media murmured. "We have declined all of the bowl bids offered to the team this year. The program was simply running at a level off the field that is unacceptable. This firing in no way reflects Frank Flaherty's role in any of the off-field incidents. As far as I know, Frank conducted himself professionally at all times."

Karen looked up at the cameras and the flood lights.

"We simply need a change in the way things are done with the football team."

54. Home

Jake Steffon awoke just in time to catch *The Frank Flaherty Show*.

Like the other players, Jake had been in shock when Karen Strassel announced to a room full of naked football players that their coach had been fired. He felt bad for Frank, but also remembered seeing Craig bleeding on the sidelines.

No one had heard from Craig since then.

Jake rubbed his eyes and saw Rachel Randall's tanned back under the covers next to him. She'd ignored his immature ways and still believed in him. After all the trouble he'd put her through, she still wanted to be with him.

He tiptoed through the apartment. At the foot of the entrance sat the thick Sunday morning newspaper. Jake cracked open the paper to see who would be on the cover. Would it be him?

Nope.

Two large pictures graced the front page, side by side, one of Craig on the gurney to the hospital and one of Frank walking out of the locker room.

"ZELLNOFF CRITICAL; FLAHERTY FIRED."

Jake read that the quarterback was to spend the night at the hospital after losing two pints of blood. Craig had slowly regained consciousness as the paper hit the press. The story also recapped Frank's firing with the announcement from Karen Strassel.

What a waste, Jake said. What should have been a day of such joy was now a mess.

"Good morning." Jake heard Rachel's voice from behind. He looked at her feet and slowly worked his way up. Her tan legs glistened in the morning sun. His silver boxer shorts looked especially delicious around her waist.

"I got a scoop for you."

Rachel shrugged it off. "Not until I get some coffee."

"Now that Flaherty's gone, I feel the need to spill what happened," Jake said.

Rachel started mixing coffee grounds. "What do you mean, what happened?"

"I'm going to call the NCAA today and tell them everything," Jake admitted. "Everything."

"What? I don't get it."

"Tyrone Collins was right. There was gambling going on in the program. Before the Northwestern game, I got a phone call from someone telling me to miss the kick. I missed it, but not because I wanted to. I just missed it."

Rachel forgot about the coffee.

"I don't know who did it, but I'll tell the NCAA and let them take care of it. With the coaching staff gone, I don't have to stay silent any longer."

Rachel turned from a girlfriend into a journalist.

"Mind if we bring a camera along for the phone call?"

Jake laughed and kissed her. 10:30. Time for the coach's show. Rachel was one step ahead of him.

"Oh, there's no Flaherty show on today. I think they were going to put an infomercial there instead."

Jake wanted to see it for himself. Instead of Clark Cattoor and Frank Flaherty, a man selling a compact yet powerful sausage maker was on the air.

Randy had one last phone call to make before heading west. As he approached his favorite pay phone, he thought of all the business that single telephone helped him accomplish.

"Hello?" said the voice on the other end.

"Tyrone Collins, please."

"Yeah, this him."

"Tyrone, Randy Munson, how you doin'?" Randy asked.

"Randy Munson. Well, well, well. I figure you're the only happy coach today," Tyrone said from Miami. "I heard about what happened on ESPN last night. Man, I see you headin' west to San Diego, though."

Randy smiled. "Yeah, we're driving west in a few hours. We're all packed up."

"Little Brett, too?"

"Yeah, little Brett, too, thanks for asking," Randy said. "I'll tell him you said hi."

"Cool. Cool. I like little Brett."

"Tyrone, I've got to ask you, with all of the stuff coming out here about the gambling allegations, what's the truth? I ask because I don't work for the school anymore. I just want to know where it stands. Has the NCAA gotten to you yet?" Altruism masked Randy's need for information.

"Nah, nah, the NCAA doesn't care about me anymore. It's old news that I took money from Copperzweig. Old news, man. Once my eligibility was gone, they were done with me. Now I just got the NFL to look at."

Randy chuckled at that. TDT really was close to the NFL.

"Well, did you really throw those games?"

Tyrone laughed 2,000 miles away.

"They only saying that because I split with Copperzweig," Tyrone said. "He was overcharging me, and I decided to shop my services around, you know what I'm sayin'."

"Yeah?"

"Copperzweig and that flunky of his—"

"Uh, Colquist."

"Yeah, Colquist, short little Latin dude, has it in for me now that I bailed. I bailed right before all that talk came out. There's nothing to it. Look at my numbers those games. I was on fire, the only reason we weren't shut out."

"Why didn't you come out and just deny it?"

"C'mon, Coach, think about it," Tyrone said. "The NCAA

already kicked me out, I took the money, even if it was hardly anything."

"Why did you take it?"

"Randy," Tyrone said. "I don't have anything. Copperzweig gave me two thousand to get through the year. I didn't have enough money for food, for clothes, or anything like that."

Randy let Tyrone tell it all.

"And the reason I didn't go to the papers was because I had no reason to. I should have won the Heisman, but my damn agent came out and said he gave me money. Some professional, huh?

"Look, Randy, this is my only shot to get out. To take care of my family. I may be leaving Copperzweig, but I'm not gonna rock the boat. Not when I'm this close to making it. Gotta get that cash now, ya know."

"So, no one else has got to you?"

"Nope, no one else," Tyrone said. "Why, you got some info for me?"

"No, Tyrone," Randy said. "I just want to make sure you're doing all right. I'll never have another receiver like Touchdown Tyrone."

After more small talk, Randy hung up and returned home. His arrival in San Diego was 40 hours away and counting.

"STEFFON: WAS TOLD TO MISS VS. NU" boomed Monday morning's *Dane County Tribune*. NCAA investigators were on the way to Madison by the truckload the day after Jake offered the scoop to Rachel.

But Rachel had it first.

As the interim sports director and the only current employee in the Channel 11 Sports department, Rachel enjoyed finally outgunning the other stations.

"Wisconsin State placekicker Jake Steffon told the NCAA today that he was contacted…" Rachel began the early news on Sunday afternoon. For one glorious Sunday, the story was hers. All hers.

Monday morning found John Wilcox cleaning out his office. It didn't take long. He always tried to keep his desk tidy so that the day the big call came for a head coaching job, he'd be ready to bolt.

Karen Strassel had let all the coaching staff go. She claimed the program needed a fresh start. The new head coach could bring in his own staff, and John knew what that meant.

He had to find another job. Along with the other dozen coaches.

With Jake talking to the press, John knew his days as a college football coach might be over forever.

This was the underreported side of coaching, the trials of the loyal assistants. Coaches who moved families across the country as they worked their way up the ladder.

John was loyal to Frank. But he'd been loyal to Randy that day in McFarland. If the NCAA called, John would step up and take the bullet.

Epilogue

"Daddy! Go farther back by the waves! And throw it high!"

Brett was having his best birthday ever. Nine years old as the February breeze rolled in off the Pacific.

Randy Munson threw a weathered baseball as a pop fly to his son. Brett camped under it barefoot, his feet leaving prints all over Mission Beach.

"Nice catch!" Randy called as Brett splashed his toes in the whitecaps.

Those poor saps are freezing their asses off back in Wisconsin, Randy said to himself with a smile. Wisconsin State still hadn't hired a football coach to replace Frank Flaherty. All the big-name coaches had turned the job down because of the uncertainty. The threat of NCAA violations hung over the program like an eternal storm cloud.

Karen Strassel had even gone so far as to call Randy again about returning to Madison as the head football coach. But he knew the farther away from Wisconsin he was, the less likely he would slip up.

Randy didn't have to worry about John Wilcox being disloyal. Randy had thrown him a lifeline just after the New Year, naming him San Diego's offensive coordinator. Randy had stipulated that John stay up in the press box and out of the play-calling business.

The idea of doing the right thing tore at Randy as he watched his son leave footprints on the beach. Maybe the right thing here would be to stay quiet. He justified The Plan in his mind. He'd never collected any money. The paper trail did not come back to him.

According to the papers, Frank was sinking deeper and deeper. Frank had moved back to his native Michigan but couldn't escape the long arm of the NCAA. Its investigation was turning over every rock and pebble of Frank's reign. Punishment was certain, but the timetable was not.

Randy, on the other hand, was starting a three-year dream. He could feel it.

San Diego College was on the cusp of something good, Randy said often to journalists and boosters that spring. The Warriors had been 2-9 the year before but brought nearly everyone back.

Brett threw the baseball back to Randy as the coach beamed in the sunshine.

The Munsons' home way out in Sweetwater demonstrated their new wealth. Set high on a hill, the four-bedroom home gave the family room to grow. Starter homes and clipping coupons were a thing of the past for Randy and Lisa.

Randy would even get to see his daughter more. After spending her first warm Christmas in San Diego, Melissa had decided that UCLA would now be the best choice for her.

The one nagging problem for Randy was on the field. He felt good about his first team at San Diego College. Good except for one position. He needed to make a call on that one.

"Is Jake there?" Randy was at his favorite pay phone in San Diego, just three miles from home.

"Yeah, this is he."

"Jake, hi, Coach Munson calling from San Diego. How are you?"

"I'm good, Coach." This was a surprise to Jake.

Jake's football career was in limbo. Without a head football coach at Wisconsin State, Jake didn't know when his scholarship would kick in. The athletic department told him nothing. The other schools were getting itchy. The coaches at Minnesota-Duluth and Western Illinois had told him to take his time, but as March approached, they, too, needed answers.

"The reason I'm calling, Jake, is that you still don't have a coach," Randy said. "I need a kicker, one who knows how to make clutch kicks. You've done that."

"Yes?" Jake liked where this was going.

"First, this phone call never happened. Schools don't like that, even though you're a walk-on. That makes what I'm about to do acceptable. You're still non-scholarship, right?"

"That's right."

"Here's the deal: I have a few scholarships open here in San Diego. I'd like to spend one on you. Of course, you'd have to sit out next year as a transfer, but the next fall you'd be our starting placekicker with two years of eligibility left."

Jake was concerned about the lost year if he transferred within Division 1A. Duluth and Western Illinois weren't in the same league. Jake could play right away there.

"I can tell you're not quite sure what to do," Randy said, sensing Jake's hesitation like an expert car salesman. "At least out here, you'd get to kick on a D1 level. We're on TV five times next year, including three times on ESPN. If we win, we could be on more the next year. Our road trips in two years are Michigan, Hawaii, Arizona, Wyoming, Colorado State, BYU, and Vegas. Not bad, huh?"

"That's not bad at all," Jake admitted. That was much more alluring than riding a bus to Eastern Illinois or St. Cloud State.

"Tell you what," Randy resumed after giving the kicker two phone numbers. "That's my office number and my cell. Call anytime. Once you make the initial contact, I'll formally offer you the scholarship and mail you the transfer forms to get into school. Here's the catch."

There was always a catch with these coaches, Jake thought. Even ones he admired, like Randy Munson. "Yes?"

"I've gotta have your application by March 15. That's the cutoff for fall admission."

"March 15?"

"Yes. Can you do that?" Randy asked, trying to close the deal again.

"Let me think about it," Jake said. "I have your numbers."

"I'll be at the office in 20 minutes. You know it's sunny here, right? 72 degrees as I talk to you. A great place to kick footballs. No wind. No snow. No rain. Give me a call."

"OK. Thanks." Jake saw a framed picture from New Year's Eve, he and Rachel Randall in various stages of revelry. The delightful memories of the past three months bounced through his head. The thought of dealing with John Wilcox out in San Diego flashed through his mind. "Ya know what, coach?" Jake said.

"Yes, Jake?"

"Save the ride," Jake said. "I'm going to stay here and see what happens. Wisconsin State's my team. This is my home. It won't be easy, but I'll ride it out here."

"Are you sure?"

"Yeah, coach," Jake said. "Besides, I just got an invitation to Touchdown Tyrone's NFL Draft Party down in Miami in two months. We're Boars until the end."

Randy laughed. Word among the NFL executives was that Tyrone Collins would land in the late first round of April's NFL draft, even with the recent headlines.

Jake hung up and walked to the bathroom. Rachel was taking a shower before heading off to work. Jake knocked on the bathroom door.

"Rachel, guess who just called me?"

"I don't know." Rachel's voice echoed off the yellow tile.

"Randy Munson. He wants me to transfer to San Diego College. Full ride, too."

"And you said?" Rachel asked nonchalantly.

"I told him I'm staying in Madison."

Rachel paused a few seconds before answering.

"I can handle keeping our relationship on the down low," Rachel said through the wooden door. "That is, for a couple more weeks." Rachel had just given her two weeks' notice at WMA. Lou Proctor had hired an inexperienced, ex-lawyer from California to be the sports director. Instead of sulking, Rachel had landed a job at the top station in Milwaukee after only three weeks of searching. Jake and Rachel could quit hiding their relationship once she worked in Milwaukee. No more meeting in dark restaurants or smoky bars.

"Jake?"

"Yes?"

"Just don't go transferring to the Gophers or anything like that, and we'll be just fine."

Randy retreated to his lush office in San Diego. The sight of palm trees and tank tops eased his frustration. His office phone rang. Randy's secretary had the week off.

Maybe this would be a kicker, any kicker, calling to offer help.

"Randy, it's Aaron Schutz from the *Dane County Tribune*."

"Yes?"

"I've come across something very incriminating," Aaron said. "I wanted to offer you a chance to respond before we put it in print."

"What's this about?"

"Former WMA-TV reporter Harvey Walsh has uncovered a gambling ring inside the Wisconsin State football program," Aaron said. "He found through on-line sports books that both the Northern Illinois and Northwestern games were thrown. Is this true?"

"I'm not sure what you're talking about."

"Is that your quote on this?" Aaron challenged.

Randy's silence begged for more details. The tick-tock of his oak wall clock boomed through the office. Aaron filled the quiet.

"Harvey told us all this because he and Channel 11 couldn't come to a contract agreement," Aaron continued. "He moved to another station in town, so he's spilling it all."

Anger at John Wilcox exploded through Randy. Wilcox had to be the one who was chirping.

"It was actually pretty easy to find," Aaron said. "We reached someone at some outfit called the Gold Sports Book. A guy named Stephen Crossland won a huge amount of money this year, betting against Wisconsin State on—"

Randy knew he was done. His fear was not quitting in disgrace but having to tell Lisa about how The Plan was about to ruin their lives. He'd be stuck coaching the prison teams at San Quentin.

"Let's see," Aaron shuffled papers over the phone. "Losses to Northwestern and Northern Illinois plus wins against Indiana, Kansas. Looks like he blew it against Hawaii.

"That field goal did him in," Aaron added, just for spite. "Seeing that Crossland was a former roommate of yours, I would say it's extremely suspicious on your end, and that's giving you the benefit of all doubts."

The silence returned.

"Coach Munson, do you have any comment?"

Randy felt like an arm wrestler with his right knuckles a half-inch from scraping the table. The scam was up, and he knew it.

"No," Randy said quietly. "You'll have to speak with my attorney. Here's his number."

A fat white man with a thick brown mustache looked at the resumé and pondered the sunshine on the palm trees outside.

"Nine years in sports and you want to be a news photographer," he said. "May I ask why?"

Clark Catoor was getting back into the business.

"I came into some money a few months back," Clark said. "I've decided to pick a place I want to live and simply live off my salary there."

"We start off our photographers at 11 bucks an hour," the man said. "That won't get you very far in Honolulu. Do you have a car?"

"Yes."

"Reliable car?"

"Yes."

"You might be able to squeeze out a place out west, but that's a 30-minute drive into work each day."

"That's not a problem."

"OK, then, you just have to pass a drug test and we'll see you Monday morning at 9. Welcome to Honolulu."

"Thank you."

Clark walked out to his Dodge Intrepid and drove to Waikiki Memorial Hospital for the required drug test. He'd been fed up with Las Vegas after just three months. He'd worked odd hours at an all-sports radio station, but found the easy access to sports gambling too much. Clark made a small fortune betting obscure early-season college basketball games but gave it all back on the NFL playoffs. The Packers blew it again for him.

He sold all his bulky stuff and shipped the rest to Hawaii. Clark found a one-bedroom apartment in the sleepy beach town of Kailua.

He'd had the time of his life driving west in November. After seeing family and friends scattered throughout St. Louis, Kansas City, and Denver, Clark dropped into Grand Junction unannounced and gave his ex-wife an envelope with 70 $100 bills in it.

"It's all there. Keep the change." Clark said six words to his ex-wife before turning back to his truck. Carol had simply stood in the doorway in her bathrobe, unable to deliver a comeback line.

Moving to Hawaii was his own fresh start. A new station with new responsibilities. Being a news photographer was the bottom of the newsroom hierarchy. Long hours. Terrible pay. No woman would come up to him in a supermarket and say, "Hey, aren't you..."

Recognition was like a drug for Clark. Money wasn't an issue anymore, but he walked the streets of Honolulu without strangers nodding at him or stopping to say hello. Las Vegas had been the same way. He missed being a player in the market. Even after scratching the feds a check for $57,000 on his gambling taxes, he still had over $110,000 in cash from The Plan. And his grandmother had left him $100,000 in a money market account back in Missouri when she passed away two months before.

Clark sat in an anonymous hospital waiting room, awaiting the cup to prove he was not a dope or coke junkie. He flipped through that morning's *Honolulu Star-Bulletin*, in the tired hope of seeing if one of the island's sports anchors had just quit or been fired. On page two, an item jumped off the page between surfing reports.

"San Diego College football coach Randy Munson resigned after allegations of fixing games last year as an assistant coach at Wisconsin State. *The Dane County Tribune* reported Tuesday that Munson was instrumental in the team's home losses to Northern Illinois and Northwestern. A former roommate of Munson's reportedly made over $200,000 betting for and against Wisconsin State across a five-game stretch during the 2003 season. Munson, hired as head coach at San Diego College in November, had no comment."

Clark nearly lost the specimen meant for the drug test by the end of the paragraph. The story went on to say that Harvey Walsh had uncovered the story, but there was no mention of Clark or any "Madison sportscaster" in on the scheme.

He got up and started hitting the channel button rapid-fire

before locking into ESPNEWS.

On the screen John Wilcox appeared, standing at a podium. An obvious press conference.

"Holy shit," Clark said aloud, his jaw hanging low.

"Clark Cattoor, we're ready," a young nurse with skin the color of Waikiki sand called out.

"Just a second, please," Clark said, turning up the volume.

There stood John Wilcox, wearing a black-and-green San Diego College baseball cap. Under his image, a line read, "John Wilcox/Interim San Diego College Football Coach."

He had finally gotten his big break.

"This program is going through a trying time," Wilcox said with the school logo draped behind him. "I had no connection to these allegations. My hands are clean in this, but all of our hands will be necessary to rebuild the program here in San Diego."

Clark knew that he was on the legal side with his winnings, if not the ethical one. He told himself that as he walked down a bright hall, sample cup in hand, following the nurse as he attempted to start his career over from the bottom.